D0753241

A WILD CARDS MOSAIC NOVEL

THREE KINGS

The Wild Cards Universe

The Original Triad
Wild Cards
Aces High
Jokers Wild

The Puppetman Quartet
Aces Abroad
Down and Dirty
Ace in the Hole
Dead Man's Hand

The Rox Triad
One-Eyed Jacks
Jokertown Shuffle
Dealer's Choice

Solo Novels
Double Solitaire
Turn of the Cards
Death Draws Five

Deuces Down

The Card Sharks Triad
Card Sharks
Marked Cards
Black Trump

The Committee Triad
Inside Straight
Busted Flush
Suicide Kings

The Mean Streets Triad
Fort Freak
Lowball
High Stakes

The America Triad
Mississippi Roll
Low Chicago
Texas Hold'em

The British Arc
Knaves Over Queens
Joker Moon
Three Kings

A WILD CARDS MOSAIC NOVEL

THREE KINGS

**Edited by
Melinda M. Snodgrass**

**Assistant Editor
George R. R. Martin**

And written by

*Mary Anne Mohanraj
Peter Newman
Peadar Ó Guilín
Melinda M. Snodgrass
Caroline Spector*

TOR

A TOM DOHERTY ASSOCIATES BOOK
New York

THREE KINGS

A Tor Book
Published by Tom Doherty Associates
120 Broadway
New York, NY 10271

www.tor-forge.com

Tor® is a registered trademark of Macmillan Publishing Group, LLC.

Library of Congress Cataloging-in-Publication Data

Names: Snodgrass, Melinda M., 1951– editor. | Martin, George R. R., editor. |
Mohanraj, Mary Anne, author.
Title: Three kings : a wild cards mosaic novel / edited by Melinda M. Snodgrass ;
assistant editor, George R. R. Martin ; and written by
Mary Anne Mohanraj [and four others].
Description: First edition. | New York : Tor, 2022. | Series: Wild cards ; 28 |
"A Tom Doherty Associates book.
Identifiers: LCCN 2021046238 (print) | LCCN 2021046239 (ebook) |
ISBN 9781250167934 (hardcover) | ISBN 9781250167927 (ebook)
Classification: LCC PS648.S3 T52 2022 (print) | LCC PS648.S3 (ebook) |
DDC 813'.0876208—dc23
LC record available at https://lccn.loc.gov/2021046238
LC ebook record available at https://lccn.loc.gov/2021046239

Our books may be purchased in bulk for promotional, educational, or
business use. Please contact your local bookseller or the Macmillan Corporate
and Premium Sales Department at 1-800-221-7945, extension 5442, or by
email at MacmillanSpecialMarkets@macmillan.com.

First Edition: 2022

Printed in the United States of America

0 9 8 7 6 5 4 3 2 1

Saturday

FEBRUARY 29TH

FASCINATING.

It should have been impossible to ambush Badb, goddess of war. Every crow in Belfast lent her their senses. She soared over a bleeding city, from one pocket of violence to the next. From the women shaving the head of a weeping collaborator to the screams of a man shot through the back of the knees. The city had half the population it should have had. Its buildings crumbled, paint flaking away except from slogans that every day were refreshed: NOT AN INCH!, BRITS OUT!, NO NATS HERE!

She had caused it all. Manipulating the angry; creating heroes and renewing herself through their sacrifice.

But she hadn't expected this.

Three teenaged boys with hurley sticks caught her in an alleyway.

"Hand it over!" cried the nearest, his voice breaking mid-sentence. He had blond hair and a shamrock tattoo that might get him killed only three streets from here.

Behind him, a second boy, darker this time, pushed forward. "Yeah," he cried. "We want all of it!" Despite the braggadocio, this was their first robbery. Badb could tell such things. Their knuckles were white on the wood of the hurls. Their Adam's apples bobbed and bobbed.

"Let me get my purse."

She really didn't have time for this. Something was very wrong. She left her body, flicking from crow to crow, finding nearby streets to be far too quiet. No bombs went off. No snatch squads screeched out of police stations.

"Smash her, Paddy!" the second boy said as she returned to her body. "She's delayin'. It's on purpose."

"I have it here," Badb said, allowing a quiver of fear into her voice to make them feel more manly. "Please don't hurt me!" She knew what they were seeing. An old, old woman. Which she was. With aching joints to slow her movements and additional indignities they couldn't imagine—constant bleeding from cracks in her skin that only a layer of sopping bandages hid from view.

"Hit her, Paddy."

But Paddy probably had a granny of his own at home, and a conscience too.

"No," he said, and licked his lips. "Not if she hands over the pension money. An Irishman keeps his word."

Badb's arthritic fingers got the purse open as the three boys crowded closer. Inside was a razor blade. With shaking hands, she drew it across Paddy's throat. While he stared, amazed, still on his feet, she hobbled forward two more steps and got the second boy too.

Badb's hips stabbed at her as she turned. She would need to regenerate very soon, or old age would leave her incapable of any movement at all.

By now the third boy was turning to flee. But she had a crow waiting. It swooped down from a nearby building, a missile of beak and black feathers, aimed straight at the teenager's eyes . . .

And that's when it happened. A pain such as the goddess had not felt in the longest time. A wrongness that jerked her out of her body and flung her awareness across the city to Sandy Row.

Disoriented, she tried to understand what had brought her here.

It had begun to drizzle. Boys and girls stood by the gable end of a house where patriotic hands had painted Queen Margaret on the day of her coronation. Badb watched the children from the eyes of one crow and then another until, suddenly, the gang sprang forward as one. A boy and a girl carried a net between them, she in sneakers, he in boots, the laces dangerously trailing.

What are they hunting? Badb wondered. But only for a second, because then, the net came down over the crow she occupied. She flicked to another bird and then, another, but they too had been caught. Other children smashed at the birds with planks of wood. With rocks. With the soles of their Doc Martens. The pain! The pain!

Half the flock escaped, and Badb with them. What was going on? Who had ever heard of such a thing? Even in this city where the spilling of blood had not slowed in fifty years?

Badb wheeled with the other crows, toying with the idea of sending the flock back to peck some manners into the children, but she knew better than to give herself away like that. Over the last decade she could count on two hands the number of people her flock had killed. Even so, the idea had leaked out into the city's subconscious. "Crow" had become a slang term for treachery or for informers. Criminals and terrorists regularly warned each other to "keep your beak shut."

She led the surviving birds over the Peace Wall between Sandy Row and Belfast's jokertown, known locally as "the Island."

They would be safe there, she felt sure, while she tried to figure out what was going on.

She returned to her body in the alleyway to find the third boy had escaped. Inconvenient. A loose end that would need snipping and she—

The crows in the Island were under attack now, too. Again, it was children. Misshapen ones that not even Picasso or Dalí or Goya might have imagined. Their assault on the crows was less organized, but several birds were taken out before the flock could flee once more.

Finally, the exhausted crows came down in the grounds of St. Louise's Comprehensive School, where thirty girls stopped their game of camogie to stare at the arriving flock. As one, they charged forward and began stamping on wings and feathered bodies. A nun and two other teachers looked away, as though indifferent to what must have been a shocking sight.

♣

Each time Roger Barnes felt he had adapted and made peace with his body, it found some new way to betray him.

He sighed and took off his robe. He always liked to consider himself a practical man, but of late, the rituals of self-care left him glum, all too aware of how much he had changed, and was still changing.

He stood before an antique full-length mirror with doors that contained additional side mirrors when opened. The frame was scuffed by time and travel, but still sturdy. *Appropriate,* thought Roger. Like all the things he owned, it was purchased with cash, and by someone else. There were no accounts in his name; the cards and phone that he sometimes carried were not registered to him and they were cycled at regular intervals, just to be on the safe side. They, much like the basement he currently dwelt within, were transitory parts of his life; functional, impersonal, disposable.

The fingers of his right hand were too thick to manage the delicate clasps holding the doors of the mirror in place. Roger knew this but tried anyway. It was a little game he played with himself. *Perhaps this time I'll manage it,* he'd think. As if the passing of the seasons would grant him more manual dexterity rather than less. Three times, his thumb was tantalizingly close to hooking the thin strip of gold metal, but it soon became clear that it wasn't going to happen, so he switched to his left hand and the clasp opened easily, though not, he noted, as easily as it once did. Compared to his right hand, his left was positively normal, but the wooden fingers were still longer and thicker than they once were.

For years Roger had not thought of himself as Roger at all, but as Green Man. Green Man was many things to many people. To some he was a prominent figure of London's underworld. To others he was a benefactor to be approached by those unwilling or unable to call on the authorities. And to a select few he was the head of the Twisted Fists, an infamous group of joker terrorists. In the three and a half decades since his card had turned, Green Man had been labelled killer, savior, traitor, and monster; simultaneously a champion of the oppressed, an opportunist thug, and a dangerous revolutionary.

But at these times, when he stood naked, exposed, his Green Man mask sitting on the desk next to his wardrobe, he saw something of the man he once was. A small, neat man. Conservative in politics and manner. A man of principle. A family man.

Nearly all traces of that man were gone. Roger Barnes had been short, and Green Man was now well over six-and-a-half feet tall. Roger Barnes had been slight, and Green Man was, while still long-limbed, undeniably sturdy. Roger had kept his hair neat, while Green Man had no hair at all, unless one counted the persistent moss he was forever having to trim.

Roger sighed a second time, picked up a pair of clippers, and started to prune the shoots sprouting from a spot on his chest. He'd been shot there, many, many years ago, and like all of his injuries, it had healed swiftly, but never quite the same as it was. This was most evident in his right arm, which he'd lost in a fight with . . . with . . . He paused, shocked that he couldn't immediately recall her name.

He could picture her face, could hear her voice in his head; swearing, predictably. But her name eluded him. *How could I forget the name of that foul-mouthed creature?*

A twinge in his shoulder brought his attention back to the mirror. His body hadn't forgotten. Thanks to her, one arm was now thicker than the other, rough to the touch, and prone to sprouting leaves, which he found terribly embarrassing. He flexed the bark-heavy fingers on his right hand, working them until they were no longer stiff.

Wielding the clippers awkwardly in his left hand, he trimmed his right as best he could and then turned his attention to his back. There were several old bullet wounds there. All caused by his daughter when she'd tried to kill him—*do not think about Christine,* he admonished himself sternly, *not today.* Though they'd healed, they'd now become a never-ending source of itching and unsightly growths. Being on the middle of his back, they were devilishly hard to reach too.

There was one he just couldn't get. It was tempting to call Wayfarer and ask her to clip it for him but he resisted. In part because he would be crossing a line—*What next? Have her clip my toenails? Polish my head? Ugh, the very idea!*—but mainly because it would be showing vulnerability. It was fine for Roger Barnes to ask for help, but not Green Man.

He took another look at the mournful face in the mirror and then redoubled his efforts with the clippers. And there, at last, was the satisfying clip, and a whisper of pain that meant he'd got the bastard thing.

The clippers were put back down, and the mask picked up. It was lavishly carved, every leaf lifelike, from stem to tip, linked together to form the shape of a face. A trio of leaves stood proud at the forehead like a badge of office. It was larger than life, larger than Roger Barnes, both a shield for him to hide behind and a symbol to inspire others.

He put it on.

Green Man again.

Then he reached for his suit, not the dark green he usually favored, but his funeral suit. One of his jokers had died, and though any public appearance carried its risks, Green Man must be seen to pay his respects.

Green Man must be seen.

It took longer to dress than usual. His trimming had been less than perfect and he had to ease his shirt over his arms and back for fear of tearing it. The knot in his tie threatened to be too much for his fumbling fingers, but in the end, it succumbed to his slow, persistent assault.

When he was done, however, the lines of his suit were crisp, the tailoring doing much to smooth his uneven limbs. He silently thanked Bobbin for his skill. Such a blessing that one of the few tailors willing to cater to the needs of jokers was the protégé of London's finest.

"*Yes,*" he said to himself. "*This will do.*"

With a satisfied nod, he shut the mirror, trapping Roger Barnes and all of those old, ugly thoughts inside.

♠

It wasn't the cold, gray, misty day that made Constance cross. London weather was so predictably appropriate for a funeral. It wasn't even the crush of mourners—that was to be expected when a celebrity died. It was knowing that Glory lay in the casket before her, that the flowers on Glory's head—the expression of her joker—were rotting away, soon to be joined by Glory's flesh.

With a shudder, Constance remembered the time Glory's flowers were brutally shorn from her head. The blood. The dying lilies. Constance tried to shy away from the memory, but it was still there, same as ever, sharp and clear as glass.

Bobbin took her hand in his. It was warm and surprisingly soft despite his constant handling of fabric. He was careful not to squeeze too tightly. The bony protrusions between his long, spindly fingers—so often helpful when he was sewing—could also hurt like nothing else. She glanced down and was amazed by their wrinkled, veiny hands. When had they become so old? She didn't feel old at all. It was but a breath in time and here she was seventy-six and Bobbin but a few years behind.

Bobbin tucked her hand into the crook of his arm, then gave it a pat. The small gesture almost made her cry. But Constance wasn't a crier—at least not in public. If there was any crying to be done, she'd do it in private, where such things belonged.

"How're you holding up, m'dear?" Bobbin asked. His face, as familiar to her as her own, was blessed by beautiful and kind, gold-rimmed, cerulean eyes. She let that kindness wash over her. Normally, she might have shied back a bit from it—even with Bobbin she was careful not to get too close—but today was an exception.

He knew the answer to his question. After all, they'd known each other for forty years. He knew her moods. Knew when to jolly her and when to let her be. She leaned on him. Depended on him. And yet had kept one thing from him. (*Not just one thing, my girl,* she thought.) The dark, secret thing she and Glory shared.

She studied the mourners. The cast from *Wannabe a Hero* were clumped together. She appreciated them showing up. Glory had been a guest judge on the episode where the American ace, Golden Boy, had humiliated all comers—just as he had on the American version of the show.

But the majority of the mourners were jokers. Normal people whose lives had been destroyed by the alien wild card virus.

Certainly, there were jokers who had managed to do just fine. Jokers like Turing or the woman with the talk show, Peregrine. But that wasn't the bulk of them. And her anger grew, because she burned with hatred for the Takisians, and—fair or not—that included Dr. Tachyon.

And hating jokers? It didn't supplant the old animosities; it just gave people an extra, new thing to hate.

Bobbin squeezed her hand again and she managed a quick smile at him and some of her rage drained away.

Bobbin had grown so important to her and the business that making him her partner seemed sensible. And in addition to hiring as many female tailors as they could, they also made a point to hire jokers, no matter the gender. If you wanted a Constance original, then you had to accept that it was lovingly made by women and/or jokers.

But that all seemed rather unimportant standing here beside Glory's casket. At the head of the casket was Mick Jagger in his lycanthrope form. It seemed as if time had taken its toll on him only in the sprinkle of white on his muzzle. Tears wetted the fur under his eyes, turning it dark.

A massive blanket of white roses covered the casket. Constance knew this gesture was Mick's because Glory had sprouted those flowers whenever he was near her. He may have had a lot of other women, but his only real love had been Glory. And that had been a tragedy.

On the other side of the casket, hanging back near the edge of the cemetery, she saw Green Man. He was shadowed by a few dangerous-looking jokers. But then he was almost always in the company of dangerous-looking jokers. She knew he was a gangster and might even have ties to the Fists. Everyone in the East End suspected as much. It didn't matter that she'd moved away decades ago; she still had deep roots in the community and was perfectly well aware of what was happening there.

The vicar began intoning yet another prayer. Constance tuned him out. Her eyes burned, and things got blurry. She told herself it was because the wind had picked up, but that was shite and she knew it. The sharp pain of losing Glory wouldn't leave and, unconsciously, she gripped Bobbin's hand tighter, not even noticing when his thorns pierced her knuckles.

"I'm always here for you," Bobbin said softly. "I know I'm not her, but you can count on me."

"I know," she replied just as softly. There was a hitch in her voice and a lump in her throat that made it hard to swallow. The vicar kept droning on, and Constance thought she might scream, *Get on with it, you git!*

At last, the vicar was done, and the mourners began to make their way past the coffin. White flowers—lilies, chrysanthemums, and gladiolus—were lovingly placed around the casket. She saw Green Man begin to make his way through the crowd, carrying a delicate bouquet of violets.

It made her like him a little, but only just a little.

◆

It pained Green Man to arrive anything less than early, but it wouldn't do to be hanging around. He'd learned long ago that the trick to maintaining any kind of mystique was to give people as little time to talk to you as possible. And so, at the very last minute, he slipped in quietly at the back of the cemetery.

Manor Park had lost none of its gravitas over the years. Even under a drab London sky, it managed to look stylish and timeless, from the clusters of mature oak, ash, and birch trees; to the wrought iron gates tipped with gold; to the neatly kept grass. Where many places of this caliber would have turned their back on the resident jokers, Manor Park and the rest of the East End had welcomed them with open arms. To them, jokers were just another quirk of an already vibrant community.

A good-sized crowd had assembled to pay their respects to Glory Greenwood. She'd been something of a star during the sixties, and always popular. That was the thing about being different: to be accepted, you had to be easy on the eye, and mostly harmless.

Glory had been both, and charming with it. A little bit of brightness in the East End that would be sorely missed.

He allowed himself the slightest smile as the crowd became aware of him. Furtive glances were cast his way and a little ripple of reactions passed out from where he stood. He watched carefully, noting which faces seemed pleased, which afraid, and the few that were openly hostile—he'd make a point of talking to them later.

Somewhere nearby, Wayfarer would be sitting in an innocuous-looking van with the engine running. A few of the more discreet Fists were also around, ready to run interference if need be. It was unlikely anyone would be crass enough to move against him here, but it always paid to take precautions. In his pocket, his phone was set to vibrate if Wayfarer got word of trouble. The old code: one buzz for police, two for armed units or military, and three for the Silver Helix.

So far it had stayed as quiet as the park itself.

His turn soon came to step up to the grave, several of those already in the queue giving up their place out of respect. Among them he saw one of the few nats present, Constance, alongside Bobbin. They stood together, almost like an old married couple, but not quite. Green Man favored them with a slight nod as he passed.

Despite the somber nature of the day, it felt good to be outside. Too much of his life was spent cooped inside the back of vehicles or belowground. He relished the feel of the wind on his body, virtually immune to the cold these days, and was delighted when the rain descended from above.

When he reached the grave, he stood for a while, head bowed, to give the impression of deep thoughts and feelings. The truth was, he didn't really know Glory at all. Their lives had followed very different paths. She'd always seemed too much of a hippie for his liking. He much preferred tidy, practical people. And she would likely have found him dull.

Still, regardless of any personal feelings, it was important Green Man be seen to care and, in a vague way, he did care. Jokers like Glory were rare and important to the cause. The world would always see him as a monster, but she'd been able to touch people, joker, ace, and nat alike. She was the other side of the coin. The Twisted Fists could fight the worst of humanity, but they would never win over the best of it.

He stooped down, and laid a large bouquet of violets.

When he made his way out, he saw some of the old jokers laughing together as they shared stories of their time with Glory. He saw them cry and smile. He saw them hold each other, the misshapen bodies leaning together for support.

And he envied them.

♥

Alan Turing stood outside the door to the queen's bedchamber, collecting himself. She had summoned him, and he had come at her command, as always.

Margaret had been so beautiful as a girl. Beautiful and wild. An eighteen-inch waist, the papers had reported, and the rest of the figure to match, plus a face lovely enough to paint. Both before and after his card had turned, Alan had felt no flicker of desire for the stunning princess, but he had appreciated her beauty, like a work of art. And though time had worked its ravages, buried in the wrinkles of ninety lay the lovely bones of the girl who had flirted her way across Europe. Pregnant Elizabeth had surely been relieved when Townsend had actually proposed to Margaret; marrying a divorcé was still scandalous back then, but better than a babe born out of wedlock. She'd thrown her considerable weight behind the match, and the marriage, a mere seven months after Elizabeth's own, had featured the most splendid of cakes.

A flowering of British beauty, British glory; such a relief after the ravages of the War followed by Wild Card Day. And then, things fell apart, as the poem said. Had Yeats known, somehow? The center did not hold—Elizabeth's baby born dead, followed a few years later by Elizabeth's own passing, her health broken by the birth. She had fought so long, so hard, their princess, and the country had been heart-stricken. When George VI died a year later, Margaret had been so distraught that she'd needed sleeping pills for months. They'd tried to keep that out of the papers, but to no avail.

Still, in the end, she'd rallied. Young Henry to live for, and then Richard following a few years later. Twenty centuries of stony sleep put back to rest by a rocking cradle? Margaret I, ruling over a realm that had been, for the most part, peaceful. And if she had her lovers on the side, as some whispered, Townsend never said a word, and so neither could anyone else. He'd loved her to his grave, his wild girl, and now, finally, she would follow. Alan turned the doorknob, pushed open the heavy door, and entered.

The queen's crimson bedchamber, crowded with relatives and quiet murmurs of conversation, was lit by candles. Electric lights hurt her eyes. The flickering light caught the gilt of framed paintings on the walls, a long pageantry of prior kings and queens, with Elizabeth prominent in the room. Had Margaret spent her entire reign under her sister's stern gaze? Never quite good enough, proper enough, to satisfy? Yet Margaret had held England together, through the advent of the wild card, where other countries had faltered—surely Elizabeth would give her points for that? The candles lit shadows in the forest-green curtains that draped the bed, edged in royal purple and gold. On the flower-embroidered coverlet, the queen's hand lay, the thickness of middle age dissolved through her long years, until it was thin again, the skin gone papery.

Alan Turing had served George through the War, and Elizabeth after, served as well as he knew how, but it was Margaret he had loved. Something in her wild heart called to his own, though so few could see it, cloaked as it was in his skin gone metallic, and his mind that had always worked more like a computer's than most. Yet Alan was human after all, and when the queen called to him in a thin voice, his heart squeezed in his chest. Ah, this hurt.

"Alan?"

He spoke over the tightness in his throat. "I'm here, Your Majesty."

"Ah, look at you." The queen's eyes filled with the easy tears of age. "You're two decades older than I am, Alan, but you look in the prime of life. What I could do for England with those extra years! Henry—Henry, take them all away . . . need to speak to Alan." Margaret had to pause between breaths, but decades of command held, and the family dutifully filed out. Henry, soon to be king, with his young fiancée. Richard and Diana and their children as well. Richard's young grandchildren had been spared this deathwatch. Finally, they all left Alan alone with Margaret.

"Come here—" She raised a hand, and Alan hurried across the room to take it in his, careful not to press too hard.

Alan listened as Margaret spoke, her words slipping out of coherence, rambling at times. But he'd known her a long time; even if she dropped words here and there, it was easy enough for him to fill in the gaps. "Henry is too rigid . . . blinkered. He clings . . . to pride and privilege . . . might have pulled a kingdom . . . on the battlefield, but . . . not what England needs now."

Turing couldn't disagree with her assessment of Henry. Yeats had said it best: *The best lack all conviction, while the worst / Are full of passionate intensity.* But Henry would be king; somehow, England would survive.

Margaret's soft voice rambled on, "And my Dickie's . . . an attractive man—*you* know that, Alan . . ."

Intimation in her voice—she couldn't possibly know, could she? His metallic skin could not flush, but Turing felt the heat rise in his face. But the queen was already moving on.

"—but I don't know . . . the strength to hold the throne . . . the figure that England needs . . . symbol of our past, our future. When the throne falters, England falters!" She sighed, a pale hand fluttering on the richly worked bedspread. "I didn't understand that . . . a girl . . . Elizabeth worked so hard to show me . . . almost too late by the time I learned. Alan—*you* must find the other."

There was a gap Turing didn't know how to fill. "The other, Majesty?"

"The other heir. Lizzie's little boy. He wasn't right, you know. But still. Maybe better than my boys." Margaret was pushing herself up in the pillows, her eyes blazing now, almost feverish. Her words came fast and sharp, despite the tears trembling in her eyes. "*You* can assess, Alan, better than anyone else. You have seen decades of history, fought in our wars, served multiple rulers. You will likely see many more—you can judge better than any other living man. How would *he* be, for England?" Margaret sank bank on the pillows again. ". . . such hopes for my sons; I tried to raise them right, but the demands of the throne . . ."

And then she was crying, his Margaret, tears slipping down soft cheeks. Alan's heart turned over in his chest, listening to her speak on, babbling about this other, lost, child. Was this some figment of her old age, a dream fancy? Margaret had been so strong, so young and beautiful. It was impossible, what she asked. Even if Elizabeth's child actually existed, the country would never accept some random individual to take the throne of England, however toothless a power that might in these modern days. A secret heir, and her own sons passed over for him! If Richard found out, he'd be furious.

Alan Turing patted Margaret's hand, helplessly, and listened to his queen ramble on. He couldn't do much for her now, but as long as she asked him to, he would listen.

♣

The house smelled of food brought from a nearby pub. It was far from Noel Matthews' first choice of cuisine, but it was absolutely preferable to his mother trying to exercise her culinary skills . . . which were nil. His father, a stay-at-home invalid, had done all the cooking while his wife went off to teach at Cambridge, but since his death Amanda had relied solely on takeout and frozen dinners heated in the microwave. It showed in the fact her big frame was now packing more weight than the last time he had seen her. While he set the table, she was busy opening the containers and placing serving spoons in the shepherd's pie, the Brussels sprouts, the blackberry and apple crumble, and the green salad Noel had insisted she add to the order.

"Darling, while it's lovely having you home and seeing my grandson, what you're doing is rotten and you know it," Amanda was saying.

A sharp pain at the hinge of his jaw reminded Noel to unclench his teeth. "There was an easy solution. Niobe just had to agree to move back to Britain with me."

"Her family is all in that New England area—"

"Yeah, and they're all complete arseholes. Why she suddenly decided she needed to reconcile with them is beyond me. She seemed to think Jasper changed everything for them, but he's an ace and they'll hate him as much as they hate her for being a joker because they hate wild cards. Why she can't see that—"

"Because the ties of blood are strong. You've separated a child from his mother, Noel. I can't approve of that."

"Can't I be both?" he quipped with bitter irony in a reference to his intersex status.

"Now *you're* being an arsehole. Go get Jasper. Dinner's ready."

He checked the cozy study where he had spent so many hours with his father, then Jasper's bedroom. His son was nowhere to be found. Old habits leapt to the fore and he found himself gripping the butt of the pistol that he always carried and checking the knives secreted about his person. Could this be some of the many enemies he had made as an elite assassin for Britain's ace spy agency MI-7? Or could it be the Silver Helix itself, come for a little payback?

He felt a cold breeze down the back hall and he ran to the back door. It had blown open. His heart was hammering as he rushed into the back garden, fallow now as the final day of a miserable February drew to a close. The fact it was sunset meant he was unable to teleport if there should be a threat. He cursed under his breath and headed down the slope toward the River Cam, where fog was rising off the water like the waving tendrils of a witch's hair.

A small figure squatted on the river's edge. Noel slumped with relief and joined his son. "It's cold and wet out here, Jasper. You should have a coat."

"I just wanted to see the fog. It's so weird," the boy said. "It's like it's alive."

"Well, dinner is ready."

Jasper nodded and stood up. At nine years old he was becoming coltish, all legs and elbows. Noel dropped an arm around his shoulders and pulled him close to his side.

"Dad, are we going to go home soon?"

"Well technically this is home too. I have the flat in London, the place in Paris—"

"But they're not really home because . . . because." He looked up hesitantly. "I really miss Mom."

"We're . . . working on it. I just want you to be a good Englishman as well as an American, which is why I want to live here for a while."

"So why doesn't Mom want to come here?"

The memory of wet smears on the carpet where Niobe's and his three little ace homunculi died in a hail of bullets flashed across his memory. Niobe pressing a hand to her chest, weeping, remembering the pain of the bullets that killed her children.

"I'm not sure," he lied. *She's also worried I'll fall back into my old ways,* he thought. He remembered how he had reached for his weapons in a moment of panic, and had to acknowledge that she might be right.

They stepped into the house to hear a plummy BBC voice on the TV. ". . . word from Windsor is that it is only a matter of hours now. If so, it truly is the end of an era. An unprecedented time of peace and prosperity for mainland Britain for which she deserves some of the credit . . ."

Jasper looked up. "What's going on? What does that mean, Daddy?"

"Tomorrow we'll all be saying God save the King."

♠

Alan took a quick deep breath before opening the door to the antique Victorian he shared with his husband. It was falling down a bit, showing its years, but they'd redone the electric a decade ago, and it should hold up for some time yet.

"I'm home!" Alan called out, letting the door swing closed behind him. It was warm in the house, radiators clanking—too warm for his comfort, to be honest, but Sebastian was feeling the cold more these days, the arthritis in his joints acting up. Alan wouldn't ask his husband to turn the heat down, but he was quick in stripping off wool coat and cardigan.

Sebastian came through the swing door from the kitchen, letting through the scent of chicken curry—Alan's stomach rumbled in response. Sometimes people assumed that a metal man wouldn't eat, but Alan's skin was only metallic on the outside. His internal workings were entirely human, every part of him fully functional. And now that functional stomach was reminding him that he'd missed lunch, and breakfast had been much too long ago.

"Dinner's ready. I've been keeping it warm for us." Sebastian gave him a quick, dry kiss, lips to lips, and then headed back into the kitchen. Alan followed.

"You didn't have to wait on me," Alan said. It was late, past ten.

"I don't like eating without you. You know that," Sebastian said quietly. He was climbing on the stepstool, reaching down plates from the cupboard. The dishes they'd picked out together on their wedding day, heavy bone china in cream, with a simple gold rim. Alan usually didn't bother noting such everyday details, but perhaps his time with the queen was making him more sentimental than usual. Five years ago, he and Sebastian had promised each other they'd use the good china every day. They'd waited long enough to finally be able to marry; there was no point in waiting for anything else.

Sebastian had looked handsome at their St. Paul's wedding, in his morning coat and top hat. Oh, he had the thickness of late middle age, twenty extra pounds lodged solidly in his belly. But he'd still looked good back then. In the last five years, Sebastian had aged visibly; his hair was almost pure white now, with matching bushy white eyebrows, and twenty extra pounds had turned to forty. Alan didn't really mind—he liked a solid man, and at age sixty-two, Sebastian had surely earned the right to slow down a little and eat his fill.

Unfortunately, Sebastian minded, and that had its consequences in their rather desolate bedroom. Now his hand trembled a little, balancing the plate heavy with rice and curry, and Alan reached out to take it from him. Sebastian pulled away. "I've got it, Alan; don't fuss."

"You should've eaten. The doctor said—"

"Enough," Sebastian snapped. He took a quick breath, visibly steadying himself. "It's almost time for the news—we can watch together." He handed Alan a cold beer, and then they were moving back through the door now, heading into the sitting room, with its comfortably worn leather furniture and the big TV. "How is she doing?"

Alan let it go, settling down on the couch beside his husband. "It won't be long now, I think. Tomorrow or the next day." The curry was sharp and sweet, the way he liked it, with a little vinegar tang to balance the heat. Sebastian dark-roasted the spices, ground them himself, giving the curry a rich flavor surpassing any local takeout. The TV news was still covering the recent football results: "Watford continue their winning run, following recent promotion back into the Premier League . . ." Alan's days dreaming of Olympic gold were long past him; no one would call him a serious runner now. But he still enjoyed following sports; the TV would turn to political news again soon enough.

Sebastian took a long draught of his beer. "And the rest of the royals? How are they taking it?"

"Henry is practically chomping at the bit. How Margaret managed to raise a son like that . . ." Would Elizabeth's child have been any better? If they'd given him a chance?

"Well, Richard's a decent enough chap. Did you see him?"

Alan answered carefully, "Yes, the Duke was there, of course."

When he'd first started dating Sebastian, their relationship had been open. Sebastian had an insecure streak, though, and after a few too many angry fights, Alan had agreed to monogamy. It simply wasn't worth the arguing. He'd held to it, mostly, until the affair with Richard. Sebastian had caught him, not long after it first started, and that had almost been the end of their relationship right there. A crystal chess set, a gift from Richard, had ended up shattered in pieces on the tiled greenhouse floor. Alan's perfect memory replayed the scene on command: Sebastian shouting, "How do you expect me to compete with a fucking prince?" Tears that he refused to shed standing in his eyes.

Alan had eventually persuaded Sebastian to forgive him, promised never to slip again. The problem, Alan reasoned at the time, wasn't the affair itself—that had gone on quite pleasantly until he'd been caught. He'd been sloppy, that was the problem. That's why Sebastian had gotten hurt. He didn't want to hurt his husband; Alan loved him. But Alan had seen no point in confessing when he and Richard shared a few stolen moments, here and there, over the years.

Of course, lately, it'd been a bit more than that. Richard had grown ardent lately, intoxicatingly passionate. Sometimes, Alan thought he should confess it all—confession was good for the soul, they said. Did jokers still have souls? A morbid thought for a somber night.

"Alan?" Sebastian leaned forward, tapped Alan's arm.

"Sorry—just thinking of Margaret," Alan said hastily. "Her family's all gathered around the bedside in proper fashion. Perhaps I should have stayed . . ." The news was shifting now, on to the weather. Cold and rainy, with more cold and rainy to come. Appropriate for mourning at least.

Sebastian raised an eyebrow. "What could you do there, really?"

All manner of things, like searching for a lost heir. Not that he could discuss that with Sebastian. There had been times, over the decades, when little bits of Silver Helix business had slipped out; that was inevitable in a long relationship. But this news was potentially explosive; Alan couldn't risk a slip of Sebastian's tongue. It was almost like it had been, back during the War, when they'd all worked on the German ciphers at Bletchley in complete secrecy. Alan had long ago learned how to keep his mouth shut.

Still—"There are things I should be working on." It wouldn't hurt if Sebastian thought there was a good reason for his late nights.

Sebastian shrugged. "I'm sure, but I'm also sure the Crown can spare you for a few hours. It's not as if you're running the Silver Helix. You can have a decent meal, and get some sleep, and in the morning, maybe you can get to that leaf mold?" He gestured out the window to the back garden, where the conservatory sat at the far end of a row of trees. The birdfeeders had all been recently filled, and a host of birds were constantly swooping down and squabbling over the bounty. Robins and goldfinches, starlings and crows. "You promised you'd take care of that this weekend—the snowdrops will be smothered if you don't, and my shoulder . . ."

Alan frowned. "You've been overdoing it." He took a long draught of his beer, savoring the bitter taste that lingered on his tongue. Sebastian's new brew was even better than his last. "Maybe it's time to talk about retirement again? I make plenty for both of us, you know." Alan idly calculated the odds—yes, if he stopped work tomorrow, they could live quite comfortably for decades on Alan's investments. Probably indefinitely, barring catastrophes—but with the mind that the wild card had gifted him, Alan should be able to avoid any of *those*.

Of course, Sebastian probably wouldn't make it that much longer. Sixty-two. Sebastian's parents had died in their seventies, and his grandparents notably earlier. Alan couldn't help calculating the odds. Mortality tables had a certain grim fascination to them. Yes, his husband probably had no more than ten or fifteen years left—Alan's mind flinched away from that thought. He couldn't quite picture his life without Sebastian in it.

As for Alan himself—who knew? He was 108 this year, but didn't feel old yet—he felt, in fact, much as he had in his twenties. His card's turning might have brought him many more decades of life—or he might drop dead tomorrow. There was no way to calculate that.

Sebastian was frowning at him. "Make plenty for both of us? What are you saying, Alan—that your work is more important than mine? Just because you get paid more?"

"I didn't say anything of the sort, Sebastian, and you know it." Alan fought to keep his tone even, not letting the irritation through. That would just escalate marital snippiness into an actual squabble. Alan did get frustrated with the imprecision with which most people spoke. Sebastian should know better by now.

His husband turned away, and was staring at the TV screen now, deliberately. Punishing him. "I care about what I do, Alan. I may not be a human computer, but I'm good at my work, one of the best." His voice raised a little. "Have you seen the new maze garden at Buckingham? You can view it from Margaret's windows—have you even bothered to look? It'll take several years to fill in properly, of course, but I designed it specially for her to enjoy . . ."

"I'm sorry—I just haven't had time . . ." *to look at plants*, was what Alan carefully didn't say out loud. "But I'll look tomorrow. Maybe I can find enough time to go for a walk in it . . ." *with Richard*, which he also didn't say.

Sebastian brightened, turning back to him. "Come at noon—I can show you around."

Oh, he'd walked into that one, hadn't he? "If I can get away." Alan regretted the words as soon as they were out of his mouth; Sebastian's eyes had gone bleak. "No, I'm sure I can. Tomorrow. We can have lunch together—when you came to work at the Palace, we said we'd have lunch all the time . . ."

"Yet somehow, we never do," Sebastian said.

Alan counted to ten, at human speed. He had to try harder. Sebastian was just so much work. Richard was easy by comparison . . . "Maybe we can pick some flowers for our lunch, add them to a salad, or to a bit of dessert? Remember that cake you made me for my birthday, with the crystallized rose petals on top? That was delicious. I'm sure the queen wouldn't mind . . ."

Sebastian sniffed. "The only things blooming in the garden right now are hellebores and snowdrops. If you put hellebores in my dessert, I'll drop down dead."

"Well, we wouldn't want that." Alan put a hand on Sebastian's cheek, leaned in for a quick kiss. After a brief moment, his husband responded, lips warming under his, opening. The kiss lingered, longer than any had in some time, and when Sebastian finally pulled away, his eyes were bright.

"No," Sebastian said, softly. "I suppose we wouldn't." He snuggled into Alan's shoulder, turning back to the television and increasing the volume a bit. Even with the closed captions on, Sebastian liked to hear as much as he could.

Alan brushed his husband's hair with his fingers, letting the strands slip past, one by one. He should've felt reassured, but there had been something in Sebastian's eyes, a bleakness, that worried him. He couldn't possibly know about Richard, could he?

The TV cut away, and then there was a somber-faced announcer on the screen, all in black, announcing that the queen had passed away. *Oh, Margaret.*

"I'll have to go in," Alan said, pulling away from his husband and rising to his feet.

"Right now?" Sebastian asked. He followed Alan back to the main entry.

Alan said, as he bundled up again in cardigan, coat, scarf, "I'll have to meet with the Lion at Windsor, set up Henry's security detail for his return to London and Buckingham Palace. It will take some time—don't wait up."

"I'll try not to," Sebastian said quietly. "Though I don't sleep well until you're safely home beside me."

Alan repressed a sigh. "I'll come back as soon as I can." Time to make an effort. "The curry was delicious, love. Thank you."

Alan let the door shut behind him, and headed out into the cold.

◆

That night, the killings of the crows continued. There wasn't so much as a word spoken of it on the news channels, even though now, adults were joining in. Gunshots rang out, and even in the nearest barracks she felt crows die at the hands of common soldiers, while officers turned a blind eye.

And that's when the goddess understood.

Like any dying organism, the city stirred its antibodies to free itself of the disease. It knew, perhaps only through the shared subconscious of its inhabitants, who she was, what she was. Perhaps the time had come to spread her wings. To bring some other city to its knees so that the land might drink the blood of its heroes.

On the news, an item about farm subsidies was brought to a sudden halt.

"We apologize to viewers for the interruption. But we're hearing that Windsor Castle will be making an announcement in the next five minutes or so. The program will stay on the air, but it looks like the sad news we've been expecting about the queen is about to be confirmed. If so, it truly is the end of an era. An unprecedented time of peace and prosperity for mainland Britain for which she deserves some of the credit . . ."

Badb stayed up watching for hours. *Unprecedented peace and prosperity,* she thought. *Fascinating.*

"And what about the succession?" said one royal correspondent to another.

"Frankly, the polling prefers Richard by a wide margin. His opinions are less . . . troubling."

"Quite!"

"But just imagine the chaos if he were to try for the throne!"

Imagine the chaos. Unprecedented peace.

Badb left that very night.

Sunday

MARCH 1ST

ST. PAUL'S CATHEDRAL WAS packed with worshipers—*correction, make that gawkers*, Noel thought. There were some obvious tourists among the crowd, but it seemed to be predominately Brits filling the pews. The boys in the choir were doing their best to pull the attention away from the family in the front pew, as were the various participants leading the congregation in prayer, and everyone was failing utterly.

This was the first opportunity for people to see their new king and his young bride-to-be and they were taking full advantage. Noel studied the man: his bald pate shining in the light through one of the transept windows, the black mourning armband wrinkling the material of his suit jacket. In place of his now-divorced rather horse-faced wife of forty years sat a young woman in a chic little hat with a net veil. Her family was also present, but the whole thing was grotesque. She could have been his granddaughter.

Henry's only son, Edward, had been killed sixteen years ago while serving in one of those periodic brush wars that flare up in British colonies, and Edward's wife had lost her baby, leaving only Henry's other child, the royal daughter, Gloriana. But she had married a Norwegian prince and agreed to be removed from the succession. It amused Noel to think he had been part of the reason for that marriage. He stifled a laugh.

Gloriana was not present on this cold, gray Sunday, but Noel assumed she would attend the funeral. As for Henry, Noel could not fathom why he hadn't remained at Windsor and attended services at St. George's Chapel rather than returning to London. *Maybe he wanted to bask in the moment and show off his bride. Christ knows he's waited long enough for the crown, but Richard . . .*

Noel stole a glance across the aisle where Richard, Duke of York, sat stony faced with Diana and their brood. Despite the rumors about his proclivities, Richard had sired a passel of kids. Although based on some of the hair colors it was questionable if all of them were his.

The prayer of preparation began and Noel found his memory of the words returning. "Almighty God, unto whom all hearts be open, all desires known . . ." *Please let me keep my son.* "And from whom no secrets are hid . . ." *Please don't let him ever find out what kind of man I really am.* "Cleanse the thoughts of our hearts by the inspiration of thy Holy Spirit, that we may perfectly love thee, and worthily magnify thy holy Name; through Christ our Lord. Amen."

Despite himself, he found the music and language was having an effect, even though his belief in any sort of divine, guiding, and loving god had vanished years ago. Yet how quickly one returned to a hope that entreaties to an imaginary friend in the sky could actually help. He glanced down at Jasper, who sat with rapt attention, listening to the music. The boy's fingers were playing with the light flowing through the stained-glass windows, weaving the different colors into a fanciful design. Noel laid a hand over Jasper's and leaned in to whisper.

"Not in here. There's a lot of security." He nodded toward the various agents positioned around the church, and the three Silver Helix agents. "They might view what you're doing as a threat."

The boy gave a small gasp and released his construct. It shattered into slivers of light that flew in all directions. Rory Campbell, known to the world as Archimedes, who was up in the Whispering Gallery, stiffened and peered down. Noel caught his eye and gave him a brief salute. The ace gave him a dirty look but relaxed.

The service continued with prayers and hymns, readings and a sermon. Noel shifted a bit on the hard pew, looking to ease the ache in his backside. *The things I do to prove I'm a fit parent,* he thought. Finally it was time for the Holy Eucharist. The royals received communion first, and their security detail closed in to block access and even much of a view of the royal family from the passing worshipers.

Noel, hand on Jasper's back, guided him forward. All six foot six of Ranjit Singh blocked the entry into the royal pew and his turban added to his towering presence. He had been Noel's firearms instructor when he had been recruited into the intelligence service, and the Lion had become the head of the Silver Helix after Flint's conviction for war crimes. Noel gave him a nod as they passed and received a glare in return.

He and Jasper knelt at the altar rail as the Bishop of London, assisted by a pair of priests (no mere altar boys for a bishop), made his way down the line dispensing the host. The dry wafer caught in the back of Noel's throat, which caused him to take a rather larger sip from the chalice being offered by the trailing priest. That earned him another frown. Nobody seemed to be happy with him today. The thought amused him.

Once back in their seats, there was more singing and more praying and then blessedly, mercifully, it was over. There was a brief remonstration with Henry, the gestures from the agents both nat and wild card indicating they would prefer that the king leave through a more private exit, but Henry was having none of it. He sat stubbornly still, so the bishop then announced that the congregation should leave. Noel and Jasper joined the throng shuffling slowly out of the cathedral. Noel contemplated transforming into his male avatar and just teleporting them out of the crowd, but decided that might cause an uproar and rather undercut his image as a responsible father.

♥

The crows of London welcomed Badb as well as any had in Belfast. More so! She'd stowed away on a lorry, hiding under a pallet of frozen fish. When the vehicle came to a stop in a place called "Billingsgate" and she had tumbled out the back, exhausted, dehydrated, a spiral of crows descended around her to pay homage.

They did not flinch as she bit through the skulls of the two closest, swallowing the brains, sating her thirst on their blood. She sent the rest of them flying again, watching the glory of London through their eyes. Oh, this city! This unfamiliar city! Its might swept out below her in all directions. How it had ripened until such a time as she could come for it.

She flitted from one bird to the next, learning the shape of the river. There were towers tall enough to house every soul in Belfast. Glass glittered, steel shone. But not everywhere. She landed outside a room where twelve immigrant workers snored beside their own washing. She soared over a knot of narrow streets where only jokers walked or slithered or hopped. Divisions. Yes, there were divisions here too. Poverty lived within stabbing distance of wealth.

Down there, in a place called Greenwich, the IRA had a safe house. Less than a mile away, their sworn enemies in the UVF kept a hidey hole of their own. She knew all their secrets. They would do as they were bid.

Most satisfactory.

And then, a distant crow heard the peal of bells.

Great crowds gathered around a white cathedral whose dome would have swallowed Belfast City Hall. Security guards pushed back a forest of microphones at the main entrance, but they couldn't stop Badb drifting down to listen.

Annoyingly, the city had put in those spikes intended to discourage pigeons from landing. But the crow impaled itself willingly and would live long enough to see what came next. She left it to suffer, taking the mind of another bird and then another, circling, circling until she saw what she was looking for: weakness.

A guard absent from his post, mobile phone in hand.

She landed right behind him.

"Not now, babe," he said in a thick accent. He knew nobody could hear him. The crowd was too loud, the reporters too many. "What? Absolutely no! They find out I'm Serbian instead of Croat, what then? Home on first plane, that's what. Marriage? Ha! They'll read my war record. It will be prison not Belgrade where they send me."

Fascinating.

"Of course, I am changed, babe, but only you know. Only you. What?" He laughed. "Crazy bitch. I see you tonight."

Behind him, the doors of the cathedral swung open. A new king emerged and at his back a wealth of other important people. So handy to have them all gathered here in one place. Leaders she would follow with crows, listening to their every word for hidden cracks in this magnificent city.

♣

It was a raw day with lowering clouds and a cold rain that had ambitions of becoming sleet. Noel tightened Jasper's muffler, pulled on his gloves, and opened his umbrella. "Can we wait and watch the king leave?" Jasper asked. "It's kind of like when I play *Dragon Age* with all the kings and stuff. I mean to see one for real is kind of cool."

Noel scanned the loitering crowd and realized that a lot of people apparently shared his son's fascination with royalty. And if he was honest, he felt it too. Not for any fanciful sense of brave kings and beautiful princesses but because of what it represented about his country. Of Magna Carta and Trafalgar and the Battle of Britain and fighting on the beaches. It was that sense of history, permanence, and continuity embodied in an institution to which Noel had sworn his allegiance.

He hugged his son. "Okay, we'll wait a bit."

At the bottom of the stone steps the press and paparazzi lay in wait. Camera lenses stared up at him like dead eyes. There was a growing murmur as Henry and his fiancée emerged. The young woman walked a few steps behind her husband-to-be, which left Noel wondering about that relationship.

"Answer a few questions, Your Majesty?" a reporter yelled from the crowd.

"Certainly."

Noel noted that the equerry, a man in his fifties with the upright stance of a former military officer, blanched a bit at the response from Henry.

"So, what are your hopes for your reign, sir?"

"I'd like to bring England back to being England again," Henry responded.

"What does that mean? Exactly? Sir," another called.

"Well, take London. In my youth you heard English spoken everywhere. Now you'd be lucky to hear your own language in amongst all the other gabble."

Noel thought the equerry was going to have a stroke. The rapid fire of digital cameras was like claws clicking on ice.

"So, you don't like the fact that London has become a multilingual, multicultural, and multiethnic city?" came a third voice out of the crowd.

"It's all well and good until it isn't. If we lose sight of who we are we'll be in the suds."

"Does that mean white and European, sir?"

Henry gazed down his nose at the questioner, a tall, elegant black man. "It means Anglo-Saxon. Make of that what you will."

"Damn right, I will," the journalist muttered.

Another voice rose out of the crowd. "The Pakis are one thing, sir, but what about those freaks down in the East End?" Noel searched the crowd for the speaker and also for any sign that a riot was about to break out. It proved to be an older white man with a bulging belly hanging over his belt and the general shape of a fire plug. "I live on the edge of that mess and it's driving down property values."

"It is a problem, but now there is *that* thing up on the moon." Henry waved vaguely skyward. "Perhaps they can be encouraged to emigrate. They'll no doubt be happier among their own kind. Better for all concerned if they leave."

There were more cheers than Noel liked to hear, and only a few muttered objections, but no one booed. *We are so British*, Noel thought. Henry was the king despite the stupid words that had just fallen from his mouth, and no one was going to be that overtly rude. It was at that point that Henry's people wisely decided to rush him to the waiting car.

People began to disperse. Noel stood watching the motorcade making its way back toward Buckingham Palace and wondered if maybe a removal to his bolt-hole in Paris or even the one in Vienna was indicated. Things were likely to become tinderbox tense in the city after Henry's performance. But if he left for a foreign capital it might add to the perception that he was merely a kidnapper and not a devoted father.

He also had a performance to prepare, and getting sued for cancelling a performance was not going to aid his effort to seem like a fit parent. It was ironic that he had to keep working. His company Ace in Hand back in New York continued generating income despite him no longer doing the day-to-day management, and he was technically a millionaire because of his share of the money after that ill-fated poker game in Chicago. Still, he had mentally set those funds aside for Jasper; for his education and to set him up in life.

Jasper tugged at his suit jacket. "Dad?"

He looked down. "Hmmm?"

"Does this mean people don't like *any* wild cards? I mean, I'm an ace, but if they don't like jokers, does that mean they don't like me too?"

You're far too smart for me to sugarcoat this, Noel thought as he gazed down at his son. "We have it easier because people don't know we're wild cards, but yes, a lot of people don't like us."

"That's why you don't like me to . . ." Jasper allowed some sunlight to briefly become a physical golden thread in his hand, then quickly released it.

Noel put an arm around Jasper's shoulders and pulled him tight against his side. "Precisely."

♠

The weather was still shite and Glory was still dead.

Constance plugged the kettle in and started the ritual she and Bobbin had begun decades earlier. Every morning they would get in early—long before their employees—drink tea, and share a post-breakfast pastry. Breakfast they ate out. Cooking was forbidden in the atelier. The smell alone ruled it out. No one wanted to buy expensive clothes in a place that smelled of eggs, sausage, beans, and bacon.

Normally, they would chat about what was happening with the studio.

Constance would tell Bobbin about the designs she'd been working on and how she was planning on fabricating them. Then Bobbin would look dismayed as he mentally ran through the cost of materials.

But today, they had the TV on instead and couldn't stop watching reports of Queen Margaret's death. It hardly seemed possible to Constance. Losing two people she loved in such a short time was horrid. She had always been inclined to get angry rather than cry. And today she was livid.

Footage of Henry, that bastard, came on, and he was saying things about jokers no decent person would, except he'd wrapped it up in that royal verbal deceit. The things he said on the steps of St. Paul's were all too clear for anyone paying attention. She may have clothed his mother, but Constance was damned if she'd ever put so much as a scrap of fabric on his back.

And just as her indignation rose even higher, a Man on the Street interview began, with the reporter inquiring what *their* reaction was to what Henry had been saying.

"The Pakis are one thing," said a stout fellow with a florid complexion. He wore a snap-brim cap and an army green zippered jacket. "But those joker freaks down in East End? The king is right, send 'em to the moon."

She swore at the TV, and then there were cool fingers on her wrist. Bobbin.

"This is only going to make you angrier," he said, gently tugging her into her chair. "You should stop watching."

She hadn't even known she'd stood up. Henry was talking about *her* people, for the love of God.

"Why are you so upset?" he asked. "It isn't as if you'll ever have to deal with him."

"You know very well I made clothes for the queen," Constance said, pulling her arm away. "Do you think that's going to stop now?"

Bobbin shrugged and took a sip of his tea. "Why would he come here? There are plenty of other tailors that cater just to men that he would probably prefer to use."

The reason Henry would come to her was part and parcel of what she hadn't shared with Bobbin. Constance debated whether to tell him part of her secret, but decided against it. She'd kept the whole of it hidden for so long that she wasn't even certain how to tell anyone.

"Come on," he said. He gave her his funny lopsided smile that showed off his pretty teeth. "Tell me about your new sketch." He gestured at her drafting table.

"I couldn't sleep last night, so I thought I'd do something to honor Glory," Constance said, punching the Mute button on the remote rather than turning the TV off. She wasn't ready to let go of the news just yet.

"Florals," she said with a smile. "Of course."

She lifted the protective tissue up off the sketch. A simple, but sweeping, dress was covered by bright geometric rectangles. These provided a background for highly stylized flowers. It felt both modern and as if it were an homage to the sixties, which was what it was.

"It's quite lovely," Bobbin said. He stepped closer, looking down at the sketch, and Constance got a whiff of his spicy cologne and the Pears soap he used. There was a hint of pipe tobacco and wintergreen mint too. The combination was very Bobbin-like. She felt a little rush of happiness and calm.

"I suppose you're going to do a whole line based on Glory?" he asked.

"Yes, of course," she replied with a smile.

"And we're going to need to have a lot of new fabric made up." There was resignation in his voice.

"Indeed. As always." This was a bit of old playacting between them and it made her feel a bit better.

"And it's going to cost a fortune because your fabrics always do."

"You have the right of it."

Bobbin sighed. She knew he would figure out a way to get the fabric made without bankrupting them, and she would make sure they had designs people wanted to buy.

But out of the corner of her eye she caught a glimpse of a replay of Henry on the TV, holding forth on the steps of St. Paul's.

Bastard.

◆

Green Man sat at his desk staring at the array of newspapers, not really reading any of them. Every headline spoke of the same story, rendered in somber lettering, and those that favored a splash of color in their logo had foregone it for a funeral black.

Queen Margaret was dead.

The spiteful comments of the new king, Henry, were there too, pushed to the corner but still on the front pages. A bad sign of things to come.

Green Man wasn't a fervent royalist, but he'd always had respect for the queen. Throughout the turbulence of the War, and ups and downs of Britain's fortunes in the years that followed, she had been there. A thread of continuity and a thing of stability. It was not unlike the feeling of when he'd first left home but been told his old room was still available. He hadn't needed it, but it was comforting to know it was there. Now she was gone, the world seemed that bit less safe.

A familiar knock at the door brought him back to the present. "Come in," he said.

Wayfarer stepped inside, reliable as ever. Thank God he still had her! She'd been a young slip of a woman when she'd first started working for the Fists, but time had thickened her. Despite this, her skirts remained too short, her hair often changed color, and she still insisted on wearing sunglasses at all times. No doubt this last detail was connected to her mutation, but she'd never volunteered the information, and he'd never asked. A person should be allowed a few secrets. *God knows, I have them.*

Unlike him, however, she still had a youthful energy. A quiet spark of industry that he admired, and wished he could reclaim. "Good morning."

"Is it?" he replied, casting a glance toward the papers.

"Sorry." She closed the door behind her. "What are the plans for today?"

"No plans."

"I thought we were going to check in with the local cells."

That had been the plan, but he didn't feel up to it. It all seemed so pointless. All these years of fighting and what did he have to show for it apart from bloodied hands? Despite their best efforts, jokers were no closer to being accepted now than they were forty years ago.

The silence hung there for a while. He knew he should say something, perhaps give an order, but he couldn't summon the energy for it.

Wayfarer came a few steps further into the room. "Are you alright?"

"I don't know; first Glory, now Queen Margaret. It seems like we're losing all of the greats. And look at her replacement: the poster boy for Britain First."

"I'm not convinced we should have a monarchy at all," said Wayfarer, "but I've always liked Richard. It's a shame we can't give the crown to him instead."

"He's too soft. In times like these we need a king with a spine."

"With respect, Richard isn't soft. He's just not an arsehole." Green Man scoffed and she carried on quickly before he could reply. "Besides, a gay man might be just what we need on the throne. He'll understand persecution and social injustice better than Henry ever could."

"He's not gay, he's a married man."

It was Wayfarer's turn to scoff. "Everyone knows he's gay."

"It doesn't matter either way. The crown doesn't get passed on to the person with the most votes from the audience. It'll go to the eldest as it always has."

"I think that's a shame. We're supposed to be living in a democracy."

He sighed. "A corrupt democracy. Our elected officials get worse every year. I remember when our leaders were people of character, not these limp-wristed, career minded . . ."—he searched for a suitable insult to finish his sentence— "lawyers!"

Wayfarer shook her head. "You can't use 'limp-wristed' like that. You sound homophobic."

He'd long since learned to trust her on these matters, but it still irked him. He used to consider himself an expert on the use of language, and now it seemed as if the rules on what was and was not appropriate were changing too fast for him to keep up. "You know what I mean," he said peevishly, "In the old days we had politicians with morals. The kind you could be proud of."

"Like Churchill?"

"Yes, now he was a real prime minister."

"And a racist," she retorted, "and a killer who ran death camps."

Green Man nearly stood up, he was so surprised. "How dare you! Churchill was a hero." He was also the man that had charged Roger with the task of infiltrating the Twisted Fists in the first place. Roger had done so out of love for the great statesman and to secure his family's future. Cruel fate had seen Churchill die while Roger was deep under cover, condemning him to a life as Green Man.

"Wait," said Wayfarer as she pulled out her phone. "Here's some things your hero said . . ." She only made a few taps on the screen, suggesting that she had the quotes saved somewhere for an occasion just like this one. "'The Aryan stock is bound to triumph.' That's not Hitler talking by the way, that's Churchill."

"It's hard for me to comment without context."

"He called Africans 'savages'?"

"Well," Green Man said weakly, "it was a different time back then."

One eyebrow appeared over the top of Wayfarer's sunglasses. "And when he fought the Kurds, he said: 'I am strongly in favor of using poisoned gas on uncivilized tribes.'"

"He really said that?"

"Yes. He said it would"—she made air quotes with her free hand—"'spread a lively terror.' And you should hear what he said about the Palestinians—"

Green Man raised a hand. "Alright, I get the idea. Are you making a point with all of this?"

"Yes." She slipped her phone away. "My point is that people get nostalgic about history. They forget what it was really like and it gets buried. All children learn is Churchill's speech about fighting on the beaches and the fact he liked cigars."

"I see." Green Man had known Wayfarer long enough to know there was more going on. He waved a hand for her to continue.

She sagged a little. "The truth is, I know this sort of thing riles you and I wanted to stir you up a bit."

"Consider your gambit a success. Now, will you tell me why?"

"You've been quiet lately, and I had a feeling the news was going to hit you hard. I'm sorry, I really am, but you should be out there. The Fists need to see more of their leader, especially now that King Henry's put jokers on his agenda." When he didn't reply, she added, "If you don't say something, someone else will."

"What do you mean?"

She looked away. "There's been some talk."

"Let me guess, Seizer?"

"Yes."

"What's the old fool done this time?"

"He's saying you've gone soft, and harking back to the time of the Black Dog."

"Let him. It's all hot air."

"But the younger Fists don't know what it was really like under the Dog's rule. They're scared of what's going to happen, and Seizer's going to stir them up even more. You know what he's like once he has a crowd."

"Fine. I'll show my face and put this nonsense to bed, but not now."

"This afternoon then?"

He frowned. She'd been taking more and more liberties with him lately. "Don't push me, Wayfarer."

However, she didn't back down as he expected. "We need you."

"For goodness' sake!"

"Tomorrow?"

"Alright. Tomorrow."

♥

Alan shoved his way through the coats in the closet, heavy with damp—it had been raining hard outside Buckingham and everyone's coats bore the marks. This was ridiculous. Richard might enjoy playing like children at games of Narnia—*what's in the back of the wardrobe?* But Richard also had a perfectly comfortable flat for exactly this sort of thing, and there was no need for the two of them to fumble around in the dark. Just as Alan was thinking that perhaps he should give up and just go, Richard was there, all hot hands sliding down into Alan's pants, a warm, wet mouth on his, fiercely eager. For a little while, Alan Turing stopped thinking at all.

Afterwards, Richard held up a phone, reflecting light and a camera so Alan could repair his makeup. It wouldn't do for anyone to see a member of the Silver Helix looking badly mussed, or worse, silvery.

"I'm really very fond of you, you know," Richard said, smiling. "My metal man."

Alan's throat tightened. "Can you imagine the uproar if your wife caught you with a joker? I don't know if it'd be better or worse than her catching you with a man." Alan could joke about it now, play it off lightly, but he'd never forget how he'd been treated, during the War. Eight decades ago, but his memory was perfect now, every humiliating incident recalled in excruciating detail.

Richard looked sober now. "Worse, much worse. She and I have our understandings, but a joker might require additional negotiations. And if it went public—"

Alan nodded. "Yes, that would be a problem." He hesitated, then asked, "Are you going to respond publicly to what Henry said?"

His lover frowned. "I don't know."

Alan was fond of Richard. The prince had a good heart inside that broad-shouldered body, a cheerful generosity that people couldn't help but love. But after all these years, their on-again, off-again thing had let Alan know the prince a little too well. Sometimes Richard needed a push, to be the man he ought to be.

"Dickie. You can't let the world think England's royal family supports your brother's bigotry. Your family serves as the moral compass for the realm."

Richard hesitated, then said, "If I spoke up, do you think it would hurt my chances?"

"Chances?" Surely Richard didn't mean . . .

Richard reached out, put a hand on Alan's arm. "You can see it, can't you, Alan? Henry is unfit to be king. He will drag England back to the Dark Ages." He squeezed, and Alan's malleable metal skin hardened in response to the abrupt pressure. "The people want a brighter, more civilized future." Richard was standing up straighter now, dropping his hand from Alan's arm. The light of the phone cast his face into dramatic chiaroscuro. Handsome, with those thick blond eyebrows and mane of flaxen hair—the very picture of a king. "I should make a statement, make it clear where I stand. The people of England would support me." And then Richard's voice dropped again, hesitation returning, so that he looked almost like a boy again. "Don't you think?"

Alan couldn't resist running the calculations. It was an interesting strategic problem, considered in that light, without any regard for bloodline or right of inheritance. Who would be better for England, Henry or Richard? Richard, surely. Henry was cold, unfeeling—the sort who would cut you dead at the dinner table, would blithely ruin you and your family too. Afterwards he'd go straight to bed and sleep as well as an innocent babe, certain he'd done the right thing; men of his sort always did, by definition.

Henry was elderly too—at seventy-one, he'd make an aged king, and would likely only survive for a few more years. No doubt that's the sort of math that had had Henry setting aside his wife of forty years. Was he so sure that young Emily would be able to give him an heir? But even if she gave Henry a litter of heirs, it would be a long decade and more before any would be old enough to plausibly inherit. Richard, by contrast, was only fifty-five, a far more suitable age for a monarch, one who could serve England for a long, steadying reign.

But would the people support him? That was less clear—there were too many variables. When Alan tried to calculate the possibilities, dozens of futures spun off behind his eyes. England triumphant, a land united. England in flames, torn apart by civil war. The stakes were frighteningly high, and he could understand why Margaret had desperately wanted there to be a better option. But some lost heir, with no training, to take the throne based solely on an accident of bloodline? Nonsense. Surely Richard was better suited than that. The people would likely agree; the odds were surprisingly in his favor. Alan frowned. "I cannot promise, but I think . . . they might actually support you."

Richard took his hand then, pressed it to his chest. "And you, Alan? Would you support me?"

Another interesting question. Richard was far from a perfect man. Yet there was the warmth under his fingertips, and a man who had never flinched away from Alan's joker attributes. Under his rule, the jokers would have a champion. Surely, for England's sake, Alan Turing should support the best man for the throne? Wasn't that one of the lessons he'd learned during the War, that sometimes the right path to follow wasn't necessarily the lawful road?

Richard's hand was warm on his, his blue eyes steady and intent. "Alan? Are you with me?"

Alan hesitated, then said softly, "I'm yours to command, sir."

"Good." And then Richard was kissing him again, wildly. The makeup would have to be redone, but Alan couldn't bring himself to care. His heart was thumping in his chest, and he couldn't seem to catch a decent breath. What had he just agreed to?

King Richard IV. It did sound good.

♣

"What's this do?" Jasper asked. They were at the warehouse where Noel stored the equipment for his magic act.

Jasper was standing next to a tall wardrobe, resting his hand on the polished black wood. Noel walked over to join him. "That's where I make people disappear."

"But they don't really disappear, right Dad?"

"Correct."

"Am I going to go with you when you do the show?" Jasper asked.

"Yes."

"I'll miss school."

"Travel is also educational." Noel had a low opinion of American educational standards, but so far Jasper seemed to be doing well at the private school, so apparently American private schools were keeping up standards.

In late April, Noel would be performing in Tokyo, an eight-day run on a big stage that required large equipment that supported the big illusions. He had already shipped the stage that would be installed over the theater's actual stage. Now he was inspecting the tools of his trade. Though in a world where people could ghost through walls, turn into thousands of wasps, actually fly, and (like himself) teleport thousands of miles in the blink of an eye or (like his son) braid and craft light into intricate designs, he wondered if there was still an audience for stage magic. In truth he had started to abandon the bigger flashier stunts in favor of close magic and mind tricks with cards and numbers. Those still had audiences oohing and aahing in wonderment. For some reason the Japanese wanted the big show and they were paying well, so he would oblige them. In his pursuit of sole custody over his son, Noel had had to turn the day-to-day management of his Ace in Hand company back in Manhattan over to his assistant. He still drew a salary, but he had taken a pay cut so Dogsbody would get a raise. Which had necessitated a return to touring in order to maintain their lifestyle.

Noel returned to his work and Jasper picked up a deck of cards and laid out a hand of solitaire. "You could do your homework," Noel tossed over his shoulder.

"I know. Can you show me how to do a card trick?"

Noel sighed, but he wasn't really annoyed at his son's interest. He came to Jasper's side and gathered up the cards. It was hard to manipulate the cards slowly, but he tried to so he could demonstrate how he could control the placement of each card. "Now you try." He handed over the deck. The boy's hands were a bit small to successfully grasp the skill, but he tried until the cards suddenly fountained out of his hands, and he burst out laughing. Noel loved him for that. There was no pouting or fury, just enjoyment and a touch of self-deprecation. It was clear Jasper took more after his mother than his irascible father.

"Let me show you how to pick a lock," Noel said as he removed his lockpick case from his inner suit pocket. They went to the small door into the warehouse and Noel demonstrated. He started to hand over the tools when Jasper gave him an impish look.

"I don't need those, Dad. Watch." He tried to reach for the setting sun, but clouds had rolled in and he wasn't able to make an effective braid. Noel turned on the flashlight function on his cell phone and Jasper used that to fashion one of his creations. He then thrust it into the lock. Noel heard the tumblers fall and he gave a sharp laugh of surprise.

"Oh well done, you!" He hugged Jasper close. "It's getting late and cold. What say we stop for some takeout and go home?"

"Okay."

Noel locked the door again, and with his arm draped over his son's shoulder, they walked to where he had parked his Aston Martin. *Is this my midlife crisis?* he wondered. Or was stealing away his child more evidence of aberrant behavior? Noel had always been coldly analytical until an infant had wrapped his tiny fingers around his thumb and he was lost. He abruptly dropped a kiss on the top of Jasper's head. The boy looked up, startled, and gave him a shy smile, but sadness lurked around the edges.

"I love you, Dad, but I wish you and Mom would just . . . talk."

"We will. Eventually. And she'll come around."

"That's not talking, Dad, that's telling."

Noel was stunned speechless. *You are your mother's child. Kind and empathetic. Is there any part of me in you? I suppose your intellect, but you will be a better man than I.*

"Get in the car," he said roughly. "It's colder than a witch's tit out here."

Jasper turned on the radio as they headed toward their favorite Chinese restaurant. He was scanning through the stations in search of the music he liked—*God help me,* Noel thought, *why must it be Justin Bieber? Perhaps he will outgrow it*—when he heard the voice of the second son of Queen Margaret. "Wait. Stop." Jasper gave him an eye roll and that sigh that Noel had no doubt would become even more pronounced once he reached his teen years, but Jasper complied.

". . . think it is kind to call my brother's remarks unfortunate. I think that does not begin to describe them. Such naked bigotry has no place in our country, and it is simply unacceptable for divisive and hateful sentiment to be voiced by the king of England, who, as the head of our country's government, should be setting a moral and ethical standard for the nation, not dragging it down into the gutter."

The BBC announcer returned to say, "That was His Grace the Duke of York commenting to our own Christy Walsh on his brother's remarks on Sunday. Wouldn't you say that's rather remarkable, David—"

"Fine, that's enough. Go find some music." Jasper complied and soon the latest pop tune was echoing through the car.

"Do you think he's right? What that duke guy said?" Jasper asked.

Noel sucked in a deep breath and blew it out in gust. "I agree with what he said, but he shouldn't have said it."

"That's kinda weird. I don't understand."

"For better or worse, Henry is king. We owe him our allegiance and loyalty and I'm sure the palace advisors are assiduously working to rein in Henry and clean up the mess from Sunday. Richard is his brother, a representative of the House of Windsor, and he needs to shut up, stop undercutting his brother, and let the palace handle this."

"So, you believe in all this king stuff."

"I do. I don't think Britain would be Britain without the royals."

Monday

MARCH 2ND

THE MEETING OF THE Twisted Fists was taking place in an old industrial complex. It had been left idle for years and was steadily being reclaimed by nature. Green Man saw signs that rats had taken up residence in one building, and a crow appeared to be nesting in another. Broken paving stones made the van rattle as it came to a stop outside the first in a row of abandoned warehouses. He and Wayfarer climbed out of the van and moved as quickly into the old warehouse as possible.

Rust gathered in thick patches on its corrugated roof, and an array of holes perforated the walls. Through them, Green Man could see muted lights flickering within. He checked his watch. They would step through the doors at nine fifty-five, which would allow them to start at ten o'clock precisely. He may not work for the government anymore, but that was no reason to let standards slip.

The others were already inside. Not all of the Fists—such a gathering would be both impractical and far too dangerous—but a mix of those who had something to say, and those that would spread word of what transpired here to the other cells. A silence fell as he approached, but he noted that it was Seizer who had been doing the talking, holding court—or rather, stealing court while he could.

There was a pause as the two sized each other up. Not for the first time, Green Man took pleasure in the extra height his wild card had given him. It was a petty, primal thing, but there really was no substitute for being able to look down on someone.

Seizer had been with Fists for as long as anyone could remember. His spine curved forward at the top now, and in his overcoat, he looked like a giant beetle. Egg-sized growths of hard, calloused skin grew all over his body, including a pointed set ringing his skull that Seizer (and nobody else) seemed to think was reminiscent of a crown. Over the day these growths would flake and fall off, only to reappear the following morning. A few discarded lumps of crust had collected by his feet, no doubt dislodged by some enthusiastic arm-waving. There was a particularly unpleasant smell to his discarded flesh that everyone was studiously ignoring. Despite this, the man carried himself with the kind of arrogance one could only find in the aristocracy.

"And, at last, he arrives," said Seizer.

Green Man refused to rise to the obvious bait; he knew damn well that he was on time. Or was this a broader barb? Wayfarer had told him that he'd been too absent lately. He decided it was better not to reply in either case, giving Seizer nothing but silence. The old knave made a gesture as if conceding the floor and moved to one side.

♠

Such a peaceful city, thought Badb. Compared to Belfast, that is. But wherever there were jokers, there was prejudice and fear. Hatred for those who already suffered the most.

Who could bear such appalling injustice? Not the Fists, that was for sure.

She found herself leaning against damp bricks in the East End of London. Such were the burdens of godhood that she aged many times faster than mortals did. And bled enough over the course of the day to fill a bath.

She trembled. Coughing as blood pooled in her belly and lungs.

She would need to renew herself, and soon. This was why she had come to the East End. Passions ran high among the Fists. There were always young jokers eager to give their lives for the cause of equality. The perfect tools to pick London apart.

She closed her eyes. Never before had she tried following so many important people at once. Some she had already lost track of, when a bird was snatched by a predator or stuck in a crack. But she caught glimpses of Turing traveling alone in the back of a car—her biggest threat; of the younger prince pacing in a bedroom, eager, impatient, but for what? She would check back later, because suddenly, through the window of a rotting building, a wooden giant appeared, and she knew it had to be Green Man himself! One of his joker kin stood before him now. Despite the thumb-sized boils that mottled his body, there was no mistaking the aggression in that stance, the scorn on that face. Oh, most satisfactory. A hero in the making, perhaps. A chance for her to renew herself before it was too late.

♦

The room was already crowded with a mix of MI-5 and Silver Helix members when Turing arrived, filling the seats of the long conference table. They'd arranged to have this meeting in the Silver Helix conference room, because MI-5 would be chairing it. Of such uneasy compromises was government made.

Singh said genially, "Turing, man, you've been avoiding me. Every time I see you in the hallways, you're rushing in the other direction. What are you so busy with? You must give me a game sometime; it's been too long." Singh towered over the gathered security forces, a full head higher than most of them, with the bulk to match; when he stood, the top of his turban would be high enough to brush the ceiling. With his deep voice, he commanded attention, and if pressed, Alan would admit to having entertained a few fantasies featuring the Lion. Tragically, Turing didn't appear to be the Lion's cup of tea.

"Singh, I've told you," Alan demurred. "I don't play anymore." Singh's chess-board sat ready at one end of the conference room, two comfortable leather wingback chairs flanking it, inviting. This set, he'd heard, was one that had come from India originally, had belonged to some maharajah or another, back in the day.

"Hm." The Lion frowned. "You think, with that computer in your head, you would destroy me? My people invented the game, you know. Now bloody computers have made the whole thing pointless."

That was true, if your only purpose was to win. Alan had designed the first chess-playing computer program decades ago, and then tromped it soundly. All of that had changed, though. Now even *he* couldn't beat the new chess-playing computers—they were more powerful than his card-granted gifts. But Alan had still loved playing with Sebastian. When they first became involved; he'd been charmed by the openness of his play, the trusting nature. Sebastian hadn't been willing to play him in years though—*I got tired of losing, Alan.*

Now wasn't the time to think of that. "Chess will never be pointless, Singh. You can learn much of a man's character from the way he plays."

"Or a woman's?" One of the MI-5 people, a middle-aged woman he didn't recognize.

Alan turned to her. "Or a woman's, of course."

She offered a hand. "Sarah Edwards. I'll be heading things up today."

Turing shook her hand—a good grip, warm and forthright.

She continued, "Do you know everyone else here? Let me introduce you—"

He knew the Silver Helix members, of course: Singh had pulled in the new young Redcoat—it probably was time for the boy to get some seasoning—and Stonemaiden, so it wasn't an entirely male contingent from the Helix. Edwards added a quick flurry of additional names: representatives from Scotland Yard's RaSP division, along with a few others from MI-5. Some of them he'd met before, but Alan didn't know any of them well.

He missed Charlie Soper—after that business with Churchill, so many decades ago, he and Charlie had had occasion to work together, more and more over the years. A reliable man, the sort you could count on. A good man in a storm. It was a shame there were so few of those to be had. Soper was retired now, and enjoying a well-earned peace at last. A peace that Alan was determined to protect.

The Lion was sitting down in a broad chair that must have been specially made to handle his bulk, and the others moved to take the seats. Singh slammed a fist on the sturdy mahogany table. "Enough dillydallying, children. We must sort out where we stand, make this transition as soon as possible. When power changes hands, there is a moment, a gap, when no one is really in control. That's the danger—there are always dark figures waiting, lurking on the edges. They'll be the ones rushing in to fill the gap, and it's our job to make sure that doesn't happen."

Sarah Edwards frowned at Singh; in theory, she was in charge of this meeting.

"Yes, let's get started." Edwards leaned forward. "Did you hear that Double Helix is back? Will he be trouble?"

Alan felt the stab of regret that always flashed through him when he thought of Noel—could he and Flint have done anything different? Trained the boy better, raised a better man? Or had Noel always been walking his dark path? "He says he's retired—"

"You can't trust the bastard," Edwards said. "But I'm more worried about the Fists—they're roiling right now."

"Can you blame them?" Redcoat asked. "After what Henry said—"

The Lion frowned. "Hush! He'll be joining us any minute."

"But, Singh . . ." Alan began, but the Lion cut him off.

"Henry is king, Turing. What would you have us do?"

Alan just shook his head. He could hardly ask them all to swear fealty to Richard instead. They'd think Alan's 108-year-old brain had finally, suddenly, given out completely.

"Threat analysis, Mr. Turing," Edwards said. "That's what we need from you—please put that brain of yours to work and help us sort through this mess. I want to know every likely attack on the throne—and I want to know which ones we'll have to deal with first."

Threat analysis was worth doing for Richard too, of course. And while he was at it, maybe Alan would spend a little time chasing down Margaret's lost heir. It was hard to imagine that some lost joker child could become a serious threat at this late stage, but it was never wise to overlook a piece on the board. If you did, the next thing you knew, a pawn would make it to the far end and queen herself, or your king would end up pinned by some sneaky knight.

"I'll do my best, ma'am," Alan said, as the door opened and Henry entered the room. They all rose hastily to their feet, the chairs scraping back loudly.

Henry smiled benevolently. "Then we shall rest easy, Alan, because your best is very good indeed."

It was dangerous to say no to a king. "Thank you, Your Majesty. I'd best get to work right away," Alan said. "Calculating a problem this complex will take some time."

Stalling was his best tactic now.

♥

Green Man stood for a few moments, letting his gaze sweep the assembled. The last of the murmurings stopped. He had their attention now, the nervous energy of the room directed solely in his direction. He made them wait a moment more than was comfortable, then began to speak:

"Thank you for coming. There aren't many of us around now that remember a time before Margaret was queen. But, let me assure you, there was. I cannot deny that there will be change, and some of the change is regrettable—"

"Regrettable!" Seizer snorted. "Henry just told us to bugger off to the bally moon!"

Green Man allowed his wooden eyes to narrow behind the mask. He hated being interrupted. It ruined the flow of his speech. Seizer had always been difficult, but he was getting worse with age. More like a piece of cheese left in the sun too long than a fine wine. "They are words, Seizer, nothing more. They can't hurt us, and by next week, the papers will have moved on to something else."

"They are the words of our king and he's saying we're no better than a pack of scrounging foreigners. Everyone who has ever hated us will take it as permission to act." He spread his hands. "And then, by god, we'll have more than words to deal with."

A few of the other jokers nodded along, with one or two murmuring assent, while the others exchanged worried glances. Seizer might have no idea what he was talking about, but it was clear he'd tapped into the fears of the room.

"People are free to speak," said Green Man. "Even if they use that freedom to show the worst parts of themselves. That doesn't mean they're free to act. If Britain First or some other group thinks they have leave to hurt us, they will find themselves sorely mistaken. Kings may come and go, but the Twisted Fists will endure."

Seizer tutted. "A fine sentiment, but it won't protect us. We need to take action! Break a few heads to show them we mean business."

"If the Fists need to break heads, we will. Five for each of ours. But only if they leave us no other choice."

"Do nothing! Tha—"

He could see Seizer wanted to say more, so he stepped forward. His foot made a loud crunching noise as one of Seizer's discarded growths shattered beneath it.

"No," he added quietly. "There are many steps between inaction and bloodshed. We know Henry is not the sort of man to be won over by reason, nor by violence. If we lash out at him now, it will only prove him right in the eyes of the media. No," Green Man said again, "Henry does not care about the morality of his position, but he does care about his reputation. A discreet threat should be enough to make him back off, perhaps even retract his earlier statements." Green Man lifted his chin and raised his voice ever so slightly.

"Put out the word: I want everything we can get on our king-to-be. A man like Henry will have made mistakes and tried to bury them. Get out there. Dig them up. The dirtier the secret, the better."

The Twisted Fists were starting to move, much happier now that their nerves could be channeled. Even so, he could see Seizer considering whether to speak.

"Dismissed," said Green Man, as much to him as to the room.

The old knave deferred with a bow of his bent body, even as his eyes flashed displeasure.

Wayfarer was right, Green Man thought. *My rivals have grown bold, and like Henry it's going to take more than words to put them down.*

He flexed the heavy fingers of his right hand. It was clumsier than it used to be, but stronger. A blunt instrument. He'd used it to take lives before and, if need be, he'd take them again. But when he imagined having to crack a skull, it was not Henry's that came to mind, but a knobbly one, much closer to home.

♣

"I'm bloody well not going to do it," Constance snapped, rubbing her index finger between her eyes.

Constance gripped her phone even harder. It was difficult to keep a good grasp because of her arthritic fingers—her new iPhone was stupidly big—but she was past even noticing that they hurt.

"I'm so sorry, but there is no other choice," replied the Lion. "It's your duty."

"I won't do it," she said tightly. "Besides, I'm retired."

"If there was any other way," he said with real sadness and concern in his voice. "But your skills are known to the royals, and Henry wants to avail himself of them as soon as possible. And well you know that no one *really* retires from MI-7."

She could almost see his face, noble and filled with compassion for her, and she resented it.

"You've continued to help us even after your official resignation. You had no problems clothing the late queen, God rest her soul."

"That was *her*. Henry is nothing like his mother! After what he said? And said on the steps of St. Paul's of all places? He'd rather drink poison than be served by a shop full of jokers."

"Constance," he replied now with a weariness she hadn't expected. "This is the way it has to be. Besides, you know you'll be going to Buckingham, just as you did for his mother. He'll never see your jokers. Out of sight and all that."

"No," Constance said. "No. I won't do it. And don't you dare ask me again."

She poked at the Off button on her phone screen a couple of times before she hit it right. *Damned arthritis,* she thought as she slid the phone into the pocket of her dark gray, men's-style pants.

"Bravo, Constance, bravo."

Constance spun and saw that Bobbin and the rest of her tailors were clustered around the bottom of the staircase leading to the second-floor workrooms.

"That's one royal tradition we can afford to stop," Bobbin said. "He's an odious man."

"Thank you, ma'am." It was Brian, one of her best tailors. He'd come to Constance desperate for work. His skills with a needle were perfection, but his skin looked like dirty, chewed gum and, while he looked disgusting, he did have a fresh, minty scent. "Things are going to get worse for jokers now unless we have friends like you. Thank you, ma'am."

Constance could feel herself blushing. With two quick tugs she straightened the cuffs on her pristine white shirt.

"Very well," she said, shooing them away. "Back to yer jobs." Every so often her posh accent slipped, and the East End peeped through.

Another brief chorus of "Thank you, ma'am" and then they marched upstairs. Constance waited until she heard the doors to the workrooms shut.

"Bobbin," she said testily. "How did they overhear that conversation? I didn't have it on speaker."

"You were shouting, and all they needed to hear was 'Henry' and 'Not going to do it' and they knew very well what it was all about."

Constance nervously fussed with her outfit while worrying about letting herself be overheard. It was clumsy, and after her time in MI-7, she'd learned to be anything but.

She rocked back and forth in her Converse sneakers—her one concession to American fashion—and then stuck her hand into her pant pocket where she toyed with the bits and pieces of her craft she tucked away there. She knew the Lion would keep after her. It was his way.

"Stop fretting," Bobbin said. "You said no and that's that. Forget about it and come back to work." He took her hand then and gently led her into the back room. At that moment, she wanted nothing more than to tell him everything.

Losing Glory, then losing the queen (who insisted that Constance call her Margaret when they were alone), the weight of her secrets, and now turning the Lion down, it was a lot to take.

Bobbin took her back to her drafting table, gave her tea, and gently sat her down so she could get back to work. And she felt centered again. He did have that effect on her. Now if only she had the courage to tell him everything else.

♠

It was a lady judge and she looked forbidding but also absurd. The black robe was appropriately austere, but the powdered wig perched atop her beautiful cornrows decorated with pale blue beads was incongruous. As if a gull had decided to fly into court and perch on her head. Noel pulled his attention from the wig and tried to read her expression as his lawyer—also sporting a wig and a gown—began her argument.

Noel had made a conscious choice to hire a woman to represent him in his fight to be granted sole custody of Jasper under the theory that if he had a woman representing him, it might indicate he wasn't a complete wanker. It hadn't fooled his representative. Judith von Bredow had declared he was in fact a total wanker after their first meeting, but he was a rich wanker, so she had agreed to represent him.

They had developed the arguments together, so Noel only listened with half of his attention. Only what the judge said would ultimately matter to this preliminary hearing. Instead, he watched the face of the lawyer hired by Niobe. He was an elderly man with a comfortable paunch and the air of a kindly grandfather. He was shaking his bewigged head and tsking quietly under his breath.

After dropping Jasper off at school, Noel had paused for breakfast and a chance to peruse the papers. Richard's remarks regarding his brother had been met with a stiff and very British response from the palace. It was so polite that it could rip skin from the body.

Not so from the howling pack of tabloids. The *Daily Mail* and the *Daily Express* came baying after the Duke of York with unflattering photographs, suggestions that his and Diana's marriage was on the rocks, and veiled claims about Richard's sexual proclivities. Not so the *Sun*. The vitriol poured off the page and in the letter column a supposed irate citizen called the Duke of York a "fudge-pounder" and a "bum bandit." Only the *Guardian* offered full-throated support of the duke's criticisms of his brother.

Noel knew the kind of people who read the scandal sheets. Less educated, struggling in an increasingly unequal society, ready to blame others for their troubles—immigrants, jokers, or gays. And despite the British reputation for decorum, one only had to witness a soccer mob to realize that his kinsmen were as capable of violence as any other member of the human species.

Judith concluded, thanked the judge, and sat down. Niobe's lawyer rose to his feet. In his black robe and with his bulk it was reminiscent of a broaching whale. "Your Honor, I find honorable counsel's argument to be vastly creative, appropriate when she really has no basis in law with which to support this manifest injustice."

The judge waved a hand wearily at him. "Yes, yes, Ramsey, but spare me your oratorical gifts today. If you have a point, kindly get to it."

He bowed his head in graceful acquiescence. "Of course, ma'am. The child is nine and he has been ripped away from his mother under the guise that his status as an ace means that his mother, who is a joker, is unable to adequately prepare him for a world as a wild carder. The argument is that his father, who is also an ace, but has declined to explicate his powers and abilities, is a far better choice to raise the child than a loving mother. To rule in favor of this man would create the pernicious precedent—"

"Getting a bit florid there, Ram," Judith drawled.

The judge brought down her gavel. "I'll decide when it's too purple, counselor."

"As I was saying, it could set the precedent that jokers are inherently inferior to aces rather than treating all people, whether afflicted by this virus or not, as equal before the law. Besides which the court has always taken the presumption that a child is in most circumstances better off with their mother."

The judge cocked an eyebrow at Noel's lawyer. "I'm unconvinced that a parent should receive full custody merely on the basis of their wild card status. Therefore—"

"Your honor, may we have a postponement in order to garner expert opinion on the subject of families raising an ace child."

"Your honor—" Ramsey began.

"No, I think that's reasonable. It's rare for two wild cards to produce a viable child. We want to give this one the best chance in life. You have five days, counselor, make the most of them. We'll resume at"—she checked her docket—"nine A.M. On Monday, March eleventh. Court is adjourned."

◆

Wayfarer's knock made Green Man look up. He'd been reading the papers, trying to gauge how much support King Henry was getting now the initial story had broken. This was more difficult than it used to be. Even supposedly sensible news outlets like the BBC had fallen prey to the ridiculous idea of always presenting both sides of an argument, no matter how nonsensical or irrelevant the counterargument might be.

As a result, he knew that some people agreed with Henry's bigoted statements and that some did not. However, he'd known this before he'd read a single one of today's articles, and couldn't help feel that he was wasting his time.

The papers were put aside, and the mask slipped into place.

"Come in," he said, and Wayfarer stepped inside. He didn't need to say anything more; they'd worked together long enough that she could practically read his mind these days, even when he wished she couldn't.

"Seizer's been quiet since the meeting," she said.

"It's clear he's not quite ready to strike yet. I imagine he's waiting for me to slip."

"I agree." She absently scanned a story that only mentioned Henry's new, much younger fiancée, in terms of what she was wearing and her current hairstyle. She swept it neatly into the bin. "What are you going to do about him?"

"Nothing, unless he causes trouble."

"Which he will."

"When that happens . . . if that happens, I'll make sure it doesn't happen again."

Wayfarer nodded. "I'm no fan of unnecessary violence, but just this once I think prevention really would be better than the cure."

"It's a bit late for that, I'm afraid. Seizer is one of the old guard and not without allies. If I go after him without good reason, I'll shatter the Fists into pieces, when we need to be unified." He looked up at her. "I assume we have more interesting things to discuss than internal politics."

"There's a young man outside who has a story I think you should hear. His grandmother worked at the palace back in forty-eight."

"He has something we can use against Henry?"

"No, but I think you'll want to hear what he's got to say."

"Alright, send him in."

She opened the door again. "Theo, Green Man will see you now." She gestured for him to enter as she stepped out.

Green Man stifled a chortle when the "young man" appeared. He was well into his thirties and looked like he'd got a lot of living into those years. Leathery skin and blunt nails suggested a lot of outdoors work, probably shifting heavy materials of some kind. There wasn't much to love about the man's face, but he had a vitality to him and the kind of thick hair that Green Man would have envied even before his card turned. Theo's mutation had done something to his right leg, though exactly what was hidden under flared trousers that brushed the floor.

Green Man gestured to the only other chair in the room and Theo moved toward it awkwardly, swinging one leg forward and letting its weight drag the rest of him after. He gave a happy sigh as he finally flopped against the leather.

"I understand your grandmother used to work for the palace."

"Yeah."

"But not recently?"

"Nah, but she used to talk to me about it."

"Go on."

"Well, when you put out the word to find out about that royal cunt—Pardon my French."

"No pardon required in this case."

"Right. So I remember me nan used to work there and so I popped over and asked her about the old days." He leaned forward. "And she tells me that back in forty-eight, the princess has this baby, right."

Green Man nodded. "Yes, that sounds familiar. A stillborn boy as I recall. Terrible tragedy."

"Yeah, that's what I thought. Except me nan tells me that all them stories were lies. The baby was alive. She saw him."

It was Green Man's turn to lean forward. "But why pretend the child was dead? It makes no sense."

Theo nodded, looking pleased. "That's exactly what I said, boss. Anyway, she tells me that there was something up with the baby, and that's why they got rid of him."

"Something up?"

"Yeah, with his skin. It wasn't right. She said it weren't normal."

On the outside, he appeared as calm as ever, but inside his thoughts were whirling. *It could just be a skin condition, but what if it's more? What if there was a joker prince? And what if they'd had him disposed of?* The implications were staggering. If they'd killed a royal baby for the sake of appearances, it would send shockwaves around the world, and that was before Green Man arranged a very special revenge strike. *And even that is nothing compared to what could happen if the child is still alive!*

Before the change, his cheeks would have flushed with excitement, fueled by a thundering heart. But Green Man never blushed, his features and his heart unmovable.

"Would your grandmother mind if I paid her a visit?"

"Nah, she loves a good chat." He passed over a crumpled piece of paper. "That's her address."

Green Man took it, committed the details to memory, and slipped it into the inside pocket of his jacket. "Thank you, Theo. Now tell me, is there anything I can do for you?"

He looked down, embarrassed. "There is this one thing . . ." Green Man sat back, knowing this game well. Theo was trying to seem coy, but he'd come here with this request in mind. "There's this one foreman, his name's Gordon. We call him, well, it don't matter . . . I want some help with him."

"Gordon is causing you some trouble?"

"Yeah. He's always giving me the worst jobs and then pushing me about when nobody's looking. I take it on the chin, y'know? But sometimes he blames me for stuff and they dock my pay, and I can't have that. Money's tight."

"Would you like us to have a word with Gordon on your behalf?"

"That'd be great. Nothing heavy, I just want to be able to do my shift in peace."

"Send me a schedule with his times on it and I'll see what I can do."

"Thanks, boss."

Green Man stood and shook his hand. "Thank you, Theo."

♥

Alan spoke softly into his phone. "I'm sorry, Sebastian. Truly. I'm so sorry I had to cancel our lunch—I was looking forward to it. And I'm going to miss dinner too. Given the king's gaffe, resentments have sparked throughout the city. Now there are multiple forces moving against Henry . . ."

As Turing said the words, Richard shifted beneath the covers, his hand tracing small, wicked circles in very distracting regions. *Forces moving?* Richard mouthed, and Turing shook his head, firmly, only to be further ignored. He took a quick, steadying breath and continued.

". . . I'm going to be here all night, I'm afraid, working with some of the MI-5 chaps. Just put the TV on, maybe that baking show you like? That'll give you something pleasant to fall asleep to. Yes, yes—tomorrow, lunch, I *promise*. Why don't you make us reservations somewhere nice? Or I can do it—no, of course I don't mind. I'll go online right now and set it up; I'll text you the details in the morning. But now, please, just go to sleep; you'll be an absolute bear at lunch if you haven't gotten your rest."

Roar! Richard mouthed, making claws out of his fingers.

Shut up! Alan mouthed back. Could you say that to your king-to-be? Apparently, because Richard was laughing now, silently, thank all the gods. Laughing and gesturing to Alan to hang up, now. *Hang up!*

"I really have to get back to work now. Sleep well, husband." He hesitated, and then added, "I love you." The truth was, Alan had never really been comfortable saying that sort of thing out loud, but Sebastian needed it—he needed to hear those words every day. He'd even made Alan put it in their wedding vows, not to let a day go by without saying, *I love you.*

He'd be lost without Sebastian. Alan just didn't see why he couldn't have Richard too. When vast amounts of property—actual kingdoms—were involved, then certainly it mattered who was spending time in whose bed, and what children resulted from it. But once you stopped worrying about which man sired which baby, there was no good reason for cleaving only unto one other. Monogamy wasn't logical; the heart wanted what it wanted.

All right, maybe his heart wasn't the driving force here. Alan hung up the phone, finally, and reached for Richard, his dick already hardening—only to have the prince slip away, laughing out loud this time.

"Oh no, no, my lovely metal man. I want more from you tonight. You're the smartest man in the world, and I—I should be king. How can we take the throne from my brother?"

It was a difficult problem. The simplest method, of course, would be to kill Henry. Turing had ordered his share of deaths as a member of the Silver Helix, but killing a king carried tremendous risk. Was Richard truly willing to take that step, to commit fratricide? There was little love lost between the brothers, but murder was surely extreme. Could Turing condone such a thing, assist with it, if Richard asked it of him?

Thankfully, he hadn't asked it. Not yet. And there might be other options than murder. A sufficiently large scandal would force Henry from the throne. They had seen it with Edward VIII, after all—the country could not abide divorcée Wallace Simpson as queen, and so Edward had abdicated. There was precedent. The problem would be creating the scandal, as quickly as possible. Henry was still new to his throne, uncertain of his place. It would be far harder to unseat him once his buttocks were firmly planted on that royal seat.

"Let me think on it, Dickie. There may be a way."

Richard seemed ready to protest, to press for more—but then he subsided. He had, after all, seen Alan work on other problems before; he had some small understanding of the process. He murmured only, "Soon, Alan. Calculate quickly." And then he was sliding down the bed, disappearing under the covers. For a little while, Alan stopped thinking at all.

♣

"Bobbin," Constance began. They'd let the staff go home early and were closing up.

"What is it?" he replied. His smile was warm and kind. The patches of color on his face—faded now—were as familiar to her as the constellation of freckles on her arms. Those freckles hadn't been there when she was younger—age had left them in its passing. And age had left the gold rimming his eyes crinkled even when he wasn't smiling.

"I need to tell you a few things," she began. She pulled the drapes to the front windows and went around the room shutting the atelier down for the evening.

"You should sit down," she said.

"Very well," he replied. "But, do you want to get dinner out tonight? I know you're fond of the pies at Barley Swine."

"No," she said as she went and sat in one of the gray velvet, Danish-style armchairs arranged around the low walk where they often showed their pieces. He pulled one of the chairs around and faced her.

A queasy feeling settled in her stomach. Suddenly, it seemed like a terrible idea to tell him, but she knew she couldn't keep her secret any longer.

"What is it?" Bobbin asked. "Something awful?" He laughed and leaned forward. "Don't be afraid. I don't scare easy."

It suddenly felt very warm and Constance peeled her dark gray cardigan off.

"A long time ago," she said, clearing her throat. "There were three of us friends."

The memory was crisp and clean. It seemed as if the older she got, the easier her youth was to recall.

"Glory and I had another best mate when we was—were—growin' up. Her name was Frances. She became famous, but not like Glory and me. She became famous because she was married to Reggie Kray."

"One of *the* Kray brothers?" A shocked and slightly thrilled expression bloomed on his face. "The gangsters who ran the East End? Had movies made about them and all? Those Krays?"

Constance nodded. "What most people don't know is that his brother, Ronnie, was an ace. He was also barking mad, and that made him having such a power worse. There's not much to be done about an ace who is insane. Or even one a bit touched. And Ronnie wasn't just a little touched."

Constance rolled up her left sleeve. It had been almost fifty years, but the scars still hadn't disappeared. They'd turned a silvery white, like spider webs had been carved in her flesh, but they were still deep, the skin puckering around them.

She held her arm out where he could see it. He let out a low whistle and reached to touch her, but she shrank away. The memory of what had created those scars, a terrible phantom pain, flared.

"See, Ronnie's ace was in his touch," she continued, rolling her sleeve back down quickly, fastening the button at the cuff. "If he thought about it, he could slice someone open all razor-like." It made her stomach flip again just to talk about it. She tried to make it sound matter-of-fact, but her voice betrayed her.

"You might have told me that Ronnie Kray had taken it upon himself to carve you up," Bobbin said, reaching out to take her hand. She pulled it away. "There was no reason not to tell me. You can tell me anything."

She cocked her head to one side, considering him. She knew him so well, yet she couldn't be certain how he would react. There was only one thing to do and it was gut it out.

"Bobbin, I killed Ronnie Kray. Well, Glory and I did."

He stared at her, a shocked expression on his face. *Well, my girl, what did you expect,* she thought. Silence stretched out between them. It felt as if she was looking at him from the wrong end of a telescope.

"But . . . Reggie Kray went to prison for killing Ronnie," he said at last. She stopped feeling as if he was moving away from her. At least he was still talking.

"I know," she replied with a sigh of relief. "It wasn't an easy thing to fix."

His face scrunched up as he began to speak. "I don't understand," he said. "How did it happen?"

"I was trying to get away from them and Glory was trying to help me." The memories of killing Ronnie rose up with the terrible freshness they'd had since it had happened.

"Ronnie found us. He tried to kill us. Sliced Glory's flowers clean off. Tried to cut me up again." She remembered Glory's blood, slippery blood on the floor smelling like copper mixed with the scent of her shorn flowers.

Constance pulled her shears out of her pocket. They were her special ones. "I used these," she said, holding them out flat on her palm.

He gazed at them as if they were going to bite, then he looked back up at her. "Why do ya still have those?"

The shears teetered and she closed her hand around them and then slid them back into her pocket. "Because . . . because I didn't want to forget. Didn't want to take anything for granted."

"You were just about a girl, how could you cover up something like that?" he asked, frowning. "How did it get pinned on Reggie?"

This is where it was going to get tricky. She knew she had to tell him, but she was loath to. Maybe if he just had part of it now—the worst part, the part of Ronnie—maybe the other . . . that could be put off.

"'Twas Mick who helped us," she replied smoothly. "See, he and Glory, well, they'd always been sweet on one another . . ."

Bobbin waved his hand. "Yes, yes, everyone knew about that. It was that sort of Page Six stuff."

She laughed; Bobbin had never been one for scandals.

"Mick knew a lot of people. A lot of people who were interested in him . . . like MI-7."

Bobbin burst out laughing. "Mick Jagger?! In MI-7? Were they completely daft?"

"It was a different time, Bobbin. They were trying to recruit people. Mick was famous. They wanted a sort of counterculture face while they were recruiting."

"Seriously?" Wonder bloomed on his face. "Mick Jagger." He shook his head. "Well, we all know he isn't part of MI-7 . . . unless . . . Is he? No, and how would you know anyway." He chuckled.

"I called Mick after Glory and I, well, after. Glory was hurt bad. I thought he could get us out of the country. The Stones were going on tour . . . He called MI-7 to make a deal with them. They would help cover up the murder, help us get out of the country, and he would join them."

"Well, obviously, that didn't happen." Bobbin looked perplexed. He rubbed his palms on his pants and left little rips from his needle protrusions.

"We worked things out with them and I got to stay here and Glory went on to the States with Mick."

"And you got to stay . . ." His tone was thoughtful.

She smiled. He was taking it remarkably well.

"And then you started making clothes for Her Majesty. Do I have the right of it?"

"Yes!"

"And you were working for MI-7 then, weren't you?" he asked. "Making clothes . . . for MI-7."

"Yes." She wasn't sure what he was getting at.

"MI-7 is for aces. They let Mick get away because they had *you*. That was the deal you made." She recoiled from the expression on his face.

"I . . . I . . . It was the only thing to do! Glory got to be safe. She had Mick to take care of her. Reg went to jail. And all because I went to work for them."

"So, you're an ace then." He said it with a flat voice.

"Yes," she replied shakily. "My clothes . . ."

He shook his head and ran a hand through his hair. "I should have known. Should've realized. You making her clothes all the time. Henry wanting you to make his clothes. Being so intent on it. Must be an awfully powerful ace."

"No," she said softly, shaking her head.

"Don't lie to me," he snapped back. "You been lying enough."

"I haven't been lying! I couldn't tell anyone!" That he would think she'd been lying to him wounded her.

"You're an *ace*. Working a shop full of jokers. Working with *me* for forty years and ya never told me. Never told me we were alike. Both of us infected. And working for MI-7 . . ." He shook his head. When he looked at her again, it was with disgust.

"What exactly would you have had me do?" she asked. She tried to keep the pleading sound from her voice. She had nothing to be ashamed of, after all. She'd saved all of them and protected the queen for decades. He had no right to judge her.

"You had forty years to tell me the truth!" he yelled. "I thought I *knew* you!"

"Well, I told you now." It sounded weak even to her ears.

"Because you had to." It was an accusation.

"No," she said, reaching out to him. He recoiled. "Because I wanted to. Because . . ."

"I don't care," he said suddenly wearily, slumping in his chair. "You hid yourself from me. You pretended to be something you're not. I don't know who you are. I'm not certain I want to know you."

"You're being ridiculous," she said defensively. "I'm me. You *know* me."

He shook his head. "No, Constance, I don't. You've killed a man—one that needed killing—but even so. And you've been working for MI-7, as dirty an organization as there is one. And you're an ace. How pathetic you must have thought I was with my needled hands and piebald face."

She jumped to her feet, ignoring the pain in her hip. "I've never though ya were anything other than a fine man, Bobbin, and well you know it."

He looked up at her and shook his head slowly. "No," he said softly with a hitch in his voice that was almost worse than when he was angry. "If ya had thought I was a fine man, ya woulda told me."

It felt as if she'd been hit in the chest with a baseball. "What do you mean?" she asked, her voice high and jittery. Constance took a step toward him, but he backed away. The pain in her chest grew. She wondered if she was having a heart attack it hurt so bad.

"Bobbin," she said her voice cracking now. "Bobbin . . ."

But he'd already spun on his heel and strode out the door far faster than his usual gait. A cold burst of wind blew through the door as it swung shut.

He'd left his hat and jacket behind. She stared at the closed door with fear. It was just as she'd expected. She'd lost him. Staggering to a chair, she sat down, doubled over, and then hugged her chest.

It hurt worse than anything she could have imagined, but she knew with sudden clarity it wasn't a heart attack at all. This was what it felt like when your heart was broken.

And then she started crying.

The man sat nervously with his face to the wall, exactly as he'd been instructed. She watched him from a crow, but stood around a corner. Other crows were waiting to peck him to death if he attempted to turn around and look her in the face. But she doubted it. The goddess had used hundreds like him over the years.

"You are a war criminal," she told him, modifying her voice so that it sounded disapproving.

"I am changed man."

The bodyguard did not look so fierce without his bulletproof jacket and his shades. He trembled, as was proper in the presence of divinity. "And you think I don't know this is blackmail? You think I betray my employer? No! Do what you want. I not traitor."

Badb knew better.

"I am here to *help* the king," she told him. "I will give you Green Man."

The bodyguard twitched. "Do not look around." He froze again. He was still trembling, but with excitement now. The new monarch hated jokers and probably Muslims too. He might overlook the fact that this man had forgotten to feed a few hundred of the latter in a long-ago war.

"Here is the address," she told him. "They have booby-trapped the alley to the north, but the main street . . . well, they wouldn't get away with that, would they?"

♠   ♥   ♦   ♣

Tuesday

MARCH 3RD

ALAN TURING WOKE UP at 5:00 A.M.; he'd set a reminder in his mind that pinged him awake. Sebastian slept soundly beside him, one arm outflung to rest on Alan's body, the other tucked under Sebastian's head. He always slept in exactly the same position—in fifty years, Alan had never seen a variation.

Fifty years. How could he have forgotten? *Richard.* He had returned home from his tryst to find the dining table set formally for two, an ice-cold steak waiting on a plate, and a gold-wrapped box sitting next to it.

Alan hadn't needed to ask, *What's all this?* As soon as he'd seen the box, he'd remembered. They'd only been married five years ago, on a sunny summer day, but yesterday was their fiftieth anniversary.

They'd met in a bookshop on Charing Cross Road, both drenched from a late winter rain and ducking in to get out of the wet. Their hands had met over a book, and the rest was history. Up until the wedding, they'd celebrated on this day, every year. Guilt washed over Alan, like a wave, and he almost doubled over with the force of it.

He'd stood Sebastian up for their anniversary lunch. How had Alan forgotten? How could he possibly? His mind had been elsewhere, had forgotten to ask the right questions. Garbage in, garbage out. He was the garbage one now.

He'd opened his present—a gold watch, sporting gorgeously intricate gears—and mentally made a promise that he and Sebastian would take an extravagant vacation together after the coronation. Maybe they'd go on a round-the-world trip.

Alan was determined to make it up to him, though. Breakfast in bed would be a good start, a full English. He slipped out of bed, pulling a robe around himself, and headed to the kitchen. Alan reached for the cruet of oil sitting on the counter, but realized just in time that it was likely one of Sebastian's special herb-infused oils. His husband might have plans for it, and that would be a terrible start to the breakfast, to use up something Sebastian needed. Butter was safe, though.

Butter, mushrooms, fried tomatoes. Coddled eggs. Alan didn't actually know how to make blood sausage, so toast would have to do. He burned it just a bit, but an open window took care of the smell, and Alan scraped off the black bits and slathered the toast with lots of butter and marmalade. Orange juice and tea. Had he forgotten anything? Oh, a flower—there was a bowl full of flower heads floating in some water on the counter. Pinks and whites and reds, striped with green; they were ridiculously romantic. Perfect—he picked one out, and adorned the plate.

"What's all this?" Sebastian asked, walking into the room.

"Rather a mess, I'm afraid," Alan said ruefully, taking in the chaos he'd created. "I was going to bring you breakfast in bed."

Sebastian smiled, picking the flower from the plate and tucking it behind his ear. "I'd rather have breakfast at the kitchen table with my husband, if that's all right with you. It looks like you've made plenty for two."

"That would be perfect," Alan said, letting out a breath he hadn't realized he was holding. Finally, he'd done something right; relief burbled up in Alan, making him giddy. "You are a far better husband than I deserve," Alan said, which was only the truth.

Sebastian hurried over, pulled him into a quick embrace. "No, no, don't worry about yesterday." He tilted his face up, and Alan bent down to kiss his husband, hoping the intensity would read as passion rather than guilt. Sebastian smiled up at him when the kiss ended, and said, "It's fine. The kingdom's in transition, and the queen was a friend. You have a lot on your mind right now."

They fell to eating and chatting, in the way of an old married couple. Alan promised to rake up the leaf mold before going into the office, and Sebastian favored him with a smile radiant as a groom's on his wedding day.

It took so little to make Alan's husband happy. He'd been a fool to indulge himself so with Richard—Sebastian deserved any extra time and attention he could spare. Alan should end the affair; with that thought, a weight rolled off his shoulders, a weight Alan hadn't even realized he'd been carrying. Honestly, it was a relief to make the decision, though Richard would surely resist the end of the affair. Maybe striving for the kingship would distract him sufficiently.

Alan had half-tuned out what Sebastian was saying—an essential husband skill—but then something caught Alan's attention, so that he almost spilled his tea. He replayed Sebastian's last words in his mind: "After what Prince Henry said, it's going to be hard to see him crowned king. Richard would be a much better choice. I liked what he had to say: 'such naked bigotry should not be voiced in our country.' That's what a king should sound like."

"I agree," Alan said cautiously. "Richard would be better. If we had to pick one of them."

Sebastian frowned. "What do you mean?"

Alan hesitated a moment—but wasn't this what marriage was about? Trust; trust was paramount, and he wanted nothing more than to trust his husband. "The queen—she confessed something to me on her deathbed. She said Elizabeth had a son."

"What?" Sebastian's bushy white eyebrows shot up. "You can't be serious."
"A joker—they spirited him away."

Sebastian frowned. "If this is real, you can't try to manage this on your own, Alan. You have to tell Henry. Or better, tell Richard. He'll know what to do."

"Are you sure?" His husband must not suspect anything, if he were sending Alan to Richard. That was as it should be—there was no longer anything to suspect. It was over. Alan reached out and rested his fingers lightly on his husband's hand as it lay on the chintz-clad table. It felt right, like coming home.

Sebastian nodded firmly, entwining his fingers with Alan's. "Tell Richard. He should know that there may be another body between him and the throne."

And Henry, Turing added silently.

◆

The atelier was cold and silent. Constance had waited for Bobbin at the usual place for breakfast, but to no avail.

Without Bobbin there, she hadn't bothered with breakfast, but on the way to the atelier, she stopped for buns and other pastries, making certain that she bought Bobbin's favorites. Then she added Manchester tarts, caraway seedcake, and some cookies just in case he wanted something different. It was a mad amount of food, but she couldn't help herself.

"Hello?" she said as she let herself into the shop. There was no response. No cheery, "Good morning." Just the cold, dimly lit atelier. She went to the back and turned on the overhead light. After placing the box of pastries on Bobbin's desk, she went and turned up the heat. There was no doubt about it, he wasn't there. If he had been, the heat would have definitely been on. He hated the chill.

She went to her drafting table, hoping Bobbin might have come back and left her a note. Indeed, he had. Written underneath her Wednesday entry was TRAITOR. Above it, in her own neat hand, was *Henry?* She sank down on her chair.

When had he come back to the shop? Was it this morning? Maybe he was planning to talk things over? Or had he come back the night before? All she knew was he'd seen what appeared to be a damning piece of evidence and yet another lie and betrayal.

She pulled her cell out of the pocket of her cardigan. It got stuck and she swore.

"Dial Bobbin," she said once she'd freed it. Her voice was tremulous. The phone rang four times before it went to his voicemail. "Bobbin here, leave a message." At the sound of his voice she felt a stab of guilt and a brief unsteadying urge to cry. But there was only so much crying she had left in her after the night before.

"Bobbin," she said. She cursed to herself because suddenly she had no idea what to say. "Bobbin," she blurted out. "What you saw in the planner was because the Lion called me not long after . . . Well, after you left. I would have said anything to get him off the phone. I was in a bit of a daze, so I wrote it down, but things aren't as black and white . . ." She trailed off. How could she possibly explain?

This was something that could only be sorted in person. At least she hoped it could be.

♥

There came a crash of glass, and Sebastian ran into the Victorian greenhouse with soil on his knees and a trowel in his hand. He stood confused, breath rasping, although he'd covered less than a dozen yards to get here.

"How on Earth?" he said, or so Badb guessed from reading his lips. She watched him look from the broken pane in the roof to the shards of glass scattered among his orchids. And then, he gasped at the cheap mobile phone lying faceup right in front of him.

"Who's there?" he cried. "I'll call security!" But there was nothing to be seen on the adjacent lawn but grass and crows.

Then the phone rang and he yelped.

Again he looked around, holding the trowel with both hands in front of his little potbelly.

The ringing never stopped. And finally, finally, he picked up the phone.

"H . . . hello?"

The voice at the other end was that of a young woman, her accent Italian. "I am sorry to approach you this way Mr. Wallace, but I have a deadline and I need a comment."

"On . . . Who is this?"

"I'm desperate. They're all stuck in the last century. People don't care if a prince is gay. It is a good thing, yes? Very *now*. Prince Richard must be allowed to love who he wants, even if it is a man who is a computer. Would you care to comment?"

Sebastian froze, the phone held in front of him, his mouth working, but without sound.

Francesca was one of Badb's best tools. A real journalist. A glamorous woman who covered the whole world with little more than a microphone and a wheelchair. She only ever asked for payment in information.

"This is hard for you, of course. Forgive me. I presume you are aware your husband has rekindled this old relationship. I admire that you stand by him."

Sebastian growled and squeezed the phone as though he meant to choke it. "You think I'm a fool?" he whispered. "You think I don't know you're just fishing so you can print it in whatever rag you're working for?"

"We have photographs, Mr. Wallace. We have recordings."

"You . . . have what?"

"Your husband has a mole on his left buttock that is made of pure metal. I say this so you know I am speaking the truth. They laugh about your age. Especially His Royal Majesty, who calls you Mr. Floppy, who says that for a gardener, your sap rarely rises now." Francesca paused, like the professional she was. "Would you care to comment? What do you think of His Royal Majesty?

Very handsome, of course. Would you say your relationship with Mr. Turing has become toxic? Has it been *poisoned* by His Royal Majesty? Would you care to comm—"

With a roar, Sebastian smashed the phone onto the old tiles of the floor. He hit it with the trowel again and again, coughing. Sobbing. Furious.

"Your Royal . . . Fucking . . . Majesty!" And then the energy went out of him, all at once. Sebastian sank to the cold floor, rested his head against the tiles.

"Not again," he whispered. "Oh, Alan—not again."

♣

"Cup of tea?" asked Francine Smith.

"No thank you," replied Green Man. It had been difficult to squeeze himself into the limited space at her kitchen table, but she'd insisted he be comfortable.

She set out two cups by the steaming kettle. "How do you like it?"

He didn't. Since his card had turned, the only thing he enjoyed drinking was water. He'd been surprised to learn that refusing tea caused more offence than being a seven-foot-tall walking tree, but there it was. The British stereotype existed for a reason.

"Just black."

"Right you are. I'll be having milk and a sugar myself. I know I shouldn't, but at our age, you take the pleasures you can."

"Quite."

Francine was a small woman, mostly skin and bone, topped with a frizz of white hair. He suspected she'd looked this way for the last ten years and would go on doing so for the next twenty or more. Under the warm smile and slightly bumbling demeanor lurked a bit of old steel.

The floral kitchen was clean and neat, and he could see pictures of Theo and several other family members attached to the fridge door, all with their arms around each other, both before and after her grandson's card had turned.

"There you go," she said, putting the cup in front of him. He noted his cup had a much bigger handle than hers.

"Thank you."

"It's no trouble. Not often I have a celebrity to tea."

"I'm hardly that."

"Our Theo thinks you are. You should hear him talk! Green Man this and Green Man that. It's adorable." She smiled again. Francine had an infectious smile, the kind that must have made her work in the hospital that little bit easier. "I'm glad you're watching out for him."

Such praise was rare, and he wasn't sure if he should take it, given the other side of his work. "Theo deserves the same chances as everyone else."

She raised her teacup to that. "He's a good lad. Has his moments of course, but then, don't we all?"

"Definitely. Did Theo tell you why I'm here?"

"He did. Cookie?"

"No thank you. I'm afraid I can't stay long." He looked out of the window.

Things appeared suspiciously calm outside. A group of young children were playing with a tennis ball, using the fence as a goal, and a dog on the other side was
jumping up and down, doing her best to join in.

"Oh yes, I'm sure you're very busy."

"Francine, I need to know about the royal baby Princess Elizabeth had in
1948. It's very important."

She nodded, her smile vanishing, but said nothing.

"Theo tells me you saw it."

"Aye, I did. Saw him as clear as I'm seeing you."

"Alive?"

"Oh yes. He was a sweet little thing. They say all babies are, but they're not
really. This one was a love, though. A gentle soul, I could see it in his eyes."

"Was there something . . . different about him?"

"His skin. It was all blotchy and bumpy."

"Bruised?"

"No, but it wasn't like anything I'd seen before. Babies don't come out the
way they do on the telly, all clean and pink. They come out messy and some
of them have all kinds of problems, poor loves. I've seen babies born raw and
shivering. And I've seen them get stuck or injured. Birth is a tough thing, Mr.
Green Man. But this wasn't anything natural. At least not natural in the way
I understand it."

"So that we're clear: You're saying his condition would identify him as a victim of the wild card virus. That the young prince was born a joker?"

She nodded. "Yes. That's the truth of it."

"What happened when the palace realized?"

"Oh, there was all kinds of fuss. The first thing they did was get us out of the
room. They were panicking, you see. But it was too late by then. I'd seen, and
so had a few of the other girls. They made us sign a paper to keep us quiet. Said
that if we told anyone, we'd go to prison."

"And you're not worried that telling me might get you into trouble?"

She chuckled, and helped herself to a cookie. "Not much they can do to me
now, is there?" A little of that hidden steel emerged as she added, "Besides, I'm
sure if they did come after me, a nice man like you wouldn't just stand by and
do nothing, would you?"

"You know me too well. Now, can you tell me anything else?"

"Well, I probably shouldn't say anything more, but seeing as I've come this
far, and seeing that you've been such a good friend to our Theo, there is something else that's stuck with me to this day."

"Go on."

"I was the one holding him at the end, while they all decided what was going to happen. All bundled up in my arms, he wasn't no different to any other
baby. Better behaved than most, in fact. A bit puffy in the face, I suppose, and
like I said, funny looking. But nothing a mother couldn't love.

"I was talking to him and rocking him gently, trying to make sure he was
settled. Babies can be quite sensitive to their environment, so I thought if I was

calm, he'd be calm. I suppose I was hoping that if he was good they'd be more likely to take pity on him." She sighed. "I was a bit of a silly goose in those days."

She saw him looking at her, and then continued. "Prince Philip came out of the bedroom with this terrible look on his face and I made sure my eyes were down when I realized he was coming over to me. There was another man with him that I hadn't seen before. Well, Prince Philip whips the baby out of my arms, which makes him cry of course, and pushes him into the other man's chest. And then he says, 'Deal with it,' just like that. 'Deal with it!' Like this baby's nothing more than a mound of dirty washing."

"This other man, was he part of the palace staff?"

"Oh no. Not staff. If I had to guess, I'd say he was one of those MI-5 types."

"What makes you say that?"

"Something about his hair, I think."

Green Man raised an eyebrow but didn't comment. Instead, he stood up, being careful not to bash his head on the ceiling. "Thank you, Francine, you've been most helpful."

"Oh not at all, it's been so lovely to have . . ."

She went on like this for some time, but Green Man didn't take in any of it. He was already planning to call Wayfarer and have her begin investigating all jokers born in 1948, with a focus on orphans and adoptions.

". . . Can hardly blame him, though. There's so much on young people's plates these days. I'm just glad to see him when he does come . . ."

Green Man nodded politely and left, his cup of tea still steaming on the table, untouched.

♠

Alan hesitated outside the door of Constance's atelier. The street was noisy, with cars rushing past and crows squawking overhead; she got a lot of foot traffic in this location. He could just stand here for a little while, observe the passersby, play the little game of figuring out as much as he could about them from the tiny specifics of their lives. That game could lead to useful information; it had often, during the War. But Alan was procrastinating now, and he knew it.

This wasn't going to be a pleasant conversation, and he was fond of Constance, in his own way. They'd worked together collegially over the years, and he'd enjoyed her sharp wit as much as he'd appreciated her skill with a needle.

To make it worse, if she made Henry impervious clothes, that would make his own job all the harder. Alan had presented Richard with two plans early this morning:

The first one requires your brother's death. The second one doesn't.

Richard had wanted time to think it over, which was only prudent, though the clock was ticking and they should set plans in motion, one way or the other. But in the meantime, the Lion had called him in, demanded that he come down here and force Constance to clothe Henry. *Whatever it takes, Alan. You know the stakes.*

Alan sighed, and entered the shop. Gray velvet chairs, pale gray walls, long silk drapes at the windows, and oriental rugs on the floor. Modern and elegant;

the Seamstress had come a long way, risen high. Of course, the higher you rose . . . No sign of the tailors and seamstresses here—just a single girl, coming to greet him. But no—Constance herself walked into the room, and with the tiniest gestures, sent the girl away, behind a gray drape. Leaving Alan along with Constance.

She raised an eyebrow. "So, they sent *you*, did they? I should've known. Well, I suppose we'd best have a little chat."

Alan braced himself as she walked toward him, prepared with his arguments. Half an hour later, Constance hadn't let him come even two inches further into the shop, and he was still arguing—the woman was incredibly stubborn. "Constance, if Henry is hurt or killed, you know you'll be blamed for it."

Constance crossed her arms tightly in front of her and frowned. "Blamed by whom? Only a handful of people know about my power."

Alan hated himself for saying the words, knowing what a threat they carried. "That could change." The things he did for England.

She took a quick indrawn breath, her eyes hardening.

Alan continued, "We've kept your secret this long. But if this relationship is no longer a mutually beneficial one, the Crown has no obligation to continue to protect you. And if the world learned of your talents . . ."

She snapped, "I'd be picked up within the hour, forced to slave the rest of my life for the Fists or some other, equally horrible, group. Is that what you want, Turing?"

A few minutes ago, she'd called him Alan. "None of this is what I want. But I'm sworn to the throne"—*whose* throne, was the question—"and if you continue to refuse, Henry won't hesitate to order us to take action against you. Do you understand?"

"I'm not an idiot, Turing. I understand perfectly well. I understand that you are a barking dog, and you answer to your masters." Constance turned and paced the length of the room furiously, before returning to spitting distance of him and saying, "I hope Henry chokes on his damned soup."

"I need your answer, Constance. What's it to be?" Alan Turing held his breath and waited, hoping that she'd make this easy for him. He had enough to worry about right now—he didn't need trouble from the Seamstress too.

"Fine," Constance said. "I'll make Henry's clothes."

"I'll send a car around tomorrow." Turing said. "The same as we did for Her Majesty."

"Very well," she replied practically pushing him out the door. "Now get out."

◆

She shut the door and leaned forward, putting her forehead against the cool glass. She supposed Bobbin had been right; she was a traitor to her people. At least the Lion had been decent about it when he was pressuring her.

"So, yer gonna go ahead and make clothes for that bastard."

She turned. Her tailors were clumped together at the end of the walkway.

"Yes," she replied with resignation. "Yes, I am."

"Are you fucking mad?" It was Jeremy, a tall joker with long, delicate fingers up and down his arms. He was brilliant at finishing work and could create the most marvelous knit creations. Never had Constance heard him so much as say "damn" or "bollocks." He was the most gentle soul in her shop.

"Are you fucking mad?!" he repeated.

Constance could only stare at him, speechless. Several of the other jokers nodded.

"I can't believe you agreed to this after that whole display of 'Not going to clothe Henry. Not I.'"

"You don't understand," she began.

"We don't need to understand," Brian said. The smell of peppermint filled the air as it did when he was upset. "You said you wouldn't, and now you've gone back on your word."

Constance was wounded. Not only had Bobbin left into the night and was God-only-knew-where, but now her people, and they were her people, by God, were turning on her. And it was all because of Turing, coldhearted machine-mind he was, and Henry. She positively loathed Henry at that moment, with Turing not too far behind.

"I can't trust you anymore, Miss Russell," Brian continued, a hint of tears in his voice. "Been with you for twenty years and I can't believe you'd let us down like this." He turned and walked into the back of the shop. A few moments later, he reappeared with his coat and hat. "I appreciate that you gave me a chance, but I can't work for you while you serve him."

A few of her other tailors repeated what Brian had—going and fetching their bits and pieces, then they left the shop, the door swinging shut behind the jokers. A few were women who'd been with her for thirty years or more.

Taking a deep breath, she looked over at the rest of her tailors. Some refused to meet her eyes. "If anyone wants to join them, you should go now," she began. "I'm not going to sack anyone or give you a bad reference. It's up to you. Things look bad, I suppose, and I can understand if you want to leave too."

They stared at her mutely. She couldn't discern exactly what they were thinking, and not just because several of them had jokers that had transformed their faces into something terrible. Silently, they turned and went up the stairs to the second-floor workrooms.

Constance stalked into her office and plunked down at her drawing table. She stared at it, unseeing, uninspired, frightened. Bobbin was gone—she had no idea where. Half her staff had walked out and who knew how long she might keep the ones who'd stayed. And tomorrow, she was being forced to clothe a man she hated, to use her wild card power to protect someone who deserved no protection at all. Normally, her anger would have galvanized her, but now she only felt old, flat, and drained.

♥

The streetlights outside the MI-7 office building had come on hours ago, but there was no need for additional lights in Alan's office—the six large screens spanning the far wall gave off more than enough. Alan's eyes barely blinked as he scanned the data, endlessly scrolling. No nat could possibly make sense of the information coming so fast, but Alan's mind, which forgot nothing he asked it to store, captured it all, analyzed furiously.

These computers had gotten much faster, but were still fundamentally dumb. Even the best supercomputers needed direction from a human—true AI was just a dream. And if you asked computers the wrong questions—garbage in, garbage out. If the researchers who worked on AI had known of Alan's existence, they would have tried to draw him into the search. But would true AI actually be good for humanity, or would the machines resent their human progenitors? Might they even rise up against the humans?

Alan was too old for such questions, and it was too late to imagine such a public life for himself. This path suited him better: sitting in a quiet room, lending his unique talents to the country he loved, and remaining their closely guarded secret. Alan Turing had grown comfortable with secrets over the years. Though now, he was looking to unravel one.

If Margaret had been telling the truth, if the whole idea hadn't been some fever-dream of advanced old age, there would surely be traces of the lost prince, traces that could be found. Alan had gone back to the early sixties, examining DNA samples, looking for markers for the royal family. Richard's pattern was intimately familiar to him, and a cousin would be a close match. Alan had been at this for hours. So far, nothing.

He couldn't help imagining the life of this joker child—living in obscurity for decades, likely with no knowledge of their true parentage. Maybe it would be best to simply let the sleeping dog lie? Richard was surely better suited to the throne. And would the nation even accept a joker, however good their claim? Opening the question might bring simmering tensions to the fore, lead to riots, death, mass slaughter. Alan Turing had seen enough of that during the War. His throat tightened at the thought of such violence returning to England's shores.

♣

The delivery truck reached the barracks just outside of London. Sentries looked inside, waved wands at the tires, passed mirrors underneath. Then a pair of dogs gave it the once over and failed to bark. "In you go," an officer said.

It drove through a razor wire–topped gate; past blinking red cameras and motion detectors; it was watched by random patrols and even the vibrations of its passing were graphed by equipment sensitive enough to count the worms in the soil. Such was the paranoia of military intelligence in this age of wild cards.

Badb wondered if the operators in the building were annoyed when a scruffy crow settled right in front of one of their cameras. Beneath her, she had a view of the officers assembling in meeting room 6a. A crow had better eyesight than any nat, and she watched with interest as Henry's bodyguard was escorted right to the front of the long table.

"Look at you, standing to attention." It was a young officer who spoke, his accent like something out of an old war movie. He should have had a moustache, really, but a nasty knife scar ran from just under his nose all the way to the tip of his chin. A present from Belfast, she felt sure. Perhaps that was what put such bile into his voice, and it pleased her to think that her great work in Ireland had crossed the sea before her to plant such strong roots here. "What are you," he said, "But a glorified security guard?"

An older man, sitting at the far end of the table, cleared his throat. "Now, now, DeVere." Good cop's accent was identical to that of his younger colleague. "I'm sure this gentleman has seen military service before. Am I right, Mr. Savic? Reputable, *honorable* service?"

Their guest gave them little satisfaction. The goddess had warned him they would be fishing. "You do not need this . . . pantomime. Is that good word? I told king everything. Your Green Man is in his hideout. Now my part is done."

DeVere's snarl was all the more savage for the way it made his scar writhe like a trapped lizard. "And yet you haven't told His Majesty *where* you got your information, have you, Yuri?"

"Yuri is not my name." He shrugged, as though indifferent to his surroundings. And in a way, he probably was. His mind would be with his daughter and his British girlfriend. Every word that came out of his mouth was keeping them safe. Safe from accidents.

"My source will not be revealed to the likes of you. I will tell only Silver Helix. It is they who should handle Green Man for king."

That got their attention. Every back in the room straightened. Fists clenched. But only the young DeVere was intemperate enough to actually snarl. "Aces!" he said and not in the envying way most mortals spoke that word. "Barely once in the past decade have they laid a glove on Green Man. And why would they harm their joker cousins anyway?"

"What are you suggesting, Captain DeVere?" asked the older man. He wasn't chiding his subordinate; if anything, a slight smile tugged at the corner of his upper lip.

DeVere snapped to sudden attention. "Sir!" he cried. "Permission to clean out the vermin!"

Now there was no disguising the older man's smile. "Granted, my boy." He turned to the bodyguard. "There you have it, Mr. Savic. You're welcome to wait here until we have our man." There was no disguising the fact that this was an order. He stood up. "Some of my colleagues will continue our earlier conversation about your source of information. They are *very* patient. Now, if you'll excuse me? I have a mission to plan."

♠

The knock at the door came after Jasper had been put to bed. Noel looked up from the book he was reading and frowned. He was expecting no one. *La*

Traviata was playing softly on the Bose Wave player. He left it. It would cover his footfalls. Kicking off his loafers, he removed the pistol from his shoulder holster and approached the door staying well off to the side.

"Yes, who is it?" he called.

"Zachary Pike." The name meant nothing to him and Noel said as much. "I'm senior equerry to the king."

Well that was odd. Noel rubbed at his chin. He hadn't shaved in several days and had actually raised a bit of stubble. "May I see some identification?" He unlocked the door and opened it the width of the chain. He also took a quick three-second look through the crack and recognized him as the man from the cathedral who had reacted when Henry decided to pause for questions. Then as now he was wearing a very elegant suit with no suspicious bulges. Pike handed over a card that had the royal crest and his information. Noel opened the door fully and stepped into the hall.

"My son is sleeping, so if we could talk out here."

"Of course. His Majesty wishes to speak with you."

"Really? That's . . . odd. He wants a magician?"

Pike gave a discreet cough. "I believe His Majesty is more interested in your other line of work."

"Knowledgeable bastard, aren't you?"

"I have the honor of His Majesty's confidence."

"Look, my son is nine. I can't leave him alone—"

"A member of the royal protection squad served as my driver. Would he be an acceptable babysitter until you return?"

Curiosity warred with caution. Naturally, curiosity won. "All right."

◆

When she got to Bobbin's flat, Constance let herself in. She'd had a key for as long as she could remember, but had never used it before. There had been times when she'd been curious about how Bobbin lived and what she'd find there, but it would have been a terrible intrusion to use it unless asked. And he'd never asked.

"Bobbin?" she asked, pushing the door open. The drapes were drawn and the room was shadowed. She fumbled for the light switch, then clicked it on. She saw a comfortable room, not unlike the parlor in her own flat. Deep leather chairs and a deep sofa were arranged next to the fireplace. There was a beautiful, but well-worn, Oriental rug on the floor. The memory of tobacco hung in the air.

"Bobbin?"

She made her way into the kitchen. Like the living room, it rather resembled her own in taste. The colors were similar. Thinking back on it, she never realized just how much they liked the same things. It just seemed perfectly normal that they agreed on so much.

Though she didn't want to, she went to the bedroom. She worried that she might find the worst there. She breathed a sigh of relief when she saw only that the bed hadn't been slept in. But then she wondered, with no small worry and annoyance, where the hell he could be.

"Bugger," she swore softly. Then she stepped forward and touched the cover on the bed. It was a soft wool blanket, and she gave it a little pat before she turned and made her way outside.

♥

One did not shake hands with a king. One paused in the door and bowed one's head. Noel had been taught that in his earliest days at the Silver Helix when Flint and Turing had been busily coaching a sixteen-year-old how to dress, how to dance, how to seduce, and how to kill. The etiquette around royals had been drilled into him in the off chance that he might someday meet one. Now twenty-three years later he was. He was not to offer his hand unless Henry did. Henry didn't. He just waved away Pike, who withdrew and closed the door to the study behind him.

The room was fussy and cluttered with heavy furniture that sported dull gold upholstery and a faded Oriental carpet underfoot. The bookcases were filled with leather-bound volumes. Noel wondered how long ago they had actually been touched. The room smelled of cigar smoke with a faint underlying scent of perfume. This had obviously been the queen's study before her death, though Noel had suspected as much given the Dresden figurines on the mantelpiece. The charming shepherdess and her beau didn't seem in keeping with the personality of the man who stood before him.

Unlike many of the other Windsors, Henry had the benefit of being the child of the vivacious Margaret and Peter Townsend and the vestiges of handsomeness remained, though right now his expression was a mix of fury and frustration. He moved behind the desk and sat down. He didn't offer that Noel should do the same.

"So, you don't look like much."

"So many have said, sir."

"According to this," he laid a hand on a file. Noel recognized the tabbing; it was from the archives of the Silver Helix. "You were one of the Helix's elite agent specializing in . . . er . . . cleanup until your . . . retirement."

Noel realized why he was here, and his impression that Henry was a son of a bitch was now solidified. He strolled closer to the desk.

"Shall we dispense with the euphemisms, sir? I killed people for the Helix and by logical extension with the blessings of the British government. And I didn't *retire*, I kicked the slats out of the place and blackmailed them to leave me the hell alone. I presume my particular skill set has been taken on by another, but you're not talking to that person, so I must conclude that this conversation isn't taking place."

The response from the king wasn't what he expected. Henry laughed. "They told me you were a cheeky bastard."

"Dare I ask who?"

"A couple of your former colleagues. They said they trained you."

Noel couldn't imagine the Lion or Turing saying such a thing. It sounded much more like the lowborn, uncouth Spraggs, a married couple who had beaten him to a pulp during hand-to-hand training and enjoyed it far too much.

"So, let me get to the point, Mr. Matthews." Henry left the desk and moved to a large mahogany bar in the corner. "Drink?" he offered lifting a bottle.

"Please. I suspect I'm going to need it."

Henry returned with two highball glasses. Noel took a sip. It was a dark, smoky scotch and it was very good. Henry now motioned them to a pair of armchairs in front of the fireplace. "You know that my aunt Elizabeth bore a child."

Noel cast his mind back to history classes at Cambridge. "Yes, it was still-born . . ." His voice trailed away and he looked up to meet Henry's gaze.

"Ah, I see I don't have to elaborate. It was a boy and a joker. It was alive when it was taken from the palace. I need to know if that infant grew up and is still among us."

"I see . . . and if he did I gather you'd like me to change his status?"

"I can see you are a very circumspect man, I like that," said Henry.

"I'm also a traditionalist and a royalist." Henry looked pleased at that, but the expression curdled when Noel continued. "Which means that this child, should he have survived, is king, and I owe him my loyalty." He stood. "Thank you for the opportunity to visit the palace. Interesting to see something beyond the tour or on the telly."

"It's considered rude to leave until you are dismissed. You might want to hear me out."

"Going to offer me a knighthood?" Noel tried to prevent his lip from curling, but suspected he had failed.

"No. Though if you were to do a service to the Crown you might be rewarded. No, this is more in the nature of a warning." Henry also stood and they measured gazes. "I understand you are locked in a legal battle regarding the custody of your son." An oily sickness began to fill Noel's stomach. "I expect the Crown Prosecutor could be persuaded to take an interest in whether the child was taken by force and whether you are in fact a kidnapper."

Have a stroke, have a stroke, have a stroke. It had become a mantra running through Noel's mind as he stared at Henry. The satisfaction on the man's face made him want to use some of the more esoteric skills he had been taught that resulted in death.

"Conversely, efforts could be made on your behalf so that you achieve the desired outcome."

For long moments the only sound in the room was the ticking of the eighteenth-century clock on the desk. Ironically, it sported a figure of resting justice reclining against the clockface, her sword a flash of gold in the shadowed room. A counterpoint tapping joined the clock as a crow pecked at the glass of the window.

"Fine," Noel snapped. "Have you anything that might aid me in this pursuit?"

"I'm afraid not. Just the date: November fourteenth, 1948. Good hunting, Mr. Matthews. And now you are dismissed."

Noel inclined his head. Not as much as when he had entered. A small piece of rebellion against the bonds that now held him.

OVER THE YEARS, NOEL had come to Constance Russell several times for one of her special suits. They had saved his life when targets or their guards had tried to shoot him or knife him. He didn't expect a seventy-two-year-old joker would pose much of a threat to him, but experience had taught him to be cautious and assume nothing.

He caught a glimpse of himself in one of the mirrors in the elegant outer room of the shop. There were lines in his face now, and his brown hair held flecks of gray. The years had certainly taken their toll since he'd first entered these doors as a sixteen-year-old. He wasn't even counting the scars that littered his body.

He also deliberately left off the word innocent when describing his sixteen-year-old self. He doubted he had ever been innocent. One of his victims had called him a psychopath; personally he thought he was more of a sociopath. He had adored his father and had loved Niobe until she thwarted him, and his love for Jasper would drive him to any lengths, up to and including killing an elderly joker.

"Noel, my dearest boy, how are you?" Her bell-like tones were blurred a bit with the quaver of age, but Constance was still the vivacious, elegantly attired woman he had first met twenty-three years ago.

"As good as can be expected with forty looming, but you . . . you are timeless and beautiful." Though if truth be told he thought she looked stressed and haggard.

She placed her hands on her hips and gave him a suspicious look. "So, what are you after?" A hint of her East End roots slipped through the cultured accent.

He pulled her off the side away from any employees. "I need a suit."

She did not mistake his ask. "Why? You're retired. Or so I was told by your compatriots, who by the way are none too happy with you, so I'm gathering your parting wasn't all that amicable."

"That would be an understatement. Let's leave it at this—I have been tasked with a job by a government official, and since I don't want to leave my nine-year-old son fatherless, I'd like to take no risks. That's why I came to you for

help." He gave her his best smile, and mentally checked off one of the psycho-
logical traits—*manipulativeness*.

She stared up at him, brushed the hair back off his forehead, sighed. He knew
she was seeing the boy, not the man. "All right, let's get you measured. Though
I doubt you have changed much."

"Perhaps a bit heavier since the last time. Middle age, you know."

She led him into a private fitting room. He removed his suit jacket while she
gathered up her tape measure. "Did you think you'd live to see it?" Constance
asked as she took the first measurement down his back.

Noel thought about that for a moment and realized he wasn't actually surprised by his conclusion. "Yes, I actually did." He glanced back over his shoulder and gave her a smile as she wrote down the number. "You see, I'm smart as
well as vicious, and most of my opponents, while they excel at being vicious,
haven't been very smart. Or at least not as smart as me."

She had been continuing to measure while he talked, and now as she drew
the tape around his chest, she felt the ridged tissue around his left pectoral.
Her eyes lifted to meet his, and she unbuttoned his shirt. Her fingers were cool
against the scars that ringed his breast and crossed his abdomen, though her
touch brought a faint throb of pain.

"Looks like someone came close," she said.

"Close only counts in horseshoes and hand grenades," he countered.

"What the bloody hell does that mean?" she asked.

"Ah, perhaps I was too long in America. It means that there is no close in
death. It's a rather binary situation. Fortunately, I'm on the living side of it."

"Well, I'm glad, though you are a bit of a bastard." She buttoned his shirt
and finished. As she was writing down the final numbers, she gave an unconscious sigh.

"Business good?" Noel asked as he donned his coat. He checked his phone
then out of habit paired his phone to Constance's.

"Yes, though my staff is on edge. I hire a lot of jokers and well—" She broke off
abruptly and he realized there was more to the story, but she didn't elaborate.
She made a vague gesture. "You see how things are. And my partner is missing."

"Partner as in romantic partner or business partner?" Noel asked.

The question seemed to stop her for a moment and Noel watched as her
thoughts turned inward. "Business," she finally said. "It's just that in this climate I'd just like to know he's all right."

"I take it he is a joker."

"Yes."

"Well, if he's smart he'll have headed for friendlier climes."

"I . . . I hurt him, and if anything were to happen to him I . . . well, I wouldn't
have a chance to repair things." She correctly read his growing boredom, and
the fact he was edging toward the door. Constance gave a sigh. "I should know
better than to look to you for sympathy. Do you care about anything . . . anyone,
Noel?"

He didn't answer, just touched two fingers to his forehead in a brief salute. "I need a rush on that suit, Constance."

She looked at him sadly. "I guess I got my answer."

♣

The door to the atelier slammed shut and Constance breathed a sigh of relief. Noel was in one of his famous snits and, though she'd only been on the receiving end of them a few times, she wasn't a fan. He was snide and cruel and, at times, a bit of a bitch.

Luckily, over the years she'd gotten faster at making her special clothing—not that she'd ever let on—and she could easily get both Noel's and Henry's suits done. The only thing that might slow her down was her arthritis and wanting to sleep, but there were drugs of a wide variety for both things.

She went to her wall of fabric and debated which would work best for Noel. He was a bit of a dandy, but in a good way. At least, he knew how to dress and understood quality when he saw it. After all, she'd taught him.

But she couldn't concentrate on fabric. Her concern for Bobbin kept ruining her concentration. She shut the doors to the case with a sigh.

The previous night she'd rung the police station and was informed, in an amazingly condescending manner, that an adult man—even in his seventies—missing for less than twenty-four hours was hardly a cause for alarm. She was none too polite in her reply and was informed that until seventy-two hours passed, there would be no investigation into the matter.

"Ya couldn't find yer ass with both yer hands," she snapped.

"Well that's as may be, ma'am," came the reply. "But I'm not going looking for my ass nor your friend until seventy-two hours have passed."

Constance had tapped the Off button on her phone, but it lacked the satisfaction she had once gained from slamming a handset into its cradle.

It was the second day of Bobbin being gone, and she didn't care what the police thought about how long someone should be missing before deciding something had to have happened to them. Bobbin was a joker and things weren't safe for jokers since Henry IX had become king. In only a couple of days, the incidence of attacks on jokers had jumped precipitously.

She considered her choices. None of them were good. There was one possibility, but its price would be high. That didn't matter. She just wanted Bobbin found as soon as possible. The number she needed was still in her contacts list after all this time. She dialed it.

"It's me," she said when her call was answered. "I want a meeting."

♠

"So, who the devil are you supposed to be this time?"

That distinctive whisper emerging from between stone lips sent Noel momentarily tumbling back in time. Sixteen, frightened, in the custody of this terrifying, towering figure that seemed carved from granite. The glowing red eyes were once more glaring down at him. It was hard to tell if Flint was actually angry with Noel or if it was just his manner due to the way the wild card had twisted his body.

"I'm your new French lawyer who is going to argue on your behalf."

"Would that you actually were."

"Never. You're going to die here." It was said with a smile.

"Or perhaps these walls might crumble before I do." Flint countered. *"Well, what is it you want, Noel, now that you have managed to allow us to meet without the inconvenience of cameras or microphones."*

It had been a hectic morning. After leaving Constance he had transformed into his male avatar and teleported to his apartment in Vienna, where he kept a stash of passports for all three of his personae, extra computers, various outfits both male and female, and an array of weaponry.

There he had collected a French passport and supporting documentation that Monsieur DeJardin was a civil rights attorney along with an appropriate attire for said attorney. He had then teleported to the Hague, returned to his own form, changed clothes, and donned a pair of fussy wire rim glasses and affected a mincing gait and a nervous tic of wiping at his nose with a large and florid handkerchief. While his French was very good, he wouldn't have attempted the ruse in France, but he was confident he could carry it off in Holland.

And such seemed to be the case, for he now found himself in a secure room with Kenneth Foxworthy, former military officer and onetime head of the Silver Helix. He was also the man who had recruited Noel into the order and decreed he be trained as an assassin.

Noel took a seat and lit a cigarette. Flint didn't risk testing the tensile strength of the chairs in the interview room, so he remained standing. "This concerns the royals, so I'd appreciate your discretion," Noel said.

"You have it . . . and my interest," Flint replied.

"Rumor has it that Elizabeth's child back in forty-eight wasn't stillborn, but was a joker."

"Well, that would certainly upset the apple cart."

"You ever hear any whispers about that?"

Flint drew his fingers thoughtfully down his cheek, drawing sparks. *"I'm afraid I can't be much help. My body had become completely immobile in forty-seven, and people believed I was dead. I was buried in my home village and my resurrection didn't occur until the early fifties. And the Helix wasn't founded until fifty-two."*

"Shit." Noel dropped the butt of his Muratti onto the floor and ground it out beneath his shoe. "Nothing lurking in the files at the Helix?"

"Do your own research. After all, you stole the files."

"I wasn't interested in ancient history. I took the more recent files, nineteen sixties forward, that detailed our less-savory activities." He stood and moved to the door. "Well, this was a waste of time."

"Who are you working for, Noel?"

"Why? Does it matter?"

"Whatever you might think of me, I'm still a patriot. I worry for my country. If what you're suggesting is true it could—"

"Tear the country apart?"

Flint nodded. *"I also know your particular skill set and that has me concerned."*

"I'll say this much. You know I'm a total bastard. You also know I love my country. I'm not working for her enemies, so if you can help me this would be the time to do it."

The fire in Flint's eyes flared and he gave another nod. *"You have to understand; after the virus was released, people were terrified. Wild cards were shunned, even the aces. None of us would have been trusted with something like this. If this rumor is accurate, any . . . arrangement for the child would probably have been handled by MI-5."*

"Is there anybody left from around that time who might know something?" Noel asked.

"Possibly. I would speak with Charlie Soper. I expect he's retired by now, but he was a clever bloke. He might know something."

◆

"He'll be here in a bit. You want a cup of tea?"

"No, thank you," Constance replied.

"Right," she said as she walked to the door. "I'm Wayfarer. If you need anything, just shout." She left the room, shutting the door behind her.

Constance glanced around the office. It was neat and tidy. The desk was made of maple, with a burl wood inset on top. Three Montblanc Meisterstücks rested neatly on the left side of the desk. She wasn't sure what she'd expected. Maybe something like the Kray's place, where there was the constant threat of violence in the air even when they were gone. This felt more like the office of a very fastidious, but also very wealthy, government official.

The door opened and she pushed herself out of her chair.

"Please," Green Man said. "Don't stand up for me."

Constance nodded, then sank back down. Like the rest of the office, the chair was simple, but comfortable.

"What can I do for you, Miss Russell?" he asked. His voice was sonorous, and Constance thought it sounded perfect for someone whose joker had turned them into wood.

"I need your help finding someone," she replied.

He rested his hands on the desk; the grain complemented his skin. Much to her surprise, Constance found herself comforted by the solid quality of him.

"How long have they been missing?" he asked. He reached out and adjusted pens that needed no straightening.

"He's been gone," she replied. "Well, since Monday night . . . late."

"He's been gone a day?"

"Day and a half!"

"He could just have drunk too much and be sleeping it off," Green Man said. It was clear he was annoyed.

"He's NOT!"

Green Man held up his hands. One of his arms looked a little like it was starting to grow leaves. "I'm terribly sorry," he said placating her. "I see you're quite concerned."

"You should be too, Green Man," she snapped. He may have been a mobster, and likely involved with the Fists, but she'd dealt with those types before. Fear was what they thrived on. "He's a joker. Just an old joker and I thought you protected jokers . . ." Anger and fear made her tremble. "He's never gone off like this. Not once! I know I'll owe you if you help me find him, but that doesn't matter. All that matters is you get him back! His name is Bobbin." She stopped and gasped for breath, balling her hands into fists to stop them from shaking.

"It's Bobbin that's been missing? Why didn't you say so? I'll do what I can."

It brought Constance up short. "You know him?"

Green Man shrugged and then looked a little sheepish. "Well, yes. He's been making my clothes for quite some time."

"He never told me that," Constance said. Now she was irked at Bobbin. It was rich that she hadn't been the only one keeping secrets while he'd walked out on her for the very same thing. "Why didn't he tell me?" she asked, exasperated now.

"Most likely, he knew you wouldn't approve." He went back to fiddling with his pens. It was difficult to tell, but it appeared he was chagrined. "He didn't want you knowing he worked for me." He looked up at her with a determined expression. "He's one of my people and I protect them. Well, not one of mine in the usual sense."

Constance narrowed her eyes. Bobbin was hers. Green Man had a lot of brass.

"Then why are you helping me?"

"You built the Greenwood Centre for jokers here in East End. And I know you've always hired jokers to work for you. I think you're one of us—even if you don't possess a wild card."

"So, I'll owe you, then," she said.

"I won't hear any talk of owing me," he said. Constance didn't believe him. "I'll find him."

"You'll be better than the police. I reckon you have far more resources on the street."

"Yes," he said. "I do indeed."

♥

Alan had been careful to arrange this meeting with Richard in a room of Kensington Palace that was private enough that they couldn't be walked in on, but not so private that Richard would risk making advances. He wanted to be a better husband to Sebastian; they could still have twenty good years together, after all. Sex wasn't everything—and perhaps, if Alan put his mind to it, he could help Sebastian with that as well. It was just another problem to solve, and Alan Turing had always been excellent at solving problems.

Now Alan leaned across the ornately carved mahogany table toward Richard, keeping his voice low. "So, that's Margaret's story. I've been searching ever since. If I find the child, that will keep Henry off the throne—problem solved." It would be such a relief, not to be discussing fratricide with the prince. If Richard asked it of him, could Alan even go through with it? It was one thing to decide Henry was a bad king, but that was a far cry from regicide. Agreeing to even consider that now seemed like one of a series of poor decisions, not fully thought out.

Richard frowned. "Finding another heir doesn't work for me, Alan, and you know it. Some random stranger to take the throne of England? A stranger who's been raised as a . . . regular person all these years, with no training in what duty to the country entails?"

Alan was certain Richard had wanted to say *commoner* but had caught himself. Alan said, "I wanted to offer you the option." Couldn't Richard see that they'd gone too far? "You could just step back—"

"No," Richard said firmly.

Alan bit his lip. There was no point in arguing with the prince when he was in this kind of mood. Retreat, regroup. "Well, the first step, regardless, is to find out if the other prince is even still alive. We can't calculate the risk factors until we know more. And if he *is* a threat, we need to move quickly to control it."

"Fine, Alan," Henry said impatiently. "Go—go figure out everything you can. Think, and think hard. Can you work at home, so no one stumbles in on you?"

"That should be manageable." Alan didn't have quite the same setup at home, but he could move some machines around and make it work. It'd certainly make Sebastian happy to have him around a little more.

"Good. I'll tell the rest of the team that you're busy with a private project of mine." Richard pushed himself up from the table, standing to his full height.

He did look handsome, with those piercing blue eyes. The sun caught his hair, glinting gold, and Alan's breath came a little faster. Alan swallowed down desire; virtue wasn't always easy. Focus on the mission. "I don't know if the Lion will—"

Richard said firmly, "Being a prince has got to be good for something. He'll do what I tell him. Now go on. Get to work." He smiled, with that wicked edge. "If you're very good, I'll give you a nice reward."

"Yes, sir," Alan said, casting his eyes down. No need to have that conversation now.

♣

Bright swirls of color covered the street-facing wall of the Greenwood Design Centre. A week ago, the wall had been a sensible olive green. Constance had the cabbie stop and she got out. She didn't mind that someone had painted the wall—the pattern was amazing and the colors were unexpected—just the sort of thing she liked—but no one had told her it was happening. And that gave her a bad feeling.

She walked briskly around the freshly painted wall to the courtyard embracing the front doors. Sitting on benches and the ground was a group of paint-splattered students. Most of them, except a handful of nats, were jokers. Usually, she would have gotten a friendly greeting—after all, she'd founded and helped to fund the Centre—but today they just looked at her miserably.

She frowned then glanced around and saw spray-painted in black and red on the interior walls: JOKER LOVERS DIE. FUCK JOKERS. GET OUT NOW.

A different pattern in different shades from the outer walls was being painted—soon it would cover the foul sentiments written there.

"When did this happen?" Constance demanded, her voice quavering with anger.

"Yesterday," one of the nat kids replied jumping to his feet. "Bastards. Cowards. They came here in the dead of night. I'm not a joker, but I spend time here all the same. Don't make no difference to them if I'm a joker or not, ma'am."

"The youngs who come here for classes after school, they saw it," a joker girl with bony protrusions tipped with stiff fibers like paintbrushes in place of hair said. "And they're taking it hard."

This is Henry's fault, she thought. *If he hadn't been all too happy expressing his loathing for jokers and anyone else who wasn't "human," those hooligans wouldn't have felt quite so safe while committing such an ugly crime.*

"What about the elders? Do they know?"

"Oh, yes, ma'am," the nat replied. "They say they're scared, but that they'll come back anyway. They're coming to help clean up later this afternoon."

Constance nodded, but she wondered how many of them really would come back. Many of them were of a similar age as her and she'd noticed it was easier and easier to find things to be afraid of now. She'd had to work at keeping that sort of thinking at bay, and it must be worse being an older joker. They might just stay home in fear, and the isolation would only fuel the fear.

"Dammit!" she exclaimed, a little spittle spewing out. She wiped her mouth with the back of her hand. It wasn't ladylike, but she really didn't care. "It's bad enough they want us out of Bethnal Green after we've been here for decades. Now this!"

"They want to move the Centre?" cried the joker girl with the paintbrush hair. Constance remembered her name was Temperance.

"Yes," Constance replied hotly. She pulled a handkerchief out of her pant pocket. "Property values are going up here, but having a Centre that caters to jokers, well, that's keeping them lower than the speculators would like."

Temperance shook her head and the bony handles on her hair clacked together. "Bastards."

"Yes," Constance replied "Bastards indeed."

Constance glared at the graffiti painted on the wall of her Centre—the Centre she'd named for Glory all those decades before. It was a blow that the neighbors wanted them gone. And who were these nasty punks who wanted them afraid? Were they some of the locals? That there was a harbored hatred for jokers after all these years in the community got her back up. Then a cold slice of fear went through her and she fervently hoped Green Man could find Bobbin quickly—before someone took their joker hate out on him too.

♠

Green Man felt the phone in his pocket vibrate. Very few people had this number and even fewer would use it. He tried to remember a single time it had rung for anything that wasn't an emergency.

He failed.

"Yes," he said into the phone.

"It's me," Wayfarer replied. Her voice was oddly low. "We've got incoming. Military, I think."

"How many?"

"Don't know."

"Sound the alarm and get clear."

"What about you?"

He knew that if there was time for her to come and get him and for them to escape together, she'd already be at his side. "Worry about me later."

He left the room alone, moving down an old concrete corridor that smelled of damp. He ascended the stairs at the end of it until he arrived at a scuffed wooden door, and heard the whispered sounds of his pursuers on the other side.

They were too quiet to give away numbers, but he guessed there were at least two or three. He would have to be quick, decisive, and a little lucky if he was to overcome them and escape. He watched the round door handle begin to turn very, very slowly.

When it had revolved about a quarter of the distance required for the door to open, he lurched forward, slamming both hands into it. The momentum tore the lock and hinges from the door as easily as rotten teeth from gums, leaving them standing proud in the frame while the door continued forward at speed.

The first of the soldiers took the force of it full in the face, and both he and the door were carried directly into the second soldier. Green Man didn't pause to see the effects. He reached up to the exposed beam above his head . . . and pulled.

There was a groan of timber and then bricks and dust fell from the ceiling. He hoped the soldiers had been pushed clear of the rubble but had neither desire nor the time to check. Instead, he rushed to the wall opposite and dived through it. Plasterboard popped and insulation blew outwards in a tiny shower of black rubber spheres.

Though the immediate threat had passed, Green Man did not relax. After dusting himself off, he rushed to the nearest window and saw a number of black vans parked outside, vomiting uniformed figures from their open doors. They'd already have made a cordon. His only hope—and it was a weak one—was to punch through that cordon and find safer streets before they could bring their superior numbers to bear.

He ran toward the main entrance only to find soldiers, too many, coming the other way. Turning, he ran toward another door as a grenade rolled into the room. Smoke began to issue from it. He wasn't particularly worried about being able to breathe, but he was worried about being able to see.

Should I surrender? He wondered. *I can't hope to win, and the more I fight, the worse my case will be.* But he dismissed the idea. His history already damned him, and anyway, he knew the way the justice system was loaded against jokers. To escape was not enough; if the soldiers got a confirmed sighting of him fleeing it would give King Henry and the media everything they needed.

Falling back deeper into the building, he noted how empty it seemed, and was pleased. Hopefully, Wayfarer and the others were well on their way to safety by now. More grenades had been thrown, the gas clouds rapidly filling the space, giving everything an unreal, ghostly feel.

A trio of soldiers rounded the corner ahead of him, their silhouettes just visible through the smoke. Green Man turned into a side corridor, feeling more and more like an animal being herded toward slaughter. A shotgun roared at his back, accompanied by the sounds of other weapons, all urging him on. Not really thinking now, he rushed on as fast as he could, the net of enemies growing swiftly tighter.

Why now? Wondered a desperate part of him while another, more logical, part already knew the answer. *It makes perfect sense. After Henry's comments they will be expecting the Twisted Fists to take action. This is simply a preemptive strike.* The irony of this being the one thing that would compel the Fists to shed blood was not lost on him.

If they killed him, it would herald a time of bloody vengeance from the Fists, but if they captured him, they would learn too many of the Fists' secrets. Not just about the organization itself, but the myriad web of connections between them and the joker community. Such connections could be used to set back joker rights another fifty years.

He could not afford to die today.

He could not afford to be captured.

He could not afford to be identified.

He emerged from the smoke, the soldiers coming fast on his heels. Another shot was fired, shredding the fabric of his right trouser leg and gouging a new groove in the back of his thigh. He grunted and stumbled against the wall as a door opened to his right. He raised his hand instinctively, but instead of a soldier, he saw an old woman standing there. Her body was wrapped in bandages, fresh enough that patches of white were darkened by blood. She held herself tall, however, black and white hair framing sharp features and a look of the purest determination.

"This way," she hissed, turning before he had a chance to answer.

Green Man did not pause to think. Did not dare. Pushing off from the wall, he lurched after her, the sounds of booted feet and angry guns loud at his back.

♦

Green Man tore through the building—quite literally. One of her crows showed how he ripped a door from its hinges and flung it behind him, while several times, catching himself on a piece of furniture, he smashed himself free.

But his pursuers were determined. She flew one crow at the barrel of a gun to put off a soldier's aim. And once, she swooped on a grenade and flew it back the way it had come. One fewer witness. Most satisfactory.

And finally, Green Man burst through the back door.

"This way," she told him, allowing the mood of "urgency" to show in her voice and on her face, although, of course, she felt nothing. Only her regenerated self knew the power of emotions.

She led him into the nest of alleys to the north of the hideout. The enemy were coming. Everywhere, her crows wheeled through the sky. Or sat still in hidden rookeries, forbidden even from cawing lest they drop the razor blades they held in their beaks. The goddess had prepared herself well.

"Pick me up," she told him.

He was stronger than he knew, and three ribs snapped beneath his wooden fingers. The pain was inconvenient. "Run straight ahead, but not on the right. Not the right, I said!"

Footsteps echoed behind them. Soldiers were coming and Green Man wasted precious seconds turning around.

Two guns were brought to bear. "Put down the hostage! Put her down!" The men stepped forward together. But then, the one on the right stood on a manhole cover and dropped away with a yelp.

"Run!" said Badb. "Go left."

Green Man obeyed, taking directions as she threaded him through streets and lanes while the hunters were always just out of sight, calling to one another; wondering why their drones kept crashing; or stumbling on comrades whose throats had been cut, although nobody knew how.

The buildings here were a crumbling nest of squats; zoned for demolition any day now so that yet more glass and steel could rise above the river.

The only working light on the street revealed a set of steps, with a door hanging from its hinges at the top.

"Quickly," she told her companion. "In there. And put me down now."

He did, and though it was pitch black inside, she was aware of him surreptitiously wiping his hands of her blood. Good.

Then, although he should have known better than to speak, the leader of the Twisted Fists, an organization little known for its squeamishness, couldn't help whispering, "It stinks of death in here."

"Junkies," she told him. "Died in their sleep."

That much was true, at least.

She knew nobody was outside yet, so she lit a match, crouching against the wall. Her bandages were completely sodden by now. Her blood oozed down onto a carpet of old needles and rat droppings. "Here," she whispered. "When I say, you must kick the wall as hard as you can. Understand?"

She couldn't read that wooden face, but the whole set of his body spoke of puzzlement. Still, she knew he would comply. Sure enough, when she cried, "Now!" His massive right leg swung forward with all the power of a cannon. The loosened bricks shot out of the wall at head height, pulping the men behind it beyond recognition despite the helmets they were wearing.

Green Man ran to the door and Badb could read the shock in him at the results of his own handiwork. "Wait!" she said. "Wait! Three more seconds."

"What? I—"

The explosion came from four streets away, and then screams followed and everything was on fire.

"What . . . what was that?"

IRA semtex. But there was no need to tell him that.

"We can go," she said, allowing exhaustion to show in her voice. She really did need to regenerate soon, although she knew her irrational, younger self might not be up to the great work that lay ahead. "The path will be free now."

"How?" he said, still bewildered. "How did you know?"

"It's in the name," said Badb. "*Finder*. I know things. I find things. Like escape routes. It's who I am. What I am. I used to make a living off it. But . . . but I'm too hideous now."

"Not to me."

She sighed. "Yet even you . . . even you, a joker, wiped your hands of me."

"I—"

"And I have nowhere to go now. But I'm glad . . . I'm glad I helped you. You're the only one who ever stood up for us. So . . . so, I . . . will leave you in peace."

"But, Finder, where will you go?"

She allowed her shoulders to sag despite the way it rubbed the broken ribs together. "The sewers are good enough for me. It's best I disturb you no further."

He grabbed her arm, fiercely enough she thought it would pop from its socket—a great inconvenience. "No!" he said. "No. Our whole organization would have died tonight without you. You *must* come with me. You deserve the gratitude of every joker in Britain."

On a nearby road, an ambulance shrieked past. Then, several more.

"Oh, God," whispered Green Man, dropping her arm. "Soldiers. How many soldiers have died tonight?"

Fourteen.

Badb was intimately familiar with the British Army and knew they could be relied upon for a good atrocity when they lost a few of their own. Whether it was an "accidental" death in custody, or the cold-blooded hunting of panicked civilians through the streets of Derry, the goddess had seen it all and found it satisfactory. This time, the weight of vengeance would fall on a joker community that already felt itself under siege.

Yes. Her visit to Britain had begun well. But the death toll would need to be a lot higher if she were to foment an outright civil war.

She snuggled against the hard sides of Green Man as he led her to "safety." Crows flew through the dark. They nestled next to windows in palace and prison alike. And she, eternal, pitiless, flitted from one to the other, watching, always watching.

♥

"And you will be the only one working on my clothes?" Henry asked again.

It was the third time he'd queried her on the topic since she'd arrived at Buckingham Palace. They were in the private residence. Constance was well-acquainted with the residence from her years of dressing the queen. "That's what Turing and the Lion told me," he continued. "My valet will give you a list of what I need. You understand, of course, that everything *must* be handled only by you."

Constance's eyes narrowed. "I sew the clothes myself, sir," she replied. "That's how my ability works." She wanted to escape now that she had his measurements, but until Henry was done with her, she couldn't.

His bride-to-be sat primly on one of the matching gold and white damask divans. Her legs were demurely crossed at the ankles. She was intended to be Henry's perfect wife, though he already had one of those. Forty years married and now he was replacing his current wife with this Silly Young Thing. Constance wasn't certain just how silly the girl was, but she was ridiculously young; young enough to be Henry's grandchild. And only someone very silly would have consented to marry him.

The Silly Young Thing poured tea and Henry took the proffered cup, barely acknowledging her. Constance took the moment to show Henry fabric swatches.

"You decide," he said briskly, sitting on the divan opposite the SYT. "I'm certain the suit will be impeccable. Your work for my mother was always of the highest quality. You have me pondering, Miss Russell, what is it about your employees that makes them so unique that you are willing to drive clients away because of them? After all, with their, ah, infirmities it must be difficult for them to perform their tasks."

"Well, they work very hard, sir," she said, trying not to let her dislike of him slide into her voice. "And often their . . . *infirmities* . . . give them more skills at their jobs rather than not."

"But then that's not fair to humans, is it? There isn't a level playing field when one group has extra talents." He shook his head. She seethed.

"Sir, respectfully, I would remind you that I have a wild card, indeed one that you are availing yourself of this very moment."

"But you're an ace," he replied smoothly. "Aces are different, aren't they? And so useful. It's a completely different matter."

His hypocrisy was breathtaking.

"Yes," she replied. "I am certainly useful. I've been useful to the Crown for over forty years. But, sir, I must begin work on your suit if I'm to complete it in time for the funeral."

For a brief moment, Henry glared at her with a shocking amount of animosity. She'd overstepped. Even so, she glared right back at him.

"Perhaps you should consider making me an entire wardrobe," he said tersely. He set his teacup down with a clatter.

Not while I still draw breath, Constance thought. *How do you think you'll make me do that? I'm an old woman. We're hard to frighten.*

"I'll consider it, sir," she said, trying her best not to lose her temper.

"Very well," Henry said pushing the button to summon his valet. The door swung open. "Please show Miss Russell out," he said.

Constance gathered her things and followed the valet. As she walked to the waiting car, all she could think was that the palace felt terribly empty with Margaret gone. Henry's presence did nothing to change that.

No matter what Henry, Turing, or the Lion wanted, this would be the only garment she would ever make for Henry.

♣

It was a small meeting late at night and, for the first five minutes, a very quiet one. It took place in Westminster, where MPs were staying late in advance of a tight vote on defense cuts, exacerbated by several resignations from the cabinet.

Birds sheltered themselves from the wind just outside. One of these was a crow.

Badb watched the home secretary reread the casualty figures in front of her, while Turing and a stiff-backed Singh waited at her pleasure.

She snarled. "I want Green Man gone," she said. "Wait!" She pointed at her secretary. "Time for your tea break, isn't it, Prashad?"

"Of course, Home Secretary."

She waited until he'd left the room, her polished fingernails tap-tapping on the table like a flock of chickens pecking grain. "I want him gone, and I don't mean in prison."

"Home Secretary? If I may?" Turing straightened in his chair. "It would be a waste, he—"

"Compost him if it makes you feel better, Turing. We have fourteen families in mourning, and we're lying to them about how they died. Add to that the bloody Italian news spreading muck about a joker king, it's only going to get worse."

"A joker what?"

"Oh, that shut you up, Turing, did it? It's all rubbish, of course, but it'll stir up the fr—," she paused, perhaps aware of who she was talking to. "It will stir up all kinds of trouble, that's all I'm saying, and we need him gone. You hear me? Gone."

Turing's eyes met those of Singh. The latter nodded, as though to say, "you speak for me in this," and Turing nodded back.

"I have read the reports from the attack. The soldiers blundered into traps. Green Man did little more than defend himself. And you didn't even order it, did you, Home Secretary? Army Intelligence took this upon themselves . . ."

She banged the table. Badb couldn't see her face but could well imagine a snarl on it. "Don't think they'll be getting out of this scot free either. There's one little hothead in there who'll spend the rest of his career removing leeches from his underwear. But now the army wants a head. A wooden one. And with this fiasco going on"—presumably, she meant the defense cuts—"We'd better give it to them, you understand me, *gentlemen?*"

They did, but Turing dared to shake his head.

"Home Secretary, what the army is asking for—" How clever of him not to point out that it was she herself who had just given him the order; Turing could be quite the diplomat when his husband wasn't involved. "What they're asking for can't work. We need Green Man to stay in place."

"You are fucking shitting me."

"I am happy to provide you with the figures, but my *analysis* shows that the frequency of violence committed by the Fists has shrunk dramatically since he replaced the Black Dog. Meanwhile, tip-offs to the authorities have led to the arrest of the more . . . unreasonable members of that organization."

"He's keeping them in check?"

For the first time, Singh spoke, his voice resonant. "It is we who keep him in check, in a way. I myself protect his family, and he knows it."

"So, where do they live?" she asked.

The tall Sikh smiled slightly and shook his head. "These days, Green Man is little more than a crime boss, acting to keep jokers safe in situations where our own police happen to look the other way. Which occurs all too often."

Her nails began tapping again, angrily this time, but Turing, who did not always share Singh's urges to be scrupulously honest, took over. "At least, let us wait awhile, Home Secretary. Jokers are a significant portion of our population and many of them, in addition to their unfortunate external appearance, possess dangerous abilities. My analysis indicates that right now, they are on the point of an explosion. I believe Green Man's authority is all that's keeping the lid on things."

"Fuck your analysis," she said. But Turing and Singh, who could both see the expression on her face, visibly relaxed.

Green Man, it seemed, would be left in place for now.

♠

Charlie Soper lived just outside London in the commuter belt town of Chesham. It was nestled in the rolling hills of Buckinghamshire, and Noel reckoned it would be green, leafy, and charming come spring. But it was a cold March night near midnight and sleet was icing the cobblestones when he teleported into the market square. Fortunately, the images on the innumerable picture-sharing apps proved to be accurate, and no one had parked a delivery lorry in front of the clock tower. A dog barked in reaction to the soft *pop* of his arrival.

Noel had managed to suss out Soper's address, a task that had taken hours, but the man was clearly a professional—*damn him*—and had scrubbed virtually all trace of himself from the net. Which meant that Noel was arriving in the square rather than teleporting directly into the man's home.

The sleet pecked lightly at his face as he allowed his body to shift back to his normal form. For some men, finding Lilith standing in their abode at eleven thirty at night would be alluring, but Noel suspected that Soper would not be one of them. Also, Noel hoped this would be a professional conversation, and Lilith made men forget to be professional.

He checked the address, fired up his map app, and started walking. In a simpler time, he would have stolen one of the cars parked along the street, but he hadn't brought along a laptop and didn't want to take the time to hack a vehicle's security system. It was bitter cold and he wanted to get this over with, since he had left Jasper alone at the flat. If things went well, Jasper would never know he had been gone.

It was a terraced house, in a line of connected red brick houses offering a blank anonymous face to the street. Noel located the proper door and noted the glow of light from behind the drapes on one of the upstairs windows. There was an archway between the houses and, as expected, it led to a parking lot with garages available for the owners. Apparently, the MI-5 pension was sufficient for rather plush home ownership.

As he approached the backdoor Noel looked for cameras and a security system and spotted neither. Pulling out his lockpick case, he paused for a moment to contemplate why he was electing to break into the house rather than knock on the front door.

Rivalry with the other service had been part of the culture at MI-7, born out of the dismissive attitude toward the aces by the nats who controlled MI-5. Was he trying to prove that he didn't needs powers for his tradecraft? Show his lack of respect with a home invasion? Or hope for a violent reaction out of Soper that could be met with equal violence? He decided the last one was the most likely reason. Henry's demand, the grinding court case, guilt over his marriage: all had him longing to hurt someone.

The decision reached, he made quick work of the lock, carefully turned the knob, slipped inside, and found himself in a kitchen. The only illumination was from the LED clock on the coffee machine set to brew at 6:00 A.M. Noel stepped into the hallway and started at the sight of an elderly man dressed in a bathrobe over pajamas, leather slippers on his bare feet and a hand in one pocket.

"Ah, Mr. Matthews, good evening. Filthy weather," he said as he walked past Noel toward the kitchen. "Cup of tea, or something a bit stronger to take away the chill?"

Noel's wish for violence vanished, replaced by amusement. The man was a professional and Noel liked professionals. "How about both? Put a splash of something stronger in that tea." He followed Soper back into the kitchen and leaned against the doorjamb while the old man set up the kettle and tossed tea bags into a pair of mugs.

"So, to what do I owe this visit?" Soper asked.

"A mutual acquaintance told me that you are the man who knows where all the bodies are buried over at MI-5."

"And which particular ones do you want unearthed, Mr. Matthews? And aren't you more in the business of creating them?" The high whistle of the tea kettle interrupted. "Also, word has it that you are no longer in the old firm," Soper said as he filled the mugs.

"To quote the Godfather, 'just when I thought I was out . . .'" Noel accepted the mug.

"Alcohol is in the study," Soper said and led the way.

Noel surveyed the room noting the smell of tobacco, the worn upholstery on the arms of the large armchair, the dust on the mantel. This was a man's space. Though a woman had clearly picked the furnishing, no trace of her could presently be observed. *Widower or divorcé?* Noel wondered.

Soper selected a bottle from an array on a sideboard and poured in a liberal dollop of whisky. He then settled into the worn armchair and waved Noel to the couch. "So, you've been pulled back in."

"Not officially." Noel paused for a sip of tea. "I've been tasked by particular gentleman to make inquiries about an event in late 1948."

"Watch it. I'm not that old."

"And I'm not that young, but no matter. You were DG at Box after that unpleasantness in 2000. You had access to everything and you have a reputation as a man who likes to have leverage, and secrets make the best leverage." Soper didn't respond, just watched Noel over the rim of his mug. This was also the problem with professionals . . . they knew how to play the game. "Look, did you come across anything regarding the royals in November of forty-eight."

Deep lines appeared in his wrinkled cheeks as Soper began to smile. "It's pretty clear who'd have taken an interest. Also why *you* would be selected to make inquiries."

Noel set aside his mug. Time was passing and he wanted to get back to Jasper. "Was the brat born alive or not?"

"Yes."

"Fuck." Agitated, he stood and began to pace. "Anything else you can give me? Physical attributes? Who took him? Where they took him? And you seem bloody pleased about this."

"Why not? That family always find a way to top up their rotten bloodline, don't they?" He reacted to Noel's expression. "Blimey, don't tell me you're a monarchist."

"I was raised to honor crown and country. I killed for them—"

"And I'm sure they were appropriately grateful," Soper said, sarcasm edging every word. They locked gazes for a long moment, then Soper said, "All I know is that the infant was alive and given into the care of an MI-5 agent who was told to handle it."

"So, do you reckon the problem was solved back in forty-eight?" Noel asked.

Soper sucked in a deep breath, blew it out again. "The Oxbridge lot will tell you that no Englishman of that era would murder an infant . . ." He gave a shrug and Noel just snorted. Soper gave him an approving look. "If whatever psychopath they picked from the pool found he couldn't do the deed, I should think they'd have taken the baby someplace else. Someplace where his presence wouldn't cause a fuss."

"Yes, I think I see." Noel drained the rest of his spiked tea. "I'd best be off. Thank you for the tea."

"You can use the bloody front door this time," Soper responded.

Noel smiled, transformed into Lilith, and teleported away. He rather enjoyed Soper's final expression.

♠ ♥ ♦ ♣

Thursday

MARCH 5TH

JUST AN ORDINARY MAN, walking his three-year-old daughter through the park. Birds sang halfheartedly for the miserable spring, but the child threw herself laughing in among the daffodils. Each one had to be smelled separately, after which, she thanked it and gave it a name.

Badb was like that once. She remembered little now of the bog near Rann na Feirste where she'd grown up, but sometimes she dreamt of tiny fields, startlingly green, with the great peak of Errigal scratching at the sky. Would this little girl live through the chaos to come? Would she grow up to murder her doting father, as the goddess had done?

"Don't look around," she warned.

The bodyguard obeyed, but the girl did not, recoiling in horror behind her father's knee. His whole body stiffened.

"I shouldn't talk to you," he said. "I was interrogated for hours."

"I got you out," she replied. She still had enough dirt from her FRU days to accomplish that much. "Did he reward you? The king?"

"Green Man got away," he whispered. "But . . . but, yes. I thank you."

"I have more," the goddess said, allowing a note of "excitement" into her voice. "But this is for the king's ears and nobody else's, you understand?"

She flicked to a nearby crow so she could see the look on his face. Terror: his pale skin sagging around eyes that blinked as rapidly as the wings of a bee. Most satisfactory. She saw anger too. He'd thought he was done with her. But no, no. Badb was not one to leave her pawns idle on the board.

"I don't want any more *help*. You . . . you have no idea. Fourteen men killed? The soldiers were on the verge of a rampage. No joker would have been safe, but . . ."

But the Met had got wind of it first. Badb had learned that much. "You're not in Belfast now!" the commissioner had said, terrified De Vere and his merry men were about to tear the city to bits. *As they would have.* Most inconvenient, thought Badb. The meddling of the police threatened to set her plans back by days. "Tell His Majesty this. His own brother conspires with the Silver Helix to bring him down."

"What? I . . . I can't be involved in such things. I can't."

The little girl started crying.

"You can. You are."

Badb slipped away then. Deeper into the bushes.

How wonderful if the two princes moved into open conflict. Oh, she knew well that kings didn't rule Britain anymore. It was all prime ministers and the like. But nobody knew better than she how willingly people fought and died for mere symbols. For flags or books. For temples and long dead prophets. Yes, yes. And it would get even better if the joker prince proved real.

A twisted king would draw forth terrible magic. Maybe even more so if already dead, for once the idea slipped into the world, a thousand pretenders would appear overnight.

Behind her, the bodyguard had yet to move, though his daughter whined into the leg of his pants. No need to follow him anymore for now. She sent the crow into the air, soaring over the city in search of blood.

♦

Noel awoke the next morning with a stuffy head and his phone blowing up with texts from Henry's equerry. As he climbed out of bed he cursed the weather, the incipient cold that was threatening after his night spent walking through sleet.

King Henry and his bullshit. In the bathroom he applied the testosterone patch on his abdomen and hoped a hot shower would stave off the cold.

He had breakfast waiting when Jasper came into the kitchen dressed in his school uniform, book bag over his shoulder. Jasper bestowed a truculent look on Noel.

"Okay, what have I done?" Noel asked.

"You were gone last night," Jasper accused. "I got scared and I came to your room, but you weren't there. You weren't *anywhere.*"

"I had to go out."

"Mom would never have left like that."

It stung and Noel snapped, "Unlike your mother, I have responsibilities."

Yes, to your son. To your family! He could almost hear Niobe's voice. Fortunately, his child wasn't old enough to have that sort of sophisticated response.

He reined in his annoyance and modulated his tone. "I'm sorry, I won't do it again. Or if I have to be away, I'll make sure Mrs. Donnelly comes over. Now eat, so I can get you to school."

♥

Turing found himself walking into Silver Helix headquarters with a young joker woman with multiple eyes all around her head. The fact that she was in the company of Jiniri provided her identity. And indeed, as they waited for the creaky old elevator to arrive, the illusion melted away to reveal Primrose, who had shaved some thirty years off her actual age even while sporting joker attributes.

"I gather you've been doing a bit of recon. What word from the street?" Alan asked.

"It's much as you'd expect," Primrose said. "The people are grieving the loss of their queen. Lots of black in the streets, reddened eyes."

Alan nodded. "Margaret was loved. And Henry?" They stepped onto the elevator.

Jiniri responded, "Less so. But it's to be expected. They'll come around when they've had some time. That's always how it is."

Less so. That boded well for Richard's hopes, and Alan wanted to ask more, wanted to ask what the people thought of Richard, but that might give the game away. These agents were sharp as tacks—he'd trained them to be, after all. He'd found the best that England had to offer, had brought them here to serve king and country. *Which king, though? That was the question.*

"Lot of anti-joker and anti-immigrant sentiment out there. Felt a bit nervous," Primrose added. Jiniri nodded in agreement.

"I doubt Henry will be making any more extemporaneous statements, so things should quiet down," Alan said.

"Hope you're right, but I'd be very sure your makeup is in place, Enigma," Jiniri concluded as the two women stepped off on the second floor, leaving Turing to ponder that ominous statement on his way to his fifth-floor office.

♣

Because he was feeling perverse, Noel stopped for a coffee, then stopped at Hatchard's to pick up a book he had ordered before finally calling back Zachary Pike.

"Where the devil have you been? Our mutual *friend* wants an update, so—"

"You're really terrible at this. Never emphasize a particular word. It always arouses interest. Usual place?"

"Yes," Pike snapped and hung up.

There was a crowd of protesters at the front of Buckingham palace. The Queen's Guard held their rigid positions, not reacting to the chants and catcalls from the mixed crowd of students, immigrants, and entitled white people, but Noel spotted only one joker in the mix. Unlike the others, the wild cards knew that if heads were going to be cracked, theirs would be the first to feel the blow.

He turned down a side street to the entrance for official visitors. His ID was checked, car examined for bombs, and he was waved through. Once again Pike was waiting, and hurried him up back stairs and into a large office. King Henry was signing papers. He handed them to a young aide and waved the man out of the office. Pike also withdrew and the doors were closed. Noel inclined his head.

"Well? What have you got for me?" Henry demanded.

"The child was alive at birth—"

"I fucking know that!"

Noel drew in a deep breath. He was used to people yelling at him. Didn't mean he liked it. Especially when it came from a place of petulant entitlement. "If I may continue, sir?" Henry gave a grudging nod. "After the birth, the infant was given into the care of an MI-5 agent with instructions to handle it."

Henry looked eager at that. "Excellent." He stood, clasped his hands behind his back and swaggered away. "So, this nightmare is over."

"In these types of situations, it's probably smarter to assume nothing, sir," Noel said. "We don't know how the agent interpreted that order."

Henry whirled. "You didn't talk to him? Dear God, it seems your reputation was exaggerated."

"With respect, sir, it has been seventy-two years. The agent in question is probably long dead, and I rather doubt your grandfather made a note in his day planner, 'gave hideous joker baby into care of agent So and So for disposal.' Frankly, it was damn bad planning on the palace's part not to keep track of the child. But I expect Prince Philip preferred not to know if the solution selected had been a lethal one."

The silence in the room felt fraught. "You come here with nothing concrete—"

Noel was beginning to think the knock of the Windsors by the republicans was extremely accurate. "You sent for *me*, sir," he reminded the king in a purr.

Something in Noel's tone and manner had Henry shifting uncomfortably. "Well . . . yes . . . quite. So, what do you intend to do now?" The bluster had returned to his voice.

"Find some old jokers or old agents."

♠

Badb crouched in the corner of the room Green Man had lent her. Her every breath bubbled as blood pooled in her lungs, and a constant trickle of it stained the bare floorboards. Rarely had she allowed herself to grow so old without regeneration. Her arms were leaden sticks. Her skin, like cooling lava, was a plane of red cracks and oozing crevices.

She would not be young again until a hero died within a stone's throw of her. But it wouldn't be long now. Badb could feel it. Like that time in sixty-eight when she had urged the B-Specials to attack civil rights marchers, and the whole of Northern Ireland had burned for days. How many young men had given their lives then? Oh, a host of them, and *so* sincere! The land drank its fill, and the goddess became beautiful and high on emotion for weeks afterwards.

Now, Britain was fattening nicely under her care. She could see it from one crow or another. She watched as the representatives of a moderate Muslim community read out a document sent to them anonymously.

"Henry . . ." said an old man, his beard huge and white as snow, his eyes squinting at the paper. "King Henry IX. He wants us out of Britain."

"We were all born here. Except Imran."

"Doesn't matter. He wants us gone. If the young men hear about this . . ."

Oh, but they *had* heard about it. The goddess had made sure of that. A few from this very mosque were already getting free lessons in the manufacture of Molotov cocktails from her contacts in the IRA. At least one was a hero in the making.

All over the city, from Romford to Slough; from Walthamstow to Croydon and along both banks of the river, every minority community was learning exactly what the new king thought of them.

And all the while, crows kept dropping pieces of paper outside people's doors: THE KING HAS ALLIED WITH BRITAIN FIRST!, RIGHTWING MURDER SQUADS! He was going to take over the government and purge the island of jokers and anybody who hadn't been in Britain since William the Conqueror made it his own.

And the goddess, watching the rumors spread, lying in a pool of her own blood, found it all *most* satisfactory.

◆

Noel's footfalls rapped on the hardwood floor. It was a measure of his irritation and probably worry that Henry had failed to send for Pike to escort Noel. Still, Noel had always had a good sense of direction, and he saw no harm in committing these private parts of Buckingham to memory. One never knew when something might come in handy.

He heard footsteps approaching from an adjacent hall. Judging by the staccato of the heels, it was a woman. Worried that there might be a fuss at finding him unaccompanied, Noel stepped through a convenient doorway. Fortunately, it proved to be an overly decorated but otherwise nondescript room without a hint of human habitation. He couldn't resist, so he left the door ajar just enough to see.

It was a plump woman in her early forties with soft brown hair, rather protuberant blue eyes, and the Windsor chin. She was dressed elegantly but conservatively. Noel smiled and allowed his body to shift. Once he was finished, his trousers were uncomfortably tight and the buttons on his shirt strained, but Noel didn't think that Her Royal Highness Gloriana would notice when faced with the magnificence that was his male avatar.

Now if only he could remember the name he'd used when he'd introduced himself all those long years ago in the library at Cambridge. It was no use. Too many years had elapsed since that first attempt at seduction, and now the number of bodies he had fucked in, in all of his myriad forms, was beyond counting.

He stepped out into the hall and checked as if startled. "Madam, my apologies."

She gave a little gasp and her eyes widened. He had seen it in countless other women's faces and even a few men's when confronted with this Ur of maleness. In this form he had hair a gleaming red gold, with golden eyes and the physique of a god. Sexuality rolled off him in waves.

"My God, it's you. Simon." *So that had been the name.* "You look . . . you look . . . You've barely changed."

He gave an embarrassed gesture toward his face. "The damn virus you know."

She laughed. "Well, if it could keep me looking twenty, I'd risk it. What are you doing here?"

"Doing a small bit of IT work. Allow me to offer my condolences . . ."

"Thank you. Grandmama . . . the queen was always very kind to me, so Haakon didn't mind when I wanted to come for the funeral. I brought our daughter as well. Sissel adored the queen."

"Well, it was lovely seeing you again, ma'am. Please don't let me detain you. I'm sure you have a number of demands on your time."

"Well, yes . . . I should be going." But she didn't; instead she smiled, unconsciously flirting, and held out her hand. Noel took it and felt her cling for longer than necessary. "Perhaps I could have your card? I'd love to chat again, reminisce about Cambridge."

He held back a chuckle. "I don't actually have a card. How about I send over my cell number?" He pulled out one of his phones. She took her phone out of her purse and he sent over the number. He also paired his phone to hers.

He waited until she had turned a corner and was out of sight. Only then did he allow himself the chuckle that had been threatening. Why had he paired their phones? Force of habit? He wasn't sure. Noel then realized that to linger longer would risk discovery. He teleported back to his car and sat contemplating his next move.

The dilemma was that he no longer had an official position in Britain's intelligence operations, and in fact was pretty much a pariah. The rivalry between MI-5 and the Helix continued, so the bright boys over at the Box weren't likely to help him. It was possible that his former colleagues at the Silver Helix might be willing to help, though again he faced the problem that his investigation was so off the books as to be written on water. And he had no doubt that Henry would disavow him in a hot second if Noel should come to grief.

Noel knew he couldn't wander about London asking after old jokers. Even if no one knew he was an ace, he was still an outsider, lucky to be normal and distrusted for that normalcy. No one was going to tell him shit. However much he dreaded the encounter, he was going to have to go to the Helix.

♥

"This way," said Finder, her voice a strained whisper against the background noise of the city.

They'd not been traveling long, and London had already worked its strange magic, transforming from rundown, to upscale, to rundown again in as many streets. It sometimes felt to Green Man as if he actually lived in a combination of several cities that had been sliced up, mixed up, and spliced back together.

They were only slightly south of the river, but the streets were much quieter here, with rubbish collecting in little drifts in the corners of alleyways. A few people took shelter in those same alleys, but for the most part, there was no one to witness their progress. In fact, the whole journey had been remarkably peaceful after the trauma of the raid. The lost tailor seemed like the least of Green Man's worries, but he had given his word.

The old Irish woman had led him via back alleys and little-known paths that often brushed against civilization but always managed to skirt it. He considered himself experienced in discreet travel, but clearly she was a master at it, seeming to have some uncanny instinct of when it was safe to move or best to wait.

Green Man watched his companion as she made her determined way forward. Blood blossomed at the bandages around her joints, and there was something about the way she moved that hinted at an incredible amount of effort going into each step. And pain. He was sure it must hurt her to walk. Yet she gave no sign of it in her face. He respected that.

"Not far now," she added, though he wasn't sure if that was for his benefit or hers.

More than once, they passed marks sprayed over posters or on walls. Predictable, apish sentiments, like:

JOKERS GO HOME!

Or:

FREEKS FUCK OF!

And:

FIRE THEM TO THE MOON!

Green Man wouldn't mind as much if the perpetrators could spell, or if they weren't so woefully uneducated about jokers. *We are home. Our lives and families are here.* He sighed. Underneath the ranting, the ugly truth was obvious: jokers were a target not because they were different but because they looked different, and despite years of evolution and civilization, human beings still held dear to their old prejudices. Britain First hated jokers with the same passion they hated anyone unlike them. In other words, anyone without white skin.

Over the past few days, graffiti and verbal abuse had become more common, and it was only a matter of time before violence followed. Henry IX had legitimized the slurry of hatred that had been fed to the public for years by the right-wing media. The city felt like an oil-soaked rag waiting for a spark.

"There," Finder rasped, breaking Green Man from his thoughts. "Your mark is just round the corner."

"Excellent work." He paused when he realized Finder had stopped. "You're not coming?"

"No. I don't listen in to the conversations of my betters." She gestured to herself. "Besides, I must change my dressings again."

"Do you need any help?"

"No," she snapped, then again, softer, "No, thank you. I like my independence."

"Of course." He smiled at her. "This is the second time you've helped me. I won't forget."

"I would do anything for the cause," she replied. "Just don't ask me to kill. I am used to my own blood, but I can't bear . . . I . . . ."

"I will never ask that of you. I promise."

She was already shuffling away and didn't reply.

♣

Given the circumstances, it seemed prudent to knock. The building was Victorian, five stories and unremarkable, appropriate for a spy agency. The door was opened by a young man with a ruddy complexion and wide blue eyes. That grew even wider when he took in Noel.

"Ah, I see my reputation has proceeded me. Do pop upstairs and tell Mr. Turing that Mr. Matthews would like a few minutes of his time."

The flooring underfoot had been replaced, but still managed to look as dingy as the old tile. He smelled stale coffee, and someone had clearly been heating a ploughman's pork pie in one of the rickety old microwaves. As he loitered in the lobby Noel reflected on his history with this place. He had entered at sixteen, and had spent the next decade and a half in service to the organization. Everything he knew and everything he was could be traced to this space and the people who inhabited it.

It seemed to be taking an inordinately long time and his thread of patience was wearing thin when the old elevator rattled to a stop and the doors opened. Instead of the slender form of Alan Turing, it was the Lion. "Really, Noel? You dare to come here after what you did?"

"Good to see you too, Ranjit. I just want a word with Alan."

"No. Now get out."

"Get a man a promotion and this is all the thanks I get? Damn but you're a bloody ingrate."

Blood suffused Singh's face and the massive fists closed. "You best go before—"

"Before you hurt me? Have me arrested? You know what happens then. The files get released and all the dirty laundry gets washed in public," Noel warned sweetly.

"You're a viper," the Sikh said wearily.

"Yes. You made me one."

The flicker of guilt in Singh's eyes told him that for an instant the man was seeing the boy he had trained. It was quickly banished and the ace's expression hardened. "Get out, Noel. You betrayed us. There is no coming back from that."

♠

Finder had been true to her word. Just around the corner were a row of dumpsters, all overflowing with rubbish. In one of them was the hunched form of Bobbin. The piebald markings on his face were smeared with dirt, and even the gold around his eyes appeared tarnished. Green Man could see bruises too, and scabs forming on some fresh cuts. Somebody had clearly played rough with the old joker. Misery and fatigue made Bobbin seem ancient rather than old, a shriveled version of the man he usually was.

"Good afternoon, Bobbin."

"Afternoon." He glanced up through a fringe of gray hair, embarrassed, and added: "I'd offer you a place to sit, but that's too nice a pair of trousers for in here."

"I'm happy to stand. And thank you, they're made by the best." Green Man paused to consider his next words. It occurred to him that most of his social interactions over the past thirty years had run along very narrow lines, and that this one fell outside of them. "She was right to be worried about you."

"Constance came to you? About me?"

"She did."

"Another secret relationship. I suppose I shouldn't be surprised."

"All of my relationships are secret, Bobbin. For the safety of the other party. But there's nothing sordid about it. Constance is part of the community I protect, as are you. These are dark times for any of us to be alone on the street." He gestured pointedly at the piles of refuse, the rats, and the lack of comfort. "What were you thinking? A man of your age shouldn't be sleeping rough."

Bobbin blinked as if taking in his surrounding for the first time. His face fell. "I didn't plan to get drunk. Didn't plan to get mugged either. Is . . . is Constance alright?"

"She's very upset, but I suspect you knew that."

Bobbin scowled. "She's not the only one."

"So I see. Why don't you go back and talk to her?"

"No. I thought I knew her. I thought we were . . ."

"Friends?"

The tone of his cheeks changed, the blue patches moving closer to navy, the reds deepening to purple; Bobbin's equivalent of a blush. "Yes. But friends don't lie to each other."

"Perhaps she was protecting you. Lord knows I've got some experience there."

"I could have handled it."

Green Man raised an eyebrow in a manner he hoped Wayfarer would approve of. "Could you? Is that why you're out here, alone, in a pile of rubbish?"

"I . . . she should have told me the truth."

"Perhaps she couldn't. Perhaps she was afraid of losing someone precious. And I daresay you've proven her right to be cautious. Now, thanks to you, her fears of being abandoned have come true."

Bobbin straightened a little and rubbed at his face with gnarled fingers. The little spikes of bone set between his fingers peeked out now and then, wickedly sharp. "I've been a right old fool, haven't I?"

Green Man allowed himself a small smile. "You have."

"What am I going to do now?"

"That's up to you, but if you're asking for advice, you need to"—he was about to say "man up" but caught himself, it was yet another phrase that, according to Wayfarer, wasn't acceptable anymore—"Be the man she hoped you were. Go back. Apologize. Be with her."

"But I've said such awful things."

"You love her." It wasn't a question.

"Yes."

"Then I say again: Be with her. Constance accepts you, warts and all. That's a rare thing. Why not do the same for her?"

"No offence, but I never thought I'd be taking relationship advice from, well, the likes of you."

"Before today, I never expected to be dispensing any."

Bobbin shivered and said, "I'm freezing and I could murder a bacon sandwich!"

"Come on," Green Man held out a hand, "it's time to go."

There was a notable pause and then he lowered it again. Bobbin's rejection wasn't surprising, but it still stung. To his horror, he realized that he liked Bobbin and that he wanted Bobbin to like him. The man had an old-fashioned decency to him. He was honorable, trustworthy. The kind of man that would always give you the truth. The kind of man he could finally open up to. *No,* he told himself firmly. *Green Man cannot have the luxury of friends, nor the weakness of needing them.*

He stood there, not quite sure what to say, feeling uncharacteristically and horribly lonely. Perhaps some hint of his emotions found a way through his wooden skin, for Bobbin cleared his throat awkwardly and said, "If you don't mind me asking, do you have someone?"

"Not anymore. The person I'd made a life with was many things, but open-minded she was not. When my card turned, that life ended. Besides, I have other responsibilities now." His hand traveled unconsciously to his mask. "Things that stop me from being close to people. But you? You are free to live as you please. I implore you, take what happiness is being offered and grasp it with both hands."

"Alright," replied Bobbin, slowly climbing out of the bin. "I will."

"Let me escort you home."

"No need for that."

"I promised Constance I'd bring you back safe, and Green Man keeps his promises."

"Really, I'll be fine."

"I was being polite, Bobbin, not asking for your permission."

There was a pause, and then he nodded, somehow remaining dignified in defeat.

◆

It was time for an afternoon tea, but Noel decided he needed something stronger. He stopped in a pub, ordered a bitters, and sat brooding over his situation. His wanderings had brought him to the ragged edges of what passed for London's jokertown. The neighborhoods surrounding the East End were still predominately the province of the normals. It had been a working-class area, now beginning to gentrify, to the fury of the nats who dwelled there and the jokers who sensed the walls of the bright young things closing in.

Noel had lived in Manhattan for a number of years and knew the environs of Jokertown, that original societal reef where the twisted outcasts had washed up after the horrific events of September 15, 1946. It had been tamed and civilized by the passage of years and the eyes of the curious. There were still dangerous sections where gangs roamed, and places spoken of in whispers, but now tour buses swayed and farted down the streets, there were Starbucks and a Hyatt hotel, and the mask and cloak shops sold more to tourists than the actual jokers. Warped and Wonderful was the latest version of Twisted and Tall, which had replaced Joker Pride; like its defiant predecessors it was actually just the pathetic cry of the marginalized knowing that they were neither wonderful or proud.

He had been so deep in his mental funk he had missed the conversations going on around him, but now one basso voice roughened by cigarettes and booze floated to him.

"Fucking freaks depressed the home values and now the bloody Sloane Rangers are moving in and buying us out."

"And not paying enough for us to get into anything beyond a studio," his companion offered with a nasal whine.

"I heard what the king said. I think he'll put pay to this mess. Otherwise, we won't recognize the country between the bloody Pakis and darkies and the freaks."

"If you think the Windsors are going to do shit, you're drunker than I thought," Nasal scoffed.

"We've got the people, and there aren't enough of them to hold us down. And even if Henry won't openly back us, I wager he'll keep the coppers off us."

"Not like that poof Richard."

They became aware that Noel was listening. Flint could have stuck sparks off the looks he was receiving. He knew in his bespoke suit and expensive watch he had abruptly become the enemy. Noel lifted his glass. "God save the king," he said.

It did not have the desired effect. Booze and Smokes decided he was being mocked. He hitched up his pants and stalked over to Noel's table. "You a damn real estate agent?"

"No, but I suppose that you aren't going to believe me since you have imbibed enough Dutch courage to think a fight is going to ease your woes. I assure you it will not." Noel allowed every rounded vowel of his Cambridge education to drip off the words.

His resentment of Henry and his predicament rose up and Noel found himself anticipating the fight with something akin to joy. He tensed every muscle and waited, vibrating like a greyhound.

Unfortunately, the man had enough low cunning to realize he was facing a predator and he backed away. "Not worth breaking my knuckles on you," he growled. He and his companion threw money on the table and hurried out.

♥

Night was falling as they arrived at the atelier. They'd been forced to avoid public transport and to walk at Bobbin's pace. More than once Green Man considered calling Wayfarer to pick them up, but he couldn't quite bring himself to do it. It was a risk being outside, but increasingly he resented living in a variety of airless boxes. Just for a while he wanted to enjoy the simple pleasure of going for a walk, like a normal human being.

Gradually, the houses they were passing became more impressive. The cars parked there, newer, more expensive. Though he'd never have been able to afford a place this close to the center of town, they reminded him painfully of the house he used to have and the life he'd lost. It had been years since he'd really thought about his wife and children, but now all of a sudden they were on his mind all the time. *It's all this death,* he thought. *It's making me think too much.*

Bobbin began to slow as they reached the entrance, but it didn't matter. Constance must have been watching out for them and was already unlocking the door as they approached.

Green Man put his hand gently against Bobbin's back, urging him forward just as Constance stepped out to meet them. She looked tired. Though smartly turned out, no amount of makeup could hide the worry lines and lack of sleep, nor the burst blood vessels in her eyes.

"I . . ." began Bobbin. "I'm sorry, love."

She threw her arms around him in a fierce hug. "Just promise to never run away again."

"I won't. I promise."

Their faces creased with smiles and happy tears. Green Man decided it was time to go, but as he began to turn away, Constance looked up. "Thank you," she said. "Why don't you come in? I'll make some tea."

Bobbin look briefly appalled but had the good grace to hide it. "I'm sure he's got other places he needs to be."

"That's very kind of you, Constance," began Green Man, but paused as he searched for the right words to politely decline. It wasn't often he had to do anything politely.

"Not at all," she said. "It's the least I can do."

Before he could say anything more, she was going back into the shop, and he felt compelled to follow. To do anything else would be rude.

The room inside felt spacious and elegant. Dover-gray walls and hardwood floors covered by rich Oriental rugs. Clearly, Constance had done well for herself.

As she walked up the stairs she glanced over her shoulder, as if to check that Bobbin was really there. And he was, right behind her. The smile she gave him had Green Man turning to the window. It was one thing to wish others happiness, but quite another to have to see it close-up. He would allow Constance five minutes out of politeness and then make his excuse to leave.

♣

Constance's hands shook as she filled the kettle with water. Bobbin was back and the relief poured through her—a river of emotion. Someone had roughed him up. Who it was he hadn't said. Maybe he didn't even know. But Constance thought if she ever found out, she would do everything in her power to make certain they suffered. Suffered horribly. She could do that. She'd learned a lot in her years.

She turned to study him. Everything was askew. His hair wasn't combed properly. There were smears of dirt on his shirt and a tear on the right cuff. The nasty scrape on his left cheek was starting to crust and he smelled of pub. She was so happy to see him it made her dizzy.

"Constance," he said again. "I'm so sorry."

"I was so frightened," she replied. She was trembling now. "I shouldn't have told you."

"No!" he exclaimed. "You had your reasons for keeping quiet—and I understand why you finally told me. Was losing Glory, wasn't it?" She nodded. "And I have secrets from you too. I was terribly unfair."

She wiped her tears on the back of her hand. "I know your secret," she replied tartly while sniffing her runny nose. "You've been making clothes for Green Man. And how you kept that quiet is beyond me."

"Well, I do have a life outside work." He gave her a crooked smile and she saw that there was a little chip in his front tooth that hadn't been there before.

She fished in her cardigan pocket and brought out a tissue, licked it, and began to dab away at his scrape. He took her hand in his own.

"Dear, dear Constance," he said. His eyes were turned down at the corner. "Please forgive me. I should never have left like that."

Constance shook her head. "No," she replied more calmly than she felt. "I should have told you the truth years ago. I should have trusted you. It was a nasty shock for you."

"It seems we were both fools," he said.

The kettle was heated and she took her hand away to put a splash in the pot to warm it up. "I suppose we've left Green Man alone long enough." She poured the rest of the water into the pot, then heaped in tea.

"He's not so bad, you know," Bobbin said. He made as if to pick the tea things up, but Constance shooed him away. "He's been right decent to me."

"He found you, and that makes him fine in my sights."

"Shall we?"

Constance nodded. Bobbin was back and everything would be all right.

♠

"There you go," said Constance, handing him a cup.

He took it awkwardly in his left hand, not trusting his right with the delicate china. "Thank you."

"Actually, that's what I wanted to say. For bringing him back."

Green Man acknowledged her with a nod and did his best to make small talk. "I've been enjoying Bobbin's work for some time now, but I've never been inside before. It's a nice set up you have here."

"Thank you."

"This is just the front end," said Bobbin. "You should see upstairs where the real work happens. There's some amazing pieces up there, all made by people like me."

"I'd be happy to show you," added Constance.

It was the last thing he wanted to do, but he set down his cup and went with them upstairs.

While well kept, the workshop was a much more practical space. Bobbin became quite animate as he showed off the various works in progress, urging Green Man to pay close attention to the different cuts or the quality of the fabric. Each time he talked about who had done which piece of work. The names, Green Man realized, were all familiar. Many of her employees were jokers.

It was hard to be sure over Bobbin's commentary, but he thought he heard an odd hissing noise coming from nearby. He looked at Constance. "Did you hear that?"

"Hear what?"

"Never mind." He listened hard as Constance and Bobbin talked. Not to the words they said, but to the world outside, wondering if the army were about to make another move on him. Perhaps the hiss was a gas grenade. He shook his head. He'd been behaving like an amateur! Going for walks. Having chats in the open. What had he been thinking? It had been utter foolishness to be out on the streets so long. Had someone seen him and reported it? Yes, that was it. But if the army were coming, there would be vehicles and a cordon, yet he could still hear the regular sounds of London traffic outside. Of course, they might just be waiting for him to leave . . .

The sound of breaking glass confirmed his suspicions.

"That was downstairs," said Constance with a look of horror.

There was more breaking glass, then the sound of things being moved violently; fabric tearing, furniture being overturned, laughter. *Not soldiers.*

Green Man put down the dress-in-progress he'd been shown very carefully as Bobbin and Constance stood there, one naturally reaching for the other's hand.

"We'll go down together," said Bobbin.

"No," Green Man said quietly. "Stay up here and barricade the door. I'll deal with this."

He went to the window, opening it as wide as it would go, and then climbed outside and jumped down to the street below. He landed more heavily than intended, rocking forward onto all fours with a thud. *This isn't getting any easier,* he thought.

Pushing himself upright, he turned to face the main entrance.

The door was kicked in, as was the display window, and the sign had been sprayed over in lurid red paint that read:

JOKER LOVER!

And just below it were the letters BF in a circle that he knew all too well.

He counted five of them inside, leaping about with manic energy. They were all wearing jeans and workman's boots, loose tops and dark jackets. They hadn't even bothered to cover their faces. Already, the neat insides of the shop had been transformed by the intruders. A pile of clothes had been dumped in the middle of the room and set on fire. He noted sadly that the delicate china tea set they'd just used was now just a scattered pile of shards. One of the men was spraying everything he could see, while three others were just destroying whatever was within reach with boots, hands, and a sharp knife. The last was standing by the door on lookout. He had already seen Green Man, and was pointing at him. "You ain't welcome here!"

"That makes six of us," he replied, stepping up to the door and grabbing the young man by his shoulder. As usual, his opponent had underestimated just how far he could move in one step, and just how long his reach actually was.

"Get your filthy hands off me," he shouted, the words coming out more like a plea than a command as he vainly struggled to free himself.

Green Man raised his voice so it would carry into the shop. "The only law I follow is five for one, and happily, there appear to be five of you."

"Oh shit," said one of them, "it's the Fists!"

"B-But we haven't killed anyone," said the one in his grasp. "You can't!"

"Oh, I'm not going to kill you. I'm going to break you, the same way you've broken this lady's property." He squeezed for emphasis, making the man scream. "And I'm going to educate you all in the process."

The one with the knife was watching him warily, looking for the right moment to attack, while the others began arming themselves with things from the shop—bits of broken wood and a pair of large shears.

"We jokers used to be like you. Ordinary. With normal lives and normal dreams, but I want you to imagine what it would be like if one day, for no reason at all, your body turned against you." He looked at the man directly in front of him. "Beg me not to hurt you."

"D-don't hurt me!"

Green Man upped the pressure until he felt the man's collar bone begin to bend beneath his thumb. "The trouble with the virus is, it doesn't care for reason. Now beg your friends to save you."

"What?"

"Ask them to save you or I'll crush your shoulder to powder."

Some snot began to dribble down the man's face. "Lads, please!"

They looked at each other for courage, then charged as one. However, they couldn't bring their numbers to bear on him, as he was still in the doorway. One grabbed his hand, trying to pry his grip open, while another grabbed his friend's back in an attempt to pull him into the safety of the shop.

"Your friends all rally round at first," Green Man continued, "but it's no use. It's too late you see. The—"

A knife thrust low, going past the man in his grip and into his side. It punched straight through the layers of his suit and shirt, and stuck half an inch into his wooden stomach. It didn't go deep, didn't really hurt, but he felt a flare of anger nonetheless. There would be a new gouge in his skin, a new place for unwanted things to grow from.

He lashed out with his left hand, catching the knife wielder across the skull. He fell like a sack of potatoes. The others, realizing the danger, sprang back. Meanwhile, he'd clenched his right fist in anger, accidentally destroying his victim's shoulder joint in the process. He let go, shaking his head. A part of him was horrified by what he was doing, but another part was angry, exultant, and would not be stopped. He dropped the screaming man next to the silent one and stepped into the shop, deliberately bringing his foot down hard on the hand of the one who stabbed him, crushing the fine bones of the man's fingers.

"These men will never be the same again. They'll find ways to go on with life, like we all do. But it will be harder than before. Do you see the comparison?"

One of the remaining men nodded, terrified, while the second spat at Green Man's feet. The third said nothing for a moment, then burped and threw up on his own shoes.

Green Man kicked the kneecap of the one who had nodded, shattering it. "It doesn't matter if you understand."

The one who had spat swung a piece of wood at him and he allowed it to bounce off as he caved in the man's chest with a single punch. Perhaps it would kill them, perhaps not. He found he didn't care that much. After all, would they have cared if they'd gotten their hands on Bobbin? "It doesn't matter if you fight."

The last man was whimpering and slobbering, trying to back away, but hampered by the detritus on the floor. *How appropriate to be caught in a mess of your own devising.* "It doesn't matter if you feel sorry. The virus doesn't care about you. And after it's had its way, the world doesn't care about you either." The man turned to run, and Green Man stamped down on the backs of his legs, breaking them as easily as dry twigs.

He went through their things methodically, ignoring the groans of pain, and was rewarded with five wallets. Five identities. "John Harris, Matthew Jones, Jason Fletcher, Theodore Wallace, and . . . Wayne Thurtle. I have your names now. In an hour I'll know where you live, where you work, where your families are. If you take action against my people again, if you say one word about what happened here tonight to the press or to your friends in Britain First, I will know. And I will make sure that it is your children, your siblings, and your parents that pay the price."

The fire was spreading now, greedily devouring a lifetime's worth of work and achievements. He left the men to fend for themselves, crying and bleeding in the debris, and raced the flames for the stairs.

◆

Constance and Bobbin met Green Man halfway down the stairs. They had smelled the smoke and Bobbin carried the fire extinguisher.

"Fire," Green Man panted.

"I know," Bobbin said, gesturing with the extinguisher. They all continued down the stairs.

Broken glass and broken mirrors covered the floor. Her tea set, the one they'd just been using and a secret fiftieth birthday gift from the queen, had been crushed like eggshells.

The cloth case had been looted and bolts were piled up willy-nilly like firewood. And like firewood they were burning. Her chairs were broken as well. Some were just kicked apart; others had been slashed and the stuffing ripped out. She'd spent decades working here, making beautiful clothing that made people feel good about themselves. And none of that mattered because it was all gone now.

"I'm so sorry, love," Bobbins said as he sprayed retardant across the flames. "We can fix it. Be good as new. We could find somewhere else . . ."

The brutes who had done this had fled. She wanted to give them all a kick. Not just for ruining the shop, but because they were the sort who would be perfectly happy to see something terrible happen to Bobbin and all the other jokers. The fact she couldn't made her even angrier.

She stalked to the stairs. Shattered glass and mirrors crunched under her feet. Up the stairs she went, faster than she had in several years, and once in the workroom she grabbed all the clothing made with her power. Among them was Henry's suit. The final fitting was scheduled for the next day.

"Enough of this shite," she said, clattering down the stairs. Her voice was harsh and angry. "I see Henry tomorrow for his fitting, and I'll be damned if I'll go there without telling him exactly where he can shove his anti-joker rubbish."

Bobbin looked aghast. "You can't do that," he exclaimed. "He'll have you . . ."

"What? Scolded?" She gave a bitter laugh. "They still need me. Maybe they could get a piece of clothing that might stop a bullet, but it won't stop a blade, or protect anyone from fire, or anything else that might come his way as long as long as he's wearing one of my special garments."

Green Man looked at her with a speculative tilt of the head. She couldn't read his expression behind the mask. "What's all this about?"

"Just my whole life," she replied. "I have a wild card. I can make clothing that is impervious to harm and it protects anyone wearing it. I've been used by the government to protect special people."

"Ah," Green Man said. "Just how involved with them are you?"

"You needn't worry," she replied. "I'm just a cog in the machinery."

"You shouldn't have said anything," Bobbin interjected. "I'm sorry, Green Man, but telling you . . ."

"I'm tired, Bobbin," Constance interrupted him with a sudden surge of exhaustion. "It was one thing when Margaret was alive, but Henry is a monster and I refuse to protect him. Margaret may have been all the things we wish the monarchy to be, but Henry is anything but. I have a small chance tomorrow to try and talk some sense into him. To try and point out what a danger he is to the country with the sort of things he's been saying. It may be a fool's errand, but I must do *something*."

♠ ♥ ♦ ♣

Friday

MARCH 6TH

THE MORNING STARTED WITH a bang. Literally—a loud banging at the door, that roused Alan from his bed at 8:00 A.M. Sebastian groaned and pulled the covers over his head—they'd stayed up too late the night before, watching more of Sebastian's beloved baking show, all the way to the grand finale, with the bakers trying to compete in the midst of a summer thunderstorm that made most of their creations flop. Well, Alan had been mostly thinking about ways to deal with the Henry situation, and not about the perils of trying to bake showstoppers in a tent. But he'd been awake and in bed beside his husband, with his eyes on the TV for some hours, which ought to count for something.

He opened the door, startled to find two members of MI-5 there, flanking the prince. His prince. "Richard."

"You didn't answer your phone."

"I turned it off. I was up late."

"Come with me. We have to talk, somewhere private."

Alan sighed. "I can't go anywhere like this," he said, gesturing to his robe and slippers. "You'd better come inside."

Sebastian had stumbled out of the bedroom and was still pulling a robe around himself. "Your Highness!" His cheeks were bright red, and his tousled white hair was sticking up in all directions. Alan had to smother the urge to smooth it down, at least.

The prince inclined his head graciously. "Sebastian. Good to see you again."

Sebastian swallowed. "Can I give you something to drink? Coffee? Tea?"

Not now, Sebastian, Alan tried to convey with widened eyes.

The prince shook his head politely. "No, thank you. I really just need to talk to your husband for a bit. Somewhere private, I'm afraid—it's Crown business. I'm going to have to steal him away."

"Of course, of course," Sebastian said. "Another time."

"Thank you," Richard said. "While Alan's getting ready, why don't you tell me about the new garden? That maze pattern is devilishly tricky—where did you find it?"

"I designed it, actually," Sebastian said, flushing even redder. Alan was tempted to stay and hear what came next, but he was too well-trained to duty; he slipped away and quickly changed into day clothes and boots.

"I'm ready, Your Highness," Alan said, re-entering the hall and reaching for his coat.

Richard smiled. "It's been a pleasure, Sebastian. We really must have you both round for dinner sometime soon. I hear you're quite the chef too—maybe you can give our cook some tips."

That last seemed to have startled Sebastian into silence—Alan took the opportunity to usher Richard out the door. "Back soon, love." The door closed behind them, leaving only the guards to overhear. "We can walk around back, through the woods. No one will bother us there."

"That's fine." Richard nodded to the guards, indicating that they should maintain their station by the car, and then followed Alan toward the woodland path.

Occasional sun glinted through the wet leaves overhead, and a matching glint of mischief lit Richard's eyes as he paced by Alan's side along the forest path. "Oh, I do like it here, Alan. Your home is lovely and your husband is so welcoming, so accommodating."

Richard could be such an ass. "You didn't come here to discuss my husband."

"No." Richard turned abruptly, stopping still. "I'm losing patience, Alan. You've had days and days—it's been almost a week now! And where has it gotten us?"

They were safely out of earshot of the guards now. "I need more time. I'm working on two fronts. I'm trying to find some leverage to use against Henry and lay to rest these rumors of a joker prince. If we can establish the man is dead—"

Richard nodded sharply. "But that's not the real issue, is it? How will we force Henry to abdicate?" He began pacing forward again, slowly, looking like nothing so much as a lazy lion.

The prince's voice had gone low, but Alan still glanced back down the path. The curve of it meant that the guards couldn't even be seen, or the house, where Sebastian was undoubtedly puttering in the kitchen. Birds swooped through the branches, and one of the squirrels that Sebastian insisted on feeding chittered angrily from his branch. Princes plotted, but the world went on regardless; that was some comfort in troubled times. But Richard's next words commanded Alan's attention. "Your way is taking too long. We should kidnap Sissel."

"What?" Sissel was a charming ten-year-old girl, Henry's granddaughter. Alan's mind raced, connecting the dots—*oh no*. Richard wasn't really suggesting they should—

"We need something dramatic to force Henry to abdicate. If we kidnap Sissel, send Henry threats that make it clear her life will be forfeit if he takes the throne, I'm sure he'll step down. He's fond of the child."

He's not the only one, Alan thought. He'd met the girl several times—Gloriana had come home for Christmases, for the queen's birthday celebrations. Sissel had recently developed an interest in astronomy and, last Christmas, had asked Alan to help her with some calculations; he'd been pleased to oblige. Sissel had a bright future ahead of her—one that did not involve kidnapping.

"This is not a good idea, Dickie." Alan could see the possibilities spinning out, various paths that led to far too dangerous places. During the War years, he'd seen, far too often, how plans might go terribly awry. "We have to find another approach."

Richard stopped walking and faced him, frowning. "I've given you enough time to find another plan, and you've failed me."

Alan stretched out a hand to his erstwhile lover, pleading. "We can't do this, Dickie. It isn't right." Over eight decades of service to England, Alan Turing had committed more than his share of morally questionable acts, always for a higher good. But this—he couldn't justify this. He had to draw a line somewhere.

Richard's face hardened. "Can't? You are over-familiar, Turing. I don't remember asking for your opinion."

Was putting Richard on the throne actually a higher good? Or had Margaret been right all along? Perhaps both her sons were irredeemably flawed. *Oh, Margaret.*

Richard took a step forward, so that he was barely an inch away from Alan. An intimate distance, but one that now felt terrifyingly far. "Look, I'm going to do this with or without you, Turing. You swore an oath to serve England. Are you with me?"

Alan bent his head, long habits of obedience betraying him. "Yes, Your Highness." He could see no path out of this trap. If he refused, Richard would take action on his own and the outcome could be disastrous.

He'd have to do it himself. At least that way, Alan could make sure the child stayed safe.

♥

"I'm not sure of the fit," Henry said, fussing with his jacket. There wasn't much to be finished with the suit, Constance had seen to that yesterday. It was simple enough to hide the few physical shortcomings Henry had. His tall, lanky frame was easily sorted.

"It's quite nice," said the Silly Young Thing with a nervous flutter in her voice. "It does show you off to your best." She smiled at Constance who didn't return it. The SYT lowered her head and Constance did feel a wee bit of sympathy for her.

Henry preened a bit and Constance fought not to roll her eyes. It did her no good to be in contempt of Henry, but he made it difficult.

"Sir," she said helping him off with his coat. He let her take it like a man well-used to having servants dressing him. *No man is a hero to his valet,* she thought. *Nor his tailor.*

"I would like to speak with you about a matter of grave importance, sir."

The Silly Young Thing held a cup of tea out to Henry after he sat down. He gave her a perfunctory nod then turned his attention back to Constance.

"Go on," he said taking a sip.

"I've been dressing the queen for the last fifty years, sir. I daresay I have plenty of experience with the sort of things a ruler might say or think. I've seen you in nothing but your socks and your liners, and it's difficult to be in awe of anyone after that."

The SYT choked back a laugh then put her fingers over her lips as if to hide what she'd done.

"I fail to see the relevance of that, but what is on your mind?" He sounded bored and a little impatient.

Constance had hoped she could appeal to his better nature, though at this point, she doubted he had one. "Sir, I watched you grow up. I heard your mother talk lovingly about you and your brother and surely you must realize she would never approve of the way you've been behaving."

There was a long pause as Henry considered Constance.

"My mother was soft-hearted," Henry began. "And we disagreed on many matters. I assume you're speaking about my position on the sort of people you hire."

A good thrashing was just what he needed, Constance thought. Instead she said, "Yes, I hire jokers, sir. They are English citizens! They need your help and protection, not this awful propagandizing!"

"My dear, you seem quite overwrought," he said, his tone still bored. He pushed the button at his side to call his valet. "I'll be expecting my suit tomorrow."

"Of course," she replied angrily. She turned on her heel and marched out of the room just as the door swung open. It was a breach of protocol, but she didn't care in the least. Henry was determined to tear the country apart, and she might be just one old woman but she was going to do everything in her power to stop him.

♣

Alan stared at the screen. He'd spent hours looking for anything that might let him apply pressure to Henry and keep Richard from this rash action. He'd started with the accounts—money was always worth following. Most of Henry's accounts were tremendously boring, if painfully extravagant. But there was one account paid out from the palace to a woman who wasn't one of the usual palace vendors. Why would Henry be giving this woman money? A secret lover? His fiancée would be furious if she found out, but it wasn't enough of a scandal to force him off the throne, not in this dissolute age.

"Another cuppa?"

"Thank you," Alan said, turning away from the screen. He didn't bother closing it—Sebastian wouldn't be able to make any sense of the columns of numbers.

His husband set a steaming cup carefully on a coaster on the polished wood desk. "Any progress lately?" Sebastian turned, frowning at the rest of the room. "I hope so—the library just looks wrong with all these screens in here. I swear the books resent it."

Alan stifled a sigh of frustration; Sebastian *would* insist on anthropomorphizing everything. It was almost as bad as his husband's insistence that there were fairies in the garden. Patience: that's what Alan needed, patience for his husband and for the process. A marriage wasn't rekindled in a day. "It's coming along. I have a search running right now; I've expanded the parameters, so it's going to take a little while for the data to come up."

Sebastian's eyes brightened. "Oh, excellent. That means now's a good time." He bit his lip, and then said, "I wanted to ask you—you know how I've been selling some of my herbal concoctions online? The artisanal vinegars and oils?"

"Yes?" It was a silly little business, and they didn't need the money, but it made Sebastian happy to write his handmade labels and send the packages off in the mail. It was sweet, really.

Sebastian glanced down, and then looked up again, gazing straight into Alan's eyes. He asked, "You don't think there's any chance of a royal endorsement, do you?"

Alan couldn't help frowning. Really? How could his husband ask this of him, put him in this position? "I don't know, Sebastian . . ."

Sebastian's eyes were dark, pleading. "It would mean the world to me. You don't usually trade on your royal connections, and I wouldn't ask, but it would really set me up. Maybe then I could retire from the gardening work, just as you wanted." Sebastian reached out, placed a hand on Alan's arm. "You could make an exception? For me? You and Richard are such good friends . . ."

Guilt stabbed through Alan. "Well, I suppose it wouldn't hurt to ask," he said reluctantly.

Sebastian grinned and squeezed his arm before releasing it. "Wonderful. Thank you, love. Does Richard like tea? Liquor?"

Alan admitted, "He's an absolute tea fiend."

Sebastian said, "Perfect. I have a new blend that I'm dying to have him try. Thank you thank you!" He bent forward and brushed a kiss across Alan's forehead. "Best of husbands."

Alan managed a smile. "Anything for you, love. But I really ought to get back to work . . ."

"Yes, yes, of course. I'm going to go work on the tea some more—I want it to be perfect!" Sebastian bustled away, smiling, and let the door shut behind him.

Alan settled in again, but almost immediately, the screen blinked to something new. His pulse raced as he read the results. One of his searches had finally borne fruit—Adelbert Boyd-Brackenbury! A DNA match, tracing his ancestry back to Queen Victoria; Margaret had been right after all. Alan's heart fluttered at the discovery. This could change everything.

Now, for the good of England, Alan Turing had to make a decision.

♠

How fascinating. Turing of the brilliant mind. Swift-thinking Turing. A man with computer circuits threaded so finely through his brain—or so Badb had once heard—that had he wanted them gone it would have killed him to take them out . . . And yet, even he committed his thoughts to paper.

He printed the findings of his search and by the time Sebastian, who'd left the window open, had shooed the crow out of the house and tidied up the documents it had scattered, it was all too late. The news was already moving out into the world.

And what news! It could hardly be better. Green Man's lieutenant, Seizer, had royal blood in every part of his treacherous frame.

Badb spread the information to her contact in Italy. All the better if the news that the rumors were true were to appear abroad first, as though it were being hidden from the British public. Which, of course it was. To add extra spice, she kept the name to herself for now. Waiting for that second shoe to drop would madden the authorities.

And then, although the pain was great, she opened blood-sticky eyes and waited.

The Fists were on high alert since the attack. Green Man had them running constant patrols around their new hideout. They stepped over her in the corridor where she lay, gingerly avoiding the dribbles of blood that had escaped her bandages and making no mention of the smell.

The goddess waited patiently. She would live forever, after all. She flicked her attention from one crow to another, all over the city, keeping them at their tasks. But every second heartbeat brought her back to her own body, watching, always watching, until the right person appeared. Maven. Seizer's own daughter.

She was the only nat here, but she burned with revolutionary fervor. Badb didn't even need to start the conversation as she had planned. It was Maven who came to her. She knelt, uncaring of the stench or the fact that the knees of the combat fatigues on her stocky frame were soaking up blood.

"Are you well, comrade?" she asked. Maven's northern English vowels couldn't have been further from her father's aristocratic bombast. She'd run away from her mother to join him. "We should look after you better. You're a woman of talents, I heard. The Cause needs you."

The goddess hung her head. "The Cause." How satisfactory. A woman such as this might make a most . . . *nutritious* martyr.

"You are too kind to me," said Badb. "The visions take a lot out of me and rarely are they of any use."

"You had one just now?" Maven looked genuinely sympathetic. She may not have been a wild card, but she had two extraordinary powers of her own: the strength to fire a gun and the fortitude to face one too, her formidable chin raised high.

How best to kill her? Badb wondered. Although there were others here who might do just as well.

"They take my strength," the goddess said, "And deliver only nonsense in return . . . I keep . . . I keep hearing a name. A silly thing, or so it seems."

"I thought your visions were real. You did incredible work to get Green Man away last time."

"Oh, yes, child. They are always real, but not . . . not always useful, you understand? Who ever heard of a joker with a name like Adelbert Boyd-Brackenbury?

It sounds made up, doesn't it? And who cares if . . . if the Silver Helix think he's the true king? It can't help the likes of us here and—"

Maven's plain features were frozen in shock. Great warrior though she was, she fell back on her bum and staggered to her feet.

"Sorry, sister. I'll . . . I'll send somebody to help you clean up . . . I must . . . I have to . . ."

She was off, straight to her father, presumably. And later, when reports drifted in from Italy of DNA pointing to a joker match, why, then he'd know who he was. What he was. It was only a matter of time before he acted on it.

All that remained was to put in place a different soldier pawn with a high-powered rifle.

♠ ♥ ♦ ♣

Saturday

MARCH 7TH

AT 7:00 A.M., THE highest bar in Western Europe was emptied of all but two white men, gazing out over the city through an immense fifty-second floor window.

Both were middle-aged. Both had the blood of innocents on their hands, but it was the shorter one, his brown hair flecked with gray, who was by far the more dangerous.

Badb knew only his first name from her days in army intelligence, Noel. She knew too he was an ace of some kind, but what his exact powers were she had yet to determine. Nor could she figure out how he had arrived up here. He certainly hadn't made use of the elevators.

He waited until the bodyguard began to shift from foot to foot and then, in an accent that in this country indicated "education," he said, "You are remarkably well-informed for a foreigner."

The Serbian jumped, but didn't make the mistake of speaking.

"What is your source of information, exactly?"

The bodyguard straightened his shoulders. "I sell knowledge, not my source. Fifty thousand and I tell you about that very special baby."

"How about five pounds and nobody ever finds out you're a war criminal?" He must have been just guessing, but still, Badb was impressed. She would try to keep tabs on this one too. It was already difficult to track all the players on the board. The goddess had not had time to eat, and she hadn't even opened her own body's eyes in over thirty hours.

Somehow, the bodyguard held his nerve under that cold blue stare.

"Make it ten pounds and you have deal." When Noel shrugged, he continued. "Let me tell you about the ship. The *Queen Mary* . . ."

In truth the bodyguard was a much more useful tool than Badb had at first realized. Perhaps if she killed his wife and child she would keep him on permanently. *Most satisfactory.*

♦

Green Man's new hideout was a definite step down from the last one, but he had a feeling there was still plenty of room to fall yet. A knock at the door, not

Wayfarer's, snapped him from his brooding. *This cannot be good,* he thought. *A new development?*

He hastily put on his mask. "Come in."

The door opened and Finder came slowly into the room, each foot placed with deliberate care and effort. She was wearing clean white bandages, but he knew they would not stay fresh for long. He gestured to the chair opposite his desk, but she waved the offer away.

"No time for sitting." She glanced over her shoulder and then shut the door, lowering her voice to a conspiratorial whisper. Green Man found himself leaning forward instinctively. "There is a woman who lives on the *Queen Mary*. A joker. Old, like us. She was there in nineteen forty-eight and I suspect she knows what happened to our prince."

"That's excellent news." Green Man stood up. "And I can find her there now?"

"Yes. You must find her. Henry and his allies are looking too. They've dispatched an agent to get her."

Something about the way she said it made a chill run down Green Man's spine. "What are you not telling me?"

"I don't know anything, but I fear."

"Fear what?"

"I fear Henry already knows the truth."

Green Man nodded grimly and walked around the table. "You don't think they're trying to find out what she knows. You think they mean to silence her."

"I cannot say for certain, but . . . I . . . yes. You know how they operate."

"All too well," he replied.

She opened the door for him as he strode out.

♥

The Docklands stank of fish, fetid water, and old mud that had sucked down more relics and bodies then could be counted. The old ship, once elegant, now like a blowsy, bloated woman going to seed, squatted on the Isle of Dogs. Signs with breathless all capital letters urged people to VISIT HISTORY! RECALL THE BRAVERY AND TRAGEDY OF THE FINAL VOYAGE! CAFÉ AND GIFT SHOP ON SITE.

Noel had actually never visited the ship. It wasn't his history. He had drawn a straight flush when it came to the wild card, and for all the talk of wild card unity there really wasn't any. Class, as in so much of British society, was everything, and by any objective standard as well as simple bigotry, being an ace was a damn sight better than being a joker.

As for the Serbian protection officer, his oblique advice to look at the *Queen Mary* was not that helpful. Noel would have made his way here eventually for information on the lost joker prince, and perhaps he would be lucky and the old pensioner had decided to retire to live out his days on the floating mausoleum, but he doubted he would be that lucky.

He headed up the gangplank, stopped at the entry kiosk and bought a ticket from the young man in the booth. His deformities were not visible on his face. Only the odd way his shoulders bulked beneath his sweater hinted at any abnormality.

Don't want to frighten off the tourist at the first go, Noel thought as he sauntered onto the deck of the old ship. Not that there were many. The March weather, and a brisk wind carrying the effluvia off the river, not to mention the tragic story of the ship, would discourage all but the most hearty or heartless of visitors. Noel wrinkled his nose and headed inside hoping to escape the stink.

There were only a handful of tourists touring the exhibits. Pictures of the crew and passengers before the disaster had struck, and pictures of the survivors after the virus had reached the ship. There was a man with three heads, a preternaturally handsome man, a man who had stretched his body to enormous heights, but Noel was drawn to the black and white photos of Brigadier General Kenneth Foxworthy as he had been before his transformation into Captain Flint. The images showed him working among the survivors during those first chaotic days. A later photo showed him in his knave form. *When did we stop being heroes and start being bastards,* he wondered? He looked about for a docent who might be able to give him a bit of history and point him toward any old-timers, but there were none in evidence. He spotted signs guiding him toward the café and the gift shop. Often the people hired for the shops knew a bit more than the average person, so he headed that way. As he walked past the photos and memorabilia, he thought about that night in forty-eight.

A normal man walking onto this ship of monsters carrying a newborn. What did he say? Were any questions asked or did they just assume he was the father and was abandoning his child.

Noel remembered all those little fertilized eggs that were rejected because his and Niobe's child would have likely died at birth or been a joker. There was no possibility that he and his wife could ever have a nat child, given that they were both wild cards, and therefore Noel had decreed that only a viable ace embryo would be implanted. Niobe having suffered as a joker agreed and hence . . . Jasper. But what if the doctors at the Jokertown Clinic had slipped up and their child had been a joker? Would he have abandoned that baby? Or *handled* it? Uncomfortable questions. Noel shook them off.

♣

The story of the *Queen Mary* was a tragic one, and Green Man knew it well. Back in nineteen forty-six, the year that everything changed, the *Queen Mary* had been en route to New York with a full complement of passengers. They'd gotten a warning to turn back at the last minute but it had come too late. By the time the ship was making its way home, spores had already found their way on board. And by the time it reached British waters, the wild card virus was taking effect.

With most of the crew dead or dying, the *Queen Mary* finally limped as far as the Isle of Dogs and ran aground, where she had remained until the present day. Of course, that was only the start of her story. Since then, she'd had a long career, first as a prison and then as a home for the jokers created on her decks. Most of the original jokers were dead now, but something of the community remained, and the *Queen Mary* continued to make a living, albeit a more modest one, as a museum.

The van he was in pulled to a stop, and the side door was yanked open by Wayfarer. "Are you sure about this?" she asked. "It's the middle of the day."

He was already jumping out as he answered. "It's now or never."

"Do you want backup?"

"No. Just be ready to get us out of here."

She nodded. "One of our drivers is ready if we need to switch rides." He gave Wayfarer a nod and set off toward the gangplank. "I'll keep the engine running," she said, her voice betraying more nerves than usual.

Are things getting to her? He wondered. *Or is she picking up on my own misgivings?*

If King Henry had come to the same conclusions that he'd reached, namely that there was another prince, an older one with a superior claim to power, then it stood to reason that he'd want that prince out of the picture. Green Man had no doubt that Henry would be willing to break the law to see that through.

He glanced around, alert for trouble, but the sky was resolutely cheery and there were no sounds of violence. Sunlight picked out the fresh red and black paint on the smokestacks. Green Man knew that the vessel was in need of serious structural repair, with corrosion riddling its heart. Nobody had been able to raise the hundreds of millions required, but they always seemed to find the money for new paint. And so it had gone, year after year, covering its cracks from the public while rotting inside.

There's a metaphor in there somewhere.

He knew the jokers and nats who lived here, and they knew him by sight. The ones on the door let him on board with a nod. They didn't charge him an entrance fee and he didn't offer anything, though he did put a donation in the box, his haste briefly defeated by habit.

It was hard to rush, though. Everything just seemed so . . . normal. He could see a few people moving with a tourist's amble, their eyes and their smartphones darting from one detail to the next.

Among them was a familiar face, a young joker called Moseley. For him, the virus had given extra arms, all of them dead and useless, as if someone had surgically grafted the upper limbs of a baby Tyrannosaurus Rex to his chest. Moseley hid them under a baggy jumper and jacket. He'd once asked Green Man for the money to have them removed, but hadn't been able to provide any favors of sufficient value to qualify. They'd not spoken since.

Judging from the way he was pressing his back to the wall, he didn't seem pleased to see Green Man again. "We don't want no trouble."

"I'm not here for you." He tried to think about the jokers that lived here that would meet Finder's description. It didn't take long. "Is Dorothy still here?"

"Dotty? Yeah, she's minding the shop. What's going on?" Green Man narrowed his eyes, and Moseley gulped. "On you go, chief."

♠

The smell of wet wool, tea, and pasties accompanied Noel through the café. He stepped into the gift shop and closed the door after. He wanted no interruptions for his questioning. The joker behind the counter looked up. She had a thick sluglike body with an elderly woman's head perched incongruously on top.

"Please, sir, the door needs to remain open. Don't want to discourage any shoppers." It was said sweetly, but there was a flare of alarm in her eyes. Probably to be expected in any encounter between a nat and a joker, but his actions had made it more fraught.

"I was hoping," Noel began, but the rest of the sentence was cut off when a neat, dark hole appeared in the center of the woman's forehead.

Simultaneously he heard the *crack* of a bullet breaking the speed of sound as it created its own little sonic boom.

♦

It was easy to follow signs for the shop. Green Man went down one level, down several empty corridors, then up again, emerging into what had once been a grand lounge but was now a small café and shop area. A few older couples sat drinking tea and talking quietly to one another. He ignored their discreet stares as he strode past. His feet thudded heavily on the polished wooden floor, like a slow, rhythmic, but very enthusiastic drummer. Perhaps because of this, he nearly didn't hear the muffled sound of a bullet being fired. Instincts made him duck, but the sound was too far away for him to be the target. The shot had come from somewhere on the other side of the door ahead of him.

The door to the shop.

Too late! he thought, even as he ran forward.

♥

Based on the size of the entry wound and the likely position of the shooter, taking into account the location of the ship, and a tricky shot through a porthole, it had probably been an L115A3 Long Range Rifle delivering a .338 Lapua Magnum round. Noel had used the same weapon a number of times in his career. Even as his mind analyzed the details, he was instinctively drawing his pistol and taking cover behind the large bookcase featuring histories about the ship, the wild card virus, and—incongruously—children's books by British writers. The case and its contents wouldn't stop the bullet, but they would slow it down and limit the damage it would do to him. But seconds passed and no second shot followed. Apparently, the elderly joker had been the target. The question was why? Noel moved to her side despite his sure knowledge she was dead. A pool of blood with a small mixture of brain matter was creating a macabre halo around her head as she lay on the wood floor.

♣

Green Man had a good head of speed by the time he hit the shop's door and it swung open with a bang, the welcome bell joining in with manic cheer. The space here was cluttered with stands, displaying postcards, key rings and all manner of ways to spend money. History and cheap trinkets sprinkled liberally in every corner. On the other side of the shop, he saw Dorothy. Her thick, sluglike body spreadeagled on the floor. And standing over her was a man.

He was of medium height with a slender build. From the back he was just another white man with short gray-flecked brown hair. Ubiquitous and unremarkable except for two things. The first was that he was too calm. Clearly this was not the first time he'd been face-to-face with a dying woman. And secondly, he was carrying a handgun in a manner that suggested he knew how to use it. Green Man was not an expert on guns, but he doubted this one would have the power to stop him easily.

The man was already turning, his gun naturally drawing level with Green Man's chest, even as he took him in.

♠

The Silver Helix maintained a file on Green Man, all-around thug and gangster dabbling in low-level crime and always managing to push off the prosecutions onto his low-level lackeys. And right now there was murder in the eyes behind the mask. Noel also knew bullets would do little, but he hoped the kinetic impact of the slugs would give him time to transform.

They didn't.

♦

Blue eyes moved swiftly from surprise to cool detachment, and then the gun was firing. Two shots, almost on reflex it seemed, and both hit their mark. The man was clearly a professional, but unfortunately for him, the rounds did little more than ruin another shirt and add a few minutes to Green Man's next grooming session.

At full speed now, Green Man lunged for his opponent, but the man was fast, professionally trained. Instead of hitting him dead on, his wooden fist glanced along the man's ribs as he dived clear.

Going too fast to stop, Green Man crashed into, and then through, the counter, the old mahogany splintering with a groan. He ground his teeth. *I've failed to stop the assassin, and now I'm destroying pieces of history.* When he turned round, the man was already backing away, one hand wrapped around his ribs. "Hold on," he said, and made a show of tossing his pistol to one side and displaying his empty palm.

Green Man followed its arc with his eyes, and then crouched down by

Dorothy's body. As he expected, she was dead. He stood up again, fury clouding his vision. It was time for some answers.

But when he looked at the man again, he hesitated. The slender form he'd
seen before was no longer there. In its place was a taller figure, with a broader
chest and golden hair of the kind that was usually only seen in commercials.
The blue eyes had become gold too, and the unremarkable skin had taken on
a bronzy tan. If it hadn't been for the fact he was still holding his ribs and still
in the exact same spot, Green Man would have assumed they were different
people.

An ace! And one who got all the luck by the looks of it. "So," he said, trying to
keep the envy from his voice, "all it takes is a word from the Crown and the
Silver Helix show their true colors."

The man didn't reply, his gaze drifting slightly past Green Man's shoulder.
Then he vanished.

Damn! Is he gone? Or just invisible? Or small?

Green Man hoped for the latter as he glanced wildly about. His efforts were
quickly rewarded. The man had appeared behind him and had plucked an aero-
sol can from one of the shelves. The golden eyes gave nothing away, and by the
time he saw the lighter in his other hand it was too late.

Flames lashed out, golden. *Everything about this man is gold,* thought Green
Man uselessly, as he stumbled back, trying to protect his face. He felt the heat
on his arm so much more than he had the bullets in his chest. A fear rose in
him, stifling his rational mind. He was so distracted, so busy flailing in an
effort to put out his arm before the fire spread to his shoulder, that he barely
noticed the knife the man had seemingly conjured from nowhere, barely noticed him dart under Green Man's guard and thrust its edge against his neck.

Luckily, the blade didn't go that deep, and even if it had, there wasn't a wind-
pipe or a critical vein to cut. His opponent didn't know that, though, and Green
Man took advantage of the moment to grab his perfectly tanned shoulder. One
moment there was meat under his fingers, then nothing.

Damned teleporters!

Again, the man hadn't gone far. He was on the opposite side of the shop, his
head cocked to one side as he surveyed his handiwork. Green Man used this brief
pause to rub the last of the flames from his arm. He needed to land a solid hit and
end the fight before his resourceful enemy found a way past his natural armor.

Green Man picked up a piece of ruined counter and threw it across the shop.
It flew, spinning like a Frisbee's ugly big brother, and crashed through the space
where the man had been standing.

A second later, Green Man felt a weight land on his back. He instinctively
twisted, trying to dislodge it, but a firm grip was already established on his
neck and this time, the knife was coming for his eye. Desperate, Green Man
jerked his head to one side, the knifepoint stabbing just to the right of the
socket, and burying itself deep into his mask. As the man tried to work it free,
Green Man's oversized right hand closed around his forearm.

Got you!

He squeezed, and there was a satisfying crack. It was followed by an even more satisfying scream, and then the man was gone.

Green Man looked around the shop, and then a second time to be sure, but he seemed to be truly alone this time. In no way did he relax, though. He pulled the phone from his pocket.

"Wayfarer?"

"Here."

"We're too late. An ace got here first. Most likely a tame one that belongs to the Silver Helix. Be ready. I wouldn't be surprised if they call more trouble down on our heads."

"Understood."

He knelt down and closed Dorothy's eyes. "I'm sorry," he said.

Despite his appearance, or perhaps because of it, nobody stopped him as he stepped down from the *Queen Mary*. The van was waiting to pick him up, and he slumped gratefully inside. The bullets in his chest were slightly itchy—he would have to pry them out later, and he could already feel his body trying to repair the damage on his neck. There would be a scar, probably one that made its own flowers. His arm actively hurt, however, the blackened patches tingling uncomfortably.

At least it was my right arm.

They switched vans on the way to the safe house, just in case, and Wayfarer joined him in the back. Her eyes widened when she saw him.

"Anything I can do?"

He shook his head. "Not unless you happen to know about a shapeshifting, teleporting ace with a disgustingly even tan, who carries out assassinations for the Crown."

She echoed his head shake.

"I was close, Wayfarer, but not close enough to save her."

"I'm sorry."

"So am I. This was bigger than one woman. The things she knew could have changed all of our lives." He sighed. "There's only one good thing to come from this."

"What's that?" she asked.

"Vindication. Now we know that the rumor of a joker prince is true. Henry sent that agent after Dorothy. He was so scared that what she knew could get out, that he was willing to kill to keep it quiet. Now it's just a question of whether we're trying to find a living prince or a body."

"So, what now?"

Green Man sighed again. "I don't know. We're fighting an enemy that holds all of the cards and doesn't even need to obey the rules."

"That's never stopped you before."

He nodded. "No. It hasn't."

"Then what's the plan?"

"Rest, regenerate, think. Tomorrow, we pay our respects to Margaret. After that, we get revenge."

"You going to go after an ace?"

"We're going after them all. Aces, princes, anyone that's made us suffer."

♥

Bobbin and Constance were ensconced in her flat. They'd boarded up the atelier and given the remaining tailors the week off with pay. Constance had brought a rack of clothes she couldn't bear to leave behind, including Noel's suit—which she hoped to make some real progress on now that they were settled and bloody Henry had his bloody suit.

After she had placed it in the hands of an equerry and almost slammed the door behind him, Bobbin had said regretfully, "I suppose you didn't have any choice but to give that to Henry?"

"I told the Lion and Turing I would. I think Henry's a pig, but I'll protect him this one time. Lord, what a bastard. And he's giving those anti-joker bastards coverage, Bobbin. With him saying such things, it'll make it seem as if it's normal. Good Lord."

She shook her head at the memory and it made her a little dizzy. *Bollocks*, she thought. *My vertigo is acting up again.*

"Let's have some tea," she said. "It's the English way."

Bobbin nodded as he headed for the small kitchen. "What sort would you like?"

"Oh, whatever you want." She pulled out Noel's jacket and laid it on the dining room table. "I think I have everything we usually drink at the shop."

She heard the tap being turned on and then the familiar sounds of Bobbin puttering about making tea. A short time later, he appeared with two steaming cups.

"As it happens, I've never been to your flat before," he said as he placed the cups on the coffee table. "Not once in all the time I've known you. I like it, though. It's rather you, isn't it."

A bright, warm sunflower-yellow feeling expanded in her. The world might be turning to shite, but she had Bobbin.

"I saw *your* flat for the first time ever when I was looking for you the other day," she replied. She tried not to feel guilty about it. "I can't help but notice they're rather alike. I mean, the colors and all."

He smiled. "I noticed that as well. Imagine all the things we could have shared with one another. I hate to think of everything we wasted . . ."

"No," she said hurrying to his side. "Don't say that! We have what we have now and that's good enough." She grabbed his hand and began leading him toward her bedroom.

"I'm not certain what you have in mind, Miss Russell, but I'm an innocent young lad."

"I think not," she replied with a laugh. "I seem to recall a period in your forties where you were game enough for more than a few wenches."

"They weren't wenches, they were perfectly nice girls."

She gave his hand another tug, but he resisted. "Do you not want to?" she asked. There was a moment when she wondered if she had misunderstood.

He blushed. "Of course, I want to! My God! But Constance, it's been a while. I think I may have forgotten what to do."

She pulled him into an embrace and then kissed him gently. "I've forgotten too, luv. And my terrain isn't what it once was."

He took her face in his hands, careful as always about the spindles between his fingers. "You are beautiful, Constance. You'll always be beautiful to me. My God, how I love you."

"Feh, I've never been beautiful," she said shaking her head. He'd said he loved her and that made her frightened and momentously happy at the same time. "You know that very well."

"Would you say I'm beautiful, Constance? With this mug? But it isn't just your face that's beautiful. It's you. You're passionate, kind, brave, and talented. You're vast!"

"You're mad," she said reaching up and taking his hands in hers. "Come to bed with me. I'll help you remember."

Tomorrow she would be burying yet another friend, but today she had Bobbin. And she felt very much as she'd been given an immense prize at a most improbable time in her life.

"Bobbin . . ." she said as she opened the door to the bedroom. She turned back to look him in the eyes as she led him inside. "I love you too."

♣

The arm hurt like the blazes and every breath was a knife to the chest. Noel's hand was sweat-slick on his cell phone as he rang up Constance. She answered on the second ring. He didn't bother with a salutation just blurted,

"Constance, I need that suit. Need it now. May I meet you at the shop?"

"There is no shop, Noel. They burned me out." Stress, age, and sadness filled her voice.

"Oh, bloody hell. But *your* work. It would have been fine, yes?"

"I did salvage what I could. It's all at my flat."

"What's the address?"

"It's unfinished. I haven't *sewn* all the parts."

"Doesn't matter. I'll take whatever you've got."

"You're in trouble."

"Actually just got out of it . . . barely." She gave him the address.

The flat was in Soho quite close to Carnaby Street. *Still missing the glory days are you, old girl?* Noel thought as he limped to the building. He buzzed her flat from the intercom. An instant later the door clicked open.

He rode the elevator up to her floor and headed down the hall. She was waiting just outside her door, peering anxiously at him.

"Well, get in here," she snapped and gestured sharply.

"After you, madam."

"Oh, bugger that," she huffed but she proceeded him into the flat.

He had never been there, and he took a moment to notice that the good taste displayed in her shop extended to her living space. She was studying him, a frown between her brows.

"Cuppa tea?"

"Whisky if you've got it. And some aspirin wouldn't be amiss."

"Bloody hell."

She stalked off and he carefully removed his jacket, hissing in pain as it slid off his arm. When she returned, she was carrying a tumbler with three fingers of liquor and a bottle of aspirin. An older joker was with her, carrying an armful of clothes. Noel vaguely remembered him from his visits to the shop back when he had been an agent.

Noel shook out five aspirin and washed them down with the whisky. Constance was gazing at the way he was cradling his right arm. She gently unbuttoned the cuff and rolled back the sleeve. The broken arm was beginning to swell and the bruises were livid against his pale skin.

"Oh, pet, what have you got yourself into?"

Her carefully cultivated accent slipped a bit, but what hit him in a way Noel hadn't expected was her use of the endearment. Not since his father's death had anyone used that word with him.

"Just all kinds of fun and jollification."

"You need to see a doctor," the joker said.

"I will as soon as . . ." Noel nodded at the pile of clothes the man held.

Constance snatched down the coat and slacks. "Like I said, it's not finished." And indeed, one panel of the suit jacket was missing.

"I can't go about in public like that. How long would it take you to finish it?" he asked.

"Another day at least." She correctly interpreted his expression. "I get it. You want it now because . . ." She gestured at his arm. "Well, you're a damn idiot for doing such dangerous shit at your age!"

"What about the leather coat," the man suggested.

She lifted it from his arms. It was long, calf-length black leather. She eyed it and Noel. "Yes, be a bit big, but it could work."

"I'll take it," Noel said firmly.

"Pygmalion is going to be so unhappy with me."

♠

The knowledge burned in Green Man's brain as he walked to the door of Constance's flat. It wasn't public yet. The outcry was yet to come. He hadn't taken any action, but he already knew the way this would have to play out. A joker had died and the Fists would answer in kind, but louder. He could already feel the blood on his hands, oiling the wheels of recrimination, of action and reaction, as they swirled faster and faster, going from them, to the nats, and back to them, and so on, until the wheels were turning too fast to stop, too fast to see whose turn it was anymore.

His knock on the door betrayed none of this. "May I come in?" he asked when Constance answered. She nodded.

Green Man ducked into the room and closed the door behind him. "These are difficult times for all of us. You've been a friend, so I wanted to warn you. Things are going to get much worse before they get better, and you could be in danger."

"Something's happened, hasn't it?" asked Bobbin.

Green Man looked into those gold framed eyes and found that he did not want to lie. "I suppose you'll find out soon enough. An elderly joker woman was assassinated aboard the *Queen Mary*."

Constance had gone awfully pale. "And now five more innocent people are going to die."

"We live by the law of five for one. Five for every single one. If it's any consolation, I'll do my best to ensure the targets are far from innocent."

"But you can't!"

"It's wrong," agreed Bobbin. "It's just going to make things worse."

"Let me be clear: I cannot stand by and do nothing." He shook his head. "The Fists need to give an answer. And believe me, if I don't give it, someone else will. And then things really will get worse."

Constance did not seem convinced. "You're not a foolish man, you have to see this for what it is." Her voice was grim and determined. "Of course, what you've described is so awful everyone will have to condemn it. But you're not being realistic if you think that the revenge you seek won't come back on you and the Twisted Fists. You kill nats and you'll play right into their hands. That'll be the story, *not* concern over this woman who has died."

Green Man shook his head. "If the world were fair, you'd be right. But the press isn't on our side any more than the police are. This will be hushed up and brushed under the carpet. I've seen it before."

"Please," said Constance, the plea catching him as he turned to go. "If you fight, it will be people in the middle like us who suffer." She nodded at Bobbin. "We have the funds to leave if need be, but what about the people you say you want to protect?"

"Look around. They're already suffering. I intend to make sure they don't suffer alone."

For a second time, he made to leave. To his surprise he felt Constance's hand on his arm. Her grip was surprisingly strong. "I'd like to repay my debt to you."

He stopped, genuinely curious. "Go on."

"In the course of my work, I've made suits for politicians, actors, businessmen, even royalty. That doesn't make us friends, but it has given me the means to contact them. I think that if I brought what you've just told me to their attention, they could make a real difference."

"I appreciate the sentiment, Constance. But such is my cynicism for the establishment, I'm going to need more than that from you. And it doesn't seem your pleas to Henry did much good." Bobbin gave him a hard look, which he did his best to ignore. Constance merely nodded, as if expecting it. "I'm going to need results. Get me a major investigation from the police. Get me a motion to pass fairer laws for jokers. Get Dorothy's family paid a fair compensation. Get me something, anything, to prove that the life that was lost mattered and will not be forgotten. Get me a promise that this will never be allowed to happen again. If the authorities do not act to redress this tragedy, then I will. Out of deference to the queen I'll wait until after the funeral, but after that. . . ." He turned away from them, and this time she didn't try and stop him.

◆

A visit to a walk-in clinic and a tale spun about a dustup in a pub (the bruises on his arm would have given lie to a story of a slip and fall) revealed it was just the ulna that Green Man's powerful grip had broken. Noel was now wearing a fiberglass cast from wrist to elbow. On the plus side, he thought it would make a rather effective bludgeon, and he could still use his right hand though it would hurt like hell. And if necessary, he'd cut the damn thing off. He'd done it before. Fortunate also that Ranjit had taught him to be ambidextrous when it came to firearms and blades.

Noel was furious with himself for staying to fight. Once he'd transformed, he should have gotten the hell out of there. But Green Man could identify him, so silencing the joker was indicated.

Except it was a lie and Noel knew it. He had been craving a fight ever since he'd been denied the chance to vent his spleen on those two wankers at the pub.

Now that he had a chance to think, the whole thing felt dodgy. He gets a tip about the *Queen Mary*, and the joker mob boss shows up precisely at the moment a joker gets killed? Someone was pulling his strings. Was it the Lion setting him up? Or had Soper alerted the Box?

He hissed as he pulled off his shirt and inspected his left side. It really was a spectacular bruise. The doc had given him a rib belt for the cracked ribs, ordered him to take deep breaths to avoid pneumonia and to avoid any strenuous activities for five weeks so both injuries could heal. Not damn likely when he had to locate this joker prince. In the meantime, he would eat pain pills while he could, and stop when needs must. The damn things reduced your reaction time and made you clumsy.

And indeed, his reactions were slowed by the pain shot he'd gotten before they set his arm because he didn't have time to shrug back into his shirt before Jasper entered. Noel now wished that he hadn't asked the mother of one of Jasper's new chums to drop him home because his boy stared in horror at the black and blue blooming on his side and the cast on his arm, and the scars which Noel had been careful to keep hidden.

"Daddy." Dad had been replacing the more childish word, but in his alarm, Jasper had slipped back into the old habit. The book bag hit the floor and Jasper ran to him. "What happened? You're hurt. Are you going to be okay? And what are these?" He reached out as if to touch the twisted flesh but then yanked his hand back.

Noel was surprised at the blur of tears that overlaid his son's words. He hugged Jasper awkwardly. "Yes, yes, I'm fine. Just took a bad step."

"But what if you weren't? What if you'd *died*? I'd be all alone." Jasper was crying in earnest now. "I want mommy! I want to go *home*!"

It hurt more deeply than his injuries.

♥

Alan had finally gotten Noel to agree to a meeting, though Noel had insisted that he couldn't do it until late that evening, after his son had gone to bed. Alan reluctantly agreed, and had spent much of the day checking and re-checking his data, muttering to himself loudly enough that Sebastian had finally begged him to please, go to work, go for a run, go *anywhere*, as long as Alan left him in peace.

In the end, Alan had actually gone for a run, all the way to Noel's flat, hoping to clear his head. The snow had stopped in the night, and eight miles had left Alan sweaty and still deeply divided, but time was slipping away. A decision had to be made.

Now he was pacing back and forth in Noel's living room, the tension boiling off him, while his old friend—was that the right word? Surely he could call Noel a friend—leaned on the fireplace, watching him with a sardonic glint in his eye. Alan spun around one more time, and made his decision.

"Noel, you have to understand. There's so much unrest troubling the country right now. The situation is complex enough with just Henry and Richard—factions are rising to support Richard, agitating that he should take the throne."

Noel raised an eyebrow. "Are they? I hadn't noticed."

Well, there wasn't a lot of general public support for Richard yet, just a few rowdies complaining. But once Richard made his intentions clear, surely there'd be a strong contingent of patriots on his side. "Adding a third wild card—forgive the pun, dear fellow!—could tear the country apart."

Alan rather loathed puns, but he'd tried one, remembering how Noel liked a clever turn of phrase. Though had that been a roll of the eyes in response? Perhaps Alan had misstepped there. It was frustrating trying to read Noel these days; he'd changed so much over the long years. If Alan could get Noel on his side, it would be so much better—the boy was too dangerous to have running around like a loose cannon. Not a boy anymore, of course, but when Alan looked at him, he saw the child they'd co-opted, trained, and turned into a weapon. For England, of course, in a time of desperate need. How much could he justify, for the sake of England?

"What do you mean?" Alan had the feeling Noel was being deliberately obtuse.

"You must have heard the rumors . . . of a joker prince."

Noel looked interested. "So, you have a name."

"Adelbert Boyd-Brackenbury, though he goes by Seizer now. He's mixed up with Green Man." It was hard to get firm data on Boyd-Brackenbury, but there were number of actions attributed to Seizer that were less than wholesome.

Elizabeth's son had not grown up to be a good boy. There was a skittering inside the chimney that gave him a start.

"Seizer." Noel's eyes were downcast, hooded. Alan couldn't tell what he was thinking. "Do you know where he is?"

"I know where he was seen last. That should give you a good starting point."

"And what do you want me to do with this Seizer fellow when I find him?"

That was the question, wasn't it? Well, it wouldn't be the first death Alan had ordered for England's peace and security, and it likely wouldn't be the last. It wasn't as if Adelbert would be any great loss. Noel had carried out plenty of similar assignments in the past. Of course, he was technically retired now—he could refuse. But Alan didn't think he would. He wondered briefly if the cast on Noel's arm would inconvenience him, and decided it wouldn't.

Alan swallowed his misgivings. Some brute rising to the throne of England— that couldn't have been what Margaret had wanted. "I want you to handle it," he said. "For England." Noel would know what that meant.

Noel closed the door softly, leaned against it and tried to stifle his laughter. Wouldn't do to wake Jasper. *Handle it.* The living computer had actually said handle it. *Such a delicate phrase to encompass a murder.*

For an instant he felt a kinship across the decades to that unknown agent holding a squalling infant in his arms. For that man, the choice had been agonizing. For Noel it was simple. A man needed killing. He was good at that.

Sunday

MARCH 8TH

SHE FLICKED AROUND LONDON for a while. It was very early, too early for most of her targets to be active. Turing lay asleep in a room watched only by Sebastian's judging eyes. Good.

Prince Richard was working out in his own private gym, preparing to walk behind his mother's coffin. Not a hero, but the very image of one. The most beloved man in Britain right now.

And back at the safe house, Seizer, the joker who would be king, tumbled out of bed and grabbed a knife from the sideboard. Fascinating. At this time of day, the growths on his body were so large they must have pressed into his back like stones when he tried to sleep. Now, she watched him cut the worst of them off his face and arms. The pain of it made him weep.

Badb sensed an opportunity.

She took her human body down two flights of stairs. Her joints popped with each step. Her own breathing must have woken every sleeper in the house. But no, no, a quick glance through each window from the outside showed that only the sentries on the ground floor and roof were awake.

She didn't bother knocking.

Seizer spun around, bleeding, naked. Even on his cock, a thumb-sized boil had formed.

"How . . . how dare you!" he breathed. Humiliation twisted his face into a snarl. "You know what I did to the last person to disrespect my privacy?" He stalked forward, placing a finger under her chin. "I pulled out his tongue through his own throat."

Badb, although the pain was incredible, dropped to her knees and bowed her head.

"What . . ." he said. "I mean . . ."

"I know who you are," she breathed. "My lord. My king. I . . . know."

He failed to respond. She couldn't watch him from the outside because he had closed his curtains, but she knew by the way he rocked on the balls of his feet that she had confused him. Finally, he whispered, "But . . . but you work for . . . for him."

"I do. And yet . . ." she closed her eyes. "I know you go today to honor the old queen, to honor your aunt!"

She looked up, matching her gaze with his. He was loving every word of it too, she could see that. "But Green Man is too cautious," she said. "He'll give in to the establishment, you know he will. I do respect him, but this is more important. You're all that stands between us and a one-way trip to the moon."

"I am," he said, puffing out his chest so that each boil stood tall like a spare nipple.

"I have a power. I . . . I *know* things. It's how I recognized you for who you were." He nodded regally, and his boil-covered cock bobbed in time. "The Silver Helix has an assassin. A very dangerous man. You must beware today. Rely on your daughter." She bowed her head. "And stay safe, my king."

♠

It was all very well to say *kidnap Sissel*—it was substantially harder to actually do it. If it hadn't been for the funeral, Alan wasn't sure he could have managed it at all, but the bulk of the palace security was already setting up at the cathedral, which gave him a window.

"Sissel, what's wrong?" Gloriana knelt by her daughter's side, a worried frown on her lovely features.

"My stomach hurts, Mummy." Sissel was dressed in her mourning best—a black coat over a black dress, black socks and shoes, even a small black hat on her head. She looked like a palace raven, one of the flock that had gathered in the main foyer. Henry with his young fiancée, both keeping a safe distance from his first wife. Richard was by Diana's side, of course, and their children beside them. All decked out in black, gathered to pile into cars and head to the cathedral, everyone ready to go except for poor Sissel, who looked as if she were about to cry. Alan had calculated the dosage precisely in the sweet he'd slipped to her earlier—it would do her no harm. He regretted the mild discomfort the child was experiencing now. It couldn't be helped, though.

Her mother stood up. "Father—she doesn't have a fever, but I don't think she should come with us."

King Henry shrugged. "It's up to you, of course, Gloriana. It's a lot for a child anyway."

"Yes." Gloriana looked relieved at her father's words. "That's what I was thinking. If you don't think it'd look bad—"

"No, no, everyone will understand. Children catch every damn bug that comes through. Send the girl to bed. Probably no one will even notice her absence in the crush. Here, sweetheart—give your grandfather a hug." Henry reached out his arms, and Sissel obediently went over and embraced him. "Go to bed, child. Reginald will see you to your room." Henry nodded to the butler, who held out a hand to the girl.

"We'll be back in a few hours," Gloriana said. "Try to get some sleep."

"Yes, Mummy."

Sissel climbed up the wide staircase with Reginald by her side. Step one accomplished. Many more steps to go.

The royals headed off. Alan didn't have a lot of time—the Lion would expect him at the cathedral, and would note his absence if he wasn't there. But there was enough time to slip into Sissel's room, where the girl had already been tucked up in bed.

"Alan?"

He smiled down at the girl. "I wanted to see how my little friend was doing. I've brought you some homemade soup—my husband swears it heals the worst sickness."

"I don't know," Sissel said, frowning. "I don't really feel like eating."

Alan's stomach clenched, but he pushed the words out. "Just sip a little. It'll help you get to sleep."

"All right." He helped her sit up, and then fed her a spoon of soup. She blinked up at him. "It's very sad, isn't it?"

"Yes, Sissel, it's very sad." Alan urged her to take a second spoonful, and she obeyed, opening her mouth, swallowing it down.

"I didn't know her very well. Grandmama was always busy, or tired."

Alan's throat tightened. "You should have known Queen Margaret when she was younger. You would have had great fun together."

"Did she like the stars too?" Sissel asked, sleepily.

They'd danced under the stars once, oh, long and long ago, when Margaret was just a reckless young princess, and Alan, one of her favorite soldiers. "She did. But there were other things she liked more. Stories, for one. The queen loved a good story."

"Tell me a story, Alan." But the princess's eyes were already closing. Before Alan could say *once upon a time*, she was out cold.

Alan sent the message—*John, it's time.* John Davies slid in the door a few minutes later; he'd been waiting down the hall. A soldier Alan had caught stealing decades ago, John had a small joker power, a little sleight-of-mind that translated to "look away." People didn't notice Davies, not unless they had computer minds, precise enough to catch every unusual detail.

Turing had saved Davies from prison, had used him for unpleasant jobs, now and then over the years. Now John Davies was a grizzled old man, but still deft enough to slip past the thin layer of security they had left in the palace.

They didn't need to discuss anything; it had all been planned in advance. Alan gathered the girl in his arms, wrapping the blanket loosely around her, and then transferred the blanketed bundle to Davies. He hoisted her over his shoulder and Alan winced, waiting for the child to wake and scream—but no, she was solidly out. Now it was just a quiet dance, Alan's knowledge of the guard's patrol paths and Davies's "look away" combining to get them out of the room, down the hall, down three flights of stairs, and to the loading dock, where a van waited to spirit Davies and Sissel away to an old abandoned bunker. Not the homiest place for a child, full of old computers and other junk, but a forgotten space, easy to make secure. Alan had hired others to secure the approaches, though they wouldn't know what they were guarding. They'd keep Sissel safe until Henry abdicated.

Alan Turing watched the van pull out, his heart turning over in his chest.

Maybe he should have argued with Richard more. He trusted Davies to take good care of the child, but this was so very wrong. If Margaret knew what Alan had done to her grandchild, she would never forgive him.

Too late now. Onward, for king and country.

◆

The bright colors on the Greenwood Design Centre startled Noel a bit. The garish graffiti didn't seem to fit Constance's aesthetic. Through the windows he saw an old joker woman in a wheelchair playing cards with an equally old man. Outside sitting on the front steps was a gaggle of teenagers. Most were jokers. All were smoking. They eyed him, a middle-aged white man in a nice suit and long leather coat. They probably figure him to be a cop or a bureaucrat. Then they spotted the cast and like a Heisenberg experiment his status settled—he had to be a cop.

"Good morning," he said pleasantly as he walked up.

"Lo."

"Morning."

"Whatcha want?"

"I'm looking for someone, Boyd-Brackenbury. Does he ever come round here?" This had not been Noel's first stop in his search for the would-be joker prince. Turing had provided an address for the man, but Noel discovered Boyd-Brackenbury hadn't been home for several days, to the evident pleasure of his neighbor who described him as a *right old bastard*. He had tried bars and restaurants in the area and, after a few pounds had changed hands, got the tip that Boyd-Brackenbury frequented the Centre.

"Why you want him?" asked a handsome black nat kid. He had his arm protectively around a girl with organic and bone paintbrushes for hair.

"I'm a lawyer. He may have come into some money."

"Oh, he'll like that," a joker snorted.

"So, you do know him?"

"Yeah, Seizer comes around," said Paintbrush. "Tells us all how we need to do something with our lives. Like he ain't living off a trust fund."

"Isn't that why Ms. Russell created this place? To help you do something with your lives?" Noel purred. His mask had slipped and they exchanged uncomfortable glances. "Any idea where he might be now?"

"Isn't he off with Green Man and those other fools at the funeral?" Another joker offered.

"I take it you lot aren't interested," Noel said.

"Nah," said the nat kid.

"How would I recognize him?"

"He grows these bumps all over him, especially on his head, like a gross crown. Then they fall off. Stink something terrible."

"Would Ms. Russell know him by sight?"

"Yeah, she knows most of the people who come here."

"Keeps an eye out," another offered.

"Cares," the girl with the paintbrushes said softly.

"Thank you." Noel pulled out his wallet and handed over a twenty-pound note. "Go offer a toast to the old queen."

There was no doubt Constance would be at the funeral. He walked away and pulled out his cell phone glad that he had paired them. It would enable him to locate her, and then she would point out his quarry.

♥

Queen Margaret's coffin was soon to arrive in Westminster, where it would lie in state for the next three days. A brief service would be carried out, the acknowledgement of her long reign and dedication to both duty and family broadcast across the world. Green Man intended to see it in person rather than on television. And, alongside a large chunk of the nation, he was now making his way toward Westminster Hall to pay his respects.

Seizer walked alongside him, dressed in his finest funeral black. The jokers of England walked with them, hundreds of them, all here to show their love for the queen. While it was possible that such a concentration of jokers could become a target for some of the hate groups out there, Green Man was confident that even Britain First would behave themselves today.

He'd given strict instructions that his own people do the same. So far, nothing had been said of Dorothy's death. Perhaps that was why the thoughts of her sounded so loud in Green Man's skull, like a ghost seeking release.

Of course, just because all sides had come to a natural decision to cease hostilities for a day did not mean the war was over. There were many ways to fight after all, and if there was one thing he'd learned about King Henry in their recent dealings, it was that the man had no sense of decency, common or otherwise.

And so it did not surprise him to find a line of police up ahead, blocking their path. They looked grim behind their riot shields. Each face a little flag of bad news. Some had their arms folded, a few couldn't quite make eye contact, as if ashamed, and one or two hands hovered near their batons.

"Here we go," he murmured.

"They mean to stand in our way," replied Seizer, astonished. "Those bastards! Well, I'm not going to stand here and take this. We have rights. And we will be heard. And I fully—"

"You will stand here next to me and say nothing. You will stick to the plan."

"Plan? What plan?"

"Watch."

He came to a stop about twenty meters from the police line, which brought the rough lines of jokers to a stop too. More than one of the officers let out a brief sigh of relief, though the tension remained. They waited as several nats went through unmolested, saying nothing. Then, he sent Bethany and Jamila forward, along with one of his oldest jokers, the slowest and most pathetic looking he could find.

Seizer scoffed when he saw them. "I don't think they're going to do much to persuade the police. What did you send Montgomery for? He's got about as much bite as a damned lettuce. Let me go. I'll wake the buggers up."

The hands on Jamila's head were gesturing plaintively as she begged to be let through, but it was clear from the way the lead officer glared that there was no pity going spare.

No jokers allowed. Green Man narrowed his eyes. He'd been forewarned by his contacts but it still stung to have the truth confirmed. The orders had been couched in terms of security and safety, but these were just a smokescreen for King Henry's hate. Excluding the jokers from paying their respects to Margaret was the next step in the war. A powerful statement that they were not seen as normal people. Were not seen as true British citizens. Were not welcome.

Indeed, some papers would probably note the lack of jokers in Westminster Hall and accuse them of being unpatriotic. Green Man could imagine the headlines already.

He couldn't hear what was being said, but he'd briefed his people well. They would be asking, politely and repeatedly, to be let through. Two nice young girls and a gentle-faced old man who only wanted a chance to show their love for the queen. They'd get the officers to spell out why they were being blocked. And while there was an argument that a joker, no matter how small or sweet, could be very dangerous, it wouldn't hold against what was being caught on camera.

In total there were twelve cameras he was aware of recording the exchange. Three hidden ones on the jokers themselves and nine others wielded by journalists that either owed him a favor or were faithful to the cause.

When it was clear their efforts had failed, Bethany, Jamila, and Montgomery turned away, sobbing. Perhaps Jamila was overplaying it a little, perhaps Montgomery was underplaying it—he had little love of the royals, after all—but the images were pure media gold.

He saw the police tense again as the three distributed the news to the hundreds of other jokers present. He could see them wondering if this was the moment that violence would break out.

"Take my lead," he said to Seizer, making eye contact with one of the police. He held the other man's gaze for a while, then shook his head and walked forward.

Seizer did the same, and he was aware of many others moving behind them.

Several police took an involuntary step back, though several others took out their batons. No doubt they'd been handpicked for this duty, specifically because of their anti-joker sentiments.

He closed the distance slowly. From twenty meters to fifteen.

"Hold there!" called one of the officers.

From fifteen to ten.

"Hold there, I say!"

Then he paused, turned ninety degrees to the left, and marched to the side of the road. Bethany led a different section of their group to the other side of the road, taking up a post opposite Green Man.

With a mixture of slow shuffles, hops, and slides, the jokers lined the street.

He knew that others would be doing the same in smaller numbers elsewhere; flash-mobs organized by Wayfarer. Together they formed an honor guard, standing ready to pay tribute to their queen.

They watched as a string of armored cars roared by, en route to the abbey. The windows were blacked out but he knew that King Henry sat in one of them.

After the noise had faded, they heard the clop of hooves on the road as a horse-drawn carriage approached, decked out in funeral black. Within was the queen's coffin. Guards marched alongside, their eyes fixed firmly ahead. Behind them was Prince Richard, who walked slowly, the very picture of reverence. Many nodded as they saw him: a true prince, a good man, mourning his mother.

Richard paid no attention to Green Man and his people, seemingly too wrapped in his own personal grief to make a political statement. But it didn't matter. While Richard would likely steal tomorrow's headlines, they would form the backdrop for the iconic image. They would be seen.

Hundreds of mourners passed them by. A never-ending train of black clad bodies. Some ignored them or scowled at the floor, but more met their eyes, nodding in solidarity. A lot of them had phones too, videoing as they went.

Let them film, he thought. *Let the word go out on as many platforms as possible.*

Looking at the long lines of his people, all of them quiet, dignified, strong, he realized he had never felt prouder than at this moment. Tomorrow, the normal rules of engagement would resume, but today was his. He wished he could be a fly on the wall when the news of what had happened reached the bigots in the palace and in Britain First. He wished that very much indeed.

Your move, Henry.

♣

It was the same dreadful weather for Margaret's funeral as it had been for Glory's. Constance resented it even more, if such a thing was possible. She and Bobbin were making their way to Parliament Square Garden. They'd been informed the jokers were congregating there for the funeral. Rumor had it that the police had instructions not to let any joker close to Westminster Abbey. However, Bobbin was insisting that Constance go and pay her respects, since she had an invitation. Green Man had offered an escort for them to the park, but they'd declined. It seemed unlikely they'd need the protection.

They could see the crowd now, but the streets were almost silent. Just the occasional sound of people weeping. And then the aroma of flowers hit her. It made sense, she realized. There probably wasn't a flower shop in London that hadn't been stripped bare of its contents so that mourners could express how much they would miss their queen.

"Come with me," she said suddenly, tugging at his hand. She led him to the edge of the street. "We can go to the funeral together."

"Constance," he replied with a sad smile. "You know I can't. They'll never allow it."

"It will be fine. You're with me and I have an invitation!"

They were close to the barricade now and as she stepped forward, a policeman stopped them.

"Sorry, ma'am," he said coldly. "No jokers allowed."

She pulled the invitation out of her pocket. "I've been invited."

The cop glanced at it, then shrugged. "You can go in, but not him."

"But . . . I need him."

"Ma'am," the cop replied, not unkindly. "You know the rule. His Majesty was clear."

"You go," Bobbin urged. "You'll let her through, yes?"

"Of course."

"No," Constance said stubbornly. "I'm not going to. Let's go." She slipped the invitation back into her breast pocket and took Bobbin's arm again.

"You're quite horrible," she said glowering at the policeman.

"Yes, ma'am," he said as they began walking along the pavement again.

In a few moments, they entered the Garden. It was eerily silent. There was a pocket of jokers they strolled by who closed ranks as they approached. She couldn't blame them. After all, she looked like a nat, and even with Bobbin by her side, she still didn't look like she belonged. There was a light touch on her shoulder.

"I'd have thought you'd be at the funeral by now." She turned and saw Noel. Like Constance, he looked out of place.

"Hello, Noel," Bobbin said brightly. He gave Noel a happy smile and put out his hand. Noel shook it and a flicker of respect crossed his face. Constance was always surprised by Bobbin's ability to see the good in other people and how they reacted to the fundamental decency of him. Even Noel wasn't immune.

"I'm surprised to see you here too, Noel," she replied cautiously.

"You know I had a great amount of respect for the queen," he replied.

"No," she said acerbically. "Why are you *here*? This doesn't seem like your sort of place."

"You wound me." He said it lightly with a slight smile. "I want to pay my respects among the people who loved her best."

It was, and yet wasn't, the Noel she knew. There was an underlying tension about him.

"What's going on, Noel?" she asked cautiously.

"You're trending a wee bit melodramatic now." He glanced around the crowd. "I don't suppose you could point out Boyd-Brackenbury for me?"

Constance frowned. "Why do you want him?"

At the same moment Bobbin pointed and spoke up, "He's right over there, standing close to Green Man."

"Thank you," he said, then slipped away into the crowd.

"I didn't like that at all, Bobbin," she said.

He gave her a puzzled look, and she realized that while he had known Noel over the years, he didn't really *know* him. She was now worried that Noel's retirement was as conditional as her own.

"Don't fret," Bobbin said. He patted her arm again. "Now, you should go on to the funeral. I'll be fine here."

The vellum invitation, tucked into the breast pocket of her coat, felt both comforting and oddly heavy. With it, she could walk across the street and be in Westminster Abbey. In but a few more moments, she could be sitting in one of the pews waiting to pay her respects, but suddenly she found she couldn't bear the idea of leaving.

She loved Margaret and was lucky enough that Margaret seemed to consider her a friend, or at least enough of one that she'd allowed her many intimacies that no one but the two of them ever knew. Even so, Constance stayed where she was. She was an ace, but she was just like the jokers here. They'd all been infected with the virus.

And then there was Bobbin. She didn't want to leave him, not at this moment. She needed him. And she knew he needed her. "I belong here," she replied. It felt right. "I don't want to leave you alone, and these are my people. I want to be here with them."

Bobbin nodded. "I'm glad you're staying. You belong to us too."

Constance gave him a faint smile, then she took his hand and squeezed it. A light rain began to fall.

♠

As he slipped into his pew, Alan's heart seemed to be living in his throat. Richard had glanced at him as he entered—*is it done?*—and Alan had given the tiniest of nods in return. Richard went back to looking mournful, and perhaps he truly was; his mother lay before him in state, after all, and she had loved him. Perhaps she had loved her sons too much, unable to see their faults until it was too late. Perhaps Alan had done the same. It was hard to even look at Richard right now; the hypocrisy seemed painted on every handsome feature. Alan had kissed those downturned lips, had traced fingers across those frowning eyebrows, painted in bushy gold. Alan's hands fisted at his sides, undoubtedly smearing the makeup, but he couldn't bring himself to care. It had been so important to him, for so long, that he pass as just another human among them. So many thought of him as a calculating machine, during the War and after, naming him after his most famous creation. He was Enigma, but to Richard, he'd just been a man, for a little while. What had Alan betrayed in his yearning for that human connection?

The minister was leading them through the ceremony of reconciliation now. *Almighty God, our heavenly Father, we have sinned against you, through our own fault, in thought and word and deed, and in what we have left undone. We are heartily sorry, and repent of all our sins.*

By now, Alan's sins would fill a book as thick as that Bible that rested on the lectern . . . *forgive us all that is past.* Was there mercy and forgiveness waiting for Alan Turing?

. . . *grant that we may serve you in newness of life.* All he'd wanted was to serve his country. Once he'd thought that living for a hundred years and more, with the face and form of youth, was the greatest gift of the wild card. Now, Alan wasn't so sure. Looking at Richard made it hard to breathe.

But looking at Henry wasn't any better. Stiff and erect, with his fiancée beside him, not yet knowing that his grandchild had been taken. And Gloriana—oh. She wore a simple black dress, hat topped with a little veil, and when she tilted her head to listen to the minister's words, she looked more than a little like Margaret in those long-gone, hoyden days. Those fine-painted features that could stop a heart. Alan squeezed his eyes shut, turned away.

They were singing now, the fine words of an ancient hymn filling the air. *The King of love my shepherd is, whose goodness faileth never.* If only Alan could have such faith in Henry, or Richard, or even Richard's children. If he could be sure that eventually, England would be safe with young Thomas, Richard's eldest—in his thirties now, a handsome lad, with Margaret's eyes passed down, dark and limpid pools. But did he have Margaret's strength, Margaret's good heart? Alan didn't know. And the three younger children—Alan wouldn't be surprised to learn that they weren't even Richard's get. Did that matter? They'd been raised as royals, with the expectations of duty to the throne.

But duty could lead you terribly astray; England's history was full of bloody crimes, slaughters committed in the name of duty, by good men who thought they were doing good things. *Take up the White Man's burden—/ Send forth the best ye breed—/ Go, bind your sons to exile / To serve your captives' need.* Kipling had surely known how fraught that endeavor was, had judged in story after story these failed attempts of kings. *The silent, sullen peoples / Shall weigh your gods and you.* In that final weighing, how would Enigma be judged? Alan Turing bowed his head before God and his dead queen, waiting for judgment to fall.

◆

With luck Constance and her elderly beau would never know that he had identified the man that Noel was about to kill. The long leather trench coat brushed against Noel's legs as he moved through the crowd. From beneath the brim of his hat he watched the top of Boyd-Brackenbury's head, with its growths. He and his daughter were in close conversation, though her head kept turning this way and that. *Looking for celebrities? A good place to stand?*

Noel closed his left hand around the hilt of the slender blade that he carried in his pocket. He hadn't used this particular knife since he'd slit the throat of the Caliph on that long-ago night in Baghdad. He much preferred the gun, but in a crowd this large the chance of a stray bullet and ensuing panic was too much of a risk. This had to be fast and silent.

He had considered transforming, but the pain of the shifting bones of his broken arm and ribs made him decide against it. In a crowd this large he could vanish as effectively as if he'd teleported.

It was an appropriately subdued group as well as a segregated one. The nats were closer to the church, and security kept even them back from where the cars would arrive and the family and friends and sundries (ambassadors and such) would be escorted into the cathedral.

Jokers lined the street, silent sentinels to honor a dead queen. There were a smattering of nats among them, mostly immigrants and minorities showing solidarity with an even more despised group.

Noel waited until the crowd began to break up, then began sliding through the crowd, drawing closer to his target. The cast and ribs were going to throw off his balance. He analyzed how to compensate for that while he mentally chanted the mantra—*Thrust between the third and fourth ribs, with an upward direction, add a twist.*

To avoid the chance of slip or a jostle, he kept his feet pressed firmly to the pavement. The knife he held softly, ready to flip it if necessary. His grip would tighten only at the moment of the thrust.

Perhaps half a meter separated them when Maven's stare rolled across him. Gone was the pleasantly smiling daughter. They were two predators locking eyes across the body of a quarry. Noel moved fast. She was faster. Grabbing her father's arm, she spun him like a child playing crack the whip. What should have been a killing blow left the blade sliding across Boyd-Brackenbury's palm and up the arm to his elbow. Material and skin parted at the knife's honed edge.

The joker screamed. Maven remained silent, a deadly silence that Noel knew well. Just as he knew the shape of the object in her pocket. A pistol no doubt, as illegal as his own. He knew the coat would suck the round unless she was an accomplished shot and aimed for the head, and at this point he had to believe she was.

He shouted. "Hoy, a man's been hurt here!" as he slipped the knife up his sleeve.

People rushed forward and he allowed them to shoulder past him catching whiffs of body odor, perfume and aftershave, the scents of exotic lands, and the strange smells that sometimes were part of a joker's affliction. He faded back into the crowd, and had a final vision of Maven's cold-eyed stare. It promised retribution.

♥

They'd all gathered at the Queen's Library at Buckingham Palace; Margaret had spent much of her free time in that room, and the royal family was used to coming there to find her. Maybe they were looking for that sense of comfort now. The table was piled high with trays of foods that no one was eating and cups of tea and coffee sat on every available surface, at some risk to the books. Not that anyone cared about that right now.

Gloriana sat erect at the table, but her fisted hands would have been enough to betray her agitation, if the tremble in her voice hadn't given her away. "Daddy, please!"

Alan hadn't heard Gloriana call her father that since she was a small child, not since she'd grown into an elegant young woman, married, and moved away. But she had clearly given up on any pretense of sober adulthood now.

Henry frowned from his own seat across the table, flanked by a sober-faced

Emily. "Gloriana, what would you have me do? I can't let this family, this country, be held hostage to some thugs—"

"Hostage! *Sissel* is the hostage here, not you or us or England. She's just a little girl, and she's frightened, maybe hurt, missing her mother—" Gloriana broke down into tears again then. Her own mother walked across the room and sat down beside her, one hand reaching out to stroke her hair. As if that would help.

Alan's heart ached for Gloriana, and he wished he could reassure her that Sissel wasn't hurt or frightened at all. Only sleeping, and kept perfectly safe. But even raising his head a little brought Richard's eyes snapping to him, a frown on that broad forehead that said, louder than words, *shut up, Alan!* Alan bent his head again in silent obedience.

The phone rang, and one of the MI-7 people snatched it up, hit speakerphone.

"Give me Henry."

"I'm empowered to negotiate . . ."

"Henry, now, or I'm hanging up."

The agent mutely offered the phone to Henry, who took it, frowning. Alan was counting seconds in his head, and he knew Davies would be doing the same. They had very little time before the call was traced, despite all the extra servers Alan had routed it through.

"Have you made your decision, Your Highness? The little girl is looking a bit peaked."

"Bring Sissel back, you bastards!"

"You know our terms. What's it to be? Is a kingdom worth your granddaughter's life? She has such pretty little fingers—it'd be a shame if she were to lose a few."

Alan closed his eyes as the room erupted in noise and chaos, with Henry raging into the phone. Davies had been told not to lay a finger on the girl. But even the words were enough to make Alan's throat constrict. He'd been through too many operations not to know that sometimes things spun out of control; even the best plans could go terribly wrong.

Alan Turing was far from certain that this was the best plan.

♣

Embarrassment was not an emotion with which Noel was much acquainted. He viewed much of the world with cynical detachment, but seeing Gloriana's rather round face swollen and red from the tears that still rolled down her cheeks and hearing the chest-wracking sobs made him feel like a voyeur. Gloriana's mother—the rejected wife—sat next to her on the sofa, arm around her shoulders, trying to comfort her daughter while the young broodmare hovered nearby.

The real action, however, was happening on the other side of this room in the family quarters. Ranjit Singh stood stiff and expressionless as Henry berated him.

"You bloody, fucking useless raghead. My mother's funeral disrupted and my granddaughter kidnapped. What the devil good are all you aces if you can't protect my family?"

Noel could see that the Sikh was attempting to gather back the tatters of his patience and courtesy. "With respect, sir, it appears that the kidnappers had detailed intelligence regarding our security measures. I have ordered a full review and investigation. We will get to the bottom of this."

"To hell with your damn navel-gazing! What are you doing to find my granddaughter?"

"Every intelligence and law enforcement agency is working diligently to locate the princess, sir," the Lion said stiffly.

"You lot haven't been able to do bugger all since you lost Flint. Collection of useless freaks. I need someone tough enough to do what's necessary."

"And would that include the same sort of grotesque illegalities committed by Brigadier Foxworthy . . . sir?" Singh belatedly added the honorific.

Henry glared up at the big ace. He gestured sharply, ordering Noel to his side. Apparently, Noel's entrance had not gone unnoticed.

Noel joined the pair and nodded respectfully to Henry. "Sir?"

"I'm putting you in charge of the Silver Helix," the king said.

Emotions raced across the Lion's face: fury, humiliation, dread. "Sir, I must protest. Such a decision cannot be yours alone to make—"

Henry cut him off. "My mother created the Helix, selected its first director. Protest if you wish, but by the time all the lawyers and politicos have finished arguing, Matthews will have gotten the job done."

"I will make every effort to do so, sir," Noel said.

"Well then, get to it!"

It was clear they were dismissed. Noel headed for the door trailed by the Lion. Before he reached it Gloriana came to her feet and blocked their exit. The tears had ended, leaving only her face and makeup in ruin as testament to their passing.

She was once again a Windsor in full control. "Please, gentlemen. Find my daughter."

They both bowed their heads, but the Lion didn't answer. This was now all on Noel. "Madam, I will."

Now I just have to figure out how the fuck to do that.

♠

Alan had driven the two hours out from London, but parked a distance from the estate. He could have driven all the way there, but he'd needed to clear his head. The last three miles he'd ran through the gathering dusk, crossing neglected woodlands, his memory flashing back eight decades, to the War. There had been other wars, and some he'd even fought in, risking life and limb in service—but there would always be one War that ranked above them all. Alan Turing had built the Engima machine and led the team that cracked the German codes. He'd gone to America in forty-two, taught the Americans everything he knew. Was it hubris to think he'd had a significant hand in winning the War, in saving England? All of his compatriots from that time were dead; there was none left to challenge his memory of events.

It was getting harder to run these days; maybe Alan was finally aging. His breath came harder. Sweat dripped down his neck, undoubtedly smearing his makeup, but Davies wouldn't care and Sissel wouldn't be awake enough to notice. She wouldn't know he'd been there at all. The late winter woodland was mucky; Alan's shoes squished in the mud with every step. But still he ran, and it felt good, clearing the cobwebs away. If he could, he'd run forever.

Alan slowed down for the approach, paused in the shadow of a great old tree and texted Davies. Wouldn't do to get his head blown off by one of the guards, or even to have them see his face.

Davies texted back: *It'll be clear in ten—I'm sending them to the pub for a bite. You'll have at least thirty minutes.*

Thirty minutes would be more than enough. Soon the van rattled past, one of the guards dimly visible through the window. Once it was well down the road, Alan headed to the low white building that sat at the edge of the lake—a Grecian folly, built by a long-ago lord to adorn his lands. Most of the estate had been broken up by now, the mansion separated into apartments. But eighty years ago, this folly had concealed one of England's code-breaking sites, and Alan Turing had long ago arranged to have a shell corporation purchase this little parcel of land. You never knew when something like this might come in handy.

He passed through the pillars that would shortly be guarded again by two men Davies had hired. Another would be inside, at the base of the stairs, and another patrolling the bunker. Four total, along with Davies—it was overkill for one helpless little girl, but better safe. Alan descended into the darkness and fished a key out of his pocket. He opened the door to a room filled with a maze of massive computers, furniture, and filing cabinets, lit only by dozens of tiny blinking lights.

"You can turn the lights on, you know," he said mildly.

"I prefer it like this," Davies said quietly. "Peaceful-like."

Alan almost hadn't seen the man, who sat hunched over in a dark corner of the room. Had Davies always been the sort of person who hid, or had his card turning changed his fundamental character? Philosophical questions that no one had the answer to, and Alan was losing his faith that he could sort out even mundane puzzles, much less metaphysical ones.

"Where's the girl?" Alan asked. There was no sign of Sissel in the open center of the room. Davies jerked his head toward the back and Alan walked to the far end, past banks of out-of-date computers. Oh, they still worked, but there was more computing power on the phone in his pocket than on all of these machines put together. His brain still worked faster than the phone could—but for how much longer? And of course, his brain couldn't make actual phone calls. Inadequate in so many ways.

The girl was tucked into a far corner, lying on the floor, on a bed of palace blankets, with her hands loosely bound in front of her and a blindfold across her eyes. Alan's throat tightened. There'd been no need to gag Sissel, at least—even if she woke, this place was remote enough that no one would hear her screams. But Alan didn't plan to let her wake. She was still fast asleep, but the meds would be wearing off soon. Alan sighed, and pulled a hypodermic out of his pocket. He bit his lip as he bent down to inject her. Sissel twitched away at the tiny pain; her body responding, though her mind was absent. *Sorry, sorry, child.*

It was better this way—let Sissel sleep through it all, that would surely be less traumatizing. Fall asleep in her bed, and hopefully wake there again, surrounded by her loved ones. If Henry would just abdicate and be done with it.

Richard had been convinced that this would work, but so far, there had been a lot of sound and fury, but nothing significant had changed. Davies had made the first call with a voice modulator as disguise, demanding Henry's abdication in exchange for Sissel's return. Henry had only threatened dire consequences in response, and Davies had hung up before any of the intelligence and law enforcement agencies could trace the call.

Richard had said to let them sleep on it, or not sleep, as the case might be, and call again in the morning. Maybe it was time to stand up to him, to just bring Sissel back and end all this nonsense. Henry was a nightmare of a king, but would Richard truly be any better? If he were willing to stoop to this?

Yet if Alan brought Sissel back now, he'd have to explain everything. Once Henry knew Richard was behind the kidnapping—there would be blood and fury. Alan's mind raced in circles; the best path he could see out of this trap was for Henry to renounce the throne. That would solve everything.

Davies came up to join him, speaking softly. "I'll keep her safe, sir."

Alan sighed. "I know you will, Davies. Good man."

The pawns were moving on the board. Nothing to do but wait, and see which way the king would go.

◆

Badb found herself back in her own body, on the floor of the safe house. Sticky and weak. She was not alone.

"Oh god, Beth, the smell! Worse than Seizer's scabs."

"Watch it, Jamila! Don't let him hear you say that. He'll put his fingers right through your neck."

Badb kept her eyes shut, watching the two women through a crow at the window instead. The first one, Jamila, had ears in the shape of human hands that telegraphed her moods by making rude gestures or giving a thumbs up. Right now, they were clenched in horror, while one of her real hands was clamped hard over her mouth.

The younger one, Beth, encumbered as she was with a mop and a bucket, could only screw up her face against the stench of the goddess's rotting bandages.

"Let's just get it cleaned up quickly, can we, Jamila?" She didn't look much like a joker, but slim rods of metal and plastic rested against her limbs. "We can be back downstairs with a cup of tea in five minutes."

Jamila's "ears" crossed their fingers. She nodded, replacing Badb's water jug, while Beth began mopping up the blood.

"She looks dead," said Jamila.

"She's breathin', though."

"Should we get help?"

"Nah," said Beth. "Just do what Green Man says, innit? Like he never heard of woman's lib. Got boobs? Great! Mop the floors, love."

"You think Seizer will be any better?"

The mop paused. Beth's elegant head swung one way and then another, before she lowered her voice. "What you mean, 'will be'? You stagin' a coup, missis? Because I enjoy a bit of a laugh, but I'm loyal, ye hear me?"

"Nah, nah, this ain't about Green Man. It's Seizer. Ain't you heard? Seriously? He's the prince." The hands were suddenly very animated. Like Beth, Jamila kept her voice to a whisper, but it kept cracking as she spoke. "A joker prince and the rightful king. I found it written on a piece of paper outside my window this mornin'. There was a whole story. Spirited away as a baby, innit? 'Cos they couldn't stand for one of us to get his due. They think we'll just lie down and take it. But what use is us bein' Fists if we do that, eh? I've never shot no one myself yet, but I'd pop me own mum if she tried to stop us gettin' the little that's rightfully ours! I'd pop every fuckin' puppy in London, so I would!"

Jamila grinned, "What, even the fluffy ones?"

"None of your jokes, now. I mean it."

"And you really think . . . you think it's Seizer?"

"Well, he's got the voice, don't he? And he could be the right age."

"But if it's not him?"

Jamila's ears turned to fists, clenching so hard their knuckles were white. "Real or not. I'd take him over any nat. They just want us gone. Well, fuck 'em. Fuck 'em all. I'd die for that, Beth, and I'm not the only one."

A knock on the door made both of them jump. Green Man, always courteous, called, "Can I come in now? Is she decent?"

"Decent?" said Beth, staring at Badb on the floor.

The goddess needed every bit of her strength to lift herself up against the adhesive power of a thousand dried scabs that ripped all at once. The crunching, tearing sound of it made the other women flinch.

Badb didn't care. She knew why Green Man had come. She watched him more than anyone, after all.

She stood, hunched over, a horror of torn dressings and fresh wounds.

"Allow me a few minutes to change," she said.

♥

Noel paused in the doorway and studied the office. The massive desk and chair that had been able to withstand Flint's stone form had been replaced by a plain executive desk and swivel chair. The Lion was not a flamboyant man.

All that remained of Flint was a single framed photograph of him alongside the other two men who had led MI-7 since its founding: Lord Dalton Carruthers, who had replaced Flint after the Churchill assassination, and of course, Singh. Noel wondered if his picture would join them.

I may not be here long enough to have a snap taken, he thought. As if to give period to that thought, a crow perched on the windowsill gave a raucous cry.

"I'll just get my things," Ranjit said. "You'll have my resignation within the hour."

"And it won't be accepted," Noel snapped. "As much as you might want to fuck me by leaving save it until we've kept our promise to find that child, and we best do it quickly or we'll have all of Norway screaming for our blood. But first things first. We have to inform the agency, and you're going to stand at my side and look noble and faithful."

♣

Seizer was nearly shouting. "We must stand up for our people! We must fight for those who cannot!"

And he's waving his fist! He's actually waving his fist at me.

It took all of the self-control Green Man had not to take that fist and crush it in his own. How dare Seizer talk to him this way in front of the others?

But he already knew the answer to that question: *because Seizer's a prince and everybody knows it.*

Only a few hours ago they had stood together in solidarity, showing their best face to the world. He took a tiny bit of comfort in the fact that this meeting was secret, and not likely to feature in tomorrow's news cycle.

Green Man shook his head while Seizer's rant finally came to an end. He was just trying to decide if it was best to put Seizer's arguments down himself or to let someone else do it for him when he heard a most astonishing sound.

Someone was clapping.

A few people now, in fact. And Bethany, who had never liked Seizer, seemed to be nodding along like an idiot. *What is going on?* His dismay grew as he saw that the room was falling for Seizer's empty rhetoric. It was infuriating. *We must stand up for our people? What does he think we've been doing all these years? Picking flowers? And we've always fought for those who couldn't fight for themselves. That's the whole point of the Twisted Fists!*

And yet the Fists seemed to be lapping it up. Even Blue Jeans—who had once ended a long and tedious debate by calling Seizer the "clown prince of cunts"— was acting deferent.

Green Man held up his hands for silence. It took a little longer than usual to get it. "Seizer states the obvious. Of course we must stand up for our people. Of course we must fight for them. But these are delicate times that call for a careful approach."

"Sounds like bollocks to me!" shouted Peggy. The young knave had a slightly reptilian look. Shaggy hair fell down to her back, making her already thin face look even thinner. Peggy was handy in a fight, but her quick wits and quicker tongue were less desirable here. "When are we going to fucking kill something?"

Seizer displayed his other hand. It was covered in a bandage that ran from his palm to his elbow. "We have all been carrying out your delicate orders, and look where it has gotten us! Our headquarters were attacked and now I have been assaulted, only narrowly escaping with my life. What will it take to get you to act? My death? Is that what you're waiting for?"

"Don't be so dramatic," replied Green Man, but he could feel that he had lost the crowd. This was just the sort of chaotic situation he hated. He much preferred to plan for these things than react in the moment. *I never wanted to have to make the speeches,* he thought bitterly. *Just write them.*

"I demand an answer! Will you see me avenged for this vicious attempt on my life?"

"We're the Fists, Seizer. We avenge death. Nothing more, nothing less."

A nasty smile spread across his opponent's face, making his eyes vanish amid the wrinkles. "Then what about Dorothy McDonald? She died in front of you and yet you have done nothing."

"I—" began Green Man, but Seizer carried on in a louder voice.

It didn't matter, neither could be heard over the crowd's angry roar.

Who could have told Seizer about Dorothy's death aboard the Queen Mary? It didn't matter now. The news had broken in the worst possible way and he had to pull it back, quickly, before Seizer made a successful bid for power. He cursed himself for listening to Constance. Her ways were not his. He'd allowed himself to get soft and now his enemies were taking advantage.

Green Man held up his hands again and waited for quiet. "All of our people who have died will be avenged. This, I promise you."

"You sound like a politician," said Peggy, giving the most savage of all her insults.

"You know me," he said. "I take my time but, in the end, I always act. As it happens, I was already planning the strikes. I hadn't told you yet as I'm still choosing the appropriate targets. I want to be sure that we send the right message."

"Fine words," retorted Seizer. "But while you pontificate, more of our people die. It simply isn't good enough. We have to fight against what has been done to us and what is about to be done. For"—he raised his unbandaged fist a second time—"Henry's latest speech has cast us as Sissel's kidnappers. Though he is the one to lie, we will be the ones to suffer! And so I say again, and will keep on saying: it is time for us to act! Not delicately. But with righteous force. Not at some vague point in the future. But now!"

The room erupted.

It was like being in the playground again, where volume trumped reason. Once more, he felt himself being swept up in the tides of inevitability. This was it. The moment he committed them to a path he would not see the end of.

"You know what this means?" asked Green Man, his voice soft, and the room settled to meet his quiet. "It means multiple strikes of a nature not seen in decades. It means risk. It means that some of you will not come back. I intend to do everything in my power to minimize that risk because I believe we have already lost enough." He sighed. "Now, I suggest you all get some rest, and spend time with your loved ones while you can. When I give the order, there will be four teams going out at once. That means very few of you will be staying here."

Suddenly, with the exception of Peggy, the urge to fight seemed to leach from them.

"We all stand ready for action," said Seizer, desperate to have the last word. Green Man didn't fight him for it, watching sadly as the old knave swept out of the room, drawing the others in his wake.

He's drawn blood now, and he must feel the change in our fortunes as much as I do. The challenge will come soon.

Green Man sighed again. It seemed like all he did was look at the world around him and sigh these days. He'd played this round badly, and would need to do something impressive if he was to avoid losing the Fists altogether.

As he was brooding on this, the last of the room emptied, revealing a bandaged figure slumped in a corner.

"Finder?" he said, rushing forward.

But the old woman was dreadfully still.

"Finder? Are you alright?"

He knelt alongside her, but when he began to prop her up, she moved in a way that was all wrong, and to his horror, he heard something rattle free inside her skull.

♠

Badb came back to herself, blinking. She was on the floor. How much time had she missed? She really was too old for this. Worse. She had missed the last part of the meeting. Everybody was gone except for Green Man.

"Finder? Finder? Are you all right?"

The pain from the ribs she had damaged a few days earlier was incredible. It took a superhuman effort to ignore it and push herself upright, although the room and the great wooden figure in front of her tilted and spun in her vision.

Green Man had one enormous hand behind her head. The other he presented palm-first. She tried to focus on what he held there, failed, and had to look through the eyes of a crow on the window outside instead. From that distance it took her a moment to realize what she was seeing.

Her own teeth. Never before had she grown so old that they fell out. Not even the time she had killed Billy Little and regenerated from his heroic death.

"I'm sorry," he said. "I can arrange a dentist for you. Or . . . or a doctor?"

"No doctor. I need to get some air. That will be sufficient."

"Please stay inside, Finder. These rumors . . . about jokers kidnapping the princess. We could be on the edge of a pogrom. I was wondering . . . Do you think *you* might find her?"

Badb tried to clear her head. It was always easy to turn nat and joker against each other. But she wanted more. She wanted the real prize of a proper civil war. She pictured tanks in the streets; entire cities burning and every week a toll of death higher than the entire history of Northern Ireland put together. Let every home produce a martyr! Then, she, the goddess, could regenerate as often as she liked. Young and joyful forever.

"The princess will be found," she said. "I have seen it. Very soon. But not by us."

She left him. Already she knew where the girl was. Henry's side must be the ones to find her. Richard might have no choice then but to make a bid for power.

On her slow, slow walk from the building, a hand tapped her on the shoulder.

"My king," she whispered, without turning around. How strange to speak with no teeth! And strange too that of all her body, only her bare gums failed to bleed. Fascinating.

"What did that rascal want? Green Man?"

"He wants you, my lord. He's the one who tried to have you killed. He'll try again. Soon."

He gasped, his hand falling away and Badb, mighty goddess that she was, staggered outside and into the wind.

◆

They had all gathered in the canteen. It was likely to be a fraught meeting, so Noel thought perhaps a nibble and a cuppa would help keep things civil, which was why he had picked that location. Noel strode to the front of the room with the Lion trailing after him. He nodded to one of the office pool girls and mouthed *tea*. She hurried to comply. Only then did he scan the assembled crowd.

There were a few familiar faces—Rory Campbell, Jiniri, Robin Shawcross, and one glaring absence—*where was Turing?* Also several new recruits. Noel had pulled their files before coming downstairs. A new Redcoat, Jason McCracken, had been recruited since Noel had left, and he fit the preferred model for that title. He was tall, handsome, and square-jawed, and Noel suddenly felt very old because McCracken looked to be no more than twenty.

Kerenza Tremaine was also very young and intense, and preferred to be called Stonemaiden. It was an affectation that Noel could not understand. He hated being called Double Helix, the nom de guerre he had been saddled with by Flint and Turing in one of their more waggish moments. It drew attention to the thing that made him a freak—not the wild card but rather the fact he was intersexed. No one in the room was looking particularly happy, but Stonemaiden was also looking at him with pure hatred in her eyes. Given her deadly power, Noel decided to never turn his back on this one.

Noel waited until most had secured a cup and a plate then said, "Yes, it's a balls-up, no one knows that as acutely as me, but it's where we are and there's a ten-year-old who's terrified and alone and it's our job to find her. So do put aside your loathing for me until we get the job done. Agreed?"

There were a few nods from some of the old-timers. The rest remained silent but didn't demur. All except Kerenza. She raked the room with a hot look and, jumping to her feet, said, "He betrayed you all. He put the Captain in prison! And you're just going to let him waltz in and do this?"

Ranjit cleared his throat and stepped forward. "No one has more cause to be resentful then I, Kerry, but whatever else he might be I have always known Matthews to be a patriot and a professional. As director he has my full support." She subsided back into her chair, but did not seem mollified.

Noel took back the reins. "Very well, if there are no more complaints let's get to it. The Met is no doubt reviewing the security feed." Noel nodded toward the tech boys. "Get in touch. Jiniri, the immigrant community has more than enough reason to resent the king. See what you can find out. And where the hell is Turing?" Blank looks and shrugs slithered through the room. "Well, get to it."

As they dispersed several of the agents and support staff came up to offer their congratulations and promises of support. Perhaps this wasn't going to be a complete cock up.

Monday

MARCH 9TH

ALL OVER THE EAST End, joker families woke to the sounds of, "Police! Open up!" And before any opening up could occur; before there was even time for a father and mother to exchange glances, to tell the children that everything would be OK; the doors slammed inwards, raining splinters. Armored figures, faces masked and inhuman, all hard surfaces and loud voices screamed, "ON THE FLOOR, ON THE FLOOR!"

The Police had been warned to expect resistance in their search for the princess, and while none came—the raided families were perfectly innocent—mistakes were made. Grenades dropped out of the sky. Firecrackers fell through open windows on the tenth floor that none but a crow could have reached, and when they went off, the police reacted.

The results were most satisfactory.

Badb watched a joker toddler die under panicked gunshots. She saw an asthmatic grandfather choke on tear gas. A girl with purple skin fell from a balcony while horrified neighbors looked on.

"They're exterminating us!" cried a man on the street from his three different heads. "I always knew this day would come!"

"Only the Fists can protect us now."

"We'll go down fighting! Fucking nats! Five for one, five for one!"

♥

Badb walked into the dawn. And farther.

It was starting to rain, the drops frigid on her skeletal frame. Each one that found its way between the weave of her bandages set off a painful round of shivers and would have had her teeth chattering if any remained in her head.

Her time was short, and still so much work lay before her. Here and there, as she soared above the city, cleanup crews were hoisting burned-out cars from the streets. Bulldozers allowed life to return to normal by shoving barriers aside, and even joker children were going back to school.

All of London breathed a sigh of relief, failing to recognize the false, brief recovery that sometimes came on the sick mere hours before death.

If the goddess of war could get the supporters of the two princes into a more open conflict, why, the barricades would be permanent, and all this rain would be replaced by blood that would fill every gutter and make its way deep into the soil.

Along the street, ordinary Londoners veered away from her. A woman clutched her child protectively. An old priest blessed himself. A busker under an awning stopped playing right in the middle of "Five Years." None of them were in the game. None knew who she was or what she was, or even realized that the building behind them was the headquarters of the Silver Helix.

She ignored them, her rickety walk taking her right up to a well-dressed man on his way out of the anonymous double doors. "Your housekey," she rasped.

He looked up, astonished. He winced, as he tried to move his right arm before remembering it was injured. Then, as the smell of her rotting body reached him, his nose twitched.

"You left it on the nightstand," she said. "It is still there."

"Who the hell are you?" he asked. He was used to answers and fine tailoring. But it hadn't always been so. Badb could read such things. She saw duty in him too, or rather, she sensed it. It was the very quality that fed her after it had matured into heroism. Perhaps she would consume this man too. But not yet.

"The brandy," she said, "was taken by your son. It made him sick. He refilled the bottle with cold tea."

The man's face contorted. He wanted to strike her, but was either too decent or too controlled to give in to the urge. Interesting.

"And congratulations on your appointment," she added. "The king has chosen well. God bless him. How happy he will be when you save his granddaughter."

He froze, and then, rather admirably, regained complete control over his face. He looked up and down the street.

"My name is Finder," she said. Her legs wobbled beneath her and she had to lock them to prevent a complete collapse. "I find things. And people too. I saw the girl in a vision."

He stared, waiting. "She is in the countryside, guarded by soldiers. A bunker beneath a pretend Greek temple. Very large. Full of old machines from the War." He didn't ask her which war, of course. For the English there was only ever one. She would teach them otherwise.

Badb closed her eyes as though she could still see the building, although, in fact, it was his face that she was watching through a nearby crow.

"Machines for what?" he asked.

"Code-breaking, sir. Do you know anybody in this field? I doubt there's any still alive who worked in it."

His face twisted; he couldn't help it. He'd be thinking about Turing, of course.

Most satisfactory. How would Henry react when he learned that the kidnapper was his own brother? And what of his supporters?

Noel turned to leave, more agitated than she had seen him yet. She opened her eyes. "You are familiar with this place?" she asked. "Take me with you, sir! I could be useful, I—"

"Enough! Thank you, but enough. You'll get your reward if this turns out to be true." She hadn't asked for a reward, but with that, he sprinted away and off around the corner. Then, he skidded to a halt, leaning against a wall beneath her nearest bird and awkwardly working his phone with one hand.

"Turing!" he growled. "Where the fuck is he?" And then. "You tell him he's staying put. I'll be there in five minutes." He walked into a café from which she never saw him emerge. And yet, moments later, the same man was confronting Turing on the far side of London.

Fascinating.

♣

The door to Alan's study slammed open and Noel stormed in.

"Shut the door, Noel." Turing glanced out the window—yes, Sebastian was safely in the conservatory, his shadowed figure visible through the double layers of glass, bent over his transplanting. But still, there were security protocols to follow.

"Turing, you fucker."

Ah. It was going to be that kind of conversation. Alan walked over and quietly closed the door himself. "Is there a problem, my dear boy?"

"Don't even think of calling me that. Not with what you've done."

"And what do you think I've done?" *Did he really know?*

"I know you're behind it. That you've stolen that child—" Noel was practically choking in his rage.

Alan could deny it, of course. Noel couldn't have any proof. But maybe—maybe this was the right path forward. For days, Alan had felt as if he were stumbling through a dark wood, but now, there was a smooth road ahead of him, well-lighted, begging for a run. All he had to do was tell the truth, and then events would unfold as they must.

He was curious, though. "How did you know?"

"That doesn't matter. You admit it then? You kidnapped Gloriana's kid?"

"She's perfectly safe, I promise you. We can just go get her, bring her back. You and I, together." Alan stood up straighter; he felt as if he might grow wings.

Noel snapped, "But why, Turing? Tell me that, before I rip it out of you."

Alan spread out his hands in supplication. Noel would understand, surely. "You don't need to rip anything. It was Richard; he was going to act no matter what I said. I had to try to contain the damage."

Noel snarled. "Oh—I should have seen it. Oh, goddammit, you know what this means?"

"What?" Why was Noel so furious?

"I can't bring in any other aces on this. No one else can know, or even guess, that Richard was involved. If they know that you had anything to do with it, they'd trace that line straight back to Richard."

Alan frowned. "Why? I work for the Silver Helix, after all."

"Oh, Alan, you cunt. Everyone knows you've been fucking Richard. Did you really think you could keep that a secret?"

Well, apparently Alan had miscalculated. Of course, *everyone* didn't mean

Sebastian—Noel meant everyone in the Silver Helix, surely. Perhaps Alan and Richard hadn't been quite discreet enough at work. It was a good thing that was all over.

Alan flushed. "Ah. Well, then yes, we probably shouldn't bring in the others. But it'll be all right—I can call off my men . . ."

"Call them off? We can't leave them alive, you idiot."

Alan's heart sped up. "What? You can't kill them! They're just following orders—three of them don't even know what they're guarding."

Noel spoke slowly, as if to an idiot. "If they reveal that you're behind this, that leads to Richard, and then the whole fucking country's in flames, isn't it? That's the nightmare you'd be consigning us to. So I'm going to have to kill all of them, to be sure they keep their mouths shut, and that's your damn fault too. Thanks for that!"

Dammit, dammit, dammit. Noel was right, was right about all of it. Alan's head felt as if it were going to explode. How had he miscalculated so badly? Davies had served him faithfully, and he didn't even know the names of the other men.

"I see," Alan said, his voice gone weak and hollow. "I guess it's up to us then."

Noel snapped, "Let's go. Now!"

♠

It was another mobile phone, lying in among the bags of woodchips as though it had dropped out of the sky. Sebastian pretended not to see it. He knew by now that if he so much as looked at it, it would ring and one of a number of voices on the other end would tell him things. Awful, awful things.

Or it might just be a recording, like the time he'd been treated to the sound of his own husband, gasping that way he had the first time Sebastian had taken him in his mouth. And then, the unmistakable breathless voice of the prince. "You don't get that at home, I'll wager!"

"You would," Sebastian whispered. "You could." But it was more anger than self-pity that ground his teeth together.

"I hate him," he whispered. Nobody heard him but for a nearby crow. Who else could he talk to about the issue that stole his sleep?

Then, the phone rang and he jumped, dropping the tray of cuttings, spraying compost over the plastic bags of wood chippings.

It kept ringing and ringing. As always, he tried to resist its lure, its promise of nothing but more pain. As always, his hand, of its own accord brought it to his ear.

This time, the voice on the other end was old enough that it might have belonged to death herself. "Richard," it said. "Likes tea. The fancier the better. Considers himself a connoisseur."

"How . . . ?" Sebastian swallowed. The voice sent a shiver throughout his whole body. He wasn't sure he could bear to finish his question and have her respond to him.

The woman, that ancient woman, spoke anyway.

"He's not just a vigorous lover. He's a prince too. People give him gifts all the time. You . . . could give him one."

Sebastian swallowed. Terrified.

"What . . . what do you mean?" But he already knew, and she was gone anyway.

♦

Badb leaned against the ivy-covered wall and waited for Turing's Jaguar to screech to a halt right in front of her. She had been watching through the eyes of a crow in London, even as her own body was on its way here, bouncing around in the back of a van while the driver cursed in Serbian.

Noel and Turing had climbed into the car. Why only the two of them? Badb had hoped that with a princess at risk, the full might of the Silver Helix would descend on the kidnappers. Bullets would fly, and in the chaos, royal blood might be shed and who knew how many precious aces would lie staring at the sky when all was done?

Nor was that the only puzzle. Because although Badb had watched Noel get into the car in London and had flown behind it all the way, when it arrived here in Oxfordshire, it was a stranger who sat in the passenger seat: a young man over six foot tall with the face of a magnificent warrior, perfectly, mathematically symmetrical.

His piercing eyes fixed her. They were the color of burnished gold.

"You!" he said, as if he knew her. And of course, he did. The newcomer's arm was in a cast, just as Noel's had been. His mannerisms were identical and he bore the same tiny scar above the left eyebrow. Noel was an ace, after all. He must be able to alter his shape, to become this perfect specimen of youth.

Fascinating.

"What . . ." Turing began. "I mean, *who* is this?"

She could see herself through a bird's eyes. Layer upon layer of sticky bandages, oozing gently beneath a face of wrinkles and sagging, flapping skin. Turing was getting the smell now too. He was edging away from her, probably not even aware he was doing so. "I am Finder," she told him. "I found the princess. I will be of great use inside. I can take you to her." She stared at Turing with her own body's eyes, seeing the strain in his every movement. "*If* you want her to be found."

"Of *course*, he does," drawled Noel. He was checking various pockets for weapons, but he never took his eyes off her. "It appears we can't stop you following. But this is a question of national security, now. We will not coddle you."

Badb inclined her head. She barely had the strength to raise it again.

He turned his attention to Turing. "I take it you are familiar with the layout?" She recognized the sarcasm. "Then, lead the way."

♥

The mud squelched beneath his shoes as Noel moved forward toward the Grecian pavilion. It was a ridiculous affectation on the grounds of the old estate.

How typical that Turing would have picked a place where he had worked during the War. All these old men still trying to live in the past, from Henry to Flint to Turing, *And fucking it up for the rest of us*, Noel thought. The cast was cutting painfully into his avatar's more muscular arm.

Around him snowdrops covered the ground, their blossoms drooping like white bells. He took cover in the shadow of a large Scots pine and studied the situation. The folly had seen better days. Dark stains marred the white marble, and the steps leading up to the interior were cracked. One guard stood in the center of the pavilion, rifle cradled in his arms. The other was outside walking a slow circuit around the structure. Noel had not anticipated the men being in such close proximity to each other. It would make things harder. He noted the wires running from earpieces and the throat mics, and rejected using the garrote. Noel pulled the pistol from his shoulder holster and screwed on a silencer. Despite what one saw in the movies, silencers weren't all that quiet. Still, it would be quieter than the sound of a man being choked to death.

Sucking in a quick breath, Noel teleported behind the man in the pavilion and shot him in the back of the head. Another quick jump to the second guard. Unfortunately, he was turning in reaction to the *pop* of displaced air and the muffled gunshot. Noel's first shot sheared away his lower jaw. It took a second one to the temple to finish him. He then teleported back to where Turing and the old woman waited.

"Okay, the way is clear. Now we go in the front door. You said there's one guard at the base of the stairs?" Noel asked.

Turing gave a jerking head nod. "Yes."

"Presumably he knows you?" Another tense nod. "Good. Then toddle on down there and kill him."

♣

Noel pounded down the stairs at the sound of a gunshot, a yell of pain, and running footsteps. Clearly the plan had not survived contact with the enemy.

"Damn bird wrecked my aim." Turing panted. Noel put it down to more nerves than exertion. Whatever the cause they were royally buggered now.

"What's it like further in?" Noel asked.

"Cluttered . . . To put it mildly."

"Well, let's go play hunt and seek." He turned to tell the old Irish woman to stay back, only to find her gone. *Well, bugger all, she was on her own. If she got hurt that was her lookout.*

♠

Badb allowed the men to get ahead of her, disappearing into the chaos of cabinets and old equipment. There was a quicker way to the back of the bunker if you were skeletally thin and careless of damage to your body. The goddess eased herself to the damp floor. The builders had put pipes between the rooms, for wiring perhaps, or sewage. Only rats lived here now in the perfect darkness.

They fled as she slithered her way through, her rasping breath echoing ahead of her.

But halfway along, with the pipe sloping downwards, a hidden hook of rusted metal stabbed through the soft flesh of her shoulder and pinned her there, too weak to lift herself free.

She called for a crow.

The metal wouldn't give under its beak, leaving her no choice but to have the creature worry at the flesh around it until, all of a sudden, gravity tore her free and sent her slithering down to the end.

Most satisfactory.

She sent the crow on ahead. Yes. This was the place. A stench of dust and damp. Three rooms away, bunk beds rusted amid piles of tea chests, rolls of wire, headsets, and bizarre-looking typewriters. That's where the last guard waited, alone but for the princess.

The girl was asleep. And no wonder! Her hulking captor was only now putting down a bottle of chloroform. He began throwing feminine clothing into a bag. No doubt, he was planning to get her out of here before the shooting got any closer.

The goddess moved toward him with perfect concentration, never once stepping on broken glass or giving in to the many weaknesses of her body. She wouldn't be able to keep this up for long. The trip through the pipe had exhausted her. And indeed, by the time she stood at his back, she had barely enough energy to slide a knife between the vertebrae on his lower spine.

He flopped to the ground, a monstrous whining fish. But still dangerous. He might cry out at any moment. Those arms of his could crush her, and she was not sure that if she bent over to finish him off, she would ever be able to rise again.

How inconvenient.

◆

Drawing his gun, Noel moved through the bunker. The lighting was dim. Many of the ceiling sockets gaping like blinded eyes. The stacked desks, chairs, old-style computers, boxes spilling papers, and rusting filing cabinets were shadows in the gloom. There were pathways between the mess like a hamster's Habitrail.

Noel had a sudden flash of Jasper's face when he'd brought the creature home to the Manhattan apartment. Jasper had named him Jetboy, except Jetboy had turned out to be Jetgirl and bestowed upon them three babies, so Jetboy had become Bubbles. The ache in Noel's chest was no longer due just to his cracked ribs.

And then it hit him . . . *Bugger all, the court hearing!* He'd forgotten completely. Forgotten to tell Judith and have her ask for a continuance. This could kill his chances.

On the other hand, distraction would most certainly kill him. He shook off the memories and the worry—he had to hope that his service to Henry would smooth out the problem. Noel motioned to Turing to go right while he went left.

In this environment his ace power was virtually useless. He would move a few steps then hold his breath and listen. Eventually he was rewarded with the soft ring of metal against metal. Apparently one of the guard's keys were clipped to his belt. It marked him as either a rookie, or a man too confident in his own skills. *Which could be said of you,* Noel warned himself.

He needed to draw the man to him, but first he had to find a spot where he could arrange an ambush. A few more turns and he spotted some stacked furniture that culminated in a large metal table. Reaching up, he gave the leg an experimental shake. It seemed solid. He then nudged another desk loaded with old computer tape. The rolls slithered to the floor with a sighing hiss. A few seconds later, he heard slow footfalls.

A blink of his power and he stood on top of the table. It shifted a bit under his weight, and there was a short rasp of metal on metal. A few seconds later, the guard came around the corner of some stacked boxes. Noel froze, held his breath. The man crept past him. Noel leaned down and shot him in the top of the head, then gave an involuntary yell of alarm as the body fell against the stack of furniture, sending his perch toppling. He teleported to an open area, but when he reappeared, several boxes had decided to occupy the same space. He lost his footing and fell hard onto his back, losing his grip on his pistol.

The final guard came into view. Time seemed to dilate. Noel watched the knuckle on the man's trigger finger whiten as he began to squeeze. He pictured his flat but before he could teleport, the man's face exploded into gore and bits of bone.

Noel cranked his head around toward Turing. "Nice shot."

"You're welcome."

♥

In the end, she opened the bottle of chloroform and knocked it on its side so that its contents poured down over the guard's face. He swallowed twice before realizing the danger, but already it was too late. Then, holding her breath, she hobbled to the bunk where the princess slept.

A quick slice of the throat, Badb thought. That would do it. Then, she would drop the knife beside the guard's right hand. Henry would be enraged . . . She sat on the thin mattress, her old hands shaking with the effort. She paused.

Perhaps she had a better idea.

Surely, the kidnapping was already extreme enough to bring the princes into conflict. But the goddess wanted to build for the future too—a war that would never end. So, instead of the throat, she plunged her knife into the girl's cheek, twisting it to make as cruel-looking a scar as possible.

Yes, yes, most satisfactory. Never again could this girl appear in public without reminding Henry's supporters of the need for revenge.

She would make sure the king found out. And the people too. Using her phone, she snapped a photo, just as she heard two shots from just around the corner. The would-be rescuers were already here.

"Help!" cried Badb. Hurriedly, she dropped the knife down beside the guard. "Help us!" She put as much panic into her voice as she could. "I think . . . I think he killed her!"

♣

Noel staggered a bit as he landed on the soft turf of Green Park. Carrying three people, even for the few seconds it took for him to translate through space, had left his arm and ribs grinding with pain. And they had barely beaten the setting sun.

He released Turing and Finder. The stink of corrupting flesh off the old woman had him fighting down nausea. Turing had made a makeshift bandage of his handkerchief, securing it against the deep cut on Sissel's cheek with his tie. It was soaked through with her blood. Just like the bandages that covered Finder's hands and throat. Noel's leather jacket was streaked with both sets of gore.

No time to clean it off. He had to get the child into the hands of the palace physician and the arms of her mother. He took the little girl out of Turing's arms, leaned in close, and hissed, "You don't get to play the hero after orchestrating this entire damn mess."

"That's fair," the old man said softly. "But I see you're not above playing it yourself. Must be an odd role for you." Spite coiled around the final words. Noel resisted the impulse to punch that metallic face. Sweat had streaked Turing's makeup.

Noel paused briefly to look down at Finder. The old woman had collapsed onto the grass. The first time teleporting was always disorienting.

"Thank you for your help. I'd like to know more about your *visions*, but it can keep."

Bones shifted, and his clothing sagged as Simon vanished with the setting sun. Noel crossed Constitution Hill, located a gate and a guard, and was rushed inside.

A torrent of people surrounded him. Gloriana snatched her daughter from his arms. She was crying but her face held the cold and ancient rage of an Erinys. Noel reflected that the men who had guarded the girl should be glad they had died so gently.

Faintness washed over him, and Noel leaned against a wall. A hand clasped his shoulder. It was the king. "Well done. Knew you were the man for the job. Once Sissel is cared for, we'll be leaving for Windsor. I'll be in touch."

"Yes, sir."

♠

How had everything gone so wrong? Alan Turing wasn't a man who cried. He was physically capable of tears, but had left them behind in childhood, along with schoolyard taunts of *faggot!* He'd learned to keep his emotions inside, where they belonged. But now tears stood in his eyes. He angrily dashed them away once Noel had deposited him in Green Park and taken Sissel to the Palace.

Alan sent the prince a curt message: *Meet me.* Grabbed a car and took the roads too fast. He arrived at the flat to find Richard already there, looking mussed. Alan wouldn't be surprised to learn that Richard had been in the midst of an assignation when he'd received Alan's text—it might, perhaps, have stung on some other day, that Richard would bring someone else to the apartment Alan had arranged for them. None of that mattered now.

"Alan!"

"Richard." The formal name, putting Richard on notice.

Richard said, "I've gotten word from the palace doctor. Sissel will be fine, though it will take some time for her recovery, of course."

Alan replied angrily, "Fine? We've terrorized the child. Do you understand what she has just experienced? Her life was in grave danger. Sissel could have easily died in that chaos . . ."

The prince frowned. "You're exaggerating—she slept through the whole thing. And the mess that this operation turned into is your fault, not mine!" Richard's voice grew louder, "*You* said that we could trust these men!" He took a breath, visibly calming himself. "In the end, Alan, the important thing is that you kept Sissel safe."

Alan sputtered, "Me? What do you think I did? How is *thinking very fast* supposed to compete with guns and teleportation—oh, never mind. That's not the point."

The prince tilted his head, raising a shaggy golden eyebrow. "What *is* your point, then?" Richard asked.

Alan snapped, "I should never have gone along with this absurd plan. And now the country is being ripped apart, jokers assaulted across London! The police adding to the chaos and hatred!" Exactly what Alan had hoped to prevent, now created by his own hand. The misery of it made his gut churn; he had to force back the urge to vomit. "We have to come forward, admit that we were behind it." He was pacing circles in the small room, like a trapped beast in its cage.

"Are you mad?" Richard said, his eyes gone wide. "What do you think it would do, if a prince of England admitted to kidnapping a royal child? You think you're seeing chaos now—we'd have civil war, blood running in the streets!"

Outside the flat's open windows, great swoops of black birds filled the sky. If only Alan could fling himself out the window and join them, fly far, far away from all of this. "I'll do it myself, then. We can't let the violence against jokers continue, Richard!"

It had been Alan's mistake, all of it, and now good men were dead because of his foolishness. He'd let his dick lead him around. That, and some confused notion that Richard would be a better king than Henry—that wasn't Alan Turing's job to decide, was it? He should never have let Richard talk him into this. "I'll tell them it was all me. I'll keep you out of it completely, I swear." Sebastian would never understand, but Sebastian would be better off without him.

Richard said, "I forbid it."

Alan's head snapped up. "What?"

Richard stepped closer, took Alan's chin in his. "I forbid it. I need you—England needs you. Working in Silver Helix, doing your damned job. With Noel in charge, clearly working for my brother, gods know what's coming next. You have to keep your head down, your eyes open, figure out what they're planning."

"But—" He'd been so clear, so sure that he finally knew the right thing to do.

"Alan." Richard's voice had gone low, caressing. "You are the only person who can protect England right now. Are you really willing to take your piece off the board?"

Alan's heart seemed to slow to a crawl. The clock on the mantel ticked, but each beat took an infinity. A million futures spun out in front of him—too many to calculate. The wrong push on the pendulum could shatter the clock, send fragments flying everywhere.

"Alan? What are you going to do?"

He pulled his chin out of Richard's hand, stepped back, trying to get enough distance from the prince that he could *think*. "I don't know."

◆

The image was everywhere before the authorities had time to ban it. In the papers. On social media. On TV screens in darkened pubs where normally only sports were shown. It was a single photograph, but there was no hiding it, no hiding it at all. The stolen princess had been found. The girl whose absence had inspired police raids and massive, nightlong vigils all across the nation, and in Norway too, lay bleeding on a cot somewhere.

The poor thing looked terrible. And worse. So much worse. The scum who took her—everybody knew it was the jokers, everybody! Except for those who knew it was Prince Richard or the king or the foreigners . . . Well, the monsters had ripped a jagged cut right across her cheek. In the photo, half the child's face was literally hanging off.

The time for vigils was over. Only blood would pay for this now.

Tuesday

MARCH 10TH

ALAN HAD FIVE SCREENS set up in his library now. Three of them monitored various local news channels, with the fourth bringing in a feed from overseas. Sometimes one could be too close to see the problem clearly; ugliness could grow under one's very nose. All of those screens showed growing violence against jokers—again and again, they cut to anti-joker graffiti, the destruction of property, physical attacks. Blood on the screen. The last screen was feeding him data—a host of financial information. Richard had convinced him to hold off on confessing to the public about Sissel's kidnapping—but only while Alan gathered more information. He needed data. He couldn't think clearly without it.

"More tea, Alan?" Sebastian hovered in the doorway to the library, a mug at the ready.

Alan barely glanced him before turning back to the screens. "Sebastian, *please*. I asked you to leave me alone this morning."

"Sorry, sorry." The door slammed shut behind him, and Alan felt a twinge of regret. Though Alan had pledged to be a better husband, it was hard to keep that in the forefront of his mind when there were such urgent matters afoot. He'd raked up the damned leaf mold, hadn't he? And he'd stopped having sex with Richard. Not that Sebastian knew that.

What if Adelbert weren't the true heir? It would mean he'd sent Noel to kill a man for nothing. He'd ordered the kill with the best of intentions, for the national defense. Yet guilt stabbed through Alan. Could that have been another terrible mistake? Maybe there was something wrong with him—computers did break down eventually, after all. Maybe Alan Turing had become obsolescent.

Alan had to talk to Noel; he needed absolute proof that Adelbert was Elizabeth's son. The press would demand proof, and the government would too—anyone he brought forward would have to be able to withstand a firestorm. Even with his own metal skin, Alan wasn't sure he'd make it through what was coming un-singed. But he couldn't worry about that now—whatever the consequences, he had to make amends for all his past mistakes.

Alan hurried out of the room, headed into the kitchen. The tea was still sitting on the counter, his mug still warm—he gulped it down. The great English restorative, and he needed its power now; Alan couldn't remember a time when he'd felt more shaken, not even that time he'd been assaulted in the park, beaten bloody by a group of men who thought his activities somehow impugned their manhood. Nineteen fifty-eight? Sixty-three? He couldn't remember, and that was almost more frightening than anything else.

Sebastian opened the back door and stepped into the kitchen, letting in a gust of cold air. Forever in that conservatory; the man practically lived out there.

"Ah, Sebastian." Alan managed a forced smile. "I'm sorry I snapped at you earlier. Is this the new blend? It's wonderful. I'll take some in to Richard, shall I?" Maybe he could start mending things here. Start at home, and the rest would follow.

His husband smiled. "Yes, that'd be lovely." He reached out to the counter, collected a paper bag, and handed it to Alan. "Here's a batch, all made up. I've been waiting for the right moment."

"I'm sure he'll appreciate it." Alan leaned forward to give Sebastian a quick peck on the cheek—but his husband turned at the last minute, so that lips met lips, and the kiss turned more intense, more passionate, than any they'd shared in quite some time. Ah yes—Alan had been on the right path before, choosing to invest in what he had once held so dear. This much was clear, at least.

He broke off the kiss reluctantly. "I'd best be off," Alan said. He hesitated, then said, "I know things have been busy, but I'll be able to fill you in on everything soon. We just need to get past this current crisis." His husband would understand, surely.

"I understand," Sebastian said. "Goodbye, dear." He reached up and touched a few fingers to Alan's cheek, fondly, and then went back out through the kitchen door. For a moment, Alan wanted nothing more than to chuck it all in and join Sebastian in the conservatory, amidst the tropical plants and flowers. Their own little romantic holiday.

He was just tired. No time for that now; when all this was done, he'd take Sebastian on a proper holiday—to Greece perhaps, or maybe even Sri Lanka. They'd always planned to visit there someday.

Right now, Alan had to talk to Noel.

♥

Edwards was new to him. It was just past eight, and they were meeting at MI-5's headquarters. Noel had Singh with him, since the Lion knew the woman and could advise him. As they entered, she was saying, "The Fists are going to respond. They won't have a choice."

"Goddam the Met," said a man from MI-6.

"Why are you blaming the Met? It's the goddam jokers who kidnapped the princess," snapped a man from military intelligence.

Noel cleared his throat. "Pardon me, but we have information that indicates it was *not* the knaves."

"Then who the hell was it?" Sarah Edwards demanded.

"We're running that down," Noel said. *Finding a convenient scapegoat.* He moved to the coffee tureen and poured himself a cup. His phone vibrated and he took a surreptitious look. It was Turing. *Need to meet.*

Noel texted back *Damn it, Turing. In charge now. Not your dog to fetch and carry. Also Busy.*

It's important, please

At the peacock statue. Noon. Noel slipped his phone back into his pocket just as a man with the bearing of a former military officer came up next to him.

"To be fair to the Met, they claim some of what happened was not due to their actions. Firecrackers and whatnot, and a damn grenade. Bet that was the IRA," said the man as he topped off his coffee with a large dollop of cream and returned to the table.

"That's similar to what the army reported," said a man who had the demeanor of a bank clerk.

"I'm telling you they have a bloody ace," gritted a man in uniform with a grotesque scar beneath his nose. "We need to go in there and—"

"We need to do nothing," Noel snapped. "I've had word from the home secretary that she has an intermediary between herself and the Fists. There will be no retaliation."

"Who is this *intermediary?*" Edwards demanded.

Noel gave her a limpid look. "I'll show you mine if you'll show me yours—"

"Bloody aces," muttered the Scar.

Noel continued. "But allow me to assure you she's someone we can trust. And they will tell me if the situation is about to change."

The meeting dragged on for another twenty minutes. Noel could sense Singh's impatience and curiosity as they stepped out of the building. Overhead, a murder of crows arrowed into a smaller quarrel of sparrows who blew apart like the fragments of a grenade.

"So, who is this go-between?" the Lion asked.

"Constance."

"How the hell . . . ? Green Man . . . ? How the hell?" he repeated.

Noel shrugged. "It's Constance."

♣

Rain and wind rattled the windows of the warehouse. Joker guards on the roof shivered and dripped, holding onto their hats instead of watching the street. But no attack was coming. Badb knew that much, and knew too that the Twisted Fists had far more to fear from the inside: spies and informers; selfishness and ignorance; and above all these others, ambition.

She flicked her attention back inside where Seizer held the floor, daring to wave his fist at Green Man. In the past, his impertinence might have spread anger. His upper-class vowels would make lips curl and fists clench. But now, at the back of the crowd, a woman wearing an exoskeleton gazed at him adoringly. Others bowed heads, and Blue Jeans, a notorious heckler, kept his mouth zipped shut—literally. His metal rivet eyes he cast down in what could only be respect.

Seizer may have been a fool, but his voice was resonant. "We must stand up for our people! We must fight for those who cannot!" Minute by minute, he grew in confidence.

Badb allowed her body to sag against the back wall. She had work to do.

She flicked to a classroom where Loyalist fugitives from Belfast unpacked a crate of guns for their amateur but enthusiastic brethren in Britain First. "See here, lads," a balaclava muffled the speaker's voice. "These here will clear them jokers right out of the city. They declared war on our king when they took his daughter from us."

"How'd we know it was the freaks?" asked one of the more thoughtful thugs.

"Oh," blue eyes glinted through holes in the wool. "I have evidence to show yez." And he had too. Badb herself had commissioned it. Hackers working out of Macedonia were flooding the internet with videos of twisted creatures manhandling the figure of a young girl. It didn't matter that her hair was the wrong color; that she was too tall. People would believe anything about jokers, so long as it was bad.

Out on the rainy streets, two men pissing in an alleyway shared their disgust in the hearing of a crow. "An ordinary bloke spends his life pretendin' not to be disgusted. He even works next to the monstrous fuckers and then, they go doin' a thing like this? To our princess? Throwin' all our tolerance back in our face."

"Send 'em to the moon," said his companion, shaking himself off. "Where we don't have to look at 'em."

♠

Noon. Which gave Alan three hours to kill, and he had spent them walking. The Buckingham Palace gardens were perfect for walking, even in the steady rain that had begun to fall mid-morning. The rain was, in fact, perfectly suited to his mood, as Alan strode the long pathways, not quite breaking into a run. It wouldn't be dignified or prudent for a member of the Silver Helix to run on the Palace Grounds; people would get worried. *Not that there wasn't plenty to be worried about.* Still, he kept his pace to a very brisk walk, and managed to cover quite a bit of the grounds with that. If he walked fast enough, Alan Turing could almost not think about just how angry he was at Richard.

Richard had put him in this position, had played upon his loyalty, his devotion to king and country. Alan had made his own decisions in the end—he was a grown man, and 108 years old was certainly plenty grown. But if Richard cared for him at all, he would never have asked Alan to chart such a questionable course. And if Richard could treat his nearest and dearest with such callous disregard, how could Alan trust him with an entire country? A country that Alan had fought for, had bled for, had almost died for, over and over again.

For seventy long years, Alan Turing had been England's champion—at least, that was how he had always thought of himself. A quiet champion, misunderstood and disregarded, but still steadfast, honorable. When had Alan started to compromise his own honor? When he sent a sixteen-year-old to commit assassination? There were younger soldiers in the War, of course, but there was a difference between a soldier on the battlefield and a knife in the night.

Alan could ask Noel where he'd gone wrong. Maybe Noel would know. Noel would certainly have an opinion.

His swift pacing eventually brought him to the part of the garden he'd probably been subconsciously avoiding—the grounds that fell beneath Margaret's window. Sebastian had been so hurt, that Alan had never come to visit them. His husband's work, his art. He turned the corner and there it was—the new hedge maze, intricate and lovely. Alan had no heart for puzzles today, though.

He turned away, walked a little further to an older part of the garden, an area that Sebastian had allowed to go a little wild. Let the French and Italians have their formal gardens—a proper Englishman would always love a wild wood best. And here were flowers, at last—a flood of snowdrops cascading through a pleasant wood.

It would be sun-dappled on another day, with birds chirping merrily above—today, the birds clung to the branches and cast baleful glances in his direction. Still, the effect was glorious, a river of white flowers bursting forth, as if to say, oh yes, spring is here, come at last! And beneath the trees, those pink and white perennials bloomed, heads nodding down—what had Sebastian called them? Alan asked the question, and his brain tossed the answer back—hellebores. For this, it could be useful, reliable. For this.

Alan stood there a moment more, drinking it in, memorizing every aspect. Tonight, he would go home; whatever else happened with crown and country today, tonight, he would tell his husband how much he'd enjoyed his garden.

But it was full day now, and England needed him. He rendezvoused with Noel by the large stone peacock—not the most felicitous statue on the grounds, but certainly distinctive, and since it stood in the midst of a large grassy sward, impossible for eavesdroppers to come near. Noel was quite clever sometimes.

Noel snapped, "I'm busy, Turing, running the Silver Helix, and on that little assignment *you* gave me. If you want me to get anything done, you can't be dragging me in for meetings every five minutes."

"It's not as if it takes you any time to get here."

Noel laughed shortly. "Well, there is that. So, what's this about?"

"I need you to stand down. That matter with Adelbert—let it be, for now."

Noel frowned. "You're going to have to give me a reason, you know."

Turing hesitated—but hadn't he just been thinking that he should talk to Noel more? Maybe that was the problem—maybe he'd been keeping things too much to himself, in his own tangled head. "I'm not sure Richard is our man."

Noel laughed, and it wasn't a kind sound. "After all that?"

"After all that," Alan agreed, bitterly. "I thought—well, whatever I thought back then, what matters is now. And now, I think Adelbert might be a better choice for England. I don't know, and I need to know. He's a mystery. Maybe Adelbert can be steered in the right direction, especially by the men who made him king?" Turing had no desire to be the puppet master behind the throne; the very thought made him want to retch. But was there anyone else better qualified?

Noel was regarding him steadily, rain dripping off the brim of his hat. "Are you sure about this, Turing?"

"I'm not sure of anything, Matthews. But can we risk it, if we're not sure?"

Noel snorted. "We'd damn well better *get* sure. I'll hold off for a day. I'm not promising more than that—it depends on what I find out. Henry's an ass, but would this joker be any better? That's the best I can offer."

"Fine. If that's the best you can do, I'll take it." Alan snapped. A headache had started pounding behind his temples. *Dammit, Noel.* Nothing was ever simple with him.

Noel frowned. "Careful, Enigma. You're starting to sound as human as the rest of us."

Alan took a deep breath, let it out again. "I have to go."

◆

Alan went looking for Richard after the garden meeting, finding him in the Queen's Library, among the books and teacups. Alan was still carrying Sebastian's little paper bag of tea, jammed in his pocket. He offered it to Richard as something of a peace offering. "Sebastian sent this along for you. Maybe we can sit, have a cup together."

Richard took the bag, but dropped it on the table impatiently. "I don't have time for tea now, and neither do you. You're supposed to be working on Henry. We need a new tactic now that you've completely bungled the Sissel project." Richard's face had gone red, ugly with frustration. "Go, think! Use that massive brain of yours. That's what you're good for, isn't it?" No hint of affection left, no remembrance of pleasant times past. Just orders. Just as well, really.

Alan nodded curtly and left the prince to seethe alone. Down the hall, down three flights of stairs, out the door and buttoning up his coat, bracing to face the rain. And then, like the last word of the Sunday crossword, or the final Jenga piece that pulled out, bringing it all tumbling down, something clicked in his mind. Finally, finally, a pattern came together, the way it had in the old days. Alan Turing spun around and sprinted back. Through the door, up the stairs, down the hall to the door that was still half-open. Finding the nightmare waiting for him on the other side.

Alan kept grasping for the right words to describe what he saw, but nothing seemed to fit. *A feint? A fool's mate?* No, he was the fool, surely. It was so obvious, in retrospect. If Alan could reverse time, run it backward to where— Margaret's death? Restarting the affair with Richard? Meeting Sebastian, perhaps. The moment in that bookshop when their hands reached for the same book, and a bit of makeup brushed off, revealing the silver skin, but Sebastian didn't flinch away. He just smiled and said, "I think you have my book."

I think you have my book.

Alan should have let him have the damned book, should have turned and walked away, disappeared into the streets of Bloomsbury. Instead, here he stood, witness to the death of a prince of the realm.

Richard looked so small, lying there. Tea spilled out on the floor, the cup smashed on the fireplace tiles. That brown paper bag, unlabeled—had Sebastian thought he might get away with this? When he sent his creations out into the world, they usually came with a jaunty little label, a charming, scribbled name. Not this time, though. That alone should have made Alan suspicious.

Did Sebastian think Alan would cover for him? It would be simpler not to say anything, less humiliating. It would all come out, if they knew Sebastian had done it—the affair would be a headline in the *Guardian*. The end of Alan's career, surely, assuming Noel didn't think he'd had a hand in it too.

But if Alan didn't give Sebastian up, then they'd all be hunting for the murderer. The entire country would be up in arms. Most people would assume some joker had done it—what nightmare would that unleash?

And either way, Henry would remain king. Henry! Elizabeth's child was out there. The old stories would say that it was the lack of a true royal on the throne that was leading to England's downfall. Everything had started falling apart with Margaret's death. Alan Turing wasn't a superstitious man, but at this point, he felt willing to clutch at any straw.

That's what he had to do. Alan had to know, for once and for all, what to do with Elizabeth's child. Was Adelbert the heir that England needed? He turned and walked out of the room. Someone else could find the body, start the hue and cry. Alan had work to do.

♥

Noel was getting damn tired of being summoned at all times of day and night. He was frankly exhausted after the events of Monday, and his ribs and arm were aching terribly. He couldn't face transforming again, so he ordered one of the junior staff to sign out a car and drive him to Windsor rather than teleporting.

During the drive he had sat in the backseat reading reports and texting with his manager that the Japan tour would have to be rescheduled. He couldn't do magic tricks with a broken arm. That was going to cost him. Noel spent a few seconds mentally cursing Green Man. He then realized the absurdity of his thoughts. He led the Helix now. His other life was gone.

The young driver kept sneaking glances at him from the rearview mirror. Noel couldn't tell if it was admiration, curiosity, or fear. Perhaps a mix of all three. He had become director in the late hours of Sunday night and rescued a princess by Monday evening. Perhaps the boy really was impressed.

Once through the gates and onto the palace grounds Noel had ordered the driver to park and find himself a warm place to wait until he was called for. It was once again the ever-present Pike who led him across the quadrangle to the private royal apartments. As they walked across the grass, Noel reflected that he was getting an in-depth tour of the private lives of royalty in their natural habitats.

♣

Sebastian's hand shook a little as he lowered his teacup to its saucer; it clinked, quite loudly.

"You're cold. Let me get you your cardie." Alan rose from the sofa over Sebastian's muffled protests, and went to the entryway, where the tweed brown cardigan hung on the closet door. Alan was forever telling Sebastian to just open the door and hang it on a hook inside, but Sebastian couldn't be bothered. *It's cozier this way, husband. Do you want to live in a show house, or in a home?*

Alan paused in the entry, contemplating the William Morris wallpaper they'd chosen together. Stylized rabbits tumbling endlessly down a flowery field. The paper was in good shape, despite decades in this house. The two of them did manage to keep things reasonably tidy; they'd had a calm life. Nothing like the life they might have had, if they'd ever had children running through here; the wallpaper might not have survived. Sebastian hadn't been interested, and Alan had been too busy to push.

But now he had to wonder—if they'd had children, would that have been the path that saved this marriage? Or not. Perhaps the children would have driven Alan out of the house and into Richard's arms even faster. Maybe choice was an illusion, and every move you made led to the same damned result.

The doorbell rang. So, they were here already; Scotland Yard could be efficient, on occasion. Sebastian came to stand under the archway to the living room, while Alan opened the front door.

"Sir. We need to speak to your husband."

There would have been fingerprints on the paper bag, of course. Alan had no fingerprints himself now—the wild card had stripped him of those. But if Sebastian had worn gloves—there was the briefest microsecond when hope rose, a fluttering bird in Alan's breast. They could fight this, they could beat it, and go on as if it had never happened! Sebastian was only sixty-two; Alan had been too conservative with the odds before, thinking he'd only have another ten to fifteen years. They could easily have thirty more good years, or even forty. Mortality tables weren't everything. Alan Turing turned to his husband.

Sebastian was gazing at him, but it wasn't love in his eyes. Just a bitter desperation. "Alan?"

No complicated calculations needed to solve this puzzle—just a husband's request, plain as day. *Help me, take care of me, use your considerable powers and the might of the Silver Helix to make this all go away.* Alan could probably even do it, and surely, he owed Sebastian that?

Or not. The bird fell dying to earth, burned and crisped to ash. A prince of the realm had been murdered; the peace of England gravely threatened. Alan would not, could not, betray his country. If Alan Turing had been wrong, if he'd done damage, he had always at least been *trying* to do right. Alan couldn't give up on the last shreds of his honor now.

He shook his head, the tiniest of gestures.

Sebastian's face fell into dull, despairing lines. He turned deliberately away from Alan and stepped forward, toward the waiting men. "I'm ready," Sebastian said to them. "I did it, of course. I killed the prince."

They grabbed him, yanked his arms behind him and into cuffs, bundled Sebastian out the door.

"I'm sorry, sir," the last man said, in a voice caught halfway between respect and pity. "We'll see you back at the Yard? We'll need to take your statement."

"Yes, yes, of course. I'll be there shortly," Alan said. Of course.

His face impassive, as if turned to stone. Alan closed the door behind them and then carefully, slowly, hung Sebastian's cardigan back on the closet door.

♠

Inside a servant took Noel's hat, overcoat, and umbrella, and Pike took him to the study, announced him, and discreetly withdrew. Henry was frowning down into the flames dancing in an ornate fireplace.

Noel waited but the king didn't speak. Finally he asked, "How is the princess, sir?"

"Frightened. Hurt. Terrible thing to see a child in pain. Still, I suppose it could have been worse."

"Much worse, sir."

"Who were they? What have you learned?" Henry demanded.

"Unfortunately, they were not amenable to capture."

"God damn it! I want to know who was behind this!"

Noel remained prudently silent.

Henry crossed to the sofa and indicated that Noel should take a seat in the chair across from him. Henry's hands were clasped between his knees, and exhaustion and worry had sharpened his features so he rather resembled a skull.

"I think we can safely assume that Elizabeth's child does exist."

Noel opened his mouth to answer, to tell the king about Boyd-Brackenbury, but before he could speak Henry removed a sheaf of paper from his pocket.

"I have here a list of all living male jokers born in the latter half of 1948 from the Wild Card Registry." He skimmed it across the polished surface of the coffee table that separated them.

"That information is confidential—" Noel began.

"*L'etat c'est moi,*" Henry snapped.

A sick certainty began to grow. "With respect, sir, Parliament might not agree. Also, *la tête est sans repos qui porte une couronne,*" Noel retorted.

"Quote *Henry V* to me?"

"If the crown fits . . ." Noel's voice trailed away.

"It does and I'd like my head to rest easily."

They were matching stares. It was a miracle the paper that lay between them didn't burst into flames. The silence stretched on and on. Finally, Henry said, "Pick it up."

Righteous indignation was not an emotion with which Noel was intimately acquainted. Cynicism about human nature and a life spent in a very dirty business had left him feeling numb to outrage. *But not now. Especially in the face of such absurdity.*

Noel surged to his feet. "Good God, sir, you would go to such lengths just to spit on your brother's grave?" Blood rushed into Henry's face leaving it a mélange of blotchy red and white. "Especially for what is merely a ceremonial position.

While we may be sentimental, the Crown's only useful purpose is to boost the tourist trade. So no, sir, I will not do as you are ever-so-subtly requesting. I will not kill innocent British citizens."

Henry glared at him. "Very well, Director, but I'll have your resignation, and you'd best develop amnesia or unfortunate things might happen."

"You know, I've always been very happy to kill people who are simply begging for it or whose removal would improve the state of the world . . ." Noel knew his tone was dangerous.

"My people know you are here," Henry warned.

"I know. That's the only reason you are still alive." He turned to walk to the door and reflected on how they were both so very *English*.

"You have not been dismissed," Henry snapped.

Noel paused at the door, hand on the knob. "And you are not the king. Good evening, sir."

Wednesday

MARCH 11TH

NOEL LOOKED SERIOUS. THERE wasn't a hint of the usual cool, detached, mocking attitude about him. Constance was shocked to see an expression of real concern, and maybe even a little fear.

"Good Lord, Noel," she said, opening the door wider and letting him in even though it was a ridiculous hour, a little after 3:00 A.M. "What's happened to you?"

"It's not what's happened to me, it's what's about to happen to Bobbin."

Constance glanced over at Bobbin, and he returned her confused expression. "What on earth is about to happen to Bobbin? Aside from the current climate where terrorizing jokers is a perfectly fine thing to do."

"Henry showed me a list. The names were all those of male jokers born in 1948. Not sure how old Bobbin is, but figured I'd best warn you." He ran a hand nervously through his hair.

"Warn us about what?"

"He wanted me to kill them. There are fewer of you than one might expect."

Constance's hand fell to her pocket where her scissors were tucked away. It would take but a moment to stab Noel. He wouldn't be expecting it from her, and he didn't know that she—and only she—could harm her impervious creations. That was a secret she guarded fiercely. But she was old and Noel, though he was almost forty and beginning to be past his prime, still had thirty good years on her. Bobbin needed to be protected.

"Bobbin," she said softly. "You should clear out."

"What are ya talking about?" he asked. He looked from Constance to Noel. "Good Lord, woman! After what you told me about Matthews, if he'd wanted me dead I'd be deader than a . . . well, a very dead carp."

"Noel," she said as she slipped the scissors from their sheath and started to slide them from her pocket. "Then I think you should leave."

"I'm an assassin, Connie! Put those shears away. Bobbin is right. If I wanted him dead, well, that's what he'd be. And you as well. I'm here because you've always been good to me. Even when I was a lad. I can't support Henry anymore." A wry smile, more like the normal Noel, slipped across his face. "There are some things even I won't do."

"You were a good lad, Noel," she replied warily. "So, why are you here?"

"I want you and Bobbin to get out of the country. It's not safe. I won't do what Henry wanted, but that doesn't mean there aren't plenty of people who will."

"This is madness!" Bobbin cried. "People won't stand for it!"

"The people won't know," Noel said coldly.

"When seventy-year-old jokers start piling up like cordwood they will," Constance snapped.

"Connie," Noel began in a pleading voice. It frightened Constance. "I need you and Bobbin to leave now. It's too dangerous now and I can't protect you."

"I've never seen you like this," Constance said. "I don't like it."

Noel ran a hand over his face. He looked haggard and his clothes were askew, not at all Noel's normal state. "If I didn't think you were in terrible danger, Bobbin, I'd never ask this of you. There are other matters I must attend to and I can't play nursemaid to a pair of geriatrics."

Constance stepped forward thinking it might do to give him a good slap. "We don't need a nursemaid, Noel," She growled. "We are quite capable of taking care of ourselves."

"Think, Connie! You're not ready for what's coming. These are men who kill for money. Professionals. You're out-matched."

It took Constance aback. Seeing Noel worried, almost frightened, was beyond disconcerting—it was terrifying. And she didn't scare easily.

Bobbin reached out and took Constance's hand. "Very well, Noel," Bobbin said in a remarkably calm voice. "We'll go. I bought a house in France for Constance a few years ago. We'll go there."

"You what?!" Constance exclaimed.

"Investment and security, my dear," he said with a slight smile. "You make rather a lot of money through your licensed properties and clothing lines. I wanted you to have a retreat and maybe even a house to retire to. Of course, you like working too much to take a real holiday."

"So, I've had a house in France for how long?"

"About six years."

"And you never told me about it?"

He shrugged. "You didn't seem interested in anything other than work. I knew eventually you'd retire and I could tell you then."

"But . . ."

"This is all very sweet and affecting, but the two of you need to fucking stop," Noel drawled, then snapped. "You have somewhere to go. Go there! Now!"

"We'll just grab a few things," Constance began.

"Have all the stores in France suddenly vanished?" That was the Noel she knew. "Just go to the station and get a ticket on the Eurostar and get to France as quickly as possible."

"But . . ."

"No. Connie. Go."

◆

Green Man stared at his hands. They had curled into two creaking fists, the one on the right thicker and uglier than the one on the left. He was finding it hard to maintain his usual calm, which was bothering him because he was far from alone. Constance was still standing in the doorway. Seizer sat in the chair opposite, mercifully at a loss for words, and Finder was leaning against the wall, looking as if a strong breeze would be enough to knock her over.

He forced himself to look up at them all. "You're sure about this?"

"Yes," said Constance. "It's real."

"I was coming to warn you as well," added Finder, the words coming out with a slight lisp. "The order comes from Henry himself."

"But . . ." began Seizer, then trailed off.

For once, Green Man felt some empathy. It was difficult to put into words. To say it out loud seemed ridiculous somehow. Henry's secret order to wipe out all male jokers over the age of seventy was hard to swallow. It felt like something that belonged in a story from the Old Testament rather than the modern age.

Seizer flapped his arms and huffed. "But this . . . It's . . ."

"We're going to leave the country," said Constance. "I wanted to warn you before we left."

Green Man nodded, glad that she and Bobbin would be spared whatever came next. "When do you go?"

"Today." She came further forward into the room. "Don't worry about us. What are you going to do?"

That was the question. How did one respond appropriately to something so patently monstrous? He was so angry, he was finding it hard to speak.

"It's a bloody outrage!" shouted Seizer. "This is war!"

"It is," agreed Green Man.

"No!" said Constance. "There's still time to stop this. Go to the press, go to the courts. If you tell them what Henry is planning, they'll take action."

Finder nodded from her corner. "Yes, get the people to turn against him."

"How?" scoffed Seizer. "With the word of a seamstress and, forgive me, a vagrant?"

Constance's nostrils flared. "And the former agent of the Silver Helix that Henry asked to do it."

After a show of checking the room, Seizer replied. "I don't see any agents here. Do either of you have any evidence at all?"

Finder and Constance exchanged a look. Clearly, they did not.

"That cad, Henry, must be stopped, and I am the one to do it," Seizer continued. "It is time for me to step forward and declare my rightful claim to the throne."

"You?" asked Constance, unconvinced. "A prince?"

"Yes, and Henry knows it! That's why he tried to have me killed. Look closely at my face and you will see the truth. My royal blood cannot be denied!" An expression flitted across Constance's face that Green Man couldn't interpret.

"Be that as it may," interrupted Green Man. "We need proof of your lineage. Our own genetic test to confirm what we've heard, and someone with an untouchable reputation to carry it out and publish the result. That will take time. Henry's threat to our people is imminent and needs to be acted upon." He glanced at Constance. "Thank you for bringing us this information, but now it is time for you to leave."

She looked like she wanted to argue, but then nodded and she and Bobbin left.

Green Man turned back to the others. "We need to get word to every one of our people that will be targeted by this new edict. Fortunately for us, there aren't many male jokers of that age to protect. We'll bring those who are willing into our custody."

"And those that refuse?" Asked Seizer. "Some of them are stubborn buggers."

"We hope there aren't many, and place a watch on them. But that isn't enough. We have to go on the offensive."

Finder was nodding, an eager light in her eyes.

"About bloody time," muttered Seizer.

"Britain First have already shown their hatred toward us," Green Man continued, "and are poised to escalate things. Which is why we're going to go after them first and preempt whatever they're planning. We'll start with their leaders and work our way down.

"This is war, and Britain First are not the only front we're fighting. To be honest, everyone will be expecting us to make a move against them, and that's what I'm counting on. A team will draw their attention with a strike against Britain First while I go after the real problem." He looked at Finder, and then to Seizer. "Henry. As long as he's alive, our prince, the true prince, will be in danger, and our people will never know peace. This all started with him and it will end with him too. Tomorrow."

Seizer hauled himself out of his chair. "I know we haven't always seen eye to eye, old man, but by God I'm with you on this one." He held out a hand. "Let me come along when you go for Henry. Let's bring the oaf down together."

Green Man stood up and took it, hiding any misgivings. "Together, then."

♥

The tips of his fingers felt numb; in fact, he felt as if his entire body were disengaged from the planet. Noel stood in Jasper's bedroom, holding the boy's favorite Lohengrin tee shirt. The open suitcase on the bed yawned like a devouring mouth. Jasper was nattering, though it seemed to come more from nerves than happiness as he dumped clothing into the case.

"Is Momma coming? Will she be at the airport?"

"No, you'll be traveling alone," Noel finally said. "But the nice people at the airlines will look after you."

Henry's vengeance had been swift and surgical. Mid-morning Noel had received word that the court had ruled, and Jasper was to be returned immediately to his mother in New York City. Niobe's lawyers had procured a ticket shortly after the court appointed a guardian ad litem for Jasper. The man had accompanied Noel to pick up Jasper after school, and now the moment was fast approaching when a court-appointed lawyer would arrive to take Jasper to Heathrow. Noel's hands clenched on the material.

Jasper looked up at him a frown wrinkling his brow. "Why don't you just take me, Dad?"

Why indeed? Why don't I transform, grab him, and go? But not to Niobe. We could vanish. And what kind of life would that be for a nine-year-old: on the run with a fugitive father, no school, no friends, no stability? Whatever he might have become, Noel had had a stable and loving family life at the start of it. Pity he had done such a piss-poor job of providing that for his own child.

"I . . . I don't think that's a good idea," Noel finally said.

"Momma would understand. You could work it out. You did before. Please, Dad. Let's go home."

Home. But this is home for me, and it's being destroyed from within, Noel thought.

And soon several hundred old pensioners were going to die because in this toxic atmosphere, there was no doubt that Henry would find someone who would carry out his wishes. Those extralegal murders might already be underway.

Child or country? Which would it be?

He knelt in front of the boy and gripped his shoulders. "Jasper, you know I love you. More than anything in the world, but there is something I have to do."

"No, Daddy, please." Jasper threw his arms around his neck, pressed this face against Noel's shoulder, and began to sob.

Noel stood and thrust his handkerchief into son's hands. "Jasper, sometimes a man has to give up what he wants in order to do what he must. You'll understand . . . some day. When you're older." He dropped his arm over Jasper's shoulders and guided him back to the closet. "Now finish your packing. I'll come and see you in America as soon as I'm able."

♣

Being in the Silver Helix bought you some privileges, even if your husband had killed a prince. A little time alone, just outside his cell. If he'd wanted, Alan could have slipped Sebastian something to end things quickly. But all he really wanted was to talk.

"I just can't figure out where I went wrong, Sebastian."

"Oh?" Sebastian's voice was haggard, as was the rest of him. The guards hadn't been gentle dragging him here; he cradled an arm against his body. A good husband would get him some medical attention. "Maybe it was when you started fucking Richard again?" The words laced with rage and bitterness.

Alan heard them, but they weren't relevant to his current problem. "None of this makes any sense. Maybe my love for you is clouding my judgment."

Sebastian reached a hand through the bars, grasped Alan's, and pulled it close. "You do still love me, don't you, Alan? I love you, you bastard. That's why I did it, you know."

"Yes, I know," Alan said absently. His hand felt strange in Sebastian's—cold and icy, like metal. *My lovely metal man.* But it helped him, talking out loud to Sebastian, instead of running in circles inside his own head. Alan kept feeling like he almost had all the pieces of the puzzle, and then they slipped away again. It would be easier to think if Sebastian didn't keep talking about other things; it was distracting.

Sebastian said urgently, "I almost killed you, you know. Or me. Both of us. I thought about that a lot. But I thought it'd be so much better to kill Richard instead . . ."

Alan sighed. "You should have talked to me, told me how unhappy you were."

Sebastian let go of his hand, stepped back in his cell, out of reach. "As if that would have done any good."

Alan frowned. "No, you're probably right." He should be grieving, broken-hearted. Alan was sure he was, on some level. But everything that touched Sebastian seemed to live far away, behind a thick pane of clouded glass. It was over and done with; Alan had failed utterly to see the murder coming, had failed both Sebastian and Richard.

But he couldn't think about any of that now. The country was still at risk, and there were a thousand small details screaming for Alan Turing's attention. "There's still too many things I don't know. What I need is someone who knows the joker community, knows it intimately."

Alan turned away from Sebastian's cell, pulled his overcoat more closely around himself and buttoned it tight. He'd get in touch with Green Man. Constance could help Alan find him. They'd known each other a long time, and Green Man owed Alan a couple of favors at this point. Maybe it was time to collect.

"Alan—where are you going? Alan? Alan???"

♠

The court-appointed lawyer had taken Jasper. His son hadn't cried, just given him a last pleading and hopeful look that turned to despair when Noel had shaken his head.

The only sound was the slow clicking from the electric tea kettle as it cooled. Noel felt that if he moved too quickly, he would fly into pieces. He forced a swallow through a painfully tight throat, pressed his fingers briefly against his eyes. Told himself the moisture on their tips was nothing.

What was clear was that he could not stay an instant longer in the silent, empty flat. He grabbed up his leather jacket and walked swiftly out the door. He had a job to do, so he forced aside his bitter grief and loss.

The most pressing matter in this moment was determining to whom Henry would turn to carry out the murder of the elderly jokers. Logic suggested that it was probably the Britain First crowd, but logical or not it was still just a guess, and Noel never trusted to guesses.

As he strode through the sleet and fog Noel mentally kicked himself for not recording that final meeting with Henry. If he had he could simply go to the Lion, now back in charge of the Helix, and dump this mess in his lap, but he had no proof, and would Ranjit believe him without it? *Probably not.* Still, he should probably try. *But not without evidence.*

A snort of amusement bubbled up. He who had been the blade and the bullet for the Silver Helix was now trying to prevent the death of few hundred men. It was an odd role in which to find himself.

The justifications for his state-sanctioned murders had been the belief that a death or two was a small price to pay to save potentially hundreds, thousands, or millions. He suspected the people in the Helix who still had a conscience comforted themselves with that fragile fig leaf. He had never bothered. He knew what he was.

◆

It was hard to hear the truck's engine through all the layers of wood, but Green Man could feel the vehicle decelerate, stop, and then slowly reverse.

He'd been in trucks and vans and boxes before, but he'd never been inside a box, hidden inside a box that was inside another box, inside a truck before. It was not something he was keen to repeat in a hurry.

They'd debated for some time the best way to break into Windsor Castle and kill King Henry. A direct attack was out of the question. The castle was too heavily guarded to fall quickly, and the moment Henry got wind of their attack, the military and Silver Helix would be called. Given the castle's status as tourist attraction, it was technically possible to buy a ticket and walk inside. However, Henry's hatred of jokers meant that only Maven would be allowed to get in that way, and then only if she left her guns outside.

For the attack to work, they'd needed a more discreet method of entry. A way to bring in people like him without raising the alarm. There had been lot of arguments about the best way to achieve this goal which, given Seizer's involvement, had been both long and tiresome. In the end, they'd fallen back on the classics for inspiration and opted to employ a Trojan Horse. Or in this case, a Trojan Wardrobe.

Instead of a hollow belly, the wardrobe had a secret chamber built into the back. They had constructed it around him, the panels pressing hard against his shoulder blades and chest as they were bolted together. It was like being buried in a vertical coffin. He barely had room to clench his fists. The little bits of space between his legs and around his head had been filled with coiled rope and foam to ensure the hidden chamber didn't sound too hollow. He'd been assured that the ornate design of the wardrobe was as close a match to the one ordered by King Henry as they could manage, and it also served to disguise how deep the back really was. Ideally, he'd have approved the final illusion himself, but given that he was part of that illusion, he'd been forced to hand it over to Wayfarer.

Men grunted as they moved him from truck to forklift. He couldn't make out their words, but imagined they were moaning in that good natured way people did when working.

He felt the shuddering movement as the crate rose up, out, and was then lowered down; heard the occasional shouted instruction and then the lurch as the forklift took him to wherever it was they stored furniture in Windsor. After they had deposited him, he soon heard the forklift return. With Henry's coronation imminent, it was no surprise that he'd splashed out on a number of new items to stamp his identity on the royal home.

More movement, labored this time, as they took him inside. He felt sorry for the poor souls who were carrying him up the stairs. Despite the fear, there was a delicious thrill to being carried past security by the very people tasked with keeping out intruders.

Then, with a final thud, he arrived. Somewhere in the castle.

A crisper sound of wood creaking caught his ear as royal staff pried open the crate. *Here we go.*

By now they would have already scanned the contents for metal, electronics, and any other telltale signs of explosives. He wasn't worried about these things. Indeed, he no longer gave off heat the way a normal person did, nor did he have a heartbeat to give him away. The chances of them picking him up with regular equipment was extremely low. However, the chances of their ruse tricking a thorough physical examination were much less certain.

Footsteps echoed in the space, moving around him. He heard the dull throb of chatter, mainly one voice with a second punctuating it with the occasional word. All measured. All suggesting that they had not realized they had an intruder less than three feet from where they stood.

More boxes arrived, and these too were checked. The same voices were heard again, but further away this time. Green Man allowed himself a little relief. For now, the ruse seemed to have worked.

He waited until the footsteps could no longer be heard.

He waited until the voices had faded away.

He waited some more for good measure.

Then, very carefully, he pressed against the false back of the wardrobe. There was a soft creak and a crack as the seal broke. He didn't open it all the way, just enough to allow any light to spill through. There wasn't any.

Good.

He pushed through entirely and stepped forward, opening the main doors of the wardrobe to peek out, the rope coiled around one arm. To an observer it would have appeared like a magic trick or a scene from one of the stories he read to little Roy so very long ago. *A wooden man returning from the wilds of Narnia.*

A little light shone white through a crack in a pair of curtains, and he watched it patiently as the hours ticked by, waiting for it to dim. He couldn't see much of the room, but it was of a decent size, with a high ceiling, and no doubt would be beautifully decorated.

It was impossible to know how things were going outside or if Henry's insanity had already started to claim lives. But it was good to finally take direct action.

Peggy was right. We didn't join the Fists to do nothing. He nodded to himself. *These hands will shed royal blood tonight and I am content with that. For once, I really am sure that I'm doing the right thing.*

He knew that the Silver Helix would come for him after this, in a way they never had before. In all likelihood, this night would be his last as well. But now he was here, committed, he found it didn't worry him.

He nodded to himself again, and settled in.

Meanwhile, very slowly, the light outside began to fade.

♥

Constance and Bobbin sat facing each other in the Blue Elephant Café in St. Pancras station. They each had a small pot of tea and were sharing a plate of cookies. At least, that's what they were pretending to do.

The cookies were untouched, as were their cups of tea. The tea had long gone cold. There were stares and whispers from some of the tables around them, but they just barely noticed.

"You bought me a house, then," Constance began, but trailed off. Right now, she didn't give a shite about houses in France, no matter how lovely they sounded.

"Yes," Bobbin replied, but he kept staring off into space while tapping his spoon on the table.

"Stop that, please," Constance said tightly.

"Stop what?" Bobbin asked.

"Spoon."

"Spoon?"

"Stop tapping the . . ." She caught herself. It wasn't Bobbin or the tapping of the spoon. It was what they were doing.

"I can't go, Constance," Bobbin said, shaking his head.

"I know," she replied with a smile. "Neither can I. There's too much at stake. Too many things going wrong. I'd feel like . . . "

"Like you'd run from the fight just when you were most needed?"

"Yes," she replied. He understood her so well. No, they understood each other so well.

"Well then," he said, sharing in her sudden conviction. "We need to go and fight the good fight. Yes?"

"The more I thought about leaving . . ."

"Yes, my dear. Yes."

"So, where to now?" Constance asked as they began gathering their things.

"We could go back to Green Man. Try to help," Bobbin said. "Wouldn't be the worst person to throw in with . . ."

Constance thought it over. Noel would be furious if he found out they hadn't left the country.

"If you think we should throw in with him, then we will," she said. "It's a mad, long-odds, throwing-in-with-shady-sorts idea. What could possibly go wrong?"

♣

Noel's removal from the Helix had been so abrupt that they had thus far neglected to strip him of his identification. That oversight had allowed him to request information from Scotland Yard.

He was in the busy computer center where reports from all across Britain were received and processed and decisions were made about whether to send a Met officer to assist in a local crime. It was late evening, and Noel wondered how quickly Henry might have set his murderous plan in motion. He would soon find out.

The young woman police officer manning the computer pulled a printout from the printer next to her desk and handed it over. "Here you are Director, every reported murder of male jokers born in 1948."

Noel scanned the list. It wasn't that long, five men, but it was suggestive, and he couldn't risk waiting longer to have suggestion become certainty with the proof being the bodies of old men.

He thanked the officer and left. He just hoped it would be enough.

♠

It was finally time.

Green Man moved to the window and opened it. The room looked out onto part of Windsor Castle's gardens and surrounding grounds, tastefully lit so that the paths were still safe to walk at night.

Somewhere out there, his people would be waiting. He left the window open as arranged, and five minutes later lowered down a rope. Shortly after that, he felt the rope jerk in his hand—three sharp tugs, the agreed signal—and began to pull.

The room gradually filled with jokers and knaves. One after another, they arrived through the window, each wearing night goggles. Peggy, grinning, a cricket bat in one hand and a silenced pistol in the other; Seizer, also armed; Blue Jeans, metal eyes wild with excitement; Jamila, looking oddly childlike as she clutched her gun to her chest; and Maven, in military black, a sniper rifle on her back, and lord knows how many other devices of death strapped to her body or kept in special pockets.

She handed him a pair of goggles and he put them on, turning the world green and black. The others looked strangely ghoulish rendered in this way, but at least he could see clearly. "Remember," whispered Green Man. "We're here to kill Henry, no one else. If others have to die, so be it, but it will be our failing if that's the case."

Jamila nodded, as did Blue Jeans. The others didn't.

Maven confirmed where they were in the castle. She also confirmed that Henry was still in residence, and, as luck would have it, that his room was not far from their current location.

The castle was quiet, all sane and decent people having long since gone to their beds. Of course, there were guards on night watch, but much of the security was deployed to stop people getting in, rather than to stop people who were already inside.

They arrived at Henry's door without incident. Two men stood guard outside. Neither was particularly big nor scary, but given that they could be Silver Helix, that wasn't very encouraging.

Green Man signaled Maven and Peggy to deal with them. The plan was to silence them quickly, but if the men put up a fight or turned out to be superhuman, the others would slow them down while he went in and dealt with Henry. There was an escape plan for afterwards, though none of them besides Seizer were very confident in it being necessary.

Maven lined up a shot, and a moment later a dart appeared in the neck of one of the men. Even as he was putting a hand up in surprise, Peggy was moving. One moment she was at Green Man's side, the next she was sliding to a stop in front of the second guard, her cricket bat held horizontal in two hands and pressed against his neck, pinning him to the wall. His gasp was choked off, and a minute later, both men were unconscious.

No alarms had sounded. The castle remained quiet. So far, so good.

While Blue Jeans and Jamila moved them out of sight, Green Man started toward the bedroom, Seizer matching him step for step.

"I want to be the one to finish Henry," Seizer was trying to whisper. It didn't come naturally. Green Man frowned at both the sentiment and volume, making his night goggles bob. "It's fitting," added Seizer, "one king being killed by another."

Green Man wanted to argue but he didn't dare. Idle talk really could cost lives in this case. Seizer seemed to be under the impression that being a prince gave him the right to murder people, whereas to Green Man, the opposite was true. There was no time to get into an argument here, however, so, under his breath, he replied: "Fine."

The night goggles picked out Henry in his bed, asleep. Even from this distance and rendered in green, there was no mistaking him. Seizer advanced across the room, sacrificing stealth for speed. Green Man closed the door behind them, wincing with every creak of the floor. *Surely Henry will hear and wake up. It will only take one scream . . .*

But by the time Henry was starting to stir, Seizer already had a hand at his throat. "Hello, Your Majesty," he said far too loudly. "I'm afraid you won't be able to make the coronation after all." He pressed the index finger of his other hand against Henry's forehead and began to push. Apart from a habit of making and then shedding very crusty skin, Seizer's wild card had given him the ability to sever organic material by touch. He could, quite literally, unzip a person by running a hand across their body, or he could bore a hole through their flesh by pressing through it, penetrating bone as easily as someone might push a hand through jelly.

Green Man had seen it happen more than once in the past, so he was just as surprised as Seizer was when this time, it didn't work.

Henry sat up as Seizer raked his fingers across his belly, trying to open up his guts.

Again, nothing happened.

"This bugger's hard as—"

Whatever Seizer was about to say was cut off as Henry punched him in the stomach, driving the old knave to his knees. It was hard to tell through the goggles, but now that Henry was moving, something didn't seem quite right. He looked a tiny bit too slim, and maybe a little younger than he should. And where Seizer had been holding his throat, the skin looked . . . smudged? Was that the right word for it?

Seizer scurried back, trying to get away, a few of his scabs breaking loose as he went.

Henry assumed a mockery of a martial arts pose and beckoned for Seizer to attack. There was grace and humor in the movement, of a kind the king had never once displayed.

It's not Henry. Henry isn't here. He was never here. They knew we were coming.

There was a gun in Seizer's hand now, and he fired it into Henry's chest. Henry rocked with the impact, but again, not in a natural way, and three puffs of chalk blew into the air where he'd been hit.

And that's when Green Man understood. About five years ago, King Henry had commissioned a famous sculptor to make a statue of him to celebrate his first tour of military duty. Somehow, this statue was now in Henry's bed, made up to look like him, wearing his pajamas, and moving!

There's only one Silver Helix Ace I know of who can animate statues, thought Green Man as "Henry" swatted the gun from Seizer's hand before admonishing him with a finger. *Pygmalion!*

That meant the ace would be close, close enough to see them. Green Man looked around wildly. Crazy thoughts of secret passages and spy holes ran through this mind, but then, when he realized where Pygmalion was most likely hiding it was all he could do not to laugh. *The wardrobe! He's hiding in the wardrobe.*

One of the doors was open slightly, enough to allow anyone inside a view of Henry's bed.

"Help!" called Seizer. He'd continued moving hastily backward until he'd bumped his head against the wall. The statue of Henry made a show of cracking its knuckles and then advanced with an authentically smug version of Henry's smile.

Green Man skirted the room to approach the wardrobe from the side. One way or another, he would soon know if his theory was correct. He grabbed the back of the wardrobe and toppled it forward. There was a high-pitched yelp from inside as Green Man slammed it down on the ground, doors-first, trapping whoever it was inside.

The statue of Henry froze mid-step, and then slowly fell sideways, the smug grin still frozen on its face.

That proves it, thought Green Man, but there was no time for congratulations. He ran back to the door, beckoning Seizer to follow.

The others were still outside.

"Well?" hissed Peggy. "Did you get the cunt?"

"They're on to us," he replied. "We're aborting and getting out."

"Wot?"

"This is a trap. Henry isn't here."

"Someone's sold us out. When I find the—"

"Not now, Peggy!"

He could hear running footsteps coming along the corridor, lots of them. Too many for them to face. Maven had obviously had the same idea and ran past him into Henry's bedroom. They all followed automatically. The statue remained on its side, unmoving, and someone, presumably Pygmalion, could be heard banging on the inside of the wardrobe.

Maven ignored him, rushing to the far side of the room to open the window. She hooked something into the wall that trailed a cable to her belt and got ready to jump. "Keep up," she said to Seizer, and threw a canister back over her shoulder toward the corridor that immediately began to spew smoke.

Then she leapt out and began rappelling down the wall.

Seizer looked at the open window dubiously. "We'll be like bally ducks in a shooting gallery."

"It's your funeral, mate," said Peggy as she dived past him.

They could hear people calling orders in the corridor now. The smoke canister had bought them a brief reprieve, but it wouldn't last long.

Desperation sent Seizer after his daughter.

Meanwhile, Green Man tied his rope to the statue's leg and around the leg of the bed, and then started to lower Jamila and Blue Jeans down together. He didn't have time to make it gentle. As soon as they were clear, he followed them out into the rain, lowering himself hand over hand.

He was halfway down the wall when he heard a young man's laughter. Looking over his shoulder he could see foliage below. Just beyond it was a large circular area of stone with multiple pathways leading from it, including the famous long walk—a tree-lined path that ran for over two miles. In that moment it looked very appealing to follow it off into the night. Unfortunately, the path to freedom was blocked by five figures. Two women and three men. Even before he'd put names to faces, the lack of weapons combined with their confidence told him who they were straight away: the Silver Helix.

Damn.

They weren't going to walk away from this easily, if at all.

He resisted the temptation to jump and concentrated on getting to the ground as fast as possible. All the while he was trying to work out who they were facing, and what their chances were.

He'd seen two women. One was smartly dressed, with her hair worn up, athletic-looking, Persian. Not old but not young either. He had a terrible feeling it was Jiniri, one of the literal big guns of the Helix.

The other woman was petite, pale, and focused in a way that reminded him of Maven, and dressed in a simple uniform. *Stonemaiden?* He wondered. He'd only heard rumors: a woman that killed with a single touch.

Of the three men, one was easily identifiable by the distinctive coat he wore. A mantle passed from one Redcoat to the other over the years. The man wearing it now was square-jawed, tall, and surely far too young for the role. *Shouldn't he be in school?* If he was anything like the other Redcoats, he'd be an ace, most likely one with physical superiority. The second man was slight of build and dressed in a casual suit. His skin was dark, and he looked the most worried of all of them. Green Man had never seen or heard of him before. The third man was older, portly, his red hair thinning, and dressed in a naval dress uniform. He was also standing significantly further back than his fellows. *Archimedes.* A well-known ace that was due for retirement. Famously, he'd taken down HMS *Juno* on his own.

There was no sign of the teleporting golden ace from the *Queen Mary*. It was possible they were still in recovery, but he doubted it.

As Green Man made the last part of his descent, he saw more soldiers both inside and outside the castle. Some were coming to the windows, but none followed them out, nor did the ring of soldiers in the grounds advance.

They're holding a perimeter and leaving us to the Helix.

It looked like the only way out was to go through the enemy. Green Man jumped down with a heavy thud and raised his fists.

So be it.

◆

Bobbin and Constance gasped as a blast of cold air hit them. It was sleeting and cold and had gotten rawer since they'd come to the station.

"We'll get a cab," she said, walking to the taxi stand. For a moment, her vision was obscured by her hair as a sudden gust whipped it around.

"I can provide you with transportation."

It was another altogether too familiar voice. One she'd hoped not to hear again. Turing.

She shoved her hair behind her ears and glared up at him.

"I thought I made it clear the last time we spoke that I wanted nothing more to do with you or MI-7. And how did you find us?"

He looked pained. "Constance, you wouldn't answer my calls, so I had your phone location traced. Once we knew that, well, Constance, it's London, there are cameras everywhere . . ."

She narrowed her eyes. "I'm going to put that cursed phone in the rubbish. What do you want?"

"I need to get to Green Man. There's a joker with him I need to locate. Goes by the name Boyd-Brackenbury. Constance, I think he may be the real heir to the throne."

Constance and Bobbin exchanged a look.

"You decide, Constance," Bobbin said. "I trust your judgment."

She considered Turing. He looked almost as shite as Noel had. "Why should I trust you, Turing? You aren't exactly my favorite person right now."

"Because I'm trying to do the right thing! I need to make amends for . . . so many things."

"I'm not standing out here in the cold," she said.

"I have a car," Turing said. "Let me help you with those bags." He led them to an illegally parked Mercedes sedan. "Privileges go with the job," Turing said opening the backseat for her. Constance slid in. He let Bobbin into the passenger side, then quick-stepped it to the driver's side. Once in, he punched the buttons for the seat warmers and turned up the heat.

"I know you have connections to Green Man. All I want is an introduction so I can find Boyd-Brackenbury and determine if he is indeed the heir. There's so much in play. But the main thing is we find the person who might be king."

"You do know Boyd-Brackenbury is already claiming he's heir to the throne," Constance said, re-tying her scarf. "You might not like what you find."

"It doesn't matter," Turing replied, remorse tinging his words. "I must right things."

Constance shook her head. "I'm not even certain Green Man will see *us* with you in tow."

"Bobbin," Turing said. "He'd likely listen to you. And I am a joker, after all."

"I'm not certain I'd play that card, given your history," Bobbin said. "But I'll do what I can."

♥

"Give up while you can," said Redcoat.

Green Man half expected Seizer to answer, but the old knave was too busy catching his breath.

"Let us leave and nobody has to die," replied Green Man.

Redcoat laughed. "We're not going to kill you. We're going to bring you to justice."

"For all your powers, that is one thing you cannot offer us."

"What?"

Peggy pointed her gun in Redcoat's general direction. "I didn't come here to fucking talk to people!"

For once, he found himself in agreement with her.

Time to find out if this iteration of Redcoat is bulletproof.

But, before Peggy could fire, she swore loudly, as if in pain, and dropped the gun.

"Thanks, Payback," said Redcoat with a broad grin.

Green Man narrowed his eyes. The worried-looking man had taken out a long needle and was holding it in one hand. *What has he done? What is his power?*

Before he could think further on that, however, Jiniri began to run toward them. With every step the surrounding lights flickered, and when they came on again, she had grown in height. Step.

Flicker.

And now she was as tall as him, her clothes splitting at the seams.

Step.

Flicker.

Twice his height.

Step (the footfalls much louder now).

Flicker.

Three times his height. Over twenty foot tall and covering the distance between them at terrifying speed.

Those still with guns opened fire but the bullets did nothing to slow her. Their power reduced to little more than gnat bites by Jiniri's wild card.

The Fists scattered, but Jiniri didn't care. The giant wasn't going for all of them. She was going for him. He raised his hands just as her foot connected with his chest, firing him backward into the wall of the castle.

Both the impact of her kick and the hard crunch of stone on his back were muted. Green Man rarely felt pain these days. Even so, it took him a few moments to get up again, and in that time, everything had changed.

Several of the outside lights had exploded as Maven shot them out one by one. Without the lights, their night goggles would give them an edge, and it would be easier to escape.

Jiniri tried to land a punch on Peggy, who kept dodging, swearing, and rapping the giant's knuckles with her cricket bat.

Meanwhile, Redcoat and Blue Jeans had begun trading blows.

Archimedes stepped forward and held out his hands. Green Man's heart sank but he wasn't sure what the ace was doing.

Suddenly, the green-black world of his vision went white, and he felt heat on his face, painful and sharp, and he heard the others crying out in alarm.

My goggles are on fire! My face! No!

He tore them from his head and hurled them aside. The other Fists had done the same, but the distraction had been costly. Peggy now dangled from Jiniri's grasp. Blue Jeans was doubled over and staggering, with Redcoat lining up for a finishing shot. And Stonemaiden had started sprinting toward Jamila.

The terrified joker realized it too late, and by the time she was bringing her gun to bear, Stonemaiden was on her. The ace didn't slow down, just tapped the girl on the shoulder as she went by. *Like children playing tag,* he thought.

As Jamila recoiled, trying to twist away, she began to judder, the color leeching from her face, from her clothes, from her eyes, as they all faded to gray. Then, she stopped moving altogether, the hands that served as ears going rigid, freezing in place. Dead, like the rest of her.

To his horror, he realized that he'd stopped reacting to the fight and started to simply watch it. He lumbered toward Redcoat, aware that Stonemaiden was heading their way as well, her eyes intent on Blue Jeans.

Maven set off a smoke grenade between her and Jiniri, but it only came up to the giant's shins. A few more bullets bounced harmlessly off her arm, but she didn't drop Peggy. *We're going to lose,* thought Green Man, as Redcoat sent Blue Jeans reeling backward with another punch.

Despite the noise and confusion, Redcoat heard him coming and turned to face him, craning his neck to meet Green Man's gaze. "This is more like it," he said, and came in fast.

Green Man felt the punch. Just. It was a good punch. Superhumanly strong. Compared to Jiniri, however, it was nothing. Redcoat followed up with three more, all just as good, then tried to sweep his legs. It was a good sweep. A normal person would be on the floor.

Green Man grabbed Redcoat's arm and ripped it out of its shoulder joint.

As Redcoat screamed, he lifted him overhead and turned toward Stonemaiden, who was frighteningly close now. It was possible his wooden skin was immune to her touch, but he didn't want to risk it.

Stonemaiden was running full tilt at them, and so, when he threw Redcoat at her, there was little she could do. There was a satisfying thump as the two went down in a heap. He doubted either of them would stay there, but it would buy him a little time.

The smoke was clearing now, and it didn't take long for Jiniri to find where Maven was hiding. "Last chance to give up," she boomed, waving Peggy at her. "Or I'm going to club you to bits with your friend here."

Maven just fired at Jiniri, not because it would hurt, but because Seizer had also been hiding in the smoke, and now he was in position to strike. His hand slashed across the back of her ankle and she screamed, dropping Peggy as she fell to one knee. Whatever powers Jiniri possessed, they did nothing to protect her against Seizer's wild card.

He slashed again, and blood ran freely down the back of Jiniri's leg, causing her to groan and swipe backward. With a flip, Peggy was back on her feet, cricket bat in both hands. She hopped up onto Jiniri's knee and swung hard at her face. There was a crack as the bat snapped in two, and then Jiniri was toppling.

Green Man was trying to decide what to do next, but there was so much happening all at once, he was struggling to process it all.

Seizer was moving in to finish Jiniri off.

Blue Jeans was going after Payback.

Stonemaiden dragged herself out from under Redcoat and faced off against Seizer.

A red light from Maven's sniper rifle appeared on Stonemaiden's forehead—

—Then it flickered and went out.

A second later, Maven swore, and threw her smoking rifle on the floor.

Archimedes. Again.

Green Man decided it was time to deal with him next and set off.

To his right Seizer was shouting. "Are you sure you want to try your power against mine, Stonemaiden? My hands are deadly too." And he waved them in what was presumably meant to be a threatening manner.

"I'd love to, my handsome," replied Stonemaiden without pause, taking a step forward, then twisting suddenly, lashing out.

The feint was clever, because it not only fooled Seizer, whose bravado vanished as he tried frantically to get away, but it also fooled Peggy, who was Stonemaiden's real target.

The knave recovered quickly, and she turned with the blow, so that the strike was reduced to a graze. It was nothing really, a slight brush of skin on skin. Peggy thrust the broken bat handle toward Stonemaiden's face, but halfway through the action, her arms locked up.

"You bi—" began Peggy, but the sentence never finished, as the air in her body wasn't strong enough to move vocal cords made of stone.

Stonemaiden turned her attention back to Seizer.

Seizer turned away to Maven. "Help your father!"

Without comment, Maven pulled out a pistol and fired two rounds into Stonemaiden's stomach. Stonemaiden went down, but if the lack of blood was anything to go by, not for good.

Green Man was nearly at Archimedes now. He could hear Blue Jeans crying out rhythmically as he rolled around on the floor. Payback was doing something to him, but Green Man didn't have time to worry about what. The soldiers that had been holding back were starting to close in. Hundreds of lights bobbed on the end of rifles as they jogged closer. But he didn't have time for that either.

Galloping ahead of them on a horse made of stone was King Charles the Second. The living statue had a smug gleam in its eye. If it weren't bearing down on him, he'd have to admit that it looked magnificent, picked out by all of the spotlights against the grandeur of Windsor Castle. *Pygmalion!*

There was no way he'd be able to find the puppet master behind all the soldiers. Gritting his teeth, he continued after Archimedes who, realizing the danger, turned and tried to run away. Luckily for Green Man, his quarry wasn't young anymore.

His larger right hand closed around Archimedes' throat, as he leaned down to whisper in his ear. "Use your power now or you're dead."

"On what?" he gasped, his Scots accent unmistakable.

"Everything."

Green Man squeezed lightly for emphasis, and Archimedes nodded.

One moment, they were surrounded by lights. The ones in the grounds, the ones in windows, the hundreds of smaller ones strapped to weapons or helmets. The next, all was black. All around him, the night air was full of gasps of surprise and fizzing and breaking glass. The sudden removal of the light had made them all equally blind.

But Green Man had known it was coming, and was already on the move. He cast Archimedes aside and ran. Soft bodies cracked against his and were brushed aside. He kept running. He hit something harder, dented it, was turned by it. He kept running. Sometimes a branch dragged across his chest. Sometimes he tripped, but he kept running.

He wasn't the quickest wild card out there, but his legs were long and did not tire. Seconds passed, then minutes.

They'd be on to him soon; he was sure of it. But would they?

There would be no working communications at the castle now. No working vehicles. No lights. Perhaps he had a chance.

Then he heard the sound of a helicopter. Soft at first, then louder, then horribly loud, directly overhead.

His heart fell as a white beam appeared to his left, then swung over, picking him out. He squinted against the brightness and glanced around for a fencepost, or any loose object he could use as a projectile.

Something was dropping toward him.

He was going too fast to avoid it, but managed to get his arms up in time as it smacked against his shoulder.

It was a ladder.

And now he looked, the helicopter wasn't military. Fairly sure whatever was up there was better than staying where he was, he skidded to a stop, grabbed it, and started to climb.

As he did so, the helicopter rose higher into the sky, leaving the castle quickly behind.

When he reached the top, Wayfarer was waiting to help him inside.

He blinked at her a few times, unable to think of anything to say.

After she'd pulled the ladder back in and shut the door, she looked at him. "I had a look at your escape plan. It was terrible, so I decided to prepare one of my own."

He blinked again; no words came out.

She raised an eyebrow. "You're welcome."

♣

Badb realised she had fallen asleep again. Unconscious, rather. She was stuck to her own blood on the floor, and for the first time in her life, no amount of determination could substitute for the strength needed to get her up.

Fascinating.

Fractured bones had never stopped her before. She had once lost an eye without breaking concentration. She'd kept her mouth shut when an armored car drove over her feet, although, that time, she had been forced out of her body and into that of a crow. Pain and weakness were no impediments to one whose every thought was divine.

She needed to regenerate. Her younger self was prone to emotions more powerful and foolish than those of mere mortals, but it was either that or risk the breakout of peace.

And so tonight, she would accompany the Fists to Windsor, and when Pygmalion and the others sprang their ambush, the goddess would drink in the death of the heroic young Jamila. Yes, that would be *most* satisfactory.

She listened to the quiet. Perhaps, as these groups sometimes did, the Fists were each sitting by themselves, contemplating their own mortality. It was dark in the hideout too. Very dark. Almost as if night had already fallen. As if her blackout had been severe enough to miss an entire day . . .

No. Impossible.

She threw her consciousness to the nearest crow. The sun had long since set. Streetlights shone everywhere. To the east, sirens and burning buildings. She flitted from bird to bird, shaking them from their slumber; sending them flying from the eaves of houses, the tops of trees; from warm factory roofs and empty centers of worship. Her mind crossed hundreds of streets in mere minutes, but even so, by the time she caught sight of Windsor, all that was left of the raid was the massive figure of Green Man clinging to a rope ladder that dangled from a helicopter.

Too late.

She had mere days left to shatter this city for good or the land here would go unfed. Time to move her plans forward.

But who would wield the blade for her?

And then, a quick flick revealed a familiar figure trying to sneak away from the site of the raid. Seizer. Too many soldiers were rushing in now from all directions. He'd never make it. Not without the aid of a goddess.

♠ ♥ ♦ ♣

Thursday

MARCH 12TH

GREEN MAN SAT ON the decaying office chair, head in his hands. He and the remaining London Fists were hiding out in an abandoned set of flats scheduled to be demolished.

Just like us. I wonder which will be destroyed first?

It had all gone so terribly, terribly wrong. After the botched attack on Henry at Windsor Castle, the Twisted Fists had gone to ground, aware that the Silver Helix would be hunting for them, no doubt backed by the army. Of course, the authorities wouldn't know which jokers were members and which were innocent. Many of them wouldn't care either. Constance had been right: by attacking Windsor, he'd given his enemies all the evidence they needed to bury him.

The door to his room was somewhat lacking in integrity, and he could see Wayfarer on the other side of it as she made a game attempt to find something solid enough to knock on.

"Come in," he said, fixing his mask into place.

She did so, and placed a chipped glass of water next to him. She waited as he sipped, the familiarity of their ritual comforting despite the squalor. "Report," he said, not without a trace of reluctance. "How bad is it? Did any of the others get out or was it just me?"

"Blue Jeans is in custody. We don't know where they've taken him. Jamila and Peggy are—"

"I saw." Both had died at the hand of Stonemaiden.

Wayfarer nodded sadly. "I'm sorry."

"And Seizer? Maven?"

Much as he despised Seizer, they needed him. The old knave was their king. He tried to convince himself that a tarnished symbol for their people was better than no symbol at all. It was hard to swallow, though.

"They made it out and are on their way," replied Wayfarer. "Do you want to leave before they get here?"

He looked up at her. "You think they'll be followed?"

"No. I think they might have made a deal with the Helix and sold us out for a reduced sentence."

It made sense but he couldn't bring himself to move. "If you're right, I'll be their target. I'll be sure to make plenty of noise so that you can get away. If something happens to me, Wayfarer, it will be up to you to make sure the Twisted Fists continue."

"Me?"

"Is there anyone else you'd trust to keep everyone in line?"

She smirked at that. "No, but I'm happy where I am. I've no wish to paint a target on my head, especially not when the country seems to be falling apart. Which is why it isn't going to be relevant. I'm going to make sure nothing happens to you."

He sipped the water again. "If it does, though, you'll need a mask. And a strategy. I thought I'd brought the Fists into the modern age. Perhaps I had for a while, but things are pulling too far away for me to keep up. I'm tired, Wayfarer. I'm getting too old for this. It's time for some new blood."

Wayfarer shook her head, ignoring her phone, which had started to ring. "If you give up now, what they'll get is Seizer on the throne and Seizer in control of the Fists."

He shuddered and stood up. "Heaven forbid!"

She gave a lopsided grin, "That's the spirit," and stepped out to attend to a call.

"We need a plan," he muttered to himself. "Some way to salvage this . . ."

He began to pace, his footfalls thudding heavily on the cracked floor. He was still pacing later, when Wayfarer returned.

"One of our people just picked up Miss Russell and Bobbin near the old hideout."

"Constance? Is she alright? I thought she'd be well clear of London by now."

"Apparently not. She wants to speak to you."

Even in these circumstances it would not do for Green Man to turn away a friend of his people. He returned to his chair, sinking heavily into it with a sigh. "Send her up."

♠

Green Man looked exhausted. There was a pall over his hideaway. And no wonder. The news had been filled with stories of the fight between the Fists and the Silver Helix on the grounds of Windsor Castle.

"I appreciate you seeing me," she began. Convincing Green Man to see Turing after the events of the night before was going to be tricky.

Green Man nodded slowly. "I can't believe what a massacre it was." He sounded bewildered.

"You shouldn't have tried to take on the Silver Helix," she said. "It was always going to be an unfair fight."

He nodded. "I'm not certain how I could have led my people to such a disaster. But I had to take a stand."

She steeled herself, then said, "I need you to talk to someone. And you're not going to like it." She hoped this wasn't a fool's errand. But what was happening was bigger than either of them. She hoped he would see it the same way.

"I'm in contact with Turing," she said. There was thunderous clap as Green Man's hands slammed down on his desk.

"Why? Why would you have anything to do with that evil bastard?"

"Because he might be able to prove Seizer's claim to the throne," she said more calmly than she felt. There was enough *sturm und drang* to go around, she didn't need to be fanning it. "Henry can't be allowed to continue—isn't that your position? Isn't that what last night was all about? Henry's son is dead. Gloriana has given up her claim. And Richard . . ." Her voice trailed away then she rallied. "But if Seizer is the true heir, Henry can be replaced and we can right a terrible wrong."

Green Man shook his head. "How could I possibly trust Turing?"

"Don't trust him," Constance replied reaching out and taking his hands in hers. "Trust me. I've worked with him for decades—I don't have time for me to explain the details, but believe me, he wants to make things right. This is how he can."

Green Man slid his hands away from Constance's. She hoped she'd done enough. He stared down at his desk, shaking his head silently. At last, he looked up at her and said softly, "Bring him in."

◆

The morning papers had made it clear why Ranjit hadn't responded to any of Noel's requests for a meeting. Finally, Noel had taken matters into his own hands. Assuming his male avatar he had teleported directly into the director's office.

The look bestowed upon him had been both weary and aggravated. "What now, Noel?"

Noel laid the printout in front of the big Sikh. While the Lion flipped through the copies of police reports, Noel laid out his encounters with Henry. He could only hope these murders of seventy-two-year-old male jokers would bolster his unsupported word.

Ranjit looked up from the pages and met Noel's gaze. "Our intelligence indicates that these people are all members of the Twisted Fists."

"That is utter bullocks!"

"Really? Then explain to me why our people fought a pitched battle with the Fists on the grounds of Windsor last night?"

"Maybe because they heard about this?" Noel gestured wildly at the printouts. "They have their ways, and then there were the joker deaths *without* the normal five for one killing. I'd say limiting their response to just that bastard Henry showed incredible restraint on their part."

"This was an assault upon our government. We can no longer leave Green Man in place. Whatever his role in the Fists might have been he has become a danger. There is a warrant out for his arrest." The Lion stood and handed back the papers. "Stonemaiden will show you out."

"Ranjit, no, please wait, the joker prince is real. It's why Henry—"

"Good day, Noel. I have a country to protect."

♥

"Are you daft?" Constance hissed, staring at Turing with complete dismay. "I *just* brought *you* to Green Man, and now you want me to bring Noel to him as well? It's mad. Completely mad."

Turing paced and nervously ran his fingers through his hair. It surprised her because normally Turing never looked anything other than cool and collected.

"You must," he said quietly, but with real urgency. "I have the DNA, but I want to be absolutely certain. Noel can make inquiries without the inconvenience of travel."

"If you have the DNA, why bother checking out his childhood?"

Turning turned away and murmured, "I have to be sure. No more errors."

Constance shook her head, exasperated and exhausted with it all. Would this madness and the ripple effect it was causing her country never end? And now Turing, by far the most coldly logical person she knew, was obsessed—as if putting Boyd-Brackenbury on the throne would fix something and make the world suddenly right. She allowed that having your husband poison an HRH might cause you to be in quite a state, but really . . .

"Please," he pleaded. The tone was one she'd never heard in his voice before. It was a shock after the forty-some years they'd worked together. "Please. We must."

"Fine," she said impatiently. She grabbed his wrist. "But you're coming with me."

She gave a sharp knock on Green Man's office door and heard his muffled, "Enter." As they did so, a slight joker with a rather startling resemblance to a demon from a Goya painting scuttled out of the room.

Constance shut the door and Green Man looked them over with an expression that was both wary and puzzled.

"Is something else wrong?"

Turing started to speak, and Constance gave his wrist a hard squeeze. His mouth clamped shut.

"Yes," she began carefully. "I know I've asked a lot of you what with bringing Turing here, but his aims coincide with your own. He tells me that in order to completely verify Boyd-Brackenberry's claim to the throne, he needs to use the powers of another ace."

There was a dour expression on Green Man's face. She hoped she hadn't pushed him too far.

"And who would this miraculous ace be?" he asked.

"He's someone I know as well," she said quickly. "I've known him since he was a lad. And I know he very much wants to help find the true heir to the throne."

"You're hedging," Green Man said, leaning back in his chair. "Just how bad is this ace?"

"It's No—" Turing blurted out. Constance shook his wrist and glowered at him. "We need to tell him," Turing insisted.

"His name is Noel and he's a teleporter," she began. "Turing can send him wherever he's needed to get the information we need, and he can do it in the blink of an eye."

Green Man leaned forward. "A teleporter? What does he look like?"

Constance described Noel and his power quickly. She left out the bits about his other avatars because that was Noel's business to tell.

"I think I've already had the privilege of a fist-to-fist introduction," Green Man growled. It was a deep resonant sound as if amplified by his wooden body. "He's a murderer. He killed Dorothy. Why would I let him near me at all?"

"Dorothy?" Constance asked in confusion.

"A harmless old joker, worked in the shop aboard the *Queen Mary*. I found him standing over her body with a gun in his hand."

Turing spoke up, "I know this case. We coordinated with the Met, fearing you and the Fists might take action. The woman was killed by a high-powered round fired from a sniper rifle. It could not have been Noel."

"You wouldn't lie to me, Turing," Green Man asked, though it was more a threat than a question.

"No, I'm not such a fool."

"And what do you have to say about this?" Green Man asked. "You're asking for quite a lot. And whatever happens is all on you, Constance."

She had to think for a moment. In the rush of everything that was happening, she'd just given over to Turing's opinion. She looked at Turing, then dropped his wrist. He hadn't been one of her favorite people of late, but she still *knew* him. She turned back to Green Man and said, "I've known Noel for a long time and he can be a bit of a bastard. Actually, he's rather terrible in his own way, but you could do far worse than trust him. He's the one who warned me about the plot against the old jokers. I guess I'm saying, you should trust both of them. Heaven help us."

♣

Badb blinked against the light. She had fallen asleep again. Very dangerous indeed. Even worse, was the fact that she could not remember where she was, or for an instant, who she was.

An old woman leaned over her, her eyes full of concern and kindness. "You poor thing. You poor, poor thing."

This was Constance! A mere seamstress and yet so respected by the likes of Green Man that the goddess had followed her once or twice, only to come up with nothing.

"Is there anything you need? Water, perhaps?"

Information, thought the goddess. That's what she needed. It ought to flow into her as fast as the blood seeped out. She flicked to a crow that lay in waiting just outside and saw, with shock, the men she had allowed to rescue the princess. Noel and Turing, both.

They must not see her here.

"Help me stand."

"Of course," said the woman, but she was interrupted by a man behind her. Badb's eyes were so poor now, she had not even noticed him in the dim light of the corridor.

"Let me do it," he said.

"You always think I'm too delicate, Bobbin," said the woman.

Neither of them worried about the blood, although the man wore thick leather gloves so that Badb wondered if he might be hiding a joker deformity beneath them.

Meanwhile, Turing hoisted a box of heavy equipment out of the back of his car.

"I'd *love* to help," said Noel. "But my arm, you see?"

What were they up to? What were they doing *here*? She had to know. She cast her mind around for a crow. Most satisfactory! She had remembered to hide a few around the building before she lost consciousness. Mostly, they waited quietly under piles of rubbish and would remain there unmoving until they starved.

"Has she fainted?" Asked Constance. "Oh, the poor thing."

"No," Badb told her. "Please." She allowed her voice to sound grateful. "I prefer to be out of the way. In . . . in here. On the old couch. Yes, so kind. But . . ." she took in a big gulp of air. "Please, don't mention that you found me in the corridor? Don't . . . don't mention me at all?"

"Why would we?" said Constance.

Already they could hear Noel's voice coming toward them. "You really think your machines can prove all that, Alan? I got close to him, and I'm telling you now, I didn't like the look of him one bit."

He paused as Constance and Bobbin made their way back into the corridor.

"Well, will you look who it is?"

♠

It had been fraught meetings all around. At their introduction Green Man had unconsciously touched the arm where Noel had burned him, and the eyes behind the mask were cold and deadly.

Noel had come right to the point telling the big knave, "I didn't kill that woman. Sorry about our little misunderstanding. Truce?" He offered his hand, hoping the cast would underline that they were even now.

For a few heartbeats Green Man made no move to accept the handshake. Then he said, "Truce. We have a country to save," he added as they shook. Noel's hand looked like a child's as it was enfolded in that enormous wooden appendage. "But I will kill you without hesitation if you play us false."

"Never thought otherwise."

Green Man's meeting seemed positively effusive when compared with Maven and Boyd-Brackenbury. The old knave had been actually spitting with fury, saliva dampening Noel's face as he shouted, "You tried to kill me you bastard! I'll see you punished when I come into my own."

Noel pulled out his handkerchief and made a show of wiping his face. "Well, that's gratitude for you. Since I'm here to help you come into your own, you best hold off on any retribution until we get that settled." As he finished speaking Noel glanced at Maven. The look she bestowed on him promised retribution.

Yep, one or the other of us is coming out of this dead.

After all the threats and drama, Noel went in search of Constance, figuring he was probably back in her good books. He found her in another room, sitting on a broken-down old sofa with her elderly beau. The crone was sleeping on another couch. Blood soaking into the fabric. Constance and Bobbin were holding hands, and for a brief moment Noel felt a stab of pain. He shook it off and crooked a finger at Constance. She followed him into the corridor.

"What, Noel?" Her tone was sharp and suspicious.

"Nothing. Just wanted a friendly face, more fool me." Her expression softened. He lowered his voice. "I don't have a lot of friends here. What do you know about the old Irish lady?"

"Nothing. Why should I?"

"Because you're both old?" Noel quipped and earned a slap on the arm for it. "There's something . . . she helped me—us—find Sissel."

"Green Man said she helped him find Bobbin."

Noel took another long look at the bandaged figure. "A woman of many talents, it seems."

◆

"A joker on the throne . . . it could change so much . . ." Bobbin trailed off. Constance glanced at Boyd-Brackenbury and Maven, who were sitting together on a divan on the opposite end of the room.

"Depends on the joker," Constance replied softly. "I always thought Boyd-Brackenbury was a bit odd with his whole I'm-the-rightful-King story, but now, who knows. He wouldn't be my first choice."

Bobbin took her hand, ever careful that his spiny protrusions didn't stab her. "There will be an uproar if he succeeds, but . . ."

"No, there will be riots in the streets," she said. That much she knew. The Britain First crowd would burn the country down before letting a joker sit on the throne. Especially one like Boyd-Brackenbury. "What are we going to do about *that*?"

"We try and create calm. There has be an outreach between jokers and the normal folk. Bring aces into it. Maybe even you, Constance."

The very idea of exposing her power made Constance woozy. She'd spent her life hiding her power as best she could. But Bobbin was right. If the face of a wild card was just an old lady who makes clothes—very special clothes, admittedly—then maybe people wouldn't be so afraid.

"Maybe, luv, maybe," she said with a sigh. "Do you think the country even wants a monarchy anymore? After all this . . . this madness, I wonder." Suddenly, she felt weary and every moment of her age.

"I'm a simple man," Bobbin said. "All I know is that we Brits might complain about the monarchy, but no one else had better disrespect it. Perhaps with a joker on the throne, things will get better for all of us."

Constance considered Boyd-Brackenbury again. "And you think he's the one to do that?" Bobbin followed her gaze.

"I hope so, Constance."

♥

Noel had never visited Wolferton, the village where the palace payments had been sent and Boyd-Brackenbury had been raised, but his parents had once brought him to the nearby village of Sandringham, site of the queen's private home and shooting retreat. It had been years, but Google maps and city view were his friend, so Noel in his male form managed to make a relatively undramatic arrival in the larger village.

Turing's instructions had been clear: "Find out all you can about Boyd-Brackenbury. There will be a massive reaction once we go public, so we want no surprises. If we are going to challenge Henry, we must be absolutely certain of our facts."

So now he arrived in Sandringham with a *pop* of displaced air that startled the hell out of a shop owner busily sweeping off his front stoop, and caused an elderly Pekingese being walked by its equally elderly owner to go off on a fit of hysterical barking, followed by desperate wheezing.

The old lady glared at Noel. "You aces have no concern for public safety. Why can't you take the train like normal folk?"

Noel was in a foul mood. In his male form the cast was abominably tight, and the transformation had hurt his ribs so much he had to work to suppress the urge to dropkick the yapping dog. Instead he murmured an apology. He then turned to the shop keeper. "Is there someplace I can hire a car? I need to get to Wolferton."

"It's not so far, two miles or so. I'd just use a taxi."

"Or walk," the old lady sniffed. "Young people today don't—"

"Yes, quite; I am, however, in rather a bit of a hurry."

He turned his back on her, and receiving the message, she moved off, towing her dog. The shop owner guided Noel to the nearest hotel, where he snagged a cab.

Wolferton's close proximity to the sea had Noel's nostrils tickling with the scent of brine and seaweed. He had the driver drop him at the address for Boyd-Brackenbury's mother. She was long dead, but he hoped there were some gossipy oldsters who might be able to provide information about the sudden arrival of an infant to that home in late 1948.

The residents of the terrace were a bust; most seemed to be transplants fleeing the cities for the charms of country living. He stood on the sidewalk smoking and trying to put himself in the place of a woman who suddenly had custody of an infant. He found himself recalling Jasper's first two years, the visits to the pediatrician for routine vaccinations, earaches, and bumps and bruises. Niobe had been more than a bit overattentive.

He needed to get information on the local doctor. Of course the records would be private, but Noel was good at stealing things that were supposed to be kept private. He had a momentary worry that the NHS bureaucracy would make this a tough search, but a quick check of Google revealed that the National Health Service had been founded in July of 1948.

♣

"In the late forties? That would have been Doctor Bevins. Long dead of course, but his patient notes are just delightful. Not at all dry."

She gave a gurgling chuckle. Doctor Nalakini Khatri was an attractive young woman with a bright smile. Noel was seated in her office after having spun a tale about being a lawyer trying to locate an heir. She continued, "You can see how much he cared for the people here, but he also had some rather acerbic commentary about them."

Khatri was probably saying more than she should, but that was no doubt due to the fact Noel was presenting as his male avatar. Women and some men went weak in the knees when faced with the overwhelming sexuality that was Thomas Landry, the latest identity Noel had taken for himself. He sometimes wondered why Lilith was always Lilith but the male form had had so many names—Simon, Bahir, Etienne, Ilya, and now Thomas? Perhaps because Noel himself thought of himself as a man, so the sun god avatar seemed more false? He had a momentary wish he could talk with the Helix's on-staff psychiatrist again. Actually, finding a therapist probably wouldn't be a bad idea—

Noel forced himself back to the moment. This was not the time to lose focus. "I'm interested in any information about a woman. Marjorie Boyd-Brackenbury and her son." He leaned across the desk. Khatri's lips parted and her breath quickened.

"I really shouldn't . . ."

"It's been seventy-two years and it might mean a very large inheritance for our client." *No shit*, Noel added mentally. *Just the throne.*

She gave in. Everyone always did.

♠

Consternation and frustration were his dominant emotions as Noel started at the elegant handwriting on the yellowing papers. Doctor Bevins had been the exception to the rule about doctors' handwriting. His penmanship was perfection.

And the tale written in the notes changed everything. They detailed the progress of a pregnancy. *So why in the hell had the palace sent her a stipend for all those years? One that had continued to her son,* Noel wondered.

"Do you know of anyone who might still be around who would have known this woman?" he asked the doctor.

"Well, there is the Doctor Bevin's daughter, Sandra. She's up in her eighties now, but she used to assist him in the office."

◆

"She's eighty-eight. Who knows if her memory is accurate," Turing objected.

Turing shrank back as Noel pushed in too close. Despite the fact they were of a height, Noel projected predator, and no one knew that better than Alan.

"I've seen the fucking doctor's notes. She was *pregnant*. And while it took a while, and enough tea and sherry that I'm more than a little drunk and my bladder's bursting, the old lady did finally give up the village gossip. Boyd-Brackenbury was a maid at Sandringham. Rumor about the village at that time was that she got knocked up by Prince Philip."

"But the markers were all there for Victoria," Turing argued. He then broke off and shook his head. "Of course, Philip and Elizabeth were cousins. They would both show markers back to Victoria." He began pacing. The flesh-colored makeup he wore was streaking, giving him bizarre silver slashes across his face and neck like robot war paint. "This is suggestive, but not dispositive. She might have been pregnant when she took in the baby, or the pregnancy was faked to explain the infant. This might have been mere gossip, or she was known to the palace because of her work at Sandringham and was therefore an appropriate choice to foster the child. And finally, one must take into account the age of your interlocutor."

"So how do we prove it one way or the other?" Noel asked.

"Mitochondrial DNA to compare with Boyd-Brackenbury's. So, I need a sample of a close family relative. Margaret's would be ideal—"

"I am not grave robbing the queen or sneaking into the morgue to take a little nip out of Richard," Noel snapped. "And right now I have *got* to go take a piss, so let me know when you've decided on our next move."

Noel had almost made his escape when Turing's voice stopped him. "Gloriana. You were acquainted. Go to her and bring me back a sample."

"Acquainted? I tried to seduce her. And why in the Hell would she give me a DNA sample that would cost her father the throne?"

"Which is why your . . . *acquaintance*," Turing gave another little cough. "Could be . . . helpful."

"So, you want me to fuck the wife of the Norwegian monarch?"

"We did train you for it," Turing said simply.

"Among other things," Noel drawled. He sighed. "Fine, but I'll need to do this tomorrow. I don't think Gloriana would be enticed by Lilith. Also, my arm and ribs are killing me. And I've got to get some sleep."

"Time is of the essence," Turing responded.

"And some of us are still just flesh and blood, Alan."

♥

There were several good things about this bright and cold afternoon. The first being the sun. Second, Constance had cut the cast off Noel's arm. While it throbbed, it meant he could finally reach that annoying itch that had been driving him mad for the past two days.

Their paired phones had revealed that Gloriana was not at Windsor. Instead, she and her daughter were ensconced at Claridge's prior to their return to Norway.

It had been absurdly easy. Gloriana had expressed a desire to thank the man who had rescued her daughter. Turing had arranged a meeting. As he walked into the lobby and headed for the elevators, Noel reflected on Turing's final instructions.

"Blood would be best, but saliva, hair, really almost anything will do for a sample."

Irritated Noel had snarled, "How about I just wipe my dick when we're finished?"

Turing, pedantic as always, had frowned and said, "Your semen would complicate matters."

Noel had told him to factor for it. Assuming of course that Gloriana was even open to seduction. If not, he would at least get a look at the rooms and could return later and try a little light burglary.

There was discreet security in the hallway, but they had been told to expect Noel, so he received a nod and one of the guards murmured into his throat mic. By the time Noel had reached the door it was opened by an efficient young woman in sensible heels, a knee-length skirt, and a cardigan sweater tied around her shoulders. Her blouse was starched and pressed and almost as blue as her eyes.

"Mr. Grenville-Lacey, welcome." (Thanks to Turing's eidetic memory Noel now had the name he had given Gloriana all those years ago.) "Her Highness is waiting for you." The woman had a pronounced Norwegian accent. "May I take your coat?"

Noel relinquished the leather jacket and followed her to a set of sliding doors. A muted knock, a murmured *come in*. The aide closed the door behind him.

Gloriana was seated on a sofa but she stood and gave him a quizzical look. "So, not an IT tech," she said.

"I do have a few skills in that direction, but no. Do accept my apology for lying to you at our earlier meeting."

She looked better than when he had last seen her, but she had lost weight and the shadow of fear was still in her eyes. She waved off his apology. "Doesn't matter. I understand you're the agent who saved my daughter. I can never repay you for that."

She held out her hand and Noel touched the tips of her fingers, "It was my honor, ma'am," but he then clasped her hand in both of his. Her breath caught and a flush rose in her cheeks. "Forgive me, ma'am, but I've never forgotten you."

"We didn't have much time together at Cambridge, did we?" Her tone was an interesting combination of coquettish and regretful. She didn't remove her hand and in fact she stepped in closer to him.

"No, ma'am. Life swept us apart."

"Only to bring us together now," she said. "Perhaps it's kismet."

All of his practiced words deserted him as Noel experienced an odd moment of shame. The woman was vulnerable, defenseless to the overwhelming sexuality of his avatar, and he was about to use her in the most callous way imaginable.

He wondered if he could pull off a reverential Victorian request for a lock of her hair, then decided he would sound like a complete prat. Also, he didn't do reverent and sincere all that well.

Gloriana decided it for him. She pressed her body against his and gave him a gentle kiss on the lips. Their desperate need for proof swept away Noel's brief moment of scruples and he swept her up into his arms while passionately kissing her.

"Bedroom," he growled against her mouth.

She threw out a hand indicating the correct door while frenziedly kissing him.

At sixteen he had no idea how to undress a woman. Now he did in ways designed to delight and arouse. They shared the task of removing his clothing. There was a moment when she first saw the scars and recoiled, but then recovered and gently drew her finger across them.

"You have suffered in service to our country," she said softly. He didn't answer, just gently eased her onto the bed.

The Helix had seen to it that he was trained in the art of lovemaking by experts. In all of his forms he knew how to bring a woman or a man to an intense climax. He did so now. Her nails raked his back as she arched against him, their bodies slick with sweat. As he drove himself deep into her, approaching his own orgasm, the calculating part of his mind wondered if he would ever again make love to someone and *not* have it be a job or involving the exchange of money.

With a hoarse groan he climaxed, shuddered, rolled off her, and lay panting on top of the sheets. Gloriana propped herself up on an elbow, smiled down at him, and ran her nails across his chest.

"Was it worth the twenty-year wait?" she teased.

"Twenty-four years actually," Noel corrected, then pulled her down and kissed her. "And very much worth it." He slid his hands down to cup her breasts. Gloriana sighed and gave a regretful head shake.

"As much as I would like to test your stamina, I think we had best end our tryst before Bodil begins to wonder."

"Completely understand, ma'am," Noel said. "Thank you though for this opportunity to have a young man's dream come true." He then rolled off the bed. "May I use your bathroom?"

She nodded and he gathered up his clothes, went into the bathroom, closed the door, and collected the mix of his cum and her spunk, which he placed in a plastic envelope. A quick look around the bathroom revealed a hairbrush. Noel pulled out a number of strands of her brown hair and placed them in another envelope. He then quickly washed up, dressed, and reentered the bedroom.

Gloriana had already returned to the sitting room. Her assistant, Bodil, was talking with her about the upcoming flight home to Oslo. Noel could only assume there was another bathroom or Bodil was the most discreet of discreet aides.

Noel bowed his head. "Thank you, ma'am—"

"No, thank you for the opportunity to *properly* thank you."

♣

Alan carefully reached out a gloved hand and took the swab from Seizer. This was no proper lab, of course, but appropriate procedures could still be observed. When everything was falling apart, protocol could sometimes save the day—he'd seen that on the field of war, and Alan had precious little else to hold onto now. The machines were waiting for his input—hopefully not garbage in this time. If Seizer were Elizabeth's son—well, they would at least have a path forward. It wasn't nothing.

He started the analysis. Now it was just a matter of time.

♠

"Is that a rat?" asked Noel suddenly. It might have been a joke to break the tension as everybody waited for the results of Turing's test to come through. But he stared suspiciously into the corner where the ailing crow had twitched beneath its pile of old newspapers.

Badb held it firm, ignoring the agony of its crippled wings until Noel turned away again. At least the bird's spasm had shifted the papers enough so that now she could see out.

Everybody in the basement room so far below her seemed nervous about the outcome of the test. Turing fretted over his machine, as though willing it to work faster. Noel and Maven stared daggers at each other. One day, surely, those daggers would become real.

Bobbin and Constance leaned against a wall, close together, their shoulders touching in the tight confines of the basement, made all the more cramped by the towering, hunched figure of Green Man, his body all but thrumming with tension.

And finally, there was Seizer.

He had a corner of the room all to himself, as if already they deferred to him.

He grinned, his chest swollen like a rooster's before a rival, his chin up proudly. This was his moment, and he knew it. A joker king, his heart more poisonous than his appearance could ever be. People would die to keep him from the throne, oh yes.

♦

Alan read the results from the screen, then turned the monitor to face the others. They crowded around, uncomfortably close, and he pulled back. Maven stood back from the others a few steps, but Seizer was practically vibrating with intensity, and Green Man wasn't much better. Constance took a quick glance, and then pulled back, turning to face Alan.

"Does that mean what I think it means?"

The data didn't lie. Everybody else might, but in the end, the one thing you could rely on were the facts. "Seizer is Philip's son. There's no trace of Elizabeth's markers."

Green Man sagged against the table, one hand reaching out to brace himself. "So, that's it, then. He's not the bloody heir."

♥

Seizer wasn't speaking. He stood frozen, still grinning for several seconds after Turing broke the news. But Maven got it right away, Badb could see that.

"Oh, you have got to be fucking kidding me!" she cried. Before anybody could react, a pistol was in her hand.

"I wouldn't," said Noel quietly.

"No," she sneered. "You would not." Steady as any machine, she swung the barrel around until it was pointed in Turing's face. "You couldn't stand it, could you? You couldn't stand to have a fucking joker in charge."

"That's not—" Turing stopped speaking as she stepped closer and pressed her gun against his lips. Noel had his good hand inside his jacket. As for Green Man, he merely watched. The chances were that any bullets that found a mark today would only make him stronger.

Finally, Seizer stirred himself. The skin on his face had turned almost as red as his blisters. He grabbed the page of the printout from Turing's hands and began backing toward the door.

"Come on, girl," he told Maven. "We have the proof here. Right here! We'll find our own expert to look at it. They're cheating us. And not just us, but every joker in Britain. In the world, even!" He swung his index finger around, his eyes wild, his voice far higher than normal. "Don't try to stop us! Don't even think about it. I have a power of my own that will make every one of you sorry."

He shoved Bobbin aside to get to the door. "I'm releasing this into the world. The jokers will rise up."

And with that, father and daughter were gone.

"Well," drawled Noel. "I'm *certain* that's the last we'll ever hear of them."

But Badb was already following them as they ran out of the building. Such fury they had! It was most satisfactory.

♣

Noel, Turing, and Constance stood at a table studying the list names that Turing had hacked from the wild card database. Constance's elderly beau had been quite dejected when Seizer had been revealed as a mere royal by-blow. He was busying himself at the camp stove boiling water for tea. Personally, Noel could have used a shot of whiskey. Green Man had retired to the far side of the room. With the mask in place Noel couldn't tell if he were as dejected as Bobbin or relieved that Seizer had been proven not to be the lost heir.

Seizer and Maven had withdrawn, muttering threats and imprecations. Noel wasn't worried about Seizer, but Maven had him very worried. She was trained, skilled, and dangerous as all fuck . . . and he was injured. He had no idea how he was going to protect this gang of geriatrics, especially if they did manage to locate the actual heir.

"He has to be here somewhere, assuming he hasn't died in the intervening seventy-two years," Noel said.

"Or been killed in the past two days," Constance added darkly and shot him a glare.

Green Man joined them. "I could try talking to the nurse again." He didn't sound hopeful.

Constance turned on Noel. With her arms akimbo and her back stiff she reminded him of a bantam hen. "We've got this list, and you've got a power that you're bloody well going to put to good use!" She pointed toward the wall and the nation beyond. "Now you get out there and warn these people!"

Even contemplating the shift into Simon had Noel wincing, but he sighed and nodded. "All right, though whether they will believe me . . ."

"Let me go over the list, remove any who are deceased," Turing said. He smoothed the sheet of paper with nervous fingers. "That will save you some time."

"I'll need an iPad with Wi-Fi so I can access Google Maps. I haven't been to some of these places."

♠

Turing scanned the list—nothing out of the ordinary until one glaring omission leapt to the forefront. Bobbin wasn't listed in the registry.

Noel was complaining, Constance scolding. Bobbin stood off to the side a bit, trying to keep the peace. Likely a futile effort. Alan stepped up beside him and said quietly, "Bobbin? Can I have a word?"

They walked a short distance away. "What is it, Turing?"

"I'm not sure I understand how you ended up mixed up in all this."

"Well, it's really just Constance, you know. I'd follow her anywhere." Bobbin hesitated and then said, "I heard about Sebastian. I'm sorry."

"Yes, well. Apparently we didn't have what you two have. Have you been together long? Childhood sweethearts, perhaps?"

Bobbin laughed. "Oh no. I grew up on the *Queen Mary*, just another joker kid in among the hideous throng."

"Your parents were jokers too?"

"No parents for me, not until Handsome Harry adopted me."

The others had quieted down while they were talking, had finally noticed that Alan had pulled Bobbin aside. Constance opened her mouth, but Noel shook his head and she closed it again. Bobbin continued his reminiscence, smiling. "Harold Hugesson was his real name; he's the one who trained me as a tailor. He gave me his name, so I became Arthur Hugesson."

"Arthur. I see." Turing glanced at Noel, whose eyes had gone wide. Then he turned his attention back to Bobbin.

"We had a decent little shop, Hugesson & Son. Nothing like as fancy as

Constance's place, of course. But these"—Bobbin gestured with his needle-studded hands—" did come in useful there. I like being useful."

"Yes. Bobbin, I think I must ask something else of you now." Turing turned and took a swab from the rack, then presented it to Bobbin.

The man's pied face somehow managed to pale. "Oh no, Turing. You can't be serious."

Alan placed the swab gently in Bobbin's hand. "I think I have forgotten how to joke. Nothing is funny anymore."

◆

The basement room with its makeshift lab seemed an incongruous place for such a pronouncement. It should have echoed with the clarion call of trumpets and the voice of a sergeant-at-arms. Instead, Turing's voice had seemed as cold and muted as the space.

The announcement had Green Man sinking down onto the battered couch as if his legs could no longer support him.

Noel watched Bobbin . . . no, that nickname had to be lost, forever left behind. He watched *Arthur's* eyes slide to Constance. His expression was impassive, but those eyes could not hide his grief.

Noel stepped forward and inclined his head. "Sir, how may I be of service?"

Green Man recovered himself, stood, crossed to Arthur, and took a knee. It should have been ludicrous. Instead, it was oddly moving.

Constance spun on her heel and left the room. Noel listened to the clatter of her heels as she ran up the stone steps toward the nave.

Arthur took two steps, only to be stopped by Turing. "Forgive me, sir, but duty calls and decisions must be made."

For an instant, Noel thought Arthur would acquiesce; then he gave a quick, small shake of his head. "And sometimes those have to wait on the demands of friendship," Arthur said. He followed Constance out the door.

Noel, Turing, and Green Man gathered in a huddle. "So, what the fuck *are* we going to do?" Noel asked.

♥

A cold, dry chill slid up her back. She thought she might vomit as she watched Noel acknowledge Bobbin. No, he wasn't Bobbin anymore. Not her Bobbin. She couldn't bear it.

The sleet and snow had cleared off, but the cold remained. She welcomed it. It was real and it bit her skin and was something to hold on to now that her world had shifted. It was as if someone had pushed her hard into a new place. A place where her dearest friend and her love was no longer himself, but a royal—*the* royal—and destined to sit on the throne and try to help mend a nation torn apart by hatred. And to her dismay, she thought he might be able to do it.

After all, Bobbin was the most decent person she knew.

The door slammed behind her. She knew who it was. She didn't have to look. Of course, he would be there. He had always been there.

"Constance," Bobbin said as he walked around to face her. "Constance, please, luv. It can't be right. I can't be the one."

Tears began rolling down her cheeks. They stung from the cold. "Oh, Bobbin, you know it is. Noel and Turing would never make this kind of mistake. Not after Boyd-Brackenbury. They hid you well, didn't they? They protected you. Oh God, what am I going to do without you?"

"I can't do it, Constance. I'm just an ordinary bloke."

There was a moment when she just wanted to scream, but coming hard on its heels was the realization that her ordinary bloke was anything but. His kindness, good sense, consideration, and deep sense of fairness were the very qualities that would make him perfect for this point in time.

She shook her head then touched his cheek. She was surprised by how warm it was. "Lord, Constance," he said. "We need to get you inside. Your hands are like ice."

"Not just yet," she said, caressing his cheek. "This is the last time we'll be like this. Like regular folk."

"Constance, don't!"

"You know it's true. You're the lost king. And you *will* do the right thing. An ordinary bloke is just what we need right now. Someone solid. And decent. And you are those things and so much more. We stayed so we could do the right thing by the country. Well, this is it, my darling. This is the sacrifice."

"I'd be gaining so much," he said, somewhere between a laugh and a cry. "What am I going to lose?"

She held his gaze. "You know what it is, Bobbin. It's the only thing that makes sense."

"No, Constance," he said with real fear in his voice. "I can't lose you now."

♣

The door swung open to admit Noel.

Green Man noted that he hadn't knocked. "Yes?"

"We've got a problem."

Just the one? he thought, but kept it to himself. Noel did not look in the mood for sarcasm. "Go on."

"You saw how Seizer was when he got the news?"

He tried not to smile at the memory. "Oh yes."

"Well, I don't trust him. And I don't trust Maven either. They're pissed, they have guns, and they know where we are. That's a bad combination. And then there's our mysterious Irish witch. She's . . ."

"I agree. What do you suggest?"

"That we get out of here before trouble finds us. Do you have a place? Somewhere that Seizer doesn't know about?"

Green Man frowned. "Seizer has been with us a long time but . . ."

"You've got a place?"

"Not a hideout exactly, but a sympathetic priest. I suspect he'd let us stay under his care for a night or two."

"Us? Hiding out in a church?" Noel rolled his eyes. "Perfect."

"I'm open to other suggestions if you have them."

Noel shook his head and made for the door. "It's fine, really. Let's just get our king and get the hell out of here before things get messy."

After a long sigh, Green Man stood up and followed him.

Friday

MARCH 13TH

IT WAS LATE, BUT Green Man didn't feel tired at all. Hope swirled in his chest, as welcome as it was unusual. They had found their king, and though he wasn't the most assertive person in the world, he was a good man. The symbol that his people—no, that *all* people—sorely needed. Apart from him and Noel, everyone had gone to bed. Turing and Constance on pallets in the rectory. Arthur upstairs in a room at the top of the tower where he and Noel could guard the stairs. The old church was quiet.

"You still with us?" asked Noel.

"Yes. I was just thinking about Arthur and how best to help him."

"Oh?"

"Yes I was trying to . . ." He paused, unused to sharing such thoughts with a stranger.

"Oh, spit it out man. It can't be any sillier than this entire cocked-up situation."

Perhaps the lateness of the hour created the illusion of intimacy, or perhaps he felt the change in the air, the chance to be someone better for the new king. Or maybe he was just lonely. Whatever it was, the usual inhibitions fell away. "To write a speech. For Arthur, I mean."

"You good with words?"

"I'm passable at delivering them, but I'm better at composing them. I used to be speechwriter, a good one, back before . . ." he gestured to his body " . . . this happened."

"Rather hard to imagine you as a normal guy, no offence."

"But I was. The very definition of normal. Well, for an upper middle-class man of my generation anyway. I had a wife, a family, a steady job, a nice house, a car, a decent pension," he laughed, "life insurance! It turns out they don't cover jokers any more than my marriage vows did."

"I'll give you the insurance," Noel replied, "those guys are bastards, but jokers don't get the monopoly on broken marriages. Trust me, we all have trouble there."

They fell quiet for a while. Noel rubbed his hands together for warmth, then uncapped a flask of whisky and tipped some into his now-empty teacup. "You want some?"

"No thanks, I don't drink."

Noel's face fell. "If any man had a reason . . . but have it your way. So tell me, how does a teetotaling family man turn into a terrorist? You seem too smart to buy into all of the Fist rhetoric."

"You really want to know?"

"I'm not the kind of guy who asks questions and doesn't expect an answer."

He looked Noel up and down. "I see that. Alright. I'll tell you." Except, he didn't. Not at first.

Noel took another sip of whisky. "Ain't neither of us getting any younger here," he drawled.

"I'm sorry. It's just I've not told anyone this before."

"Now you gotta to tell me."

"After my card turned, things looked bleak. I had no job, no prospects, and no way to support my family. When I look back on it, I realize I was in shock. I was certainly not in the right frame of mind to meet Churchill. Anyway, I did meet Churchill, and he told me that he needed me. I was a joker he could trust, you see, one that could infiltrate the Twisted Fists for them. He said that if I did that and helped to bring down the Black Dog, it would be a great service to my country. He also said that he'd provide handsomely for my loved ones and that when it was all over, he'd clear my name. He said he'd speak to Wendy, my wife, personally—"

"And you believed him? That wily old bastard?" Noel gave a sharp laugh.

"I wasn't as cynical as you back then. So, yes, I did what he asked. I got into the Fists, became one of them. I killed for them. Did everything they told me to, worming my way up the ranks until I became one of the Black Dog's inner circle and found out what I needed to bring him in. That way I could come home."

"Funny, I don't recall that happening."

"Quite. The trouble was, only Churchill and I knew the truth. When he died, there was no way back for me."

"You trying to tell me you didn't have any choice?"

"Of course not. There's always a choice; I just didn't have any good ones."

"I'll drink to that," said Noel, "even if you won't."

"Believe it or not I tried to make the best of things. To twist the Twisted Fists, if you will. We still kill, but I keep us to the code, and I try . . . it sounds naive to say it out loud, but I try to help people where possible. Not just jokers, but all the people our society abandons. I used to believe in the system. Now I believe the system needs to change."

"Yeah, things are pretty fucked alright, and I'm certainly not the man to disagree with your methods, but I'm sorry you lost your kids. That's rough, believe me, I know."

"Thank you."

"How many do you have?"

"Two. I imagine they're about your age, actually. Christine, my eldest, has really made a name for herself. We always knew she'd do well." He sighed. "She hates me. Now she's works for the government, trying to bring people like me to justice. I don't know what Roy does. I haven't seen him since before all of this. In my mind, he's still a little boy."

"You should go and find him. Kids need their parents no matter how old they are."

"He's better off without me." Green Man held up a hand before Noel could protest. "Please. They have their own lives. Happy ones, hopefully. Roy and Christine don't need me in them any more than they need the Silver Helix on their doorstep. I stay away because I love them. Let them live in peace."

Noel was quiet for a while, a variety of emotions at play on his face, all suppressed and hard to read. "You told me about your kids but you never told me your name. Your real one. What is it?"

Green Man reached up and took off his mask. "Roger."

"Hey Roger," said Noel, holding out his hand. "Nice to meet you."

♠

Roger fell silent. Noel uncapped his flask and poured another dollop of whisky into his cup. He gestured with the flask toward Roger's cup filled only with water.

"You sure, mate?" Noel asked. "If this whole thing goes tits-up it's your last chance to get pissed."

The church tower was cold. Noel gave a shiver, rolling his shoulders to loosen stiff muscles. Beyond the stone walls he could hear the muted sounds of the Barbican Estate. He checked his watch: 2:20 A.M.

"If you want to take a bit of a lie-down," Roger began, but broke off at Noel's upraised hand and urgent look as a soft metallic *tink* filtered down from the tower roof. It was followed by a man's scream from the floor above where Noel and Roger kept watch on the landing just below.

"Shit!" Noel snatched up his pistol and ran for the stairs. Arthur was sleeping on the top floor. *Should have stayed in the same room with him. To hell with him wanting privacy.* A regretful thought that was coming way too late.

He could hear Roger's crashing footfalls behind him like the clatter of a thousand wooden canes on the stone steps. His ribs sent pain driving through his chest with each breath. Gritting his teeth Noel kept running, taking the steps two at a time.

He hit the door to the upper room and bounced off, falling back against the big knave. Either Arthur or his assailant had locked the door.

"Locked," Noel managed to croak out.

Green Man knotted one enormous fist and slammed it into the door. Wood splinters flew into the room beyond; two hard kicks and the rest of the door was reduced to flinders. Noel darted through. Arthur lay on a pile of blankets that were now turning red from the slashes on his forearms, stab wounds in his chest, a long cut down one cheek, and a shallow slash across his throat.

Noel's peripheral vision caught a flicker of movement to his right. He twisted hard to the side groaning in pain as his ribs protested. The sharp turn sent the leather coat flaring and his attacker's blade slashed across his side, cutting through his sweater and deep into his flesh.

He screamed and tried to swing around to bring his pistol to bear, but Roger was blocking his shot. Sweat bathed Noel's face and his vision seemed to be narrowing.

Noel caught a glimpse of the assassin. It was Maven, dressed for wet work in tight-fitting leather; nothing to grab onto apart from the climbing rig she was wearing. The line extended out of the window, where the glass and mulls had been carefully cut and set aside, allowing her to wriggle through.

Roger attempted to grapple with her, but he was too slow. She darted to the side and threw her blade at Noel. Her aim was excellent, but instead of burying itself in his eye, the knife was blocked by Roger throwing out an arm. The knife stood quivering in his hardened flesh and then Maven was sprinting for the window.

Noel fired, but pain, exhaustion, and blood loss were taking their toll. Maven gave a grunt as she smashed through the widows, sending glass and mull posts sparkling against the night sky, but wherever the bullet had hit it clearly hadn't incapacitated her. She vanished up the side of the tower and they heard her footfalls running across the roof.

He watched the floor coming up to meet him, but before his face connected with the wood he was caught by Roger.

"The king," he managed to croak. He vaguely heard Constance and Turing calling out in grief and alarm as they ran into the room. Then blackness swallowed him.

◆

"Oh, God! Oh, God. Oh, God." Constance mouthed as she ran to Bobbin's side. She wasn't sure if she was whispering it or screaming. There was nothing but a terrible rushing sound in her ears.

It was pandemonium. She knew that Noel had been injured, but that didn't matter right now. She had but one thought—Bobbin.

It seemed as if it took forever to get to his side. He was sprawled on the floor, blood pooling beneath him. She slipped on it and landed hard on her hands and knees next to him. It didn't matter. She rocked back onto her heels—her bloody hands fluttered over his body.

"Constance," he said weakly. "Not exactly what I signed on to do." He coughed.

"Oh, God," she thought. She couldn't scream. Not now.

"Ambulance!" she shouted. "Ambulance. Someone call the ambu . ."

"Can't. Curfew."

"What do you mean, curfew?!"

"Can't go out. Can't get an ambulance. Too many questions."

She glared at Green Man, then at Noel, then at Turing. "This is all your fucking fault. Every one of you. We'd never have known about him being king if it weren't for the three of you."

"Constance . . ." Turing began.

"Get my bag," she growled.

"What?" Green Man asked.

"Get my fucking bag! Now! Make some use of yourself."

She looked back at Bobbin. "It'll be all right, my dear," she said taking his hand. Both their hands were sticky with his blood.

"This isn't how I thought I'd die."

"You're not dying today," she snapped. She was feeling better now. Drawing on her anger helped.

Turing returned with her purse. She shook the contents on the floor caring nothing for where they fell, except for one thing. Her sewing kit and special shears fell out last, thudding on the wood floor.

Her hands trembled as she began threading a needle. "Get some whiskey, rubbing alcohol, anything that'll disinfect this. Now!"

Green Man ran to Noel, rummaged through his jacket, then pulled out a flask. He slid it to her. She grabbed it, unscrewed the top, and doused the thread and her hands.

"This is going to hurt like the devil, Bobbin," she said. "But it must be done. It's the only way."

"Best do it quick then," he replied. His voice was unsteady.

There was a deep wound on his cheek, but it wasn't the real danger. With a deft hand, she cut his shirt away. Gashes covered his chest. She pinched one of his wounds together and began to stitch. After a moment, the world fell away and it was just her and him and her power. She would make him whole again. She had to.

♥

"How could they have found us?" Constance asked angrily, her eyes red with weeping. It was near dawn.

Alan rose to his feet. "I think—and I know this is going to sound a bit mad—I think it has something to do with the crows."

Noel frowned. "What? Do you mean the ravens? At the Tower?"

He shook his head. "No, no. I said crows, and I meant crows. They're everywhere—at the palace, at Westminster Abbey, at our house—even outside the windows at Richard's apartment. I've never seen so many damn crows. It must be some sort of wild card. Somehow all our secrets have been coming to light."

Alan's mind was racing. A million miles a minute, all the pieces clicking into place. "I thought it was just . . . bad luck. Word of a joker prince getting out when Margaret had told only me. Who told Henry? Who shot the old woman on the *Queen Mary*? Sent the police into joker neighborhoods? So many things going wrong for us. I even thought it was some kind of fate, the consequence of losing the true king. Utter nonsense."

"It was Finder who sent me to the *Queen Mary*. Warned me of an assassin," Green Man broke in.

"And I had an informant send me off to the ship—"

"Just in time for us to meet," added Green Man to Noel's statement.

"And it was Finder who approached me with the information about Sissel," Noel added. His tone was low and dangerous.

Turing didn't have the whole picture yet, but Alan was now sure that Finder, and crows, were intimately involved. Some joker power, setting one group against another, leading to the current chaos—but what could she possibly hope to gain? Did she have her own claimant to the throne? Could she have found Elizabeth's child and suborned him? Finder was Irish. Did the answer lie across the Irish Sea?

"Noel. You have to go to Ireland."

♣

Noel stumbled a bit as his feet hit the slick pavement of the parking lot. It was another raw day. The stitches in his side pulled as he threw out an arm to help him balance. At least the cut was on the other side from the broken ribs. And the wound wasn't as bad as he'd first feared. The faintness had been due more to exhaustion and the multiplying injuries. The air smelled of gasoline, the sea, cooking cabbage, burning tires, and damp wool. He was in his Lilith form because he didn't want to wait until after sunrise to jump to the Irish city. And indeed, as he straightened his leather coat, a faint light began to glow on the horizon and his queen of the night melted away with a grinding of bones.

He had landed in the parking lot of the Thiepval Barracks, which housed the FRU, Force Research Unit, a branch of British army intelligence. The building was one of those faceless modern monstrosities that had replaced the older barracks after a massive bomb had leveled the place back in eighty-seven. The only relic of that event was a burned tree trunk that for some reason hadn't been removed. Some sort of memorial?

Thus far he had not been spotted by security because, of course, their gaze was focused outward, over the high metal fencing. Though in this world of wild cards, someone would soon spot him. He unlimbered his Helix identification and walked toward the entrance to the main building.

Over the years he had been sent to Northern Ireland more than a few times to assist with the Troubles, so he knew the barracks well. In fact, he had made his first kill at a pub in Belfast all those many long years ago.

"Hoy!" came a basso shout.

Noel turned, hand raised, ID easily visible. Turing had provided him with the name of the current commander of the unit. "Noel Matthews of the Helix. Here to see Captain Talbot."

"Bloody aces," the soldier muttered as he lowered his rifle.

♠

Noel was listening with only half an ear while the commander of the Royal Ulster Constabulary banged on about *those bastards at the FRU.* Noel had endured more than a few minutes of similar grousing from Talbot at the FRU. The accents had changed, the song remained the same.

The rain had let up, allowing Noel to gaze at the street outside. The dingy brick walls held political (and if one was generous) art—masked men holding guns, red hands, and hunger strikes. There was a clot of black feathers in the gutter formed by a number of dead crows. In the distance the two massive yellow cranes at the Belfast shipyard dominated the horizon.

"Strange thing is the city's been scary quiet since the end of February. Hardly a single crime let alone any terrorism. It's like the whole lot of them just got tired of it all."

That jerked Noel's attention back to the speaker. "End of February you say?"

"Yeah, looks like all the troubles went your way." The added title of *English* was implied if not spoken.

"Indeed they have. Talbot over at Thiepval says you lot are leaky as a sieve," Noel said.

"He's a fine one to talk. They compromised more operations than I can list on two hands. Things have been better since that ancient bitch Badb finally shuffled off this mortal coil. Or at least I hope she has. Always acting like we were toddlers as compared to army intelligence . . ." The man's voice was becoming a dull buzz as exhaustion dragged at Noel's limbs and slowed his thoughts. *Damn Turing for sending him on this fool's errand.* Soon he would have to transform again, but suddenly the man's words penetrated again.

". . . like skin stretched over a bag of bones. Once found some blood on a chair where she'd been sitting. Damn disgusting. Don't know how she—"

Noel surged to his feet and held out his hand. "Thank you. You've been most helpful."

"Here, I thought you wanted—"

"I really must go."

◆

Alan Turing was in disgrace, of course, after his husband's murderous action. But he'd served England for long decades, and perhaps more to the point, the government was still afraid of what Enigma's brain might do if used against them. So, when Alan asked for a meeting with Henry, the prime minister and his cabinet, the Lords of House and Commons—*it concerns the fate of the monarchy*—they agreed to it. Within hours, more than a dozen serious-faced men were gathered around a long mahogany table in the palace, waiting for Alan Turing to speak. It was oddly comforting that Noel was with him, ready to whisk them away should things not go well.

It wasn't easy, looking at Henry and seeing the echoes of Richard in his face. Never to trace a finger along those bones again . . . Alan's hands were shaking, and their makeup had smeared badly at some point in the last tumultuous day, glints of silver shining through. Alan folded his hands carefully in front of him, lacing the fingers tight. *Hold fast, for England's sake.*

Then, speaking softly, he laid it out for them: Elizabeth, bearing a child with needle fingers. How badly had he cut her up in the birth process? No wonder they'd thrust the babe away in horror, a nightmare vision of what such a child would mean for England, and why another child had never been conceived. Then Alan spoke of Handsome Harry, Arthur Hugesson, and finally Bobbin.

"This is absurd," Henry said, half-raising out of his chair. At a glance from the prime minister, he subsided.

"We'll hear him out," Patel said, frowning. "You'll get your chance to respond, Henry."

Alan nodded acknowledgement, then gave them the rest as well, every piece on the chessboard, the almost inevitable maze of paths he foresaw, all leading to a new age of darkness and horror. Was this how Edmund Burke had felt, reflecting on the revolution in France, contemplating the destruction of Marie Antoinette? *It is now sixteen or seventeen years since I saw the queen of France, then the dauphiness, at Versailles; and surely never lighted on this orb, which she hardly seemed to touch, a more delightful vision. I saw her just above the horizon, decorating and cheering the elevated sphere she just began to move in—glittering like the morning-star, full of life, and splendour, and joy.* Margaret had offered England a similar vision. Henry, by contrast, offered only division and anguish.

Alan finished, speaking from his heart, "Arthur offers us the hope of a united, peaceful future. I can foresee no such future under King Henry's rule, with the jokers rising in anger, neighbor turning against neighbor. Trust me, sirs, that I know what a divided home will bring us: only chaos, civil unrest, revolution, and death." Burke had seen disaster come to life: *Little did I dream . . . that I should have lived to see such disasters fallen upon her in a nation of gallant men, in a nation of men of honour, and of cavaliers.*

Alan owed it to Margaret to defend her dying wish; he had failed her son completely. But Henry's face was cold and rigid. "No, never. This is absurd. You cannot expect me to simply step down from the throne, in favor of this fairy tale you've concocted."

Alan stiffened. "Sir, the data is conclusive." If there was one thing he could take comfort in, it was the data that supported his words, his actions. Data was entirely reliable, when no human ever was. "Arthur is the legitimate heir, and you, sir, are not."

And now the room was erupting into noise and argument. The Lord High Chancellor was banging a fist upon the table, and the president of the board of trade looked as if he were about to faint. Henry stood up, shouted across the table. "I will have your HEAD for this, Turing!" All that careful formality gone, Henry's accustomed rigid posture—spittle flew through the air, flecked onto the table.

Alan bent his head—it wasn't up to him now. He was England's loyal servant, and had finally finished the task his queen had assigned.

Now to see if these great men did their duty as well, as Noel grabbed him and teleported them away. His final thought was that it didn't seem likely.

♥

"It was always unlikely that we would be believed or that Henry would gracefully acquiesce and abdicate." Green Man was pacing, the knave's long legs taking him back and forth across the upstairs workroom in three strides.

Noel, sprawled in a chair in the upstairs workroom at Constance's wrecked atelier, looked from face to face. Arthur's expression was cautiously hopeful, as if he had been spared from a horrid fate. Constance looked fierce. Turing seemed dejected but also at peace. Noel wasn't certain how he felt. *Bad*, he concluded, as his ribs and arm ached, and the effort of teleporting them one by one had broken open the cut on his side. They had drawn all the curtains, turned on the radio, and now spoke in soft whispers in an effort to counter what they believed to be Finder's power.

Roger spoke again. "We have to use direct action."

Turing looked up alarmed at that. "Not violence."

"No. A march. On Windsor. Pulling together everyone who has been marginalized, demonized, and discriminated against. Not just the jokers but the immigrants, the poor, the young, those who love differently or worship different gods. All of us united in hope for a better Britain."

Well damn, he is good with words. And in that moment Noel felt a twinge of regret for what this man might have accomplished had his life not been destroyed by this hell-born virus. "So, how do we accomplish that?" Noel asked.

"I'll put out the word to the joker community." The big knave turned to Constance. "You have a formidable online presence. Use that. Reach out to your followers."

"I'll call the press," Turing said. "I'm enough of a curiosity, especially now . . ."—He cast his eyes down and Noel knew he was thinking of his husband—"that they'll take the call. Make sure they are there to cover the march. Make sure they report."

"And what do we tell these marchers that we hope show up?" Constance asked.

"That we gather at noon and march on the castle. Demand that Henry abdicate." Roger turned to Arthur. "Sir, I know it's dangerous, but I think you have to be there."

"I would never let any of you go alone," the king said quietly.

Noel sighed and pushed out of the chair. "I need to pick up a few things if I'm going to keep you mad people safe."

Roger turned on him. "You disapprove?"

"Oh no, I think it's our only play. One last throw of the dice." Noel steeled himself to begin the transformation, already thinking about which weapons to recover from his bolt-hole in Austria, when Turing said,

"Green Man, you can't be there. There's a warrant out for your arrest. Your presence will just bring the police down on all of us."

"I have to be," Roger said. "You need me there to keep our people calm." Green Man's tone took on a pleading note. "And let me have this one chance to make things right. That it wasn't all for nothing." Turing shook his head.

Green Man pressed again. "Please, go to the authorities . . . to the Lion. Tell him I'll surrender at the end of the march. Just allow me to walk free this one last time."

Noel waited to hear Turing agree then teleported away.

♣

They knew who she was, what she was. That much was clear. Turing had figured it out when the one called Noel, who seemed to be both a teleporter and a shape-shifter of some kind, had investigated her in Belfast. This was why they now plotted against her in secret with curtains pulled, never realizing that if a crow cared little for its own survival, it would squeeze itself even down a chimney.

The voices of the peace conspiracy were muffled, but she learned . . . much of interest.

They, on the other hand, knew nothing of all the pieces she had left on the board, nor how she would deploy them for the endgame.

She opened her eyes to a burnedout squat, where Seizer, would-be king of the Britons, paced and raged and, yes, wept too.

He turned to see her watching him.

"Is that it?" he cried. "The last of my followers a dying old woman?" In the distance were sirens and he flinched. "They're coming for me. I've been be-trayed."

"Those—" her voice was so weak, even the goddess could barely hear herself. She was aging faster than any mere mortal. Years for every day. She breathed deep and got the words out. "They search for you, my liege, but they are not coming here. Not yet."

"Then, I should turn myself in!" he cried. "Make them take me to trial and with every camera on me, the truth, yes! The truth will come out and—"

She was shaking her head, and so powerful were his fears that even Seizer's arrogance wasn't strong enough to carry him through the full sentence.

"They have decided to put a joker on the throne after all, my lord. But one *they* can control." She added the tone known as "contempt" to her voice. "One who will soothe the likes of us so the nats can live on in comfort."

"Who?" he demanded.

"The old tailor."

In the time it took her to take a breath, his face went from surprise, to shock, to outrage. "I will kill him!" he shouted. He smashed his fist against the crum-bling wall. "I . . . will . . . kill . . . him!"

He grabbed her by her bloody old coat, pulling her level with his face. "And I'll kill you too, you worthless bag of bones, if you don't live up to your name and find him for me."

Still, he had no idea that his escape from Windsor had only succeeded be-cause of her.

Badb pretended a moment of fear. "Please don't hurt me! I know . . . I know where the pretender will be. Tomorrow. We . . . we must return to the castle."

She closed her eyes again. He thought her asleep, no doubt, and in truth, she had to fight with every iota of her strength to stay awake. She needed her concentration for the birds. They flew to every bolt-hole in London with orders for men and women who knew the power of terror and how to keep it fed.

♠

Green Man wasn't sure whether to laugh or cry as the van pulled into the secluded driveway. "*This* is where I'm to meet the Lion?"

Turing nodded. "Yes. Is that going to be a problem?"

He pulled open the sliding door and looked around. The lawn was still trim but the flower beds were empty, while the garden was bare and oddly sterile. Though the kennel remained, the dog that lived there was long gone and had never been replaced. The house, his house, hadn't changed at all, just faded a little over time. What struck him hardest was how empty it looked. As if someone had sucked the warmth and life from the bricks and mortar.

He got out of the van and Turing hurried after him. "Is the location going to be a problem?"

"No," Green Man replied, though in truth he wasn't sure. He'd be hard-pressed to describe how he felt but he was definitely feeling something. Something strong.

"I hope that's true," continued Turing, "as we need this to go well. The Lion took a great deal of persuading to meet you and it will be bad for all of us if you do anything other than reach an accord."

Green Man stopped at the front door. "If there are any problems, they won't come from my end. Are you sure the Lion can be trusted?"

"Do you want the full answer or the summary?"

"The summary."

"Based on my long association with him and my understanding of the variables, he is eighty-eight percent likely to be true to his word, plus or minus five. Though this goes down to fifty-eight percent if he is given orders to the contrary, and virtually zero if he perceives you to be a threat."

Not feeling at all reassured, Green Man pushed at the door. It swung open easily at his touch.

Rectangles of mismatched colors marked where the pictures had hung on the walls long ago. The hole in the wall—the one he'd made—had been repaired. Aside from a little dust, the place looked clean. But it didn't feel like a home anymore. All of the ornaments and decorations had gone. The air was musty and cold, creating an atmosphere too sterile to generate nostalgia.

He made his way deeper into the house.

The front room seemed too large without furniture; the Lion still managed to fill it with his presence, however. Age had done nothing to shrink the man. If anything, it had given him a greater solidity. There was a calmness there, a strength that seemed to exude from every pore. Though the Lion's dark beard had whitened with the passing of time, the man had aged disgustingly well. Green Man found this profoundly unfair.

However, he was now taller than the Lion by some margin, and he took a petty kind of pleasure in being able to look down his nose at his adversary. The Lion was armed only with his kirpan, but the blade was sheathed and his hands far from the hilt.

Green Man looked at the Lion.

The Lion looked at Green Man.

The first time they'd met had been when the Lion delivered him to Churchill and the last had been in this house. It had ended in violence. While he'd been exiled with the Twisted Fists, the Lion had taken his place, protecting his family and, if the photographs were to be believed, befriending his wife and filling in as father figure.

In some ways, the Lion had taken everything from him. In others, the Lion had cared for those he loved most. Was he indebted to this man? Was he owed revenge? Did any of that even matter now?

Again, Green Man experienced a heady mixture of emotion, too tangled to identify.

Turing glanced between the two men. He opened his mouth several times, his lips mouthing the starts of sentences that were rapidly discarded before settling on: "Time is against us, and as far as I'm concerned, the terms of the deal have already been detailed. Do you agree?"

"Yes," said Green Man.

"Yes," said the Lion.

"Then I would ask why any of this is necessary?"

"Because," the Lion replied, still meeting Green Man's gaze, "I wanted to know if it was true. I wanted to look him in the eyes and hear him say it."

Green Man sighed. "Allow me to go on the march and I give my word that when it's over I'll turn myself in."

"Without trouble?"

"I'll make it clear to my people that this is my choice and that they're not to interfere. My presence at the march will help keep it peaceful, and my public surrender will send a clear signal to all parties."

The Lion looked into his eyes for a long moment, then nodded. "I believe you." He held out a hand and Green Man shook it. "And for my part, I will make sure neither the Helix nor the police act against you, so long as you remain a peaceful participant."

Turing looked relieved. "I believe that concludes our business."

"Yes," agreed Green Man, "but there's something more I wish to discuss with the Lion. In private."

Metal eyebrows were raised, but Turing didn't seem surprised. He looked to the Lion, and when he got a nod in the affirmative, he excused himself.

"I wanted to ask you about my family," he saw the Lion's expression and hastily added, "not details. I know you can't provide me with those."

The Lion folded his arms. "It isn't my place to speak of them."

"I know that."

"Perhaps, when you've done the right thing, they'll make contact. But it will be their choice."

"Again, I know that," replied Green Man, suppressing a flash of irritation. "I just want to know if they're well. Can you tell me that at least?"

"They . . ." began the Lion, weighing up what he was prepared to divulge. ". . . are alive, and in good health." He paused, then added, "You don't need to worry about them. I give you my word on that."

The emotions within settled into relief and a great deal of sadness.

"Thank you. I mean it. I know you've done more for Wendy and my children than . . . well, I know you've done a lot. Above and beyond the call of duty. When I first found out, I was angry and . . ." the words got caught in his throat. "Anyway, we're both old men now, and . . . and . . . what I'm trying to say is . . . I'm glad they had someone like you after I'd gone."

The Lion nodded. "It wasn't a duty to me."

"No, I rather thought it wasn't."

"I'll see you at the march. Don't make me regret this."

Green Man nodded. There was nothing else to say, so he turned and left, glad to be leaving the empty house behind him. Turing was waiting in the van. "We should go," he said by way of greeting as Green Man climbed inside. "Things are moving faster than I anticipated."

"I thought you anticipated everything?"

Turing looked out of the window, his face a mask. "So did I, once."

Saturday

MARCH 14TH

GREEN MAN KNOCKED ON the door.

He heard Bobbin's voice on the other side. "Come in." *Not Bobbin,* he reminded himself, *he is Arthur now. Our king.*

Aside from a set of stitches running neatly down one cheek, a bandage around his neck, and a haunted look in his eyes, there was little evidence that Arthur had been nearly hacked to death by Maven.

"Constance did a good job."

Arthur's hand went self-consciously to his cheek. "She did. Though it's not like she could make this ugly mug much worse."

"I'm sorry you were attacked but if it's any consolation, the scar is no bad thing. It shows you have suffered. People will relate to that."

"Will they? I think the tabloids will call me a thug as well as a freak."

"I think you'd best get used to being called a lot of names from now on. Arthur, Your Majesty, defender of the faith—"

"Stop it. I don't see myself that way."

"Time to start. When you go out there, and you will be going out there soon, everything you do will be scrutinized. You won't be a person anymore, you'll be a symbol. Like I am."

"Nothing personal, but I'm nothing like you."

"You're not a man that has been forced into a situation that is beyond his control? You're not a man that others will look to for guidance? You're not a man whose words will influence the fate of others?"

Arthur looked away. "Point taken. But that's where it ends. I might be a joker. I might be a lot of bloody things, but I'm not a killer."

"No. You're not."

"And," he looked back at Green Man, "don't think this is going to make us friends. I don't agree with what you and the Twisted Fists do. It isn't right."

It was Green Man's turn to look away. "No. It's not."

"No," echoed Arthur.

"Things were very different when I became Green Man. Our people weren't served by the system. They were abused. They needed someone to stand up and continue the fight. To force change to happen."

Arthur looked at him for a long moment. "Is that what you tell yourself? Because, from the outside, I just see a man with lots of blood on his hands."

Green Man held up his hands. There was blood there, buried deep in the grain of the wood. "I want the violence to stop. You and I can achieve that."

"Together?" Arthur shook his head. "No government can afford to negotiate with a terrorist, and a king can't be seen to have anything to do with one."

"I understand."

"You do?"

"Yes. You are a symbol of our future, Arthur. I am one that's mired in our miserable history. That's why, when Turing presents you as the true heir, I'm going to turn myself in."

"You what?"

"I've taken things as far as I can." He took off the Green Man mask and ran his thumbs over its familiar contours. "Green Man can never be part of the establishment, but as myself, as Roger Barnes, I stand by you, even if it has to be from prison." He handed the mask to Arthur. "I'd like for you to have this."

"I don't understand."

"Consider it a reminder of what's out there if you aren't everything our people need. I'm ready to step down and tell the world that the time for violence between jokers and nats in this country can end, but the Twisted Fists will still be watching. Should you fail in your duty to us, they'll come back."

Arthur took the mask and looked at it warily, as if the thing were a bad-tempered animal that might bite his hand at any moment. "Doesn't seem very fair to put it all on me."

Roger smiled, knowing that thought rather too well. "No, it isn't. Welcome to the joys of royal life. And good luck!"

He left Arthur in his room, still staring at the mask, and felt lighter than he had in years.

◆

"Sorry, lad," Noel whispered as he withdrew the needle from the young soldier's neck.

He patted the sleeping soldier on the back, removed his helmet, and took his place at the roof parapet. Noel had forgone the leather jacket and instead wore a flak jacket. To any other sentries he would be indistinguishable from the soldier, now that he had donned the helmet.

The entire operation—from the moment he teleported onto the roof; gripped the young man's neck and applied pressure to his carotid arteries; then, once he was unconscious, delivered a shot of ketamine to his jugular vein—had taken slightly over one minute.

Noel shrugged out of his backpack, and quickly assembled his sniper rifle. He began to scan the seething crowds below. The jokers, immigrants, and their supporters were approaching from the west. To the east, blocking access to the palace, was a mass of Britain First thugs, general bully boys who had no set ideology, but liked to drink and carouse and beat up people. This looked like a perfect opportunity.

Between the two groups was a line of very nervous looking Bobbies, worried military police, and of course the damn Helix. Turing had tried to no avail to convince the Lion not to take to the field. The only good news was that Turing reported that the military and police were armed with rubber bullets, tear gas, and pepper spray, and not something more lethal.

Unlike me, Noel thought with satisfaction as he used the rifle's scope to scan the crowd for the hunched and bandaged figure. He also figured if he spotted Seizer, he'd take out that wanker too.

♥

The crowd was huge, numbering in the hundreds of thousands, all marching through the fog toward Windsor castle. A mix of jokers and nats, royalists and activists, inhabitants of London and beyond. Green Man had called in every favor; made requests, demands, even threats to get everyone he could there for the march. He knew that Constance and Turing had done the same.

It had worked. The spontaneity of the thing counted in its favor. This was a gathering that was happening right now, without warning, and people had no time to think about whether to attend. Most had come rather than miss out.

Reporters moved alongside the group, cameras clicking, videos rolling, their individual commentaries blending into the greater buzz of humanity. The police had scrambled to get here in sufficient numbers, many of the officers controlling the spectators looking bleary-eyed behind their riot helmets. As Roger got closer, he could see members of the Silver Helix present too: the Lion, Redcoat, Jiniri. His jaw tightened as he recognized Stonemaiden. And behind them, an even less welcome sight: an angry mob of Britain First and other protesters, all sounding ready for a fight. To reach the palace, they'd need to get past both groups.

The Lion's eyes, still sharp, sought Roger out, and the two exchanged a nod acknowledging the deal Turing had struck. The Helix would not move against him so long as he remained peaceful. When Arthur had been presented, he would go with them quietly.

Roger had wanted to be here as himself. To enjoy his last day of freedom as an ordinary man and witness Arthur make history. But that wasn't possible. People hadn't answered the call of Roger Barnes. Nobody gave a damn about some old guy who used to write speeches for a long-dead prime minister. They'd come for Green Man because they owed him. They'd come because they were scared of him. They'd come because he'd left them no other choice.

Though he didn't wear his mask, he still stood head and shoulders above everyone else, wooden features instantly recognizable. He scanned his companions. There was a distant look in Turing's eyes, and Roger wondered what myriad calculations were going on in that famous skull. Next to him was Arthur, who appeared to be in a state of shock, and, not far away, Constance, proud, giving Arthur what support she could from a respectful distance.

He knew that Finder was somewhere out there, and it made him nervous. She was still an unknown, unpredictable, and willing to kill—to do anything—to achieve her aims. Noel was up on the rooftops somewhere, watching out for them. He'd sounded confident, promising them he'd handle Finder, but Roger couldn't banish the thought that life was never that easy.

The police were only armed with rubber bullets and tear gas, riot shields and nightsticks, but if Maven were here, she'd be armed to kill. There was no sign of her, though, nor Seizer. The fog saw to that, making strangers of anyone more than twenty feet away. The police looked like a line of statues, the spectators behind them little more than wraiths. Their jeers were clear enough, though.

He wished he could call Wayfarer, but he'd deliberately cut all communication with her. She was the leader of the Fists now and would be busy moving all of their assets to places Roger didn't know. He might be leaving the organization he built up, but he couldn't bring himself to betray it.

As the march drew closer to the police line the mob behind them began to chant and shout, building themselves up for something violent.

Roger looked around. With the march behind them and the police in front, they were trapped, easy targets for anyone on the rooftops above. He had the unshakable feeling that whatever was about to go wrong would happen soon.

♣

Alan didn't understand it. It had all come right, somehow. Too many losses along the way, but at least they had finally found the true king, and would soon put him on his throne. They flanked him now on the field, he and Noel and Constance and all the rest, guarding Arthur in his final moments, before his glorious ascension. It was like a great war, coming to its victorious end, but the strange thing was, there had been no careful general moving the pieces on the board. That could have been Alan Turing's job, but he had failed. The fog of war had descended, and he had lost his way.

He hadn't slept last night. Hadn't slept properly in days, now that he thought about it. The gears turning in his mind—Alan could hear them now, *click-click-click*. He was nothing but a tin man, a toy soldier destined for a sordid end. He'd lost almost everything, hadn't he? His lover, his husband, his honor. All that was left was his country, and even now, when Alan should have every iota of brain power focused on calculating the odds of where an assassin might be hiding, he couldn't seem to concentrate. *Did you get to the leaf mold, like I asked you to? The snowdrops will get smothered, you know. Do I have to do everything, Alan?*

Apparently yes. Alan Turing stood in the midst of the raucous crowd, his eyes scanning the faces ceaselessly, looking for trouble. But his mind—oh his mind was in a small cell, bars on the door and a dim flickering light, the stench of night soil suffusing the air. Had Sebastian always had murder in him? Did all men? Or had Alan done this to him somehow? Perhaps he'd brought the taint of the secret police home, that gray corruption. Alan had just enough self-control to keep his eyes where they belonged. All he wanted was to stare at his own flesh-painted hands. It made no sense, but he could *feel* the wetness on them. They were surely covered in blood.

♠

Even with sweater and flak jacket, the cold was creeping into his bones. Noel pulled off his right glove and blew on his fingers. He needed his trigger finger to be steady. He hunkered back down and did another sweep of the crowds below, but the fog was rising, twirling like ghostly dervishes and starting to obscure his view. He cursed—the fog, the cold, his aching thighs, the pain in his arm and ribs.

He briefly lost his balance and the scope tipped up. As Noel's gaze raked across the rooftops on the opposite side of the street, he spotted a figure also hunched behind a rifle. He couldn't identify the figure, but he recognized the rifle—like his it was not standard military issue.

Maven!

There could be only one reason she was there—to kill Arthur. There was no choice. He had had no luck locating Finder, and with the rising fog it was becoming less and less likely he would. His duty was clear. Protect the king. Noel teleported.

♦

They were marching for peace. Against bravery and heroism. Against greatness and the power of sacrifice. Against the very earth that had given them life to begin with.

And how foolish of them, because just as a simple mix of sulfur, charcoal, and saltpeter could turn human beings into offal, the goddess of war liked nothing better than to push rivals together in tight spaces until a random spark brought down glory on young and old alike; on the willing and the unwilling.

Far below her crow host, they teemed in their multitudes. Winding up the hill in such numbers that when they panicked and trampled each other, even rainy London wouldn't have enough gutters to contain all the blood.

Most satisfactory.

The jokers called for an end to discrimination. Loudspeakers led chants of "We are human, human too! We are people just like you!" Or simply, *"Arthur! Arthur! Arthur!"*

When she swooped lower, she saw a great profusion of impossible bodies: insectile women; men with scales or industrial rubber for skin. No two were alike but for their fervent, doomed hope of fair play.

Badb was in there too—her body was—little more than a seeping bag of blood tied to Seizer's back. It was not her wont to be at the center of things, but the Silver Helix knew her now, yes, they did. They understood her purpose in this world and they had assembled all of their might to crush her.

But she had one more thing to teach them: a painful lesson that would become apparent when, inevitably, in this huge crowd, a hero died in the vicinity of her wretched carcass. Nor would Arthur make it through the day. She would see to that. And what chance of peace then? *None. None at all.*

It might be Seizer that killed him. But the better chance belonged to the competent Maven, dressed as a soldier and hiding on the roof of a fancy hotel. The woman was scanning the crowd this very second, looking for her victim. And, suddenly, she had something! Badb could see it in the set of her body. A target.

The goddess watched her. Watched history unfold. A finger curling about the trigger of a gun and—

Another soldier appeared behind Maven. *Noel.*

Even a goddess could be surprised.

But as the two began to grapple on the rooftop, she sent a dozen crows flashing down toward them. She wanted to follow them in, she—

Badb found herself back in her own body.

♥

With a *pop* of displaced air, Noel landed directly behind Maven just as she squeezed the trigger. The sound caused her to flinch. Perhaps it had been enough to deflect her shot. It was the only hope he had. Noel flipped the rifle so he was holding the barrel and swung the stock toward the side of her head. But she rolled to the side, so he only managed a glancing blow.

She sprang to her feet and pulled a pistol from her holster. The flak jacket sucked the two rounds, but the kinetic force sent Noel stumbling back a few steps, and the three gun-shots in rapid succession set the entire seething mass of humanity below them into frenzied activity. Screams wafted up to him, but Noel had no time to worry about what was happening in the streets below.

He was still holding his sniper rifle, which increased his reach. He brought it down hard on her wrist, but not before she got off another shot. The blow ruined her aim but the bullet hit him in the thigh. Her fingers, numbed from the hit, released the gun. Noel glanced down. He was bleeding, but it wasn't the pumping blood from a femoral artery. He had a few more seconds to end this before she ended him. He charged her. In his male avatar he was significantly taller and heavier than Maven, and he drove her back against the parapet and wrapped his arms around her.

Her hands came up as she clawed for his face, trying to blind him. A sudden blow on the back of his head accompanied by a raucous *caw* forcibly reminded Noel of a new threat—the fucking crows. The beat of wings sounded like thunder in his heightened state. Birds were pecking at his hands, flying at his face. Between Maven and the crows, he could end up blind, and that terror had him teleporting just as blindly. Fortunately, he managed to keep hold of Maven, but he had no idea where his subconscious would take them.

They blinked back into existence high in the air over Tower Bridge. Disoriented and suddenly terrified, Maven went from trying to rip out his eyes to clinging to his neck.

Noel released her, but she clung like a baby monkey as they plummeted toward the pavement and the cars on the bridge. Noel butted her hard in the face and felt her nose break. Her arms slipped from his neck. She grabbed desperately at the flak jacket. Noel shrugged out of it, gave her a hard shove toward the rapidly approaching pavement. He then teleported back to the roof in Windsor.

His pant leg was red with blood. More blood ran down his cheek where Maven had clawed him. He frantically scanned the sky for murder arriving from above, but Finder had seemingly lost interest once she knew her tool was gone. Sinking down he tried to focus. He had to locate Arthur and Constance. Three soldiers arrived on the roof.

"DOWN ON THE GROUND! DOWN ON THE GROUND!"

From all around he heard gunfire, screams; smelled tear gas. Glancing over the roof he spotted Constance, Arthur, and Turing hiding behind a parked car. Noel teleported down to them.

♣

There was a *pop, pop, pop* sound and Constance suddenly found herself being pulled to the ground and dragged behind a gray Mercedes. She recognized the sound of gunfire, though which direction it was coming from she couldn't tell. She looked around and saw Turing crouching next to Bobbin.

"Where the hell are those shots coming from?" Turing asked. His normal calm demeanor was gone, replaced by barely concealed panic.

"I don't know," Bobbin said. "Constance, are you all right?"

"I am," she replied. She got up on her knees and peeped through the Mercedes' window. Before her was pandemonium. What had been a peaceful protest had turned into something bloody and violent.

"We need to get out of here," Turing said.

"We can't," Bobbin said flatly. She'd never heard him speak quite that way before. "We can't leave. It's my fault they're here in the first place."

"Arthur, don't be a martyr. We need you alive."

"That's enough, Turing," Constance snapped. "If Bobbin wants to stay, then stay we will."

There was a *pop* and Noel appeared. He was pale as milk and there was the coppery smell of blood on him.

♠

"Jesus Christ! We need to get pressure on that." Turing was staring at the sluggishly bleeding wound.

Noel had landed and fallen over, and Constance and Arthur had dragged him fully into cover behind the car.

Constance pulled a pair of scissors from her purse and cut out a panel of her coat. Quickly folding it, she pressed it against the bullet wound. Noel groaned as Turing secured it with Noel's belt.

"We have to get you out of here," he mumbled and wondered why everything sounded so far away. A hot poker seemed to be driving through his thigh. "Can't carry you all. Too weak. One at a time. Maybe."

"Don't be an idiot," Constance snapped. "The only person who matters is Arthur. Get him out of here. And get yourself to hospital."

"No," Arthur said. His eyes were on Constance. "I'm not leaving you."

"Finder, Seizer, and Maven are still out there. You're in danger," Turing argued. "You must go."

"Killed Maven. Just two to go. But yeah, got to go . . . before I faint," Noel muttered.

Arthur leaned over him, his expression intense. He then opened his hand to reveal a flattened .338 magnum round. He then gestured at the hole in his coat and shirt.

"Shit. Connie made you bulletproof," Noel murmured as darkness closed in. He vaguely felt his bones beginning to shift as he slid toward unconsciousness.

♦

All about Roger was chaos. After the gunshots, people had started to panic, and any slim control the police and the Silver Helix had was lost. The anti-joker mob surged forward, slamming into riot shields and a now-giant-sized Jiniri, battling to get through to where Arthur was crouched next to a parked Mercedes.

Constance was no longer keeping her distance, and stuck to Arthur's side protectively, while Turing watched everything with the expression of a man horrified but unsurprised by what he saw.

And then, to the left, Roger saw a familiar figure rushing toward them: Seizer.

"I am the true king!" he shouted, his booming voice just audible against the cacophony. His bulging eyes were fixed on Arthur, and full of hate. As the old knave pushed forward, he pressed a hand against the neck of a man in his path. They screamed as their flesh split, blood spraying from the wound. The crowd parted a second later, scrambling back to avoid suffering the same fate.

"Yes," said Seizer, stepping over the body, "prostrate yourself before your betters." His gaze quickly snapped back to Arthur as he took out a grenade from his pocket and pulled the pin. "Death to the imposter! Long live King Seizer!"

The grenade flew from his hand and Roger watched it, frozen. At first it looked as if Seizer had misjudged the distance, the grenade dropping well short of its target. But then it bounced, and rolled, coming to a stop under the car about two feet from them.

Arthur. Constance. Turing. My people!

Roger didn't think any more about his king or the many individuals that would be killed or injured. He didn't think about his own life or wonder about his family. Before he had time to think anything, he had flipped the car out of the way and dived forward, smothering the grenade with his wooden body.

This wasn't how he'd planned to go, but then, when had life ever gone to plan?

I suppose I should try and appreciate the iro—

The grenade went off.

♥

How did Badb end up back in her own body? There was nothing for her here but the distraction of pain, slapping against Seizer's shoulder as he broke into a run. A fist of noise pummeled her senses. Screams. The cloying odor of terror on a mass scale as thousands of people clawed for a way out that didn't exist.

But then, there was a grenade tumbling so slowly through the air. A magical thing; an invitation; a holy seed, bouncing from the curb of a footpath to roll along the street.

Badb's sluggish pulse began to quicken. The land trembled, for it knew this moment. It called forth a hero and a hero had appeared. Green Man. He threw his huge body on top of the grenade, cracking the asphalt with his elbows and knees.

Why had she never seen it in him? So much glory! She had always thought him too old. Too practical. He shuddered. The wood of his back fractured and his massive body lifted a foot off the ground. Yet not so much as a splinter struck the innocents whose lives he had saved.

Usually, a hero's death transformed Badb immediately. She became young and beautiful, with strength the match of any ace and appetites far greater still. But this time was different. Never before had she waited so long to feast. The power had been building, each day's delay winding the spring tighter and tighter.

Nor had she ever absorbed the life of a hero like Green Man—one of the great figures of this age, revered by millions, by the most desperate, the earnest, from every corner of the world . . .

For three breaths, all was still. And then she felt . . . she felt *everything*.

♣

Bits of pavement, and wooden splinters, rained down on the foursome.

A piece landed at Noel's side; a section of a face, the edges of the wood rimmed with viscous blood. *Roger*. Rage bubbled deep in Noel's chest and it seemed to burn away the pain from his various injuries. He laid a hand over the broken skull, a benediction from one ethically and morally broken man to another. They had each tried to serve in their own way, and their ways had often brought death.

"Well, no reason to repent now," Noel murmured.

Using Turing's shoulder, Noel began to lever himself to his feet.

And then a scream ripped open the sky.

♠

A great man was gone and gone forever. A beautiful soul, whose like would never walk this earth again. The pain! Oh, it was too large for even a goddess to contain. Hers was the voice of the land, the voice of the people. Her tears were theirs and she was the embodiment of every broken heart and murdered hope.

And so, she screamed.

Buildings shattered along the street, windows pulverized. One massive castle tower at the bend on Thames Street slid down on top of a thousand helpless marchers below. Animals fled or burrowed desperately into the soil of the park, and every bird for miles around abandoned the skies.

Except for the crows.

They blotted out the sun with their numbers, wings buoyed by the screech of their mistress. And when it was over, down they came, like twenty thousand arrows shot from the heavens, lethal beaks aimed at the unworthy horde for whom Green Man had given his life.

♦

Things felt as if they were moving very slowly. Noel was sprawled on the ground with Turing beside him. Green Man—*Roger*—so many new names now—was dead. Bits of him were strewn about. The hot acrid smell of blood mingled with smoke, fear, and sweat.

Floating above them, circled by a murder of crows, was what could only be described as a goddess. She was beautiful, with an incandescent light surrounding her.

Constance got to her feet and glared at the creature. Bobbin wasn't far behind

"Get down," Turing hissed.

"Do piss off, Turing," Constance said, trying to keep the fear from her voice.

Constance glanced at Bobbin and saw him nod. It took but a moment, and then she released her shears. Her special shears. She slipped them from their sheath in her pant pocket. The cold steel slid into her hand, and she turned it so the handles were facing Arthur. He took them from her and put them into his jacket pocket. His hands were trembling.

"Stay here," he whispered.

"No!" She couldn't let him go alone.

"Constance, please. I can't do this if I'm frightened for you. I've only got one chance." He was shaking. "I'm scared and I can't go if I'm worried about you too."

She looked over and saw the woman throwing bodies through the air. Her laugh was sweet and terrible and Constance was terrified down to her core.

"You did this," he said. "You saved me so I can do this thing. So I can stop this. Stop her."

"She could rip your head off!"

"Maybe, but I must try. Don't you see? These are my people. This is for all the people. Everyone. I'm no good if I can't act to save them."

A moan of resignation and horror came from deep inside Constance. "Go!" It made her sick to say it.

His hand brushed her cheek as he went past her and made his way around the car. Despite her care, he was still a little unsteady on his feet. She began to tremble as he made his way toward the woman. *That bitch*, Constance thought.

♥

How glorious: the chaos, the clash, and the challenge. They were all coming for her, the Silver Helix and their tame police.

She flashed into the eyes of one crow and then another. The dizzying fall from the sky. Terrified faces of adults and children looking up. The delirious impact of beak into flesh. There were gunshots. Shouts. Trampling feet and piteous cries; sirens; distant alarms; the crackle of flames and even bombs going off now as cowardly men pressed buttons from far away.

And here came the first of the aces. The stone maiden slipping between panicked knots of people. "You're so pretty!" cried the goddess. "So, so pretty!"

She picked up the nearest object—Seizer, as it happened.

"I am your king," he screeched. "I am your true—"

He weighed nothing to her, nothing at all and flew through air with barely an opportunity to scream. His body made mincemeat of a joker family, bounced off the street and still had enough momentum to send the maiden spinning back into the unyielding wall of a pub.

The goddess laughed, she whirled. Oh, for a kiss! Billy Little, how she missed him! And now, she was sobbing.

But her tears turned to fury.

By the shattered castle walls, a giant woman roared in challenge. Jiniri, of course. She couldn't move without stamping on the swarm of civilians about her legs, but her massive hands clawed great fistfuls of crows out of the sky.

"Murderer!" cried Badb. "Monster!"

She ran.

Never had she been so fast in her life. So powerful. The world was a blur around her. People shattered as she sprinted right through them. Now Jiniri, finally realizing her danger, tried to trample her.

Badb leapt onto the leg, laughing for the joy of it. She used the giant's silk skirt as a rope, swinging herself away from clumsy fists and around the back to where a luxuriant rope of hair led the way upwards.

"No!" cried the giant. Her head alone was three foot tall, her mouth large enough to snap the goddess in half, but nowhere near fast enough, and when Badb pulled free her left eyeball—as large as a fist—a whole fist!—her screams were magnificent too.

"For you, my children!" cried the goddess. "My loves!" She cast the brown orb high, high into the heavens, where a curtain of ravenous crows closed around it, so that barely a scrap of jelly made it to the ground.

♣

Was it just yesterday that Alan had been desperately scrounging for every bit of data he could, sure he would understand everything if he just knew enough? He had forgotten what it was to be on a battlefield. There were too many distinct moments to track, each one of critical importance. A little girl wailing that her ice cream had been knocked out of her hand—get out of the damned street, child! Some thug half a block down dragging a tire off a car, throwing it around a trapped joker's neck, and setting it on fire. A horse—why were there always fucking horses in the middle of the worst nightmares?—stampeding its way down the street. No, not a horse, a joker of some kind, a centaur, though with his human body so diminished that it took a second to parse it all.

Too much data coming in too quickly, and precious little Alan could do with it. Just stay out of the way, try not to make things harder for everyone else.

They'd stopped the bleeding on Noel's thigh, at least. Alan had been able to help with that, the swift action distracting from the pounding of his heart. Noel was a bastard these days, but Alan had made him one, hadn't he? It wasn't a grown man under Alan's panicked fingers, it was the child they'd taken and trained, and he would. Not. Lose. Him.

Noel would survive, Alan was almost sure, but all around him people were dying. The city was falling apart, buildings collapsing. All of it exploding into light and glory when a gorgeous female figure lit up the sky—for a moment, you could hear the people holding their breath, hoping that this would be the end of it, that their salvation had come. But then the crows began their manic dives, and the woman—the ace—began to laugh, a high, mad sound that promised nothing but pain.

Even Jiniri couldn't stop the goddess. Jiniri strode so gloriously through the city, ready to do combat for the soul of her adopted England—for a moment, Alan dared to hope. And then the goddess reached out and almost delicately, but definitively, gouged out Jiniri's eye. The giant woman screamed, falling to her knees, and the earth shook. Despair choked Alan, and he found himself beating his thighs with his clenched fists. Helpless, helpless, helpless. Alan was no use to anyone, and should probably have died a long time ago. Maybe if he hadn't interfered, none of this would have come to pass.

♠

The sea of chaos parted for Bobbin and left open a straight way to the murderous figure. As he reached the halfway point, the psychotic ace looked up and focused on him,

Oh God, Bobbin, Constance thought. *I've done the best I could to keep you safe. What if it's not enough?*

♦

Sometimes the universe slowed down. That was how it felt, when the calculations came together, tumblers clicking in a lock, water falling down a cascade, information finding its perfect path through the minotaur's maze—a thread, a rope to drag you out. The lift of an arm, the light glinting off the barrel of a gun, and Turing threw himself to the side—an awkward, graceless motion, but just enough to put himself in the path of the bullet. It slammed into his shoulder and oh, gods, that hurt! But his body took the impact, hardening as it had before, stopping the bullet before it pierced silver-metal skin.

Alan was never quite sure that it would continue to work; each time he walked into battle, he did so only hoping that his card might continue to protect him. And with his brain failing lately, he'd been even less sure—but it turned out that he didn't really need to think about this, didn't need to decide anything. He just needed one small good thing to come out of this day, something he had done, one tiny step toward redemption—and here it was, the gods answering his call. Where, in a rational universe, was there space for gods? Alan didn't know, but they surely walked among them today.

The Seamstress didn't even know he'd saved her life—she was turned the other way, reaching for her Bobbin. It was better that way. One small good thing.

♥

Badb had never been stronger or faster. Never more beautiful or terrible.

She picked up a car, sent it hurtling into a crowd of advancing policemen. Oh! In their crushed flesh she spied the shape of a red stallion. How lovely! Another car, another splash of gore, the colors glistening and magical and sweet. The first line of a poem occurred to her right then, every word falling perfectly into place. Ó Rathaillaigh could not have bettered it had he risen then and there from the grave . . . She looked around, but he didn't dare confront her and she laughed and laughed.

Then, for several minutes, the goddess lost herself in the simple pleasures of emotion, killing all around her from anger or joy or even a love so pure it could not bear to share these people with the world. Everywhere crows ripped at the crowd. Bodies were stampeded. Britain First sympathizers fought with jokers and police. Bombs turned shops full of royal souvenirs into rosettes of pure fire. She had arranged it all, masterminded it even. And the only thing she had to do to finish it off was to . . .

And there he was! Somehow untouched by it all. Arthur. *King* Arthur. His fall would end the game, end this entire country. The old man walked unharmed, as though he were immune to beak and bullet and bomb. He shuffled toward her, all trepidation. He had a sweet old face. It reminded her of her dear father before she'd had him killed. She felt tears at the corners of her eyes. Oh, she missed her *dadaí*! Oh, she did!

Arthur grimaced, paused like a gentleman to allow a crow-covered joker to run past. He looked up, met her holy gaze, lowered his, and came on. Did he believe his death would end all of this? Perhaps. He had such a gentleness about him. Such dignity. A beautiful, beautiful man. And finally, he stood before the goddess and opened his trembling arms.

"I have to do this," he said, giving himself over completely. He was empty-handed. Weaponless.

She wrapped her arms around him as carefully as she could. She would snap him in half so quickly he wouldn't suffer. But first, for the briefest of moments, she wanted to feel his grizzled face against hers. Oh, the scent! Old man's clothing. Old man's soap. Her heart flew all the way back to Donegal, where Majestic Errigal stood proud over the glittering bog and the wind set a thousand cotton plants to nodding and the taste of the sea infused every breath with—

Pain! How could there be pain and she so young?

She dropped him, staggering back, clawing at her own neck. What was wrong? Whose was this gushing blood? Not hers! How could it be hers? And yet, it flowed out of her own throat.

She was on her knees in a gore-spattered street as crows turned from the crowd to tear at each other. Her eyes were blinking up at the heavens. *Where? How? Who am I now? What am* . . .

The infinite sky became a tunnel. Then, a pinprick of light, that lingered three slow heartbeats and was gone.

Epilogue

IT WAS SOMEHOW FITTING that the day was soft. The lawn in the cemetery was dotted with snowdrops and sweet violets, and a haze of green filled the trees.

Noel stood, hand thrust into his pockets, studying the gravestone. ROGER BARNES. BORN SEPTEMBER 3RD, 1941. DIED MARCH 14TH, 2020. STEP SOFTLY, A DREAM LIES BURIED HERE. The Yates quote had just seemed appropriate when he'd picked the headstone.

Because of course he had. Who else was there? Roger's wife and daughter hated him. The son really hadn't known him. Noel had paid a call on the man. Told him a bit about his father. What was apparent was that Roy hadn't known how to react.

"Christine says he was a criminal,"

"He was. He was also a patriot," Noel had said.

Now he stood wondering if someone would tell his son the same. And who would pick the epitaph for his gravestone?

"Didn't peg you as the type for graveside visits."

"Beats the hell out of a jailhouse visit I'm sure," Noel drawled.

"Don't be cruel, Noel. It's unworthy of you," Turing said softly. "So, you accepted."

Noel shrugged. "As the king commands . . . and it seems the only thing I'm suited for."

"I'm sorry."

"My dear, Alan, *'things without all remedy / Should be without regard'* . . ."

Turing finished the Shakespeare quote. *"'What's done is done.'"* It emerged as a whisper. They stood in silence for a long moment. "So, Director, you'll find my resignation on your desk."

"Oh, hell no, you know where all the bodies are buried. Back to the dawn of time." He linked his arm through Turing's and they strolled toward the cemetery gate. "Besides, I need you to convince Stonemaiden not to kill me."

"I'm afraid you'll have to do that yourself. I'm out."

♣

Alan took the train out to Bletchley. Only fifty miles northwest of London, but it felt like another world, stepping back in time to the War. He hadn't been back since the restoration—they'd done a good job with it, though a part of Alan wondered if it wouldn't have been better if they hadn't saved the park. It had almost been sold off, chopped up for apartments. How much pain did people cause, clinging to lost days of former glory? What England needed now was to look ahead, and let the old folks shuffle off somewhere where they'd do less damage.

Alan couldn't bear to enter the National Museum, with photos of himself plastered on the walls. Oh, they'd have Gordon Welchman, Hugh Alexander, Stuart Milner-Barry too—the stalwarts of the old gang. But seeing their faces would be almost as bad—Gordon was lost to the mists of dementia, Hugh had died in an action in the East, and Stuart had simply died of cancer, rotting from the inside out. No more chess games deep into the night, no more arguing the fine points of Hugh's latest mathematical theory. All the beautiful old boys, gone to dust.

Block C, Block B, Huts 3, 6, 8 and more. They'd kept a surprising number of them intact, filled them with secrets that men had died to protect—there was even a pigeon exhibition. All the dark corners thrown open to the sunlight, and a stiff breeze gusting through. They'd needed the secrets back then, needed them desperately. But now the youngsters were talking about transparency. If every inner darkness was exposed to the world, maybe it could all be scoured clean. Too much festered in the dark.

Sebastian wasn't talking to him anymore. Perhaps it was for the best.

Alan didn't really know what to say to him. He had treated the man very badly—but in the end, Sebastian had chosen his own fate, raising his hand to murder. Alan Turing could blame himself for a lot of things, but that one, that was on Sebastian.

A group of students on bicycles cut across his meandering path; they were headed, by their chatter, to the just-opened National College of Cyber Security. They were so appallingly young—between sixteen and nineteen, with ruddy health glowing in their cheeks and bright futures shining in their eyes. "Oh, sorry!" they shouted, as they cut across his path. Boys and girls together, unfettered and free.

Ah, there it was. The stable yard cottage, where he had worked so long and so hard. Surely he'd done enough by now, good and bad. He had resigned from the Silver Helix; maybe he would take the trip that he and Sebastian had talked about. Go to Sri Lanka and feed the baby elephants, climb Adam's Peak and see the eye of God revealed.

"I'm sorry, sir? Sorry to bother you—" One of the girls had gotten off her bike and walked it back.

He wanted to tell her to go to hell, to leave him in his bitter peace. But she hadn't earned such rudeness from him. Alan swallowed back the nasty words, and said, "Yes? Can I help you?"

"Are you—Alan Turing?" And oh, the hope in her voice, the light spilling out from her. Like a candle, no, a great roaring blaze of a fire.

He could deny it, claim only a casual resemblance. But instead Alan nodded, and reached out to shake her hand. "Alan, yes. And you are?"

"Margaret. Margaret Evans. I'm a student at the College. I'm just so tremendously excited to meet you! We all admire you so much!"

Margaret. She looked only a little like his lost queen, but that didn't really matter, did it? This Margaret was a bright young flower of British womanhood, racing toward a future so much more free than anything his queen had known. That wild girl would have loved this one. "It's nice of you to say."

She reached forward, grabbed his hand, and pumped it fiercely. "Are you here to give a lecture? That would be incredible! Can I show you the way?"

He gently retrieved his hand—she'd smeared the makeup, and silver glistened through. Alan wanted to shove it in his pocket—that's what he would've done before today. But maybe . . . maybe she could show him the way. A new way? He'd followed old patterns for too long; they'd led him only to misery and ruin.

Alan smiled at her. "No, not today, I'm sorry. But perhaps later in the semester? We'll see. You'd better go, or you'll be late to class."

She nodded, jumped back on her bike, and pedaled off, dark hair streaming in the wind behind her. Beautiful.

Alan took out a pocket handkerchief and gently, slowly, started wiping the makeup from his face. Enough hiding, skulking in the shadows. If he were going to stay and fight for England, he would do it as himself.

♠

They sat close to one another on the plush divan holding hands. Constance didn't care that his spiny growths hurt when she squeezed; everything seemed so unreal both for the good and the bad. The hurt grounded her.

"Well, this is it then," Arthur said resignedly.

Constance stood and pulled him to his feet, then she fussed with his suit, which needed no fussing at all. She'd made it as close to perfect as was in her, but it wasn't one of her special suits. He didn't need one of those. Not right now.

"You're going to be brilliant," she said. She shoved her hands into her pants pockets.

"I'm not sure I want to be brilliant," he replied with a nervous laugh. "I think I might just want to go back to being Bobbin. Being Bobbin was easier."

She gave him a smile. "Who said life was going to be easy? You've been bone-idle for the last seventy-two years, my man, time to step up." A lump formed in her throat and she wasn't sure she could stop herself from crying.

Old woman, she thought. *Now is not the time.*

"Constance . . ."

She dropped her head. Tears started rolling down her cheeks and she gave up trying to stop them. If only he hadn't said her name like that.

"Constance," he said, lifting her chin to look her in the eye. "We could still . . ."

"No," she said. He held his handkerchief out to her. She took it and wiped her tears away before blowing her nose. "We already agreed. You've said you're only on the throne for three years, then you'll abdicate in favor of Richard's eldest. Until your three years are up, we can't be together. It will be difficult enough for you to do your duties without the constant distraction of people wondering about us."

"No one will care!" There was anguish in his voice. "We're old!"

"Of course, they'll care. Your whole story makes them care. I'm a distraction for you and the country. There have been all sorts of articles about your life and working with me. We've done a good job at hiding our relationship, but that can't last."

"God, Constance, we've only just . . ."

"I know. I can't even imagine being without you now." She reached out and took his head in her hands and then kissed him gently. Their kiss lingered, filled with sadness and good-byes.

"Now I must go," she said. "I'll be listening. Your speech is marvelous. It's just the thing we need. Go on now, Arthur. Be the king."

◆

Constance pushed open the door to the Good Knight's Brew. It was—had been—their favorite pub. She'd stayed away from it because it was filled with too many memories.

But she didn't want to watch his speech alone, and someplace familiar was what she needed.

She'd expected it would be busy, but it was packed with nats and jokers and the chatter was excited. The TV over the bar was tuned to BBC One with the sound turned off. The anchors' conversation scrolled by:

In but a few moments, King Arthur will give his first address to the nation. The shock of discovering that the true king is also a joker has rocked the country, indeed, the entire Empire. Will this man be able take up such a great mantle and preserve the monarchy given his background? Is it possible a man who was nothing more than a tailor mere months ago can lead? Ah, I see we are going to our live coverage of the speech.

The bartender turned the volume of the TV up and a chorus of "shush" and "hush now" floated through the pub until it fell silent. The screen faded to black, then the picture came back, showing Arthur sitting behind a solid-looking, dark mahogany desk. Someone had done an excellent job making him up so his blue and red piebald colors were less obvious. He coughed nervously, then began:

"There are times in the history of a nation when the country must decide what it is and what it stands for. It isn't the government—it is the people who decide what they will be. Such a moment has come to Great Britain.

"We must decide. Will we continue to embrace the hatreds that have turned us against each other? Or will we put these relics of another time aside and grow into the country we deserve? A country of kindness, generosity, and unification.

"I speak now as a simple man who has found himself in anything but simple circumstances. This is too how we find ourselves as a nation. We must help each other to mend the wounds inflicted by hatred."

A wave of sadness hit her and Constance couldn't bear to listen anymore. She slipped out of the pub, and began walking back to her atelier.

Up and down the street, she saw people stopped, looking at their phones. She could hear the speech through the tinny speakers. He was growing more earnest now, a tone she knew well. It was a terrible price to pay. Losing Glory and Margaret. And now losing Arthur left her desolate.

There was a light tap on her shoulder. Turning, she saw Brian, who had led the joker tailors from her shop the week before.

"Oh, Brian," she said trying to put a game face on. "Where did you come from?"

His light peppermint scent floated to her. "I was inside with some friends and I saw you leaving. I was wondering if you'd like to join us."

"But I thought . . . I thought . . ."

"I guess I was wrong about you," he said apologetically "We all knew the two of you were in love. And now, now you've given him up for the rest of us."

Constance shook her head. "Oh, it was never like that . . ."

His look was a knowing one and she turned her gaze away. "Come inside with me and my mates. You shouldn't be alone. Not now."

He led her back into the pub to his table. They'd left a chair open for her and she slipped into it. Brian held out his hand, and she took it. She extended her hand to the joker on her left, who took it too. And so it went, around the pub, linking them all together.

Closing Credits

STARRING	CREATED AND WRITTEN BY
Roger (Green Man) Barnes	Peter Newman
Noel (Double Helix) Matthews	Melinda M. Snodgrass
Anya (Badb) McNulty	Peadar Ó Guilín
Constance (Seamstress) Russell	Caroline Spector
Alan (Enigma) Turing	Mary Anne Mohanraj

CO-STARRING	CREATED BY
Arthur (Bobbin) Hugesson	Melinda M. Snodgrass
Jasper Matthews	Melinda M. Snodgrass
Adelbert (Seizer) Boyd-Brackenbury	Peter Newman
Maven Boyd-Brackenbury	Peter Newman
Sebastian Wallace	Mary Anne Mohanraj
Ranjit (the Lion) Singh	John Jos. Miller

FEATURING	CREATED BY
Kenneth (Captain Flint) Foxworthy	Kevin Andrew Murphy
Princess Gloriana	Melinda M. Snodgrass
Princess Sissel	Mary Anne Mohanraj
King Henry IX, Prince Richard	George R. R. Martin
Robin (Pygmalion) Shawcross	George R. R. Martin
Maryam (Jiniri) Shahidi	Carrie Vaughn
Rory (Archimedes) Campbell	Marko Kloos
Kerenza (Stonemaiden) Tremaine	Emma Newman
Jason (Redcoat) McCracken	Melinda M. Snodgrass
Wayfarer	Peter Newman

WITH	CREATED BY
John (Look Away) Davies	Mary Anne Mohanraj
Dorothy (Dotty) McDonald	Peter Newman
Sarah Edwards	Peter Newman
Payback	Peter Newman

Zachary Pike	Melinda M. Snodgrass
Eleanor (Primrose) Breslin	Kevin Andrew Murphy
Jamila, Bethany, Montgomery, Blue Jeans	Peter Newman
Doctor Nalakini Khatri	Melinda M. Snodgrass
Savic, the guardsman	Peadar Ó Guilín
Captain DeVere	Peadar Ó Guilín
Brian and Jeremy	Caroline Spector